Ten years ago, the passion was ignited...
And it's only gotten hotter with time!

Blaze

*Join the editors in celebrating
a decade of wonderful authors,
irresistible stories...and great sex!*

**Look for all six
Special 10th Anniversary Collectors' Editions
from The Original Sexy Six authors.**

Check out:

THE BRADDOCK BOYS:
and *THE PLEASURE PR*
by Kimberly Ray

HOTSHOT and *GOING*
by Jo Leigh

UNDENIABLE PLEASURES and *YO*
by Tori Carrington

COWBOYS LIKE US and *NO*
by Vicki Lewis Thomps

TOO HOT TO TOUCH and *EX*
by Julie Leto

EXTRA INNINGS and *IN HIS WILDEST DREAMS*
by Debbi Rawlins

*Harlequin Blaze—
Celebrating 10 years of red-hot reads!*

Dear Reader,

Writing romance novels is my dream job. And when you're lucky enough to have a job like that, the years go by like greased lightning! Blaze is celebrating its *tenth* anniversary this month? Impossible! But true, and I'm thrilled to be here wearing a party hat and throwing confetti around with my Blaze launch buddies (aka The Original Sexy Six) and Blaze Senior Editor Brenda Chin.

Brenda and I have been friends and colleagues for longer than either of us is willing to admit. She edited my first Blaze, *Notorious,* which is included in this volume, and my current Blaze, *Cowboys Like Us.* Both books feature yummy heroes who look great wearing jeans, boots and a Stetson. Thanks for making me and my cowboys look good for all these years, Brenda!

This is the sixth book in my Sons of Chance series, with three more arriving in the summer of 2012! I'm grateful for all of you who visit the ranch through my stories. I love hearing from you! You can email me through my website at www.vickilewisthompson.com. Please do!

And finally, thanks to all the readers who've helped make Blaze such a roaring success in the past decade. Here's to ten more years of hot heroes and happily-ever-afters!

Celebratingly yours,

Vicki

Vicki Lewis Thompson

COWBOYS LIKE US
NOTORIOUS

TORONTO NEW YORK LONDON
AMSTERDAM PARIS SYDNEY HAMBURG
STOCKHOLM ATHENS TOKYO MILAN MADRID
PRAGUE WARSAW BUDAPEST AUCKLAND

ISBN-13: 978-0-373-79634-2

COWBOYS LIKE US
Copyright © 2011 by Harlequin Books S.A.

The publisher acknowledges the
copyright holder of the individual works
as follows:

COWBOYS LIKE US
Copyright © 2011 by Vicki Lewis Thompson

NOTORIOUS
Copyright © 2001 by Vicki Lewis Thompson

Recycling programs
for this product may
not exist in your area.

This edition published by arrangement with Harlequin Books S.A.

For questions and comments about the quality of this book please contact us at Customer_eCare@Harlequin.ca.

® and TM are trademarks of the publisher. Trademarks indicated with ® are registered in the United States Patent and Trademark Office, the Canadian Trade Marks Office and in other countries.

www.Harlequin.com

Printed in U.S.A.

CONTENTS

ABOUT THE AUTHOR

New York Times bestseller Vicki Lewis Thompson's love affair with cowboys started with *The Lone Ranger,* continued through *Maverick* and took a turn south of the border with *Zorro.* She views cowboys as the Western version of knights in shining armor—rugged men who value honor, honesty and hard work. Fortunately for her, she lives in the Arizona desert, where broad-shouldered, lean-hipped cowboys abound. Blessed with such an abundance of inspiration, she only hopes that she can do them justice. Visit her website at www.vickilewisthompson.com.

Books by Vicki Lewis Thompson

HARLEQUIN BLAZE
544—WANTED!*
550—AMBUSHED!*
556—CLAIMED!*
618—SHOULD'VE BEEN A COWBOY*
624—COWBOY UP

*Sons of Chance

To get the inside scoop on Harlequin Blaze and its talented writers, be sure to check out blazeauthors.com.

Don't miss any of our special offers. Write to us at the following address for information on our newest releases.

Harlequin Reader Service
U.S.: 3010 Walden Ave., P.O. Box 1325, Buffalo, NY 14269
Canadian: P.O. Box 609, Fort Erie, Ont. L2A 5X3

COWBOYS LIKE US

To my grandmother, Nellie Sharpe,
a die-hard baseball fan. Your legacy
jumped two generations to live on in your
great-granddaughter Audrey, who eagerly awaits
that first crack of the bat every spring.

Prologue

August 8, 1963
from the diary of Eleanor Chance

NOW THAT JONATHAN'S seventeen and chasing after girls, I decided to find a hobby so I wouldn't be forever worrying about him. This summer I became a Chicago Cubs baseball fan! I figured that both Jonathan and my dear husband, Archie, would share in this new passion and we'd have some family togetherness listening to the games on the radio here at the Last Chance Ranch.

So much for that idea. Turns out neither of them have the slightest interest in the sport, but I love it! I don't care if my Cubbies don't win very often. They're historic, dating way back, and Wrigley Field is a piece of history, too. Besides, I like the team's name. Bear cubs are the cutest things ever, and I should know. Here in Jackson Hole we have bears aplenty.

I suppose I could have picked football or basketball, but I don't understand those rules as well. Baseball has always made sense to me. Hearing the crack of the bat sends a chill down my spine, especially in games like today! Ron Santo hit a home run in the bottom of the tenth to beat the L.A. Dodgers, which is amazing because the Cubs aren't doing so hot, as usual, and the Dodgers are leading the National League.

When I announced this thrilling victory at dinner tonight, Jonathan and Archie both smiled and said that was nice, but I could tell they don't give a flip. Too bad for them. They're missing some great entertainment. I've sent away for a Cubs baseball cap. I'm going to wear it, too.

1

LOGAN CARSWELL, FORMER catcher for the Chicago Cubs, had two surefire remedies for a troubled mind, and he couldn't use either one. Booze was out because he'd taken pain meds for his knee so he could dance at Alex Keller's wedding reception in Shoshone, Wyoming. As for the second method, he didn't know any of the women in this tiny town well enough.

Eventually, in spite of the meds, his knee began to bother him. Retreating to one of the Spirits and Spurs's well-worn bar stools, he swiveled to face the dance floor, where Alex was two-stepping with his bride, Tyler. Logan had known him ever since they were both kids living in the same Chicago neighborhood.

Alex had never had trouble getting girls, with his all-American blond good looks. Add to that his natural charisma behind a microphone, and he'd been able to pick and choose. Apparently he'd chosen Tyler, a dark-haired Italian beauty, or she'd chosen him.

Near as Logan could tell watching the happy couple on the dance floor, they were both quite pleased with the situation. Alex was obviously in love and seemed to have his life together at last. Logan should be so lucky. But he refused to allow his problems to cast a shadow over this celebration.

"Can I get you anything, Mr. Carswell?"

Logan swiveled back to the bar and concluded that luck hadn't totally deserted him. Of the two bartenders working the wedding reception, he'd drawn the girl instead of the guy.

He'd noticed her earlier. She wore her sun-streaked brown hair in a no-nonsense ponytail and didn't seem to go in for a lot of makeup. Her hazel eyes tilted up slightly at the corners, adding a touch of the exotic to her girl-next-door appeal.

From her enthusiasm and ready smile, he guessed she might be exactly his type—a born optimist. He could sure use a dose of optimism right now.

As he gazed at her, he realized she was looking right back with similar interest. He'd built a night of outstanding sex on less. But Shoshone was a folksy town, and one-night stands wouldn't go unnoticed around here the way they would in Chicago.

Still, he could flirt with her a little without doing any harm. He tipped back the Stetson that Alex had insisted he buy, along with the requisite jeans, boots and yoked shirt. "I think this is the part where the teetotalling stranger orders a sarsaparilla." He wished he could remember her name, but if someone had mentioned it, he'd forgotten.

She laughed. "Sorry. Don't have that. But the root beer is excellent."

"That'll do."

After placing a coaster decorated with a bucking bronco in front of him, she picked up a glass mug. Her nails were short and unpolished, her movements quick and efficient. "How do you like Shoshone so far?"

"Friendly place."

"We think so."

He grabbed the first conversational topic he could think of. "Is it true that this bar is haunted?"

"So they say. That's why it's called the Spirits and Spurs." She filled the mug to the top, and foam oozed over the lip. "Personally, I've never seen a ghost in here, but some claim they have."

Logan had never considered root beer foam erotic, but as it slid down the side of the mug, his balls tightened. Not much, but enough for him to register the sensation. Yes, a good romp in the hay with someone cute and personable like this bartender would be therapeutic, but he didn't give himself much chance of having that any time soon.

She allowed the foam to settle before putting the mug on the coaster. "I've never talked to a major league ballplayer before." She sounded fascinated by the prospect.

Oh, boy. If she had a fantasy image of him as some big celebrity, he needed to nip that in the bud. "I'm afraid you're not talking to one now, either. I'm out of the game."

She met his gaze with sympathy in her eyes. "I know. Alex mentioned it. He said if you were still playing, you wouldn't have been able to come to the wedding."

"Right." He managed a smile. "At least some good came out of it."

"Still, it can't be easy. But kudos to you for putting on a brave face for the party."

A knot loosened in his chest. Just kind words from a complete stranger, but they soothed him in a way he couldn't explain. "No, it's not." He rarely admitted that to anyone, because nobody liked a guy who felt sorry for himself. But after tonight, he'd probably never see her again, so letting down his guard was easier.

"Josie said you were a starting catcher for the Cubs."

That made him smile for real. This adorable bartender didn't follow the game, or she would have known that fact without getting the info from Josie, Alex's sister. Logan's injury had come while defending the plate against a rather spectacular slide into home, and the news clip had been replayed a lot last year.

"Yes, I was a catcher," he said. At least she wouldn't be pestering him for gossip about the big-name players. Sure, his ego took a small hit because she wasn't a fan, but all things considered, he counted it a good thing that she wasn't.

He decided to extend the friendliness. "So how long have you been tending bar?"

"Not long. I was the restaurant waitress until recently, when Josie asked me to start easing into her job so I'll be comfortable with it by the time her baby's born and she has to take time off."

"You seem comfortable with it now."

"Only because she sent me to a crash course in bartending."

Logan nodded. "I know all about those. When I was in the minors, I supplemented my income serving drinks."

"Yikes. You probably know more about this than I do!"

"Nah. It's been several years. Excuse me for not remembering, but what's your name?"

"Caro. Caro Davis."

"Karo like the syrup?"

"Caro like short for Carolyn. Josie started calling me that a while back, and I like it. I feel more like a Caro than a Carolyn, anyway."

He thought the shorter name suited her. "Is Josie a good boss?" Logan remembered Josie as a pesky little kid who was constantly tagging after him and Alex. He had a hard time imagining her as a wife and mother-to-be, let alone the proud owner of a cowboy bar in Wyoming. She'd married Jack Chance, the oldest of the three Chance brothers, and seemed blissfully happy living at the Last Chance Ranch, located about ten miles outside town.

Caro grinned at him. "As if I'd tell you if she wasn't. But she's great. She managed to promote me to this position without upsetting Tracy, who's a little young to take over Josie's job, or Steve, who's a new hire but knows bartending. Either of them could have resented me getting it. Josie handled it beautifully."

"Hey, Caro." The tall guy sharing bartending duties glanced her way. "Orders piling up down here."

"Be right there, Steve." She smiled at Logan. "Excuse me. Gotta do my job."

"You bet." He watched her walk away, ponytail bouncing. Damn, that smile of hers really cheered him up. He'd love to see more of it. He'd love to…no, he shouldn't start imagining how her perky self would react in bed. He shouldn't, but he did.

"Hey, Logan, don't be hitting on my best employee." Josie took the bar stool on his left and punched him playfully on the shoulder. She was more dressed up than he'd ever seen her, all blue satin and lace. Instead of braiding her hair in one strand down her back as she usually did, she'd created an upswept arrangement that made her look like a princess.

He winked at her. "Wouldn't dream of it."

"Yeah, right. You were sizing her up just now, and don't try to deny it."

"Just having some innocent fun." Thoughts weren't deeds, right? "By the way, you look terrific, Josie. This Jack character must be treating you right."

"Don't try to change the subject." But her gray eyes, so like Alex's, sparkled with obvious pleasure at the compliment. "Caro has enough on her plate without having you swoop in and dazzle her with your big-city ways."

"Big-city ways?" He pressed a hand to his heart. "You make me sound like an operator. I'm wounded."

"You know what I'm talking about, Logan. A guy can't live the life you have without picking up a boatload of polish and sophistication."

"Now that's more like it." He winked at her. "Thanks for the compliment, Josie."

"See, that sly wink is exactly what I'm talking about. And I can tell she's impressed with you."

"You think so?" His poor ego could take all the help it could get.

"Don't mess with her, okay?"

"I had no such plans." He'd already decided that getting cozy with a local girl would be a mistake. Now Josie was warning him off of this particular one, which was more than enough to cool his jets. He really wasn't here to cause more problems. He already had enough to handle, like what the hell to do with the rest of his life.

But he couldn't help being curious about the cute little bartender. "What did you mean when you said she has enough on her plate?"

"It wouldn't be my place to tell you."

"Man troubles?"

"No. Listen, take my word for it." Josie patted his arm. "Caro's become a close friend in addition to being an employee, so I can tell you with certainty that she doesn't have time for romance right now, and she especially doesn't have time for someone who will be gone in a couple of days."

"Is that when my guest privileges expire?"

She flushed. "Uh…no! You can certainly stay as long as you want. I just thought, with Alex and Tyler leaving on their honeymoon tomorrow, that you'd…well, you'd want to go back to Chicago."

She had no idea how much he dreaded going home. The

season was in the middle of its usual August frenzy, with billboards and TV ads reminding him every ten seconds that some guys were playing ball and he was not. He was thrilled to get away from the unspoken message that he was a washed up has-been at the tender age of thirty-two.

"Well, yeah, I need to get back eventually," he said. "But I've never spent time on a ranch, so I was thinking, as long as I'm out here, I'd like to play cowboy for a few days. Unless I'd be in the way."

"Of course not. We'd love to have you. Are you thinking about riding?"

He wasn't sure what he was thinking about, except that the Last Chance felt like a haven, and he could use one. "Riding would be great. I'll need a little instruction, but—"

"What about your knee?"

"It's my right knee that's dicey, and I vaguely remember you mount from the left, so I should be fine."

Josie smiled at him, understanding in her gray eyes. "You can stay as long as you want, Logan. Glad to have you."

"I appreciate it." More than she knew.

"But leave Caro alone."

"You've got it." And to emphasize his willingness to ignore the lovely bartender, he left his half-full root beer on the bar and held out his hand to Josie. "May I have this dance, Alex's little sis?"

"Might as well. Can't drink!"

"That's right, you're on the wagon for the next few months. I'll bet you're popular as a designated driver these days."

"I am, at that." As they arrived at the edge of the dance floor, she moved into his arms. "I must say, you picked up country dancing really fast for a guy raised in the city."

Logan guided her expertly into the crowd of two-stepping couples. "Thanks. Guess it's the athlete in me."

"Guess so." She twirled under his arm. "The Chance

brothers are famous for their dancing. You're not quite in their league, but given more practice, you could be."

Logan grinned. "See? I have the boots, the jeans, the hat and the dance moves. I'm halfway to becoming a cowboy already."

THE RUSH OF DRINK ORDERS finally slowed, but when Caro returned to check on Logan, he'd hit the dance floor with Josie. He'd left his unfinished root beer behind, though, which meant he might be back. She felt a little jolt of excitement as she remembered the way he'd looked at her with obvious interest.

And she'd looked right back. She had no business flirting with anyone right now, but those deep brown eyes temporarily made her forget her obligations. And that, she realized with a pang of guilt, was nice for a change. She just couldn't let it get out of hand.

Her grandma Bonnie, who had raised her, joyfully and without complaint, deserved all Caro's free time. Caro had been a baby when her parents divorced, and Bonnie had welcomed her daughter and granddaughter into her house. When Caro was twelve, her mother had died in a blizzard on her way home from work. Grandma Bonnie's strength had seen Caro through those dark days and taught her that a person had to be resilient to survive life's tragedies.

Her dad had started a new family by then, but Caro had never seriously considered living with him. She'd stayed with her grandma in the only home she'd ever known. Selling that beloved house so that she could afford assisted living in Jackson for the increasingly frail Bonnie had broken both their hearts.

Caro visited her grandmother every day in hopes she wouldn't feel abandoned, but she obviously wasn't happy with the move, necessary though it had been. For the first time since Caro had known her, Bonnie had lost her resilience and optimistic outlook. Caro had to be optimistic enough for both of them.

Lately Caro had done nothing but work and visit her grandma. No wonder she'd been bewitched by a heated glance. Besides, she'd been predisposed to find this ex-baseball player intriguing.

Alex had warned everyone to tread carefully around Logan, whose wicked knee injury had ended his career and the dream he'd cherished from the age of seven. He'd made it to the big leagues and then to the Cubs, the team he'd always wanted to play for. Now he was done.

Caro had never been able to resist a person in need of comfort, a trait she'd picked up from her grandma. Besides, Logan was gorgeous, the kind of gorgeous that made her think of hot nights on cool sheets. Good thing he'd be gone soon. Once Alex and Tyler left on their honeymoon, Logan would have no reason to stay.

She filled several orders while Logan whirled around the dance floor with Josie, but somehow, about the time he returned to his root beer, she happened to be standing at that end of the bar. She hadn't meant to.

Oh, shoot, yes she had. He was the most exotic man to come her way in quite a while. Mostly she dealt with cowboys. Logan might be wearing the outfit and dancing the two-step like a pro, but he was no cowboy.

Instead, he was a professional athlete from the big city. She didn't know much about baseball, but she knew Logan was hot.

He settled onto his stool and heaved a sigh. "That's challenging."

"But you do it well." The action of those tight buns on the dance floor had created a serious distraction from her bartending duties.

"Close enough for jazz." He took a long swallow of his root beer.

"What does that mean?"

He glanced up. "What?"

"Close enough for jazz. I've never heard that before."

"Sorry. It's something jazz musicians say, meaning that there's a lot of improv going on when they perform."

She felt a little bit like a hick, but she was fascinated, nevertheless. Besides, if she kept this conversation going, she'd have an excuse to gaze into those brown eyes. "Chicago's known for its jazz, I guess."

"It is. I don't suppose that's the kind of music you…"

"Not normally, but I'm always ready to learn something new." No, that statement wasn't strong enough. She *hungered* for something new, something different. She'd lived in Shoshone all her life. Travel had been a luxury she hadn't been able to afford beyond an occasional trip to Yellowstone.

But this man, who'd jetted around the country for years, represented adventure beyond her wildest dreams. She found that irresistible.

Picking up a bar rag, she began wiping up imaginary spills. "Shoshone must seem small to you after spending so much time in big cities."

"Actually, it's a nice break. I can see why Alex is so crazy about the place. The Grand Tetons are amazing."

"I agree. They are. But I'm sure the Chicago skyline is amazing, too, especially at night."

"It is," he said with a decided lack of enthusiasm.

Damn. She felt like an idiot. Of course he wouldn't want to talk about the wonders of Chicago and be reminded of losing the job he loved. "The Tetons are great, though. Wonderful for hiking. You should—" She groaned as she realized she'd made a mess of this discussion. "But you have a bad knee. You know what? I should just shut up."

He laughed. "It's okay. I forget about my knee all the time, until I stay on it too long and it lets me know."

"Can you ride? Because you could take a horse up into the mountains, if it wouldn't be too strenuous." She'd bet he would look terrific mounted on a horse. Yum.

"I'll have to brush up on my riding skills, but I've been thinking about that. Do you ride?"

"I know how, but lately I haven't had the time." She refused to allow herself to be resentful of her grandma, but still, a trail ride with Logan would have been fun.

"Caro." Steve, looking pale, appeared at her elbow. His short buzz cut was dark with sweat. The room was warm, but not that warm. "I hate to do this to you, but my stomach's going wonky. Feels like food poisoning. I must have eaten something bad earlier today. In any case, I gotta go home."

She put her hand to her own tummy, which had immediately rolled in sympathy. "That's terrible. Don't worry about the bar. Just go home and get better."

"Thanks. I can take your shift tomorrow if you want."

"Only if you're well enough. Get out of here, cowboy." She sucked in a deep breath as Steve opened the hinged bar top and headed toward the back door. She'd counted on him to get her through this first big event, but she could manage, especially if the party started to wind down soon.

But Murphy's Law was working against her. The minute Steve left, the band took a break and wedding guests swarmed the bar in search of drinks. Fighting down panic, she squared her shoulders and grabbed an order pad. No way could she keep all those drinks in her head.

"You handle the beer and wine. I'll mix the drinks."

She looked up from the order pad and discovered Logan had joined her behind the bar and was already reaching for a couple of martini glasses.

"No, you shouldn't." She put a hand on his shoulder—his

very warm, very muscled shoulder. Instantly, that heat spread through her body. Whew. "You're a guest. I'm sure Josie could—"

"She's the sister of the groom. She shouldn't have to work tonight. Besides, I want to." He set the glasses on the counter and gave her a quick glance before picking up a bottle of vodka. "It feels great to be useful for a change."

She couldn't argue with that reasoning. Didn't really want to, actually. If helping her would make him feel better about his lot in life, even for an hour or so, then she couldn't deny him that. And she'd get the benefit of working side by side with the hottest guy in Shoshone.

"Okay, then," she said. "But only until it slows down."

"Right." He picked up a martini shaker, flipped it high in the air and caught it behind his back.

Someone in the crowd whistled.

Logan winked at Caro. "You know, I'd forgotten how much I used to love this job."

Oh, baby. He was positively delicious, and Caro was the lucky girl who got to co-bartend with him for an hour or so. She would never wish ill on anyone, but in that moment, she was really glad that Steve had ended up with food poisoning.

2

BEFORE JUMPING IN TO help Caro, Logan had spent a couple seconds weighing the pros and cons. Josie had asked him to stay away from Caro, but then again, Josie hadn't anticipated Steve getting sick. Logan had seen the panic in Caro's eyes when the band had stopped playing and the surge toward the bar had commenced.

Finally, deciding Josie shouldn't have to worry about working tonight, and surely she'd rather have happy customers than obsess about Caro and Logan working together, he'd swung into action. He couldn't pretend it was a selfless act. He'd told Caro the absolute truth—doing something useful felt fantastic.

And yeah, the idea of being Caro's heroic savior for an hour or so was very appealing. The looks she gave him generated a sexual buzz he hadn't felt in quite a while, and he was enjoying the hell out of that.

He promised himself that once the rush subsided, he'd retreat to the other side of the bar. Somehow, the rush never let up. Part of that could be his fault, because he hadn't been able to resist showing off a little. Besides juggling the martini shaker, he'd built a few flaming drinks, which caused folks to order more so they could watch the process.

And damn, he was having a good time. He was also

impressing the girl. He'd caught her staring a few times, although she didn't allow herself to be distracted from her work. For two people who'd never bartended together before, they managed with a minimum of bumping into each other.

That was a good thing, because whenever he accidentally brushed up against her, he registered exactly how soft and curvy she was. That message went straight to his groin.

She also smelled of lemons, which might be her perfume or might be the lemons she'd been cutting before he took over the cocktail part of the bar duties. Whatever the reason, the scent fit her personality, which was fresh, bright, and sexy as hell.

Once in a while his knee gave him a twinge, but then he'd take his weight off his right leg and be okay again. He was grateful for that, because the party showed no signs of letting up, even after Alex and Tyler left in a shower of birdseed. One o'clock came and went. Most bars closed then, but this one was owned by the sister of the groom, and she didn't seem ready to kick people out.

Caro slipped past him holding two brimming mugs of beer. "I'm worried about your knee," she said.

"Don't be." He garnished a cosmo. "I'm fine."

"I'm not sure I believe you."

"Working back here is a hell of a lot easier than dancing." He delivered the cosmo and came back with a couple dirty glasses. "Besides, I'm enjoying the company." He probably shouldn't have said that, but it wasn't as if he planned to ask her out.

"Me, too." She sent him a dazzling smile.

That made him feel good, probably too good. He wondered what she had going on in her life that kept her from dating. She seemed like someone who was worth getting to know, on many levels, but they were too busy for him to ask any questions.

Around two, the crowd finally began to thin, and Josie came to sit at the bar.

"Can I get you something?" Logan asked.

"No, thanks, but I owe you a huge debt for filling in tonight. I hope you haven't stressed your knee."

"I'm fine."

"I'd forgotten you used to tend bar, but Alex reminded me after he saw you back here flipping martini shakers around."

"I had fun." Working in close proximity with Caro had been ninety percent of that fun, but he'd keep that fact to himself.

"I could tell. Anyway, we're all about to head back to the ranch, and most everyone else is ready to call it a night, too. Or technically, I guess we have to call it a morning."

Logan took stock of the remaining dirty glasses, popcorn baskets and crumpled napkins lining the bar and grouped on the tables. "It was some party, Josie."

"It was. Alex and Tyler deserved a blowout, so I'm glad we did it up right. When you're ready, I'll give you a ride back, along with my slightly toasted husband."

Logan gestured around the room. "Do we need to take care of the final cleanup?"

"We probably should, at that." Josie straightened her shoulders. "You're right. I don't want to leave this for the morning crew."

"Or you can let Caro and me handle it." He made the suggestion casually, but there was nothing casual about his intentions. He wanted to be alone with the lovely Caro Davis.

"I can do it, Logan," Caro said immediately. "No worries. Go home and rest your knee."

"My knee's fine." Logan started gathering glasses. "I want to stay and help get this cleaned up. It won't take long."

Jack Chance wandered over and hooked an arm around Josie. "Ready to take off?"

"Not quite," Josie said. "I really need to—"

"No, you don't," Caro said. "Go home, Josie."

"I hate to leave you with this." She surveyed the room. "It's too bad that Steve—"

"Well, he isn't here," Logan said, "and I'd really like to help out. Besides, maybe one of the fabled ghosts will show up."

"It could happen." Josie looked perfectly serious. "I've often seen them after a bash like this."

"Ghosts or no ghosts," Jack said, "I need to get my pregnant wife home. I have a suggestion. Let Logan stay and help, and then he can crash at Grandma Judy's."

Josie turned to him. "I'm not sure about that, Jack. Do you think your grandmother will—"

"She'll love the idea. She's always complaining that nobody uses her guest room. Let me borrow your pen, Caro." He picked up a napkin from a stack on the bar and sketched a quick map for Logan. "Here's where she lives. When we drop her off we'll make sure she leaves a key under the mat. The guest room is down the hall to your right."

Josie took one last look at the debris left by the wedding guests and sighed. "Okay. There's probably some fatal flaw in that plan, but I'm too tired to think of anything better, and I do hate to leave Caro alone with this huge mess."

"And the ghosts." Logan tucked the napkin with the map into his pocket, and did his best to sound nonchalant when he felt anything but. He wondered if Caro was anticipating some alone time as much as he was.

"And the ghosts," Josie said with a smile.

"Thanks, Logan." Jack stuck out his hand and the two men shook. "I'll drive in tomorrow morning and pick you up."

"Sounds good."

"Josie said you'd like to stay on for a few more days and do some riding."

"I'd like that, but I'm a little rusty."

"Anybody with your athletic ability shouldn't have any trouble." Jack touched the brim of his hat with two fingers. "See you tomorrow."

"That was very gallant of you," Caro said as the last of the wedding guests disappeared out the front door. "You must be exhausted."

He turned to her. "No more so than you, I'll bet." He took note of the wisps of hair that had escaped her ponytail and now curled around the nape of her neck. Any lipstick she might have applied earlier in the evening was gone. She looked infinitely kissable.

Her hazel eyes were bright, as if she might be feeling some of the same excitement he was. "Yes, but I'm paid to do this. You're not."

"You want to know something really sad? Getting paid isn't an issue for me anymore. I've invested a good chunk of the money I earned while playing with the Cubs, and unless I start buying yachts and staying in hotels that charge several grand a night, I won't ever have to work again." That was all true, but he might have said it to impress her. Hell, sure he had.

It obviously did, because her eyes widened. "But that's not sad, that's *wonderful*."

Her honest reaction demanded honesty in return. "You would think so, wouldn't you? But in reality, it's kind of depressing. I have no reason to go out and hustle anymore."

"You could do all sorts of volunteer things, take charge of some cause or other, travel—"

"I could, and I probably will look into a charitable cause, but I'm not much of an administrator. That doesn't get me excited. Helping people, yeah, I'd like that. But the thought of being the one in charge gives me hives." He hadn't meant to discuss this, but talking to someone who had no vested interest in his future seemed to loosen his tongue.

"What a fascinating problem to have, deciding what to do with money and free time." She walked over to the wall and put her hand on a bank of switches.

"I suppose it sounds lame to call that a problem."

"Not if you're used to being busy. Get ready. Bright lights."

He blinked. In the glare from the overhead lights the mess looked even worse. "This would be more fun with the lights off."

She glanced over her shoulder, a definite invitation in her eyes. "That's true of a lot of things."

He met her gaze. He knew that look, and instantly his cock responded. Okay then. "Oh, I don't know. Sometimes I like to see what I'm doing."

She turned back to him with a seductive smile. "Is that when you're not very sure of yourself?"

"On the contrary." Lust was quickly obliterating the memory of any warnings Josie had given him. "The more confident I am, the more light I want on the subject." He paused. "How about you?"

She swallowed, and her cheeks grew pink. "Personally, I like to retain a little mystery."

"That can be exciting, too." He'd instinctively drifted closer. If he kissed her now, they wouldn't get any cleaning done.

As if realizing the same thing, Caro cleared her throat and glanced away. "It's getting late." Pulling a plastic bin from under the counter, she lifted the hinged lid of the bar. "I'll clear if you'll wipe up after me."

He followed her out through the opening and got a grip on the bin. "I'll clear and you wipe up. You're the brains of this operation. I'm just the muscle."

Her laugh had a breathless quality that told him she was

very aware of the sparks flying between them. She let him have the bin. "If that makes you happy, knock yourself out. I'll get a damp towel. Just know that I can balance a full tray of drinks on one hand, so I'm no wimpy girl."

"So you're the brains *and* the muscle." He loaded glasses, popcorn baskets and used napkins into the bin while she followed behind and wiped off the tables. "How am I supposed to impress a girl who has everything?"

"Those flaming drinks were pretty darned impressive. I know you don't need a job, but I'll bet Josie would love to hire you. Oh, wait. You might take my job, and unlike you, I need the money, so forget that idea."

She'd just handed him a golden opportunity to ask why Josie had said she was off-limits. He cleared the last table and headed back toward the bar. "So how come you don't have time to go riding these days?"

"My grandmother's in assisted living, and whenever I'm not working, I visit her."

"You mean, every day?" Logan thought of his two grandmothers, plus two grandfathers, all living back in Chicago. His folks and his younger brother, Jeff, lived there, too. He saw his grandparents maybe six or seven times a year. He didn't see any of his relatives daily.

"Yes, I go every day. But I'm sure you don't want to hear about this."

"Yes, I do. Come back into the kitchen while I stack the dishwasher, and tell me about it."

"It's not all that interesting. You go on. I'll start putting up the chairs."

He rested the bin against the counter. "Why don't you want to tell me?"

"Because it's boring." She picked up a chair and turned it upside down on a table, and followed that with another chair, and another.

"I don't think so."

"I do." She stacked chairs in rapid succession. "I love my grandmother more than anyone in the world, but there are times when worrying about her is a real buzzkill." She paused, her hand on the back of a chair. Then she turned to him with a stricken expression. "Did I just say that? I must be a horrible person to say something like that."

He smiled gently. "Not a horrible person. Just a person who needs to get out more. And I don't mean to the assisted living facility."

She shook her head. "I can't. She knows my schedule, and she expects me to come whenever I'm not working. I need to be there for her. I *want* to be there for her."

"That's pretty intense. Can't you back off from that a little bit?"

"Eventually I hope to, once she's back to her usual sunny self. These first few months have been rough on her. I had to move her out of her house and sell it to pay for this place, because she needs constant medical supervision. It was the only answer."

Josie might be annoyed, but Logan thought of his next move as a good deed. "Didn't Steve say he'd take your next shift?"

"He did, but he might not feel up to it."

"Then again, he might. When is it?"

"Three to eleven, but he looked pretty sick to me."

"If it's food poisoning, he could be over it by tomorrow. And if he can take your shift, then you could go riding with me at the Last Chance. Your grandmother would never know." He would explain to Josie that her best employee was about to blow a gasket if she didn't get some recreation into her routine. Surely Josie would understand.

Caro hesitated. "I have to admit that sounds nice."

"Of course it does. Taking a trail ride was your suggestion in the first place."

"Josie and Jack have told me anytime I want to come out and ride, I'm more than welcome."

"There you go." His excitement grew as he imagined spending hours with her out on the trail. No doubt he'd end up saddle sore, but it would be worth it to watch her soaking up the sunshine and fresh air. And maybe a long trail ride could turn into a private little... But he didn't want to get ahead of himself.

"Now I'm really hoping Steve recovers."

"Me, too." Logan was prepared to find another replacement if Steve was still on the disabled list. He'd plead Caro's case to Josie and see what could be done. "Now let's finish cleaning so you can go home and get some sleep." He tossed that last part out on purpose, to see if she had any plan to linger around...with him.

"Okay." She started stacking chairs on tables again. "Fortunately, I don't have to go far. Josie's renting me her old apartment upstairs."

That info flashed in neon lights in his hormone-soaked brain. So her bedroom was right over their heads. "That's convenient." He picked up the bin full of glasses and headed into the kitchen.

As he loaded the commercial dishwasher, he fought with his conscience. He'd pictured some time alone, maybe a few kisses, some fondling. *But her bedroom was right upstairs.*

He probably shouldn't go there, even if he could work it so nobody ever had to know but the two of them. Then again, she might have mentioned it on purpose, hoping he'd take the hint. She might not have time for a relationship, but was there anything wrong with some good old-fashioned sex?

He sighed. Josie had specifically requested that he put on the brakes, and he was considering flooring it. She was obviously protective of Caro, and Logan admired that. But should Josie be the one to decide what happened between Caro and him? Or should she be allowed to choose for herself?

So much hinged on Caro's attitude. After spending several hours working with her, he saw her as upbeat and levelheaded, not the sort of woman who would expect one fun night together meant wedding bells.

He started the dishwasher and walked back out into the bar, where Caro wielded a push broom with gusto. The rapid motion made her breasts quiver under her red checked Western shirt. From her complete concentration, someone might conclude that the fate of the world rested on getting every last bit of debris off the floor.

Logan had always admired hustle, but he knew she must be tired. "I'd be glad to finish that up if there's something else you need to do to close the place down."

"Not really." She kept sweeping, her gaze focused intently on the job, her fingers clenched around the broom handle. "As you noticed, it was an open bar tonight, which was Josie and Jack's gift to the happy couple, so I don't have to tally any receipts."

"Want me to take out the trash?"

She shook her head and kept working. "It's better to put it out in the morning. Once in a while we have bears come through at night." She looked up. "We're basically done, Logan. Thanks so much. You can head on over to Judy's place if you want." She put her head down and continued to sweep as if her life depended on it.

"Trying to get rid of me?"

She stopped in midsweep and gazed at him. "No, but I'll bet you're exhausted."

"Funniest thing, but I'm not particularly sleepy."

"Oh." She started sweeping again, but her motions were

slower. "Then if you don't mind getting the small broom and that long-handled dustpan, I'd appreciate it."

"I can do that." He found them over in a corner and began gathering up the piles she'd made and dumping everything into a plastic-lined trash can.

"Logan, do you have a girlfriend?"

He almost choked on his answer. "No." He could think of only one reason for that question. He cleared his throat so he could elaborate as he continued to scoop up trash. "I was dating someone, but it turned out she wasn't crazy about going out with an ex-baseball player."

"Ouch."

He glanced over at Caro. "Actually, it was one of the good things about leaving the game. She had a chance to show her true colors." He paused. "Do you have a boyfriend?" From Josie's comments, he was fairly sure she didn't, but he might as well make certain.

She leaned on the broom. "I used to. Curtis got tired of me not being available because of my grandma. We broke up about six months ago." She took a deep breath. "Quite obviously, I'm not girlfriend material at the moment. There's no room in my life for a man."

Logan nodded, as if they were discussing the weather. "I understand completely."

"But…"

"Yes?" Dear God, he hoped this conversation was leading where he thought it was.

She opened her mouth, and then closed it again. When she finally spoke, the words came out in a rush. "Would you be interested in coming up for a nightcap?" Her cheeks were pink but her gaze was steady.

His heart thudded in anticipation, but he wanted to be sure this was what she really wanted. "You must be tired."

Her hazel eyes grew dark and her breathing quickened. "Not that tired."

Dear God, she wanted him in her bed. Only a fool would pass up a chance like this, and Logan was no fool. "Then yes. Yes, I would love a nightcap."

3

CARO COULDN'T QUITE believe she'd just invited Logan Carswell, big league baseball star, up to her apartment. Even more unbelievable, he'd accepted. Eagerly. She'd acted on pure instinct, and apparently her instincts were on target. They wanted each other.

The old nightcap routine was as transparent as ever. He had to know as well as she did why they were going up there. And unless Logan walked around with condoms in his wallet, he needed to make a trip into the Spirits and Spurs men's room. After Curtis had dumped her, she'd taken the remaining condoms out of the medicine cabinet and cut them up with a pair of scissors as part of some silly ritual to proclaim her new celibacy.

Once Logan left town, whenever that turned out to be, she'd be celibate again, at least until her grandmother regained her former spirit. But opportunity had pounded on the door in the person of Logan Carswell, wounded athlete. Caro was more than ready to give up her mental chastity belt and embrace that opportunity to have a little fun.

Logan dumped one final dustpan's worth in the trash. "Is that it?"

"Yes." Her heart raced. "I'll put the brooms away in the kitchen if you'll…" She found herself unable to finish the sentence. Inviting him up to her place on the flimsy pretext of a nightcap was one thing. Telling him to patronize the vending machine in the men's room was a whole new level of chutzpah.

"If I'll what?" He met her gaze. "Oh." Understanding registered in his brown eyes. "Guess I'll just duck into the bathroom for a minute."

"Okay." Her cheeks felt warm with embarrassment as she grabbed both brooms and the long-handled dustpan. She fumbled and dropped the push broom. The handle banged against the floor.

Before she could retrieve it, Logan reached for it in one fluid motion and held it toward her. "Here you go."

"Thanks. I'll be right back." What a doofus she must seem to a guy with his sophistication. Here she was, dropping brooms and sending him after condoms. She wondered if the women in Chicago always had supplies on hand before they impulsively asked someone up for a nightcap. Probably.

Well, she was a small-town girl from Shoshone. Besides, she'd been pissed at Curtis, and cutting up the condoms had seemed justified at the time. She'd wanted to destroy something, and that had been the best target for her anger.

Logan hadn't returned by the time she walked back into the bar. Her hands trembled slightly as she pulled her keys out of her pocket and locked the back door. Then she doused all the lights except for the soft ones that Josie left on for security purposes, although crime was unlikely in Shoshone.

The dim light helped calm her a little, but if Logan didn't come out soon, she was seriously going to lose her nerve. She'd almost made up her mind to cancel the plan when she heard the door to the men's room open. Then she heard it swing shut again.

She gulped. It was put up or shut up time.

He walked toward her. "Seen any ghosts yet?"

"Nope." She wondered how many condoms he'd bought and if that was what had taken him so long, but she wasn't about to ask.

"What kind of ghosts are they supposed to be?"

"Cowboy ghosts, of course." She could barely hear herself speak over the thundering of her heart in her ears. "Have you heard of the old song 'Ghost Riders in the Sky'?"

"Yeah, I think so."

"They call these guys 'ghost drinkers in the bar.'"

He laughed. "I like that. I almost wish one would show up, but not enough to hang around waiting."

So he wanted to get on with it. Gulp. "Like I said, I've never seen one myself." Her chest felt as if somebody had tightened a cinch around it. She'd never done anything like this before. Usually she got to know someone over a period of weeks or months before she progressed to this step.

But if she wanted Logan, and she did, then she had to woman up and direct him to her apartment. "We'll have to g-go outside," she said. "The s-stairs to my apartment are on the outside of the building." Damn. She *never* stuttered.

"Caro." He laid a gentle hand on her arm.

"What?" She whirled to face him, nearly stabbing him in the chest with her keys.

He rubbed her arm. "You don't have to go through with this if it makes you nervous."

"But I want to." And now that he'd touched her—on purpose, and not accidentally while they'd been working together—she *really* wanted to. Nervous though she might be, she yearned for him in a way that was shocking in its intensity.

His voice dropped to a soft murmur. "You're sure?"

Her answer came from some deeply buried part of herself, one that she'd never allowed to surface. "Kiss me and you'll find out how sure I am."

"Good idea." His grip tightened on her arm and he guided her forward while he cupped the back of her head with his other hand, fingers spread.

She stopped breathing, stopped thinking, stopped noticing anything but his mouth as he drew her closer. He had a beautiful mouth, sculpted enough to be masculine, full enough to be sensual. She closed her eyes and trembled in anticipation.

"I've wanted to do this all night." His breath was warm on her lips. He brushed her mouth with his. "You're shaking."

"I know."

His lips stroked over hers again. "It'll be okay."

"I know."

Then he settled in, and it was more than okay.

His kiss was velvet and sleek, rich and luxurious, slow and sweet. He savored her mouth as if tasting expensive brandy served in a crystal goblet. She had never felt so cherished.

Her keys clattered to the floor as she took his head in her hands. She wanted more. She wanted everything. Angling her mouth over his, she invited him deeper. He accepted the invitation with a firm thrust of his tongue.

Yes. She whimpered and he pulled her in close, sliding his arm around her waist and pressing her against his very hard, very aroused body as he continued to kiss the living daylights out of her.

Dear heaven, he really was a professional athlete, with all the toned muscles that job required. She'd known that intellectually, but experiencing it physically was more exciting than she'd imagined. She stroked his supple back, his broad shoulders, his tight buns.

With a groan he lifted his head and gazed down at her in the dusky light. His voice was hoarse. "You've convinced me. Let's go."

She struggled to breathe.

Releasing her, he scooped up her keys as if fielding a

baseball, and put them in her hand. "If we don't get out of here right now, we'll never make it up there."

"Then let's go." She moved toward the front door on unsteady legs. As she opened it, she thought she heard soft laughter coming from somewhere behind her. She turned. "What's so funny?"

"Nothing."

"Didn't you laugh just now?"

"No. I thought it was the door hinge."

She paused, playing the sound over again in her head. "Guess so." It hadn't been a door hinge, but she wasn't going to go ghost-hunting tonight. She had more important things on her mind.

SMALL-TOWN GIRLS PACKED a sensual punch, Logan concluded as he fought to stay cool while climbing the narrow set of stairs behind Caro. Her hot little body sang a siren's song with every creak of the steps. He swore steam was coming off her denim-clad fanny.

Although he hadn't indulged himself with a woman recently, in the past he'd been involved with sophisticates who dressed in expensive lingerie, women who were into sex toys and flavored body paint. Not a single one had turned him on the way Caro had with her blushing request for vending-machine condoms.

When she'd invited him to kiss her, he'd gone up in flames. Where had she learned to talk like that? When she paired her down-home cuteness with sex-kitten suggestions, she became an irresistible combo of sweetness and sin that made him wild for her.

He'd bought three condoms, and those had been hard-won. Despite a few whacks with his fist, the machine hadn't wanted to cooperate. He'd finally decided three would do. He still wanted to end the night in Grandma Judy's guest room, for appearance's sake.

Now he wondered if three would be enough, after all. He might not be able to force himself to leave before dawn, and he was a real fan of sex in the morning.

Caro reached the landing and seemed to have lost her jitters, because she opened the door without fumbling. He took the last two steps in one leap and followed her inside, his heart hammering and his johnson aching.

She hit a switch beside the door and a floor lamp in one corner illuminated a small living room on the right and a tiny kitchen on the left. Both were spotless, with cozy touches like gingham curtains at the kitchen window and colorful throw pillows on the leather sofa.

As he clicked the lock on the front door, she turned to him. "I could offer—"

"Just you." He tossed his hat like a Frisbee toward the sofa. He didn't look to see if it had landed as he pulled her into his arms. "Offer yourself, and I'll be a happy man."

"I can do that." Sliding out of his arms, she backed toward the hallway. "Follow me."

"You've got it."

"First, the shirts." She took hold of her lapels and pulled. Snaps popped like cap guns, and the cotton bra covering her pert breasts didn't fool him in the least. She might not be wearing something obviously sexy, but he saw the fire in her hazel eyes. She was a volcano ready to erupt.

He was so busy looking at what her open shirt revealed that he didn't follow orders.

"Your shirt, Logan."

He sure as hell didn't want to hold up the program. He wrenched open his shirt, shrugged out of it and tossed it to the floor as he continued down the hall.

At the doorway to her bedroom, she reached for another

switch, and lamps on twin nightstands winked on. "You said you liked light."

"I do." He gestured toward her bra. "Are you going to take that off, or shall I?"

She backed into the room with a soft smile. "I will." She reached behind her back to unhook it. "You've had a long night."

"Wouldn't trade it for the world." He started to unbuckle his belt, but his hands stilled as she slipped off her bra. She might prefer cotton, but breasts as full and perfect as hers deserved designer silk. Her wine-colored nipples puckered under his gaze.

His fingers flexed and he took a step closer. "I want—"

"And you'll have." She backed to the other side of the small room, putting the bed between them. "But I can take off my clothes faster than you can." She waved at him. "Continue with what you were doing."

He had to laugh. She was the most logical little sexy thing he'd ever come across. He had to admit she was right, especially when it came to dealing with belts and boots.

He tried to be quick about it, he really did. He managed to pull off his boots, but after that, she became a major distraction. When she leaned down to take hers off, her breasts quivered enticingly.

Then she began to wiggle out of her jeans, causing more breast shimmy. The soft denim caught on the elastic of her panties and they came off along with the jeans. She stood naked before him, and that required his undivided attention.

As she pulled the scrunchie from her ponytail and shook her hair free, she glanced over and caught him staring. "You're still mostly dressed."

He swallowed. "And you're not." He'd suspected she'd be fine to look at, but hadn't realized she'd look *this* fine. Maybe country living made a woman's skin glow like that.

Or maybe—and this was an ego-boosting thought—she was flushed with desire for him.

In any case, she was radiant, as if someone had buffed her body until it gleamed with rosy good health. He stood mesmerized, his glance traveling over the wonders he longed to touch, to taste, to lose himself in. No body piercings for this woman. No Brazilian wax, either. A neat triangle of light brown curls awaited him.

She cleared her throat, which snapped him out of his daze long enough to get rid of his jeans and his knit boxers. He had to work both of them over an erection that felt bigger than the Hancock Building. He was gratified when she sucked in a breath. Nice to be noticed.

She'd stood still while he looked, so he afforded her the same privilege. This was the first time—and maybe the last time—they would see each other without clothes. They should make it count.

He wished he was in better physical shape, but his knee had kept him from the full workouts he was used to. Her breathing picked up as she studied him, though, and he kind of thought she liked what she saw. Her gaze lingered on the purple scar where he'd had knee surgery.

Surgery hadn't put him back in the game, but at least he could walk without hobbling. In fact, he could dance for short stretches, a fact he'd proven tonight. He'd told himself to be grateful for that much.

"Looks painful," she said.

"It is, and I'm not talking about my knee."

Her mouth tilted in a smile. "Cute."

"I prefer the term *impressive.*"

She laughed and flung back the covers, which included a colorful patchwork quilt. "Are you fishing for compliments, Carswell?"

"Yes."

"Then let me just say that UPS would likely slap a surcharge on that package of yours." She climbed into bed and stretched out, facing him. "Gonna deliver it?"

"Yeah." He was really starting to like her, and that could be a problem. He might want to remind himself, beginning now, that this was only temporary. "Special delivery, overnight male."

4

CARO WAS PROUD OF HERSELF for keeping the tone light. She'd never had a one-night stand, and this was shaping up to be her first try at it. If so, she wanted to make sure the mood was carefree and playful, not intense and sordid.

So far, so good. Logan was following her lead, and as he climbed into her bed, she told herself not to mentally record this moment and think it was significant, because it wasn't. Yes, his body was incredible. He was the most muscular guy she'd ever seen naked, not counting marble statues or issues of *Playgirl.*

He was so ripped that she felt a little intimidated, as if she were about to take a ride on a monster roller coaster and wasn't sure if she'd chicken out before it began. Could she keep up with all that energy and power? She was willing to try.

Her body was more than willing. From her first glimpse of his spectacular endowments, moisture had collected between her thighs and her womb had contracted. Natural instinct had taken over, demanding that she join with him in the most basic way.

So she'd take this wild ride, but she'd better not get used to having a hard body in her bed. She'd look into his sexy eyes, which reminded her of dark chocolate, but wouldn't set that shade of brown as her new standard. His mouth not only looked sensual, she knew from experience that it felt even better. Still, she couldn't get attached to his kisses, either.

What was about to happen between them was an unexpected gift, a moment stolen from each of their regularly scheduled lives.

Then he looked into her eyes, and she was caught by surprise at the warmth and caring in his gaze. When he touched her, all her promises to stay objective shattered. He could have grabbed her. With all their banter, he would have been justified in rolling her onto her back and having his way with her.

Instead, he skimmed the tips of his fingers over her cheek with such tenderness that her throat tightened.

"I want you so much I can barely stand it," he said. "But before this gets hot and heavy, and I can guarantee it will, I wanted to say…thank you."

She swallowed the lump in her throat. "Shouldn't I be thanking you? I'm sure you can get girls by snapping your fingers. I'm the one who's in a sexual wasteland."

He smiled. "I've been in a wasteland of my own making, bogged down in self-pity. This…" He paused to sweep his hand over the bed. "This feels as if you just tossed me a lifeline."

"I'd say 'anytime,' but we both know that's not possible."

He cupped her face with one hand. "So let's make the most of right now." But his kiss was slow and easy, as if they had all the time in the world. Leisurely, he combed his fingers through her hair and nibbled his way from her mouth to the curve of her neck. "You smell like lemons."

"Homemade lemon juice hair spray." She shivered as he ran his tongue along her collarbone.

"Love it." His virile body was inches from hers, yet his mouth and fingertips were the only contact points between them.

Tension wound tight within her. She tamped it down,

fighting for the kind of control he seemed to have. In an attempt to mirror his restraint, she slid her fingers across his lightly furred chest. She'd meant to keep her caress as soft as his, but oh, the muscles on this man!

She flattened her palm against the most magnificent pecs she'd ever touched. Her breath caught as she absorbed the heat and power, and imagined his body poised over hers.

The ache that had been building ever since he'd first kissed her threatened to overwhelm her good manners. She was fast approaching the point where she was liable to move her hand lower, latch on to the object of her desire and demand that he use it immediately. That would not be classy.

"Logan?" She heard the desperate note in her voice and couldn't do anything about it.

"Uh-huh."

"Um, do you know where your condoms are?"

"Yes." He sounded amused.

"I don't mean to rush you, but..."

He chuckled softly, his breath warm against her shoulder. "Caro, I didn't want to rush *you.* I'm not a small guy, and I didn't want to hurt you because you weren't ready."

"I'm beyond ready, Logan. Rushing sounds like a wonderful idea."

He raised his head, his dark eyes sparkling with lust and laughter. "Yes, ma'am."

"Thank you." She curled her hands into fists and squirmed with impatience as he rolled to the far side of the bed, snatched up his jeans and rummaged in the pocket. The sound of ripping foil was music to her ears.

When he came back, he was ready for action. "No more foreplay, then?"

She shook her head and held out her arms. "Main event, please."

"God, Caro." He moved over her, his breathing ragged.

"You are some kind of woman." Bracing himself on one arm, he reached between her thighs. "But I still need to make sure you're—"

"Logan." She squeezed her eyes shut and arched off the bed as his probing fingers nearly made her come. She'd never wanted a man so much that she was dizzy with anticipation.

He groaned softly. "You weren't kidding."

"No." She opened her eyes and met his gaze as she cupped his firm bottom. "Now."

"With pleasure." He thrust forward and gasped. "God, that feels good."

Good didn't begin to cover what she was feeling. Pressing her fingers into the muscles of his backside, she closed her eyes again. The rightness of this connection stunned her. She'd imagined that sex with Logan would be nice, but she hadn't counted on this...perfection.

He leaned down and brushed his mouth against hers. "You okay?"

"Fabulous," she murmured.

"You're so still."

She looked up at him. "I'm just..." Overjoyed? Ecstatic? No, she couldn't say that.

"Don't worry. I'll go slow. Let you get used to me." He eased back and slid forward in a gentle motion.

That was all it took. She gasped as the first spasm hit.

His eyes widened. "Caro? Are you...?"

"Yes...*yessss.*" A powerful orgasm arced through her, leaving her shuddering and breathless.

His voice was low and intense. "Okay, then." His buttocks flexed beneath her fingers as he began a steady rhythm that urged her quivering body to tighten once again. He gazed down at her, his dark eyes gleaming with purpose. "I think you're used to me."

"Uh-huh." Her breath caught as he shifted his angle to penetrate even deeper.

He paused and gulped for air. "Still okay?"

"Mmm." She wrapped her legs around him, opening herself in complete surrender. "Don't…"

He frowned in obvious concern. "Don't?"

"Don't stop." She smiled up at him.

"Caro, you're…" He dragged in more air. "Amazing."

Logan's movements took on new authority as his forceful thrusts propelled them forward. Gradually he increased the pace, urging both of them toward the brink.

Caro abandoned herself to his rhythm as they rocked faster, and faster still, and then…heat flooded through her, brilliant, golden and intense. Through the haze of her climax she heard him cry out, and he surged forward. She absorbed his orgasmic shudders with a laugh of pure delight.

This had been an outstanding idea.

Logan felt the ripple of laughter caress his happy penis. He'd never had any woman laugh at the end of sex with him, but was beginning to understand that Caro was unique. Once he had enough breath in his lungs to form a sentence, he nuzzled her ear. "Do you usually laugh after sex?"

She laughed again. "No."

"Should I be honored or insulted?"

"Honored, for sure. I couldn't help it. I'm so happy."

He raised his head and peered down at her. Sure enough, she looked content. Her eyes sparkled and her skin was flushed with obvious pleasure. He'd like to claim credit for that, but he had a hunch Caro was pretty easy to please. Still, she had said she didn't usually laugh.

"So what brought on this happy laughter?"

She stroked his back. "Well, because I've never invited a

man I just met into my bed, I wasn't absolutely sure it would work out well. But it did, didn't it?"

"That's an understatement." He loved the way she touched him—not too light and not too heavy. Not everyone was good at that.

"See? We took a chance on each other and had a terrific time. We even managed a mutual climax, and that doesn't always happen, especially the first time with someone."

"That's true." She was adorable—and that tug at his heart should serve as a warning to be careful. But he wouldn't have much luck distancing himself while he was this close to her sweet, sunny self. He'd work on the distancing thing later, maybe on the plane ride home.

In the meantime, he planned to soak up as much of this *therapy* as he could, and give her some in return. "I'd have to say that was the best first-time sex I've ever had."

"Me, too. Hands down. Which is a good thing, because we needed to get it right the first time, all things considered."

"Yeah, not much time to practice." But he was willing to work in whatever practice they could. She ought to have some input on that plan, though. "Especially if you want to get some sleep before morning comes."

She switched from stroking his back to fondling his chest. "Are you sleepy?"

He wondered if she'd ever studied massage. Her touch was magic. "I asked you first."

"All right, then I'll be honest. I want to come at least once more before morning does. That is, if you have another condom available."

He grinned. "I have two more."

"Excellent."

"I would have bought more than that, but the machine wasn't very cooperative."

"It probably needs maintenance. I'll bet nobody would

report it to Josie or me. A guy might tell Steve, but it's not like some cowboy would come up to me and say the condom machine is malfunctioning. It's kind of a prob—"

He cut her off with a quick kiss. "Let's not worry about it. I have two more, and if you'll direct me to your bathroom…"

"Across the hall."

He eased away from her and left the bed. "Be right back." The moment he put his weight on his right leg, pain sliced through his knee. Without meaning to, he sucked in a breath.

"Is it your knee?"

Thank God his back was to her and she couldn't see his grimace of pain. "It's fine." He did his best not to hobble out of the room.

"I don't believe you," she called after him. "You're limping."

"I'll make a believer of you when I come back," he said over his shoulder. "It was just a twinge, that's all." His knee ached like a son of a bitch, but he would never admit it. He had a couple of hours with this woman, and he damned well wasn't going to be treated like some kind of cripple during that time.

He'd thought any position, including the missionary one, would be okay by now. Apparently not, especially after dancing and tending bar for hours. He'd been so blissed out by what was going on with his cock that he hadn't noticed he was stressing his knee at the same time.

Oh, well. He'd stress it again if necessary, because he wasn't about to put limits on his sexual positions. Talk about a wussy attitude. He wouldn't baby himself, and he didn't want her to baby him, either. It was only one night, and he'd enjoy the hell out of it.

He flipped on the light in her miniscule bathroom and tried not to bump his knee against anything while maneuvering in the limited space. He wasn't used to small spaces. His condo in Chicago had a bathroom three times this size.

Yet he'd much rather be here. The bathroom was decorated in the same cozy country style as the rest of the place, with red gingham curtains at the tiny window and an old oak bucket serving as a wastebasket. The scent of lemons reminded him that Caro had mentioned using homemade lemon juice hair spray.

He wasn't a big fan of hair spray, but lemon juice sounded better than the other gunk women put on their hair. She must not use much of it, because her hair slid through his fingers like silk. Everything about her was silky and smooth, in fact. She'd been wet, ready, and a perfect fit, as if her body had been created specifically for him to enjoy.

He'd had some good sex in his life, but, as she'd said, never this good this soon. Maybe that first time had been a fluke, and the next episode wouldn't deliver such a rush. He was ready to find out. Disposing of the condom, he massaged his knee for a few seconds before turning out the light and crossing the hall.

She'd propped a couple pillows against the oak headboard and was sitting up. The multicolored quilt covered her lap, but her breasts were bare. "I took the condoms out of your jeans pocket and put them on the nightstand. I hope you don't mind."

"Does it look as if I mind?" One glimpse of her waiting for him, condoms at the ready, and he was hard.

She glanced at his package and smiled. "No, not really. That's a very gratifying reaction."

"It's a perfectly natural reaction with a woman as sexy as you are." He walked over to the bed.

"I've never thought of myself as particularly sexy."

"Unconscious sexiness is the most potent kind." He tossed back the quilt and started to climb into bed with her.

"Don't get in like that. You're putting pressure on your knee."

He'd forgotten and put his right knee on the mattress, because he was used to getting in bed that way. Yeah, it hurt, but he would ignore it. Nobody was going to treat him like an invalid.

"I saw that flash of pain in your eyes, Logan. You can't fool me."

"Be quiet, Caro." On all fours, he leaned toward her, his mouth seeking hers.

She ducked out of his reach. "You're a crazy man. And I'm not kissing you again until you're flat on your back and off that knee."

"That's totally unnecessary. I'm fine." He cupped the back of her head, his grip gentle but firm. "And I'm desperate to kiss you, so hold still."

"Have it your way."

"Thank you." He lowered his mouth to hers.

She kissed him back, but while he was savoring the lush wonders of her mouth, she got both hands around his dick and instituted the kind of sweet torture that would bring him to climax in no time.

He lifted his lips a fraction from hers. "Stop that or I'll come."

"Agree to lie on your back for me and I'll stop."

"No need to be on my back, Caro." He clenched his jaw as his balls tightened and his orgasm threatened.

She toyed with the sensitive tip of his penis and used the gathering moisture to lubricate the surface. "Maybe you're afraid to let a woman be on top, where she has more control."

"It's not that." He could overpower her and make her stop, but he would never use superior strength to exert his will on a woman.

"I think you have control issues."

"I will any second if you keep that up."

"Logan, do you really want to waste precious time arguing about this?"

When she put it that way, so logically, he had no sensible response. It was a silly argument, after all. He lifted his head and looked into her eyes. "No, I don't. You win."

She stopped stroking him. "That's better."

"On one condition."

"Which is?"

"That you don't mention my knee again while we're sharing this bed."

"Why not? You need to be careful of your knee. Alex told me all about the injury, and if you aren't careful, you might—"

"Let me worry about that, okay? It's bad enough that I'm out of baseball because of my knee, without having my sex life impacted, too."

She nodded. "I see your point."

He stretched out flat on the bed. "Then I'm all yours."

5

IF ONLY HE COULD BE all hers. Caro banished that thought the minute it popped into her head. No need to be greedy about this. She had far more now than she'd had a few hours ago.

And what she had, for the time being, was one spectacular man stretched out in her bed. He was all muscle and magic to her, this man who could catch a ninety-eight-mile-an-hour fastball. Once she got a minute to herself, she'd use the computer in Josie's office to look up his stats and see if any clips were available.

But that was for later. For now, she took the package he so graciously handed her, ripped it open and rolled the condom lovingly onto his very large, very erect penis. He trembled as she did that, and his massive chest heaved.

She'd thought about exploring him a little more before putting on the condom, but she didn't think he'd last through what she had in mind. Her very presence seemed to get him hot, and that surprised her. The guys she'd known had required more obvious turn-ons, like a generous display of cleavage or a skirt slit to midthigh.

She'd been told more than once that she was too wholesome to be sexy. Logan's comment about her unconscious sexuality would stay with her for a long, long time. He was good for her, and she wanted to be good for him, too. Thank

God he'd agreed to a position that wouldn't put pressure on his knee.

She'd keep her promise not to mention that again, because she, of all people, understood when someone didn't like being reminded of an infirmity. Grandma Bonnie *hated* admitting she wasn't as capable as she'd once been. Logan's bad knee seemed like a minor problem in the grand scheme of things, but Caro wasn't the pro ballplayer who had lost his career because of that knee.

"You're driving me bat-shit crazy, taking so long with that condom." He propped himself on his elbows to glare at her. "I hope you know that."

"So you *do* have control issues."

"Yeah." He flopped back to the mattress. "I feel like I'm going to come any second, and in my world, the woman gets to come first. I'm not sure that's going to happen."

"Is there anything I can do to make your world a better place?"

He turned his head to gaze at her and his dark eyes smoldered. "As a matter of fact, there is." He caught her hand and tugged on it. "Straddle me."

"I thought that was the idea."

"Not like that." He patted his breastbone. "Up here."

"Oh." Her heart raced.

"Chicken?"

"I've never…"

"Never?"

"Well, of course I've…I mean, naturally, I've tried…but not like that."

His smile was wicked. "You'd be in control."

She doubted it. She suspected that once he began, she'd lose control very quickly.

He tugged on her hand again. "Are we going to waste time arguing about sexual positions?"

"I—"

"We're having a secret rendezvous, one that nobody ever has to know about." His voice grew husky. "You can do whatever you want, Caro. Anything at all."

"Then I want to turn out the lights."

"And spoil all my fun? Don't do that. Please."

"Logan…"

"I've wanted to taste you ever since you stripped down on the other side of the bed and I saw those caramel curls."

"You already know. You were there."

"My cock was there. I couldn't see, couldn't savor. Let me do that."

She was on fire, and she wasn't sure if the heat came from embarrassment or raging excitement. He was pushing her boundaries…and she *liked* it. He was right. They were indulging in a secret rendezvous, and if she ever wanted to be wild, this was the perfect time.

"Come on, Caro," he said softly. "Let me find out how sweet you really are."

As if drawn by the magnetic pull of his eyes, she moved toward him.

"Swing your leg over," he coaxed. "That's it. Scoot up. A little more…come to me…" He slid both hands under her bottom and then…

She gasped at the first contact with his hot mouth. Lying on her back with her thighs open was one thing, but this felt decadent, as if she were demanding it, as if she had him at her mercy, and he had no choice but to…oh, dear heaven. He had a choice and was making it, with gusto.

Trembling, she balanced by bracing her hands above his head. Gradually, she realized the whimpering sounds were hers, and the moans were hers, and the lusty cries of delight… were hers. She came once, in a shower of vibrating color, and when she tried to pull away, he held her fast and made her come again. As the contractions overtook her, she threw back her head and screamed in ecstasy.

She might have imagined that she'd have control with Logan flat on his back, but she was so wrong. While still in the grip of her second orgasm, she felt herself being bench-pressed up and back. Without quite knowing how she got there, she slid effortlessly down his rigid penis until they were locked together, a perfect fit once again.

"Got anything left for me?" He stroked her breasts and spanned her waist with both hands.

"Yes." Energized by the connection, the fullness of him deep inside her, she spread her palms on his chest. Her fingers flexed as she absorbed the warmth, the shiver of his muscles, his rapid heartbeat. "Yes."

And she began to ride him, slowly at first, and faster as he caught the rhythm and responded, his hips lifting in time with her downward strokes. They both began to pant, and the room filled with the liquid sounds of bodies pumping and straining toward the ultimate completion. Once again, they found it together, in a frenzy of rapid thrusts and mingled cries.

Caro slumped against him, boneless, unable to imagine moving, let alone leaving this bed. She realized that moment would arrive eventually, but she shoved that reality aside as she lay on Logan's sweat-slicked chest and listened to the wild beat of his heart.

He rubbed her back, his caress a soothing counterpart to the passion they'd shared. As sanity returned, she wondered where they would go from here. The first time had been amazing, but the second time had obliterated all her bench-marks. Whether that was good or bad, she wasn't sure. All she knew was that Logan had forever raised the bar and there was no use pretending she would ever be satisfied with less.

LOGAN HAD ALWAYS BELIEVED that great sex should wind down slowly, with lots of cuddling and touching to maintain the mood. But because the lights were still on in Caro's little bedroom, he could easily see his watch. He purposely hadn't taken it off.

Sadly, his watch indicated that he had to get the hell out of Caro's apartment and over to Grandma Judy's if he expected to pull off this caper. Being discovered in Caro's bed would be bad for him, but potentially worse for her. He could leave town and the gossip. She couldn't.

He wrapped his arms around her, as if he could somehow soften the announcement. "I have to go."

She sighed. "I know."

"If I leave now, I might be able to sneak into Grandma Judy's house and convince her and everyone else that I've been there longer than I actually have."

"I know that, too." She didn't move.

This was for Caro's own good, but he didn't think she'd appreciate hearing that sentiment. He'd never much liked being told that. He needed her cooperation, though. Condoms could be tricky things, especially with the woman on top.

"Just so you know, I'm going to make sure we go riding today." He hoped that would help. It wasn't as if this was the last they'd ever see of each other.

Her breath was warm on his chest. "How can you guarantee we'll go riding if Steve is still sick?"

"There must be someone else who can fill in."

"Normally Tracy would, but she's in Cheyenne for a girlfriend's wedding. We'd better hope that Steve gets well. That would be the best scenario."

"It would, but I'm prepared to make a case to Josie that you need the time off, somehow. I would probably be more convincing if I can get over to Grandma Judy's without anybody knowing I've been hanging out in your bedroom for a couple of hours."

"Right." She carefully rolled onto her side of the bed. Then she reached for the patchwork quilt and pulled it over her as she gazed at him. "Just know that if the ride doesn't work out, it's okay. We've had a terrific time, better than I even could have imagined. That's plenty."

"You'll get that ride." As he left the bed and headed into her bathroom, his heart ached for her. She was already preparing herself for disappointment. No matter what, she'd make the best of things.

Damn it, he wanted to treat her to an afternoon of riding, a carefree time in which she wouldn't have to be serving customers or taking care of her grandmother. Once he returned to Chicago, she'd go back to that routine, but while he was here, he wanted to execute a small jail break.

Walking back into her room, he discovered her standing by her closet and shoving her arms into a white terry robe.

"You don't have to see me out."

She sent him a smile. "Of course I do. I invited you up here, so the least I can do is see you to the door."

He walked over and took her by the shoulders. "Your invitation was the best thing that's happened to me in a long time."

"Good. It was a two-way street, though. I obviously needed a…" She flushed.

"A lover," he murmured, and kissed her softly on the mouth. Her lips tempted him, but he forced himself to draw back. "I feel lucky to have been in the right place at the right time."

"Me, too. Listen, can I get you anything? A soft drink? Coffee? I feel as if I shouldn't just send you off into the night without something."

"You're sending me off with something." He pulled on his jeans and sat down on the edge of the bed to deal with his socks and boots. "I feel a lot more like a man than I did a few hours ago."

"You're kidding, right?"

He pulled on a boot and glanced up. "No. Not even slightly."

"I don't get it."

He focused on putting on the other boot, because it was easier to confess these things when he wasn't looking at her. "I don't know who I am anymore, Caro, or what my future is. But for these couple of hours, I've forgotten all that. I was simply a guy who could make a woman happy. You have no idea what that means to me."

He sensed that she'd moved over to stand beside him. He felt her body heat, but even more, he felt her caring heart envelop him. He looked up, and sure enough, she gazed at him with more empathy than he'd felt from anyone in these long months.

"I wish I could help," she said.

"You already have." He stood and cupped her face in both hands and brushed his thumbs over her cheeks. "But as I'm sure you know, being the intelligent, logical person you are, this is an inside job. You've given me a chance to shift focus off myself. Maybe I can build on that and climb out of this funk I'm in."

"I hope so, Logan. I truly hope so."

"Which is why you need to come riding with me tomorrow. Show this city boy the majesty of the scenery. It will help both of us."

She smiled. "I like that. Win-win."

"Exactly." He dropped a quick kiss on her lips. "But in order to foster that plan, I need to find my shirt and get the hell out of here before the town, or worse yet, Grandma Judy, wakes up." He headed down the hall and scooped up the shirt he found crumpled on the floor.

"Yes, you do." She followed him, and retrieved his hat from the couch as he fastened the snaps. "You look good in cowboy clothes."

"It's all an act." He finished snapping the shirt and tucked it into his jeans. "Clothes don't make the man, or in this case, the cowboy. I'm still a city slicker at heart."

She handed him his hat. "That's what Alex used to say. Now look at him."

"Yeah, but he had a skill the Last Chance needed. They could use a marketing director. I can't think of any reason they'd want a washed-up baseball player."

"Now that's the kind of phrase you need to banish from your vocabulary, immediately." She put her hands on her hips and attempted a ferocious frown.

He had to laugh. She was so not the frowning type. "You're right. That's very negative on my part."

"It sure is. I've promised not to mention a certain condition of yours, but you have to promise to stop referring to yourself as a failure."

His laughter faded. "But the thing is, I *have* failed. You can blow sunshine up my ass all day, but it doesn't change the fact that I'm no longer fit for my chosen career."

"So choose another one."

Anger nibbled at his mellow mood. "Easy for you to say."

"But it's the only way to move forward."

"I suppose so, but can you begin to imagine what it's like to focus on a dream for twenty-five years, and then have it destroyed?" He heard the bitterness in his voice and winced. This was not the time or place.

"No. Truthfully, I can't." She looked contrite. "I'm sure it's terrible, and you have a right to be angry that your life didn't work out the way you'd hoped."

He sighed and rubbed the back of his neck. "But I don't

have a right to spray negativity all over the place, just because
I have no idea where I'll go from here."

"Didn't you ever think about what you'd do once you re-
tired from baseball?"

"Not really." He gazed at her and realized he'd needed to
meet this woman for many reasons, and this was one of them.
"Nobody else has had the guts to ask me that question, you
know. Everybody—my agent, my teammates, my family,
my friends—they all tiptoed around the subject. I think they
knew the answer and didn't want to bring it up."

"Well, no wonder you're so upset! You don't have a plan
B!"

"No." Which made him look pretty damned stupid. But
baseball players were a superstitious lot, and he was no exception. On some level he'd thought planning for his retirement might hasten it, and he couldn't imagine being happy
doing anything besides playing ball. Secretly, he'd hoped to
go on record as the oldest catcher in baseball history. What
a joke.

"We'll talk about it during our horseback ride this afternoon," she said. "I'm great at coming up with a plan B."

He couldn't imagine how a small-town bartender would
be able to figure out a new career path for a washed-up...no,
a *former* pro baseball player, but he didn't want to insult her.
"Thanks. I'll take all the help I can get."

"You're humoring me. You don't think I'll be able to help
you think of something."

"All right, no, I don't, but I appreciate that you're willing
to try, considering I'm just a stranger passing through."

She smiled at him. "Technically, that's what you are, but
you don't feel like a stranger to me."

He closed the gap between them and latched on to the
lapels of her bathrobe to draw her close. "Good, because
you don't feel like a stranger to me, either. But if I don't get

out of here, the whole world will know how familiar we've become." He kissed her, a down-and-dirty quick maneuver that involved tongues, but was over before it could progress to heavy breathing.

Even so, he felt his johnson respond and he backed away from her before he was tempted to kiss her again. "How soon can you drive out to the ranch this afternoon?"

She took a deep breath, as if she had to rein herself in, too. "I'll be home from Jackson around two. Assuming Steve takes my shift, I can be at the ranch before two-thirty."

"If Steve doesn't take it, I'll make sure Josie has it covered, so just come on out there."

"All right."

"I'll look forward to it." Ha. He'd be counting the seconds.

"Me, too."

"Okay, I'm really leaving." He backed toward the door.

She stood with her hands clasped in front of her, as if determined to stay in that one spot until he was out of her apartment. "See you this afternoon."

"You'll be there, no matter what, right? Because I *will* get that shift covered for you."

"I'll be there."

He groaned. "I don't want to leave you."

Unclasping her hands, she made shooing motions. "Get out of here, cowboy."

"I'm not a cowboy."

"You never know. That could be part of your plan B."

"Hell—I wish I didn't have to go, but I do, so…I'm outta here." With a supreme act of will, he opened the door, walked out and closed it behind him.

A cool breeze leeched the heat from his body and he shivered. Watching his step in the dim light, he descended the narrow stairs to the darkened street below. Caro was so warm, so full of sunshine. The afternoon seemed very far away.

6

CARO HURRIED TO THE window and watched Logan go down the stairs. He was favoring his right knee, and she battled guilt because she hadn't thought about his injury when they'd first had sex. Of course he wouldn't mention it, macho guy that he was. He had to be more careful.

She should take him to the assisted living facility and show him what real infirmity looked like. Maybe then he'd understand that carelessness now would mean depending on a wheelchair when he was eighty. He might also realize how lucky he was to be healthy in every other way, with only a bum knee to worry about.

Plus he had financial security, and he was, in her unbiased opinion, incredibly handsome. All in all, he was a fortunate man. He wasn't thinking like that right now, though. But she'd never had a single-minded drive to accomplish something like becoming a nationally known sports star, so maybe she couldn't relate properly to his angst.

She watched him cross the street and head off toward Grandma Judy's house. If Jack hadn't come up with that alternative, Logan might have been obligated to go back to the ranch instead of staying to help her. Caro owed Jack a debt of gratitude.

She wouldn't tell him so, because he'd mention it to Josie,

who might start worrying about Caro ending up with a broken heart. It would be like Josie to be protective. She'd helped, both with a truck and emotional support, during the difficult time of moving Grandma Bonnie from her little house in Shoshone into assisted living. She'd also offered this apartment at a very reasonable rate, when selling the house had meant Caro no longer had a place to live.

But Caro wasn't some delicate flower who couldn't handle a brief love affair without wilting. She'd accept whatever Logan could offer and be grateful. What woman worth her salt wouldn't? Logan was a fantasy guy who'd delivered everything that gorgeous body of his promised.

Mmm. She savored her memories of his hands, his mouth, his hard...ahem. There was no way she'd be able to sleep now that she'd reminded herself of the stupendous orgasms she'd enjoyed compliments of Mr. Carswell.

Hurrying back to the bedroom, she picked up her shirt and dressed quickly. Then she descended the stairs, keys in hand, and went into the bar. She wanted to find some information on Logan's career on the internet, and she couldn't very well surf the web on Josie's computer during working hours, or somebody would get suspicious.

As she opened the door, she heard what sounded like a soft chuckle, a very male chuckle.

A shiver traveled up her spine. "Who's there?"

No answer.

Her first instinct was to turn on every light in the place, but an early riser somewhere in the neighborhood might notice that all the lights were on at four forty-five in the morning, and report it to Josie. Caro didn't want to have to explain. So she waited, heart pounding, until her eyes adjusted to the muted glow coming from the lights under the bar.

Straining to see, she finally concluded that the room was empty. Maybe the door hinge was to blame, as Logan had suggested earlier. She moved the door back and forth, and the hinges squeaked a little, but they sounded nothing like the laughter she'd heard—twice.

But there had been nothing threatening about the laughter. The person, or the spirit of a departed person, had seemed mildly amused. Taking a deep breath, Caro decided to forget about it. Josie swore ghosts visited the bar, and Morgan, Gabe Chance's wife, said she'd seen one last summer. They'd both insisted the spirits were friendly and Caro had nothing to fear.

She walked into the office and closed the door before turning on the light. The blinds were already pulled down, so no one outside the building would know she was in here. After booting up the computer, she settled into Josie's desk chair and proceeded to look Logan Carswell up on Google.

An hour later, she checked the digital clock at the bottom of the screen and reluctantly turned off the computer. If she planned to drive to Jackson this morning, she needed a shower and lots of strong coffee. But she'd learned quite a bit about Logan, and now their time together in her apartment seemed even more surreal.

She had trouble reconciling her image of a very naked, very ardent Logan with the intense guy crouched behind home plate wearing a catcher's mask, chest protector and kneepads. Surely she hadn't just made love to that man? Yet her sexually satisfied body indicated she had.

She'd watched a few clips of him playing ball, and he'd always reacted with precision, whether he was behind the plate or up to bat. Most of all she'd noticed his intense focus, a trait he'd no doubt honed in the years he'd spent training and practicing. She understood his anger a lot better and wished she hadn't flippantly told him to "get a new career." Anyone that dedicated couldn't be expected to switch gears immediately.

She'd also watched the incident that had ruined his knee,

although seeing it made her stomach twist. He'd thrown off his mask to make the play, so his expression of agony was right there, front and center. Caro wanted to hate the player that had collided with him, but that wasn't fair. They were both simply doing what they'd been paid to do.

Moving away from the computer, she turned off the light and locked up after herself. No ghostly laughter greeted her, but then again, it was light outside, time for all self-respecting ghosts to go back to wherever they came from. She hurried up the stairs, grateful that no one was around to notice. She was terrible at making up stories.

If she wondered whether her sexual adventures with Logan had been real, she had only to walk into her bedroom and gaze at the rumpled sheets to know that he'd been there, loving the daylights out of her. Talk about a peak experience. She'd never forget a moment of what they'd shared as long as she lived.

She hoped to see him again today, but she wouldn't count on it. All things concerning Logan had to be wonderful surprises, not sweet certainties. If that time in her bed was all they ever had, she'd consider herself blessed.

After a long and reviving shower and two cups of coffee, she felt a little more fit for company, namely Grandma Bonnie's. As she was about to head out the door, her cell phone rang.

Her first thought was always about her grandmother, one of the few people who called her regularly, and the person whose welfare most concerned her.

Instead it was Josie. "Logan came to talk with me this morning," she said. "He seems to think you're headed for burnout if you don't get the afternoon off."

Warmth spread through Caro. Logan was watching out for her, and that was a great feeling. "He might be exaggerating a little." She crossed her fingers. "If you need me to work my shift this afternoon, I'll be happy to do that."

"Actually, I contacted Steve to see how he's faring after his stomach problems last night. He seems fine, and he's volunteered to take your shift."

"Thank you, Josie. I admit a break would be terrific."

"So you and Logan are going riding this afternoon?"

Excitement bubbled in her veins. She managed to sound reserved even as she mentally turned cartwheels at the prospect. "Yes, if that's okay."

"Sure, that's fine. I've wanted to get you out here to ride, but you've been so busy. It promises to be a beautiful day, and we'll saddle up a couple of cooperative horses for you and Logan. If I know Mary Lou, she'll insist on fixing you some snacks to take along."

It took Caro a moment to remember that Mary Lou was the cook at the Last Chance. "I'd hate for her to go to any trouble."

"No worries. She'd be upset if I didn't let her do that. You probably don't remember seeing her, but she was at the reception last night, and she noticed that you were working extra hard. She'll want to treat you right."

"Well, then, that sounds fabulous. Thank you, Josie."

"Don't thank me. Thank Logan. He's the one who brought it to my attention that all you do is work and visit your grandma."

Caro groaned. "Please don't think I was complaining to him. I have a wonderful situation. I love working for you, and I love my grandmother. I would never—"

"Relax, Caro. He emphasized that you weren't complaining, that you're the most positive person he's ever met. But I think he has a point. I realize that your grandma needs a lot of emotional support while she's in this transition period, but she'll think you're working. You should grab the chance to have some fun while you can."

"Okay. I just didn't want you to think I bent Logan's ear about how sad my life is, because it's not."

"I don't think that at all. Anyway, I don't know if I'll be around or not, so if I don't see you, have a wonderful ride. Here's Logan. He wanted to double-check something with you."

Caro's pulse kicked up a notch as Logan came on the line, his tone casual, as if he hadn't had to tear himself away from her a few hours ago. "So it's all set."

"Yes. Thank you."

"My pleasure."

She remembered the last time she'd heard him say that, and a zing of awareness made her tingle all over.

"Listen," he continued, "as long as you're coming out here, you might as well stay for dinner. Sarah suggested it."

"How nice of her." Caro had always admired Sarah Chance, who'd raised three fine sons and had handled her husband's sudden death two years ago with courage and grace. She was another woman who understood the meaning of resilience.

"Then you'll stay for dinner?"

"I'd love to." She made a mental note to bring lipstick along on the trail ride, in case he kissed it all off. It wouldn't be classy to appear at dinner looking as if she'd spent the afternoon making out with Logan. But she hoped she would end up doing exactly that.

"Great. I'll see you around two-thirty, then."

"I'm looking forward to it."

His voice lowered a notch. "Me, too. 'Bye, Caro."

His tone sent shivers up her spine, but she wasn't sure he should have taken the chance on Josie overhearing. He'd put a wealth of meaning into those last four words. Yes, she would definitely take lipstick along.

LOGAN HANDED THE CELL phone back to Josie. "Thanks for arranging this for her." His plan was working perfectly.

Josie had shown up to search for an old wooden cradle Jack remembered being stored in the barn. Spotting Josie's truck, Logan had gone down to the barn and offered to help find the cradle. During the search he'd mentioned Caro getting time off, and Josie had been glad to arrange it.

She tucked the phone back in her jeans pocket. "Happy to." She gazed around the barn. "I know that cradle has to be here. I can't imagine anyone pitching it out. Let's try the tack room." She started in that direction. "Did Caro tell you about her grandmother?"

"She did, and she tried very hard not to sound stressed about her schedule, but she is."

"I know she is, but I didn't think of this solution of getting somebody to take her shift. Good idea. Before the move into assisted living, her grandmother was a really cheerful sort, not needy at all, but now she asks Caro for her schedule and expects a visit whenever Caro's off work."

"Isn't that a little unreasonable?"

Josie surveyed the tack room, where saddles and bridles hung from hooks lining the walls, and saddle blankets were stacked in a large bin in the corner. "I suppose, but this is a woman who's lived in the same little house in Shoshone most of her life, and who had Caro living with her for the past twenty-some years. My guess is she's suffering from separation anxiety."

"Don't those assisted living places have counselors to deal with that?"

"I'm sure they do, but counseling isn't an instant fix for people in their eighties. Or anyone, for that matter." Josie glanced up into the rafters. "There it is! Somebody put it up there for safekeeping."

Logan gazed where she was pointing and spotted the cradle

balanced on two beams. He also saw dust and cobwebs, but maybe the cradle would look great once it was cleaned up. "I'll get it." He pulled a wooden stool over and climbed up on it.

"Be careful, Logan. I don't want you reinjuring your knee."

"I won't." He wished he could do that *Men in Black* trick and erase everyone's memory of his knee problem. He was sick of having people worry about whether his knee could withstand whatever activity he'd chosen to do.

He brought the cradle down in a shower of dust that made them both sneeze. "That's been up there a hell of a long time." He placed it gently on the floor, but anyone could see that a simple cleanup wouldn't do the trick. Something had been gnawing on the wood, and the cradle listed to one side. It didn't smell very good, and although Logan was no expert on bat shit, he thought that might explain the odor.

"It's a mess, isn't it?" Josie sounded distressed.

"I'm afraid so. I wouldn't trust my baby in that thing. Sorry, Josie."

"Jack said that supposedly his grandpa Archie built this for Jonathan. But then Diana, Jack's mother, didn't want to use it. I guess it got shoved into the rafters and ignored."

"Maybe you need to buy a new cradle."

"But I like it, Logan. Look at how he cut that heart pattern out of the head and footboards. You're not going to find that just anywhere." She glanced at him. "Could you fix it? I remember you were always building things back in high school. When you weren't on the baseball field, you were in wood shop."

Logan studied the cradle. "It's been a long time." But her comment reminded him of the satisfaction he'd felt whenever he finished a woodworking project. He'd abandoned that interest in favor of baseball, but he remembered with fondness the smell of fresh lumber.

"I'm thinking you could salvage some of it and make a new piece for the parts where the critters, whatever they were, chewed on it," she told him.

"I'd rather start over and use this as a pattern."

Josie shoved her hands in the back pockets of her jeans while she considered that. "It won't be the cradle Archie built."

"No, but it won't have bat shit on it, either. And I'm not sure those stains would ever come off."

Josie glanced at him. "I don't want my kid in a cradle with bat shit stains on it."

"I don't blame you."

"Could you really build a replica?"

He crouched down, which made him wince at the pressure on his knee, but he needed to get a closer look. The cradle was finely made, and he hated to think of all that work ending up in the trash. But it was ruined, and he could create something that would look just like it and smell a hell of a lot better. "Yeah, I think so. I'll need tools."

"Let me call Jack." Pulling her phone from her pocket, she punched in a speed-dial number. "It's been a trick getting everyone to use cell phones. It's not the cowboy way, apparently. But I think we're converting people gradually. Jack loves his phone now."

Logan no longer loved his. He'd deliberately left it in his room in the ranch house, because now that he wasn't a baseball star, nobody called. He used to be on a dozen people's speed dials, but no more. His lack of calls was so depressing that he tended not to carry it at all.

While Josie consulted with Jack about the availability of carpenter tools, Logan hunkered down and began to deconstruct the cradle. The more he thought about the project, the more he liked it. When he left the Last Chance in the next week or so, he'd be leaving behind something he'd made, something that might become the heirloom this cradle was supposed to be.

Josie got off the phone. "Jack says Archie's old tools are all packed away in a box. He thinks Sarah can locate them. Jonathan didn't have much aptitude for carpentry, I guess."

"Was he Sarah's husband, the guy who died?"

"Yes, and the only son of Archie and Nelsie—Eleanor. Jack and his brothers weren't interested in carpentry, either, so the tools have gone unused ever since Archie died."

Logan felt a little as if he might be intruding on Chance family history. "Are you sure it's okay if I use them?"

"Positive. Jack said if you can make a replica of that old cradle for our baby, he'll be eternally grateful, because, to quote him, 'I sure as hell can't do it.'"

"Then let's go find Sarah and see if she knows where those tools are. I might as well get started."

"All right." Josie headed out of the tack room. "How long do you think it'll take you?"

"I have no idea."

"Will you be able to stay until you finish it?"

Logan's first thought was that this cradle project might give him the excuse he needed to hang around longer. "I think I can manage to stay until it's done." And in the process, he'd get to see more of Caro. He wasn't remotely ready to give her up yet.

7

A COMBINATION OF ADRENALINE and caffeine fueled Caro's morning with Grandma Bonnie. More than once her grandmother asked her why she was so perky, and she blamed it on one too many cups of coffee. That was true, as far as it went.

She'd had enough coffee to float a battleship by the time she drove out to the Last Chance. She was determined not to fall asleep while riding her horse, or worse yet, while in a clinch with Logan.

Although she didn't know the ranch well, she'd been there for Josie and Jack's wedding the previous October. The double ceremony had included Jack's brother Nick and his bride, Dominique. Technically, Jack and Nick were half brothers, but there was nothing halfway about the relationship.

Caro knew some of the story from local gossip, but during one of the trips to Jackson to check out assisted living facilities, Josie had explained the whole convoluted situation. Jonathan Chance was the father of all three brothers, but each had a different mother.

Jack's mother, Diana, had left the ranch when Jack was four, never to return. A despondent Jonathan had taken up with a free spirit named Nicole for a while. She'd left Wyoming and later died unexpectedly. Baby Nick had arrived in the company of a lawyer who'd said Nicole had named Jonathan as the father and guardian.

By that time, Jonathan had remarried, and Sarah Chance was pregnant with Gabe, Jonathan's third son. Sarah had proceeded to raise all three boys as her own, and Caro suspected each of them would give his life for her.

Almost two years ago, Jonathan had died in a rollover, a tragic end to a true love story. Now Sarah shared the job of running the ranch with her three sons. Caro had always been in awe of the woman, but after hearing Josie's version of the family's history, Caro had elevated Sarah to sainthood.

The ranch buildings lay at the end of a long, unpaved road. As Caro's ancient truck bounced over the ruts, she remembered something else Josie had mentioned. Jonathan had left the road unpaved to discourage casual visitors. Sarah and his sons had continued to honor that wish. Caro hoped her shocks would hold up under the assault.

Considering the poor condition of the road, the house and outbuildings were surprisingly luxurious. Caro wasn't sure where to park, so she pulled into the gravel drive that circled in front of the main house. She could always move her truck down by the barn if necessary.

The two-story ranch house was immense, an expanded version of a log cabin. In the center stood a boxlike structure that was obviously the heart of the house. Two wings stretched out from there, each of them canted forward, like arms reaching to embrace a weary traveler.

A covered front porch ran the entire length of the house, and rockers sat quietly spaced along the porch as if anticipating a time when the family would have the leisure to sit and contemplate the view. That view, Caro noted as she climbed down from her truck and reacquainted herself with it, was spectacular.

The house faced the Grand Tetons in all their majesty.

Even now, in mid-August, snow clung to the jagged peaks. She stood for a moment and admired it before putting on her hat, a summer straw that she'd picked up a few years ago, back when she'd still had time to take trail rides from the local stable.

"Hey, Caro."

At the sound of Logan's voice, she spun in the direction of the barn, a hip-roofed structure that looked as if it belonged on a postcard. "Should I move my truck down by the barn?" She noticed two horses had been saddled and tied to the hitching post.

"Your truck's fine where it is." He walked to meet her, but kept a safe distance between them. "I'm glad you're here." His stance was casual, but his eyes, shaded by his tan Stetson, glowed with a banked fire.

Her heart thumped heavily in her chest. It could be all the caffeine she'd consumed today, but she figured it was probably the man. "It's good to see you again, Logan."

"You have no idea how good it is to see you, Caro." He studied her with such intensity that she began to tremble. "Love the hat."

"It's old."

"Looks great on you, though. I like the ponytail you wear at work, but I like your hair down like this even better. It reminds me of...well, never mind."

"I know what it reminds you of." She longed to reach for him, but that would be a bad idea. "We should probably get going, huh?"

"Yeah." He cleared his throat. "But first I want to show you something. It's in the barn."

"Sure." She fell into step beside him as they walked to the building.

"How's your grandmother?"

"She wanted to know why I'm so perky today."

He choked on a laugh. "And what did you tell her?"

"I said I'd been drinking espresso."

"Have you?"

"Yes. I didn't get any sleep last night, for some reason."

"Not even after I left?"

"No. I looked you up on Google instead."

He stopped and turned to stare at her. "You did what?"

"I looked you up on the web. I learned a lot."

His expression was unreadable. "Ancient history, I'm afraid."

"Maybe so, but I want to apologize for so breezily suggesting you find another career. You were brilliant. I understand why you can't just move on to something else. It's not that easy."

He took a deep breath. "It may not be easy, but it's the right idea. I haven't slept, either, and I've guzzled coffee, too, so my mind is probably hopped up on caffeine. But I do know that you were absolutely right to say that."

"I was arrogant to say that."

"I'd call it practical, and I apologize for being irritated. The door has closed behind me. Time to find a new door."

She met his gaze. Obviously he was making progress in his thinking, and she didn't want to wreck that. "Any ideas?"

"Not a single one." He smiled at her. "But you promised to help me come up with a plan B once we got out on the trail."

"Now that I've seen all that stuff on the internet about you, I don't think I'm qualified. It won't be easy coming up with something that absorbs your attention like that. And I know nothing about sports."

"Doesn't matter. I have to start somewhere, and I can't think of a better person to brainstorm with than you. But before we leave, I have to show you what I'm working on. It's kind of cool." He turned and started back down the pathway to the barn.

Whatever this new project was, she was encouraged by his enthusiasm. That attitude was a huge improvement over describing himself as a washed-up baseball player. Maybe he'd get lucky and this project would lead to something bigger, something he could latch on to.

A dog lay on either side of the barn doors. The one on the left had short hair and was tan and white, with a snub nose and pointed ears. The one on the right was all black, with long curly hair and floppy ears.

"Meet Butch and Sundance." Logan pointed to the left and right. "Guys, this is Caro, a most excellent lady of my acquaintance."

The dogs lumbered to their feet and came toward her for some attention. She crouched down and petted both at once. "I'd forgotten how much I love dogs. My grandmother is allergic to animals, so I couldn't have any while I lived with her."

"Knowing Josie, she'd be willing to let you have a dog in your apartment."

Caro gave each dog one last scratch and stood. "It wouldn't be fair. I'm either working or driving to Jackson. Dogs need someone who can take them out for walks, throw balls for them, keep them company." She glanced at him. "I don't have room for a dog in my life, any more than I have room for a man."

"At least the man wouldn't need you to play fetch with him."

She laughed. "No, but he'd want me to play other games, no doubt."

"Yes, he would." His eyes gleamed with wicked intent. "Come on, let me show you this real quick, and then we'll ride off into the sunset." He ushered her into the cool interior of the barn, which smelled of hay, manure and leather.

She rather liked the combination, but then, she was a

country girl. She wondered if Logan simply tolerated it for the time being.

"I don't have an elaborate workbench." He gestured toward one of the stalls, which had been swept clean. "But Jack helped me put something together so I could tackle this job. Take a look."

She peered into the stall, which had been recently modified, judging from the sawdust and the scent of cut lumber. A waist-high shelf spanned the end of the stall and a pegboard loaded with various tools hung above it. Under the shelf lay pieces of what must have been an old cradle. Judging from the newly cut sections on the workbench, Logan was in the process of creating a replacement.

She was surprised. His complete dedication to baseball didn't seem to have left room for a hobby. "You didn't mention that you were a carpenter."

"I wouldn't go that far. I like working with wood, and I did a fair bit of it when I was in high school, but after that I abandoned woodworking completely to concentrate on baseball. Fortunately, the techniques I learned in shop class are coming back to me."

"You are a man of many talents."

He gave her a lazy grin. "Thanks. Care to elaborate?"

"Not here." She lowered her voice. "Anybody could come in."

"You have a point. Emmett Sterling, the foreman, will show up any minute to adjust your stirrups before we ride out. He's already fixed mine, but you need to mount up before he can adjust yours. I wouldn't pretend to know how to do it."

"It's not that hard."

Logan laughed softly. "Maybe not yet, but it will be soon."

"Logan…"

"Couldn't resist. I love making you blush. Anyway, you've seen what I'm doing, so now we can leave."

"Hang on a minute." She wanted to explore this new side of him a little more before they left the barn and got side-tracked by…well, obviously, sex. "I assume you're making a cradle for Josie and Jack's baby, and using the old one as a guide."

"That's right."

"Where did the old one come from?"

"It should have been an heirloom." Logan crouched down and picked up one of the sections that had a cutout of a heart in it. "Jack's grandfather Archie built it for Jack's dad, Jonathan. But Jonathan's first wife, Diana, didn't use it for Jack when he was born. Instead it got shoved up in the rafters above the tack room, and has been there ever since."

"What a shame." She noticed he winced a little when he crouched down, but she wasn't about to mention it.

"It is a shame. Archie put a lot of loving care into making this. I hope I can do the project justice."

"I'm sure you can." Caro almost said what she was thinking—that maybe Logan could consider making furniture, at least until he figured out what else he might want to do with his time. But the solution seemed too simplistic. She didn't know anything about that field, and it had nothing in common with a high-profile job like baseball.

Of course, if Logan put his name on the furniture, it could become a high-profile venture. He might not like that idea, though. He didn't strike her as the kind of guy who would enjoy trading on a reputation for past accomplishments.

"I can see the wheels going around," Logan said.

"Just thinking about the cradle."

"You wouldn't be thinking that my future is in cradle making, would you?"

She looked into his eyes. "Okay, I did for a minute there. Not just cradles, but other stuff. I don't suppose that's the answer, though."

"No, it's not. I don't see myself peddling furniture I've made. I have a certain amount of skill, but I'm no master craftsman. I'd be embarrassed to charge money for making something."

"But you said you don't need money."

"I don't, but I'm not going to build furniture and pass it out to strangers on the street for free, either."

"Of course not."

"The thing is, if I make something that's a labor of love, like Archie did with the cradle, that's a joy. Mass production for customers I don't know doesn't appeal to me."

She nodded. "Totally understandable."

"But for the record, I'm not going to shoot down everything you come up with, so don't stop thinking, okay?"

"I won't. I like solving problems."

"Well, here's one." He lowered his voice. "How fast can we ride out of here and find a secluded spot so I can get you naked?"

She felt as if he'd shoved her under a heat lamp and sucked all the air out of her lungs. She gasped.

"Sorry." His grin was positively wicked. "Was that too direct?"

She had only enough breath for a single-syllable response. "No."

"It's so tempting to tease you. You're as pink as the inside of a ripe watermelon."

She wouldn't be surprised, considering the heat pouring through her.

"Anyway, I figure we've spent enough time looking at my woodworking project. Let's move on to more important things." He touched the small of her back lightly, a signal to move out of the stall and back to the barn entrance.

That brief contact was enough to dampen her panties. She gulped. "Okay."

As he walked beside her, he pulled a piece of paper from his jeans pocket and continued to keep his voice to a low murmur. "Josie drew me a quick sketch of the trails we can take. I'm not a great rider, but I should be able to stay on the horse long enough to find us some privacy."

"All right." She sounded like robot woman, but putting one foot in front of the other took all her concentration as she fought the urge to drag him back into the stall and strip him down.

"They put me up on Destiny, because he's easy, but I've been warned if we don't tie him well when we have our, uh…" He coughed. "Our *snack* that Mary Lou fixed, then he'll go back home."

"That wouldn't be so good."

"Actually, riding double sounds kind of fun."

"Have you ever done it?"

"Nope, but I'm picturing you in front of me, and I get an excellent image."

That made her smile. If he thought two people could have comfortable sex on a saddle, he was sadly mistaken, and neither of them were accomplished enough to ride bareback and have sex at the same time. Still, it was a fun fantasy.

They emerged from the barn, and the bright sunlight curbed her raging libido somewhat. Besides, Emmett would be along anytime now to adjust her stirrups and she didn't want the foreman to pick up on any sexual vibes zinging between her and Logan. She walked toward the horses standing patiently tied to the hitching post.

"That's Destiny." Logan pointed toward a brown-and-white paint with a white blaze down his nose. "The one you'll be riding is Cookies and Cream, or Cici for short. She's a mare, but Destiny's no longer in the mating game, so we shouldn't have any trouble with these two."

"I can probably adjust the stirrups myself." Caro walked

around Destiny and approached her chocolate-colored mare. She was a pretty thing, with a white mane and tail. "Hello, Cici." Caro rubbed her velvety neck. "Thanks for taking me out today."

"Or you can tell me what to do once you're up there." Logan came to stand beside her. "I watched Emmett, but I want to make sure I don't screw it up."

"All right. I'll—"

"You two ready to head out?" A square-jawed cowboy came around the corner of the barn before Caro had a chance to mount up. His mustache was mostly gray and his face was lined, but his manner was that of a much younger man. He touched the brim of his hat in a courtly gesture. "Nice to see you out here, Caro."

"Thank you, Mr. Sterling."

"Ah, call me Emmett. Everyone does. I don't get into the Spirits and Spurs very often, but I was there last night for the reception. You did a great job."

"Thanks, but I wouldn't have if Logan hadn't helped me out."

"I know." Emmett glanced over at Logan. "I saw the juggling act. Impressive."

Logan shrugged. "It's pretty easy."

"It is if you've been a top-notch catcher for years. It's too bad Nelsie isn't still around. She was a devoted Cubs fan."

"She was Archie's wife, right?"

"Yep. She started following the Cubs in the sixties, and she kept up with them until the day she died. I'll bet Sarah still has the Cubs cap Nelsie used to wear all the time. And now here's an actual Cubs player staying at the Last Chance. She would have been thrilled about that."

"That's quite a coincidence." Caro decided to say something before Logan cut in with some nonsense about not being a player anymore. "Why did she follow the Cubs?"

"Sarah has her old diary. In it she says that she picked them because they were a historic team, one of the oldest in the game. Nelsie gravitated toward anything with history attached to it."

"That's one of the things I loved about playing for them," Logan said quietly. "Being part of all that history."

Caro heard the sorrow buried in his comment, and she wished they were alone so she could wrap him in her arms and give him comfort.

Emmett put a hand on Logan's shoulder. "Didn't mean to bring up a sore subject, son."

"Hey, no worries." Logan smiled at the foreman. "I'm glad you told me about Nelsie. It makes me feel more like a part of the ranch, to know my team was her favorite."

"Well, good, then. Now let's get Caro mounted up so you two can explore the ranch. It's a pretty day for it."

Caro climbed aboard and Emmett busied himself adjusting her stirrups. In no time they were headed away from the ranch on a trail that crossed a meadow filled with wildflowers. Logan had the map, so he led.

That suited Caro just fine. She could ogle his tight buns all she wanted, because there was no rearview mirror on a horse, so he'd never know.

Then he turned to look back at her. "Checking me out, Caro?"

"Would I do that?"

"I sure as hell hope so, considering my plans for the afternoon."

"I see." Her body tightened deliciously. Rocking along on a warm leather saddle didn't hurt matters, either.

"That grove of trees seems damned far away. How do I shift this horse into high gear? It's been a while since I've done this."

"Are you sure you want high gear?"

"Okay, maybe not. I don't want to fall off. But meandering down the trail at a snail's pace is not working for me."

She laughed. "You're supposed to be enjoying the scenery."

"All the scenery I want to enjoy is currently covered up."

"Carswell, you have a one-track mind."

"So I've been told."

She considered that his ability to be very single-minded, which was probably what had made him an excellent ballplayer, also would explain why he was such a fantastic lover.

"Seriously, Caro, what signals do I give this animal so he'll move out? Do I kick him or cluck at him or what?"

"You nudge with your heels, but the next level up after walking is trotting. In my experience, it's hard to sit a trot unless you've practiced."

"So what if I skip that level and go to the next one?"

"You think you're ready to canter? How long has it been since you were on a horse?"

"Three or four years. Some buddies and I went to a dude ranch in Colorado for a couple of days."

"And before that?"

"There was no before that. That was my first and only time on a horse."

"Hmm." She thought about his knee and what sort of damage he could do if he came off the animal. "We'd better walk."

"To hell with that." He dug both heels into Destiny's ribs, and the horse broke into a trot. Logan began to bounce in the saddle. "This sucks!"

"Told you." Caro trotted behind him, but she'd had enough practice to keep from bouncing.

"Next gear, then." Logan kicked again and Destiny moved into a canter. "Better!" He jostled around some, but then settled in. "*Much* better!"

She watched in amazement as he transformed from awkward city boy on a horse to someone who could almost pass for a cowboy. Apparently that's what the gift of natural coordination could do for a person.

He was an incredible guy, the kind of man who'd be easy to fall for. She wouldn't, of course, because that would set up the perfect scenario for heartbreak. Caro was one hundred percent against heartbreak.

Logan cantered ahead of her, taunting her with his broad shoulders and tight buns. He must have been feeling really confident, because he turned in the saddle to grin at her.

As she opened her mouth to warn him that he shouldn't get cocky, Destiny shied at something on the trail. The horse crow-hopped, and Logan sailed off into a patch of wildflowers. Caro pulled Cici to a stop and leaped off; heart pounding, she prayed he hadn't landed on his knee.

8

LOGAN'S FIRST THOUGHT as his butt left the saddle was that this was no way to impress a woman. And sadly, he had hoped to impress Caro with his newfound cowboy skills. He'd seen right away that a trot wasn't going to accomplish it, but the canter had shown real promise until Destiny veered in one direction and he veered in the other.

His second thought was for his knee. He'd had a lot of experience falling during his baseball career, and in this instance he didn't have to worry about where the ball was or how other players might be impacting the situation. Twisting his body as he fell, he managed to land on his backside, which was the part that could take the most punishment.

He hit with a jolt that made his teeth click together, but fortunately, his tongue wasn't in the way. He lay there a second or two, flexing everything to make sure he hadn't broken a vital body part. Other than the fact that his butt hurt a little, he seemed to be in decent shape.

"Logan!" The stalks of wildflowers surrounding him rustled and then Caro dropped to her knees by his side. "Oh, my God. Are you okay?"

"Yes, other than feeling like a damned fool. Where are the horses?"

She glanced up. "Cici's right over there, eating flowers.

Destiny's…getting away! Stay here. I'll be right back." She jumped to her feet.

Logan sat up in time to watch her leap on Cici and trot off to retrieve his homeward-bound mount. Then he carefully got to his feet, only to find his knee was no worse than it had been. At least he wasn't totally without luck.

Meanwhile Caro, the heroine of the hour, caught up with Destiny and grabbed his reins. As Logan dusted off the seat of his pants, noting that he felt at least one good-size bruise forming there, she rode up, leading his mount. So much for impressing the woman he hoped to have sex with.

"I got him. Emmett needs to train him out of that bad habit." She gazed down at Logan. "How are you doing?"

"My pride is shredded, but other than that, I'm fine."

"You have a purple flower in your hair."

He leaned on the only thing he had left, his sense of humor. "Does it look good on me?"

She cocked her head to one side. "I think red's more your color."

"Then I'll ditch it." Combing his fingers through his hair, he dislodged the flower, plus a few pieces of grass.

"Where's your hat?"

"Somewhere in the area, I suppose." He glanced around and finally spied it upside down about ten feet away, among the prairie grass and wildflowers. He went after it, dusted it off and settled it on his head. "Time to mount up."

She handed him Destiny's reins. "We can go back, if you want."

He climbed back up and settled gingerly into the saddle. "I'll leave that up to you. Are you still interested in a guy who falls off his horse and ends up with flowers in his hair?"

"Yes."

He glanced at her and discovered she was smiling. "You are?"

"Absolutely. Some guys I know wouldn't have been able to handle being humiliated like that."

He laughed. "Humiliated?"

"Well, yeah. You were thrown from your horse while you were trying to show off for me, and then I had to recapture that horse so you wouldn't be on foot. Some men would deal with that by retreating to their man cave to nurse their damaged egos."

"Then I guess those guys have never dropped the ball for what would have been a game-winning out in the World Series. Try being humiliated in front of millions on national TV. This is chicken feed compared to that."

"Then lead the way to the trees, Mr. Carswell. But maybe we should walk the horses."

"Don't worry. I'm all about walking. In fact, I'm letting you lead."

"But you have the map."

"We don't need a map. We aren't going any farther than that line of trees." He wasn't going to admit that his backside probably couldn't take more riding than that. But he could think of one thing that would make all his aches and pains disappear.

"Okay, I'll go first then." She pointed Cici down the trail and gave her a nudge.

Destiny fell in behind the mare, and Logan realized that from this angle he could watch Caro's cute fanny in the saddle and contemplate the joys he might find at the end of the trail. As an added bonus, she wouldn't be able to observe him shifting around as he tried to find a comfortable spot that didn't press on his bruised behind.

She'd already decided he shouldn't have sex that put pressure on his knees. If she thought he couldn't lie on his back without pain, they'd be even more limited in their choice of positions. Sometimes she was too caring for his own good.

"I've been thinking about that cradle you're making," she said. "Do you suppose Josie would like a baby quilt to go with it?"

"Why, do you have one?"

"I have some quilt squares and I could make one that size. I've been wondering what to give her for the baby, but for some reason I didn't think of that."

"You're a quilter?"

"I haven't sewn for months, but yes, I'm a quilter. My grandmother taught me how."

"Did you make the one on your bed?"

"Yep."

"Nice." He would always treasure the image of her sitting up in bed with the quilt over her lap. He liked knowing she'd made it. "I suppose you don't have time to do that these days."

"I don't, but I would create the time if I thought it was important enough. But I don't know what I'd do with the quilts. I have enough for myself and for Grandma Bonnie. She said the same thing when she stopped quilting. After you've given one to each of the people you know and love, what do you do with the excess?"

"Sell them?"

"Maybe, but I'm not sure I'd want to mass-produce them for strangers, any more than you'd want to mass-produce furniture."

"I get that." He thought about the problem. "But do you enjoy making them?"

"I do. I love finding interesting scraps of fabric, and some of the patterns are breathtaking. There's real satisfaction in putting together a quilt that will keep someone warm and be beautiful at the same time."

"I used to feel that way about woodworking. I made things that looked good but served a function."

"But then you run out of people to give them to."

"I know." But he had a sudden picture of a home filled with his furniture and her quilts. A home made for a family, something he hadn't allowed himself to think about while he was totally focused on baseball.

He wasn't focused on baseball now. Did that mean he was ready for a wife and family? No. He needed to find a purpose in life before he brought another person into his. Being a husband and father was an appealing possibility, more so now than ever, but it wasn't enough to fill his days.

"How far into the trees do you want to ride?"

He glanced around in surprise. Looking back down the trail, he could see that they'd entered the stand of trees some time ago. Apparently he'd been thinking so hard about quilts and furniture and families that he hadn't noticed.

"Here." He caught sight of a little glen to the right. "Over in that clearing."

"All right." Caro guided Cici off the trail, and the horse's hooves crunched on leaves and twigs that had fallen to the forest floor. As Caro dismounted, her denim jeans stretched tight across her bottom.

Logan forgot all about families and furniture, although he wouldn't mind having a fluffy quilt right now to spread on the ground. He steered Destiny toward a sturdy-looking tree and climbed down. "I'm tying this horse up good and tight."

"Glad to hear it." Caro secured Cici's reins around a leafy branch, then walked toward him. "Got snacks?"

He turned. He hadn't meant to grab her, but he must have, because her hat fell off and she squealed as he pulled her into his arms. "I've been waiting so long," he offered by way of apology, before he crushed her to him and claimed her mouth.

Somewhere in the middle of that hot kiss he lost his hat, too. He barely noticed as they began undressing each other with frantic movements and labored breathing. Soon his shirt was on the ground, along with her shirt and bra.

"Blanket?" she asked between kisses.

"Tablecloth." He fondled her breasts. He'd wanted a blanket but hadn't figured out how to take one along without arousing suspicion.

"Never mind." She unbuckled his belt and unzipped his jeans.

Once she had her hands on his cock, he went a little crazy. He wasn't a back-her-up-against-a-tree kind of guy, but that's exactly what he did. A large pine was handy, and he leaned her against it as he fumbled for the condom in his pocket—while she caressed him with those clever hands of hers until he had to beg her to stop.

"Don't you like it?" she asked in a breathless whisper.

"I love it. But I want to be inside you when I come." He snapped the condom into place and slid both hands under her bare bottom. He wasn't sure exactly when she'd kicked off her boots and jeans, but they were lying next to the tree instead of covering her body, and for that he was grateful. "Put your hands on my shoulders, and when I lift you, wrap your legs around my waist."

"You can hold me up?"

"I can bench-press two hundred pounds. Do you weigh more than that?"

She scowled at him.

"I can hold you up." He leaned forward and nibbled at her mouth. "Open for me, Caro. Let me in." He boosted her to the level of his waiting cock, and she spread her thighs and wound her legs around him.

One thrust and he was golden. She'd paved the way for him with enough moisture to make that slide easy and smooth. Once he was locked in tight, he sighed with pleasure. "Perfect."

"Yeah…." She leaned her head against the tree trunk.

"Arch your back. I don't want you to get scratched up."

She looked into his eyes with a sultry expression. "As if I care."

"I care. Arch your back. Move your hips toward...*me*." He sucked in a breath when she thrust her pelvis more forcefully against his. The contact was intense enough to nearly make him explode.

She ran her tongue over her lips. "How's that?"

"Incredible. I could come right now, just looking at you."

"I think I could, too." She contracted her muscles around him.

His penis twitched in response. He gripped her satiny bottom, squeezing gently. "Keep doing that and I won't have to move at all."

"That would be cool, if we could just—" she tightened her muscles again "—do this."

"We can. I'm close."

Her breathing was shallow. "Me, too."

"I love it when you come. Your eyes get dark, and then I feel you squeeze me...like that...do it again...yeah ..." He was slowly losing his mind, and yet they were barely moving. No thrusting, no pumping, no gymnastics, and yet his climax edged closer each time she squeezed his penis.

Then she began to improvise. Taking one hand from his shoulder, she reached down and massaged his balls. "How's that?"

He groaned with pleasure.

She toyed with him some more until he began to quiver. "Not much longer."

She transferred her attention to her clit, caressing herself with slow circles of her finger.

"I like that, too," he murmured. "You're holding me tighter and tighter."

"Because I'm ..." She moaned softly. "I'm coming... I'm—"

Her contractions rolled over his cock, coaxing him, taunting him, until he also came in a rush, jerking with the force of it, and throwing back his head with a low cry of ecstasy.

Legs braced, he somehow managed to stay upright and hold on to her as their tremors gradually subsided. Slowly, he brought his head forward again and met her gaze. She seemed as dazed as he was. Exciting as this had been, they both needed a bed in which to recover, but he didn't have one. He had a tablecloth and a couple of saddle blankets.

It would have to do. "Can you stand here for just a little while?"

Her smile was lopsided. "Maybe."

He gently lowered her feet to the ground and reached for his shirt. Draping it around her shoulders, he gave her a quick kiss. "Wait here. I won't take long."

Picking up his jeans, he disposed of the condom by wrapping it in his handkerchief. After that he approached the two saddled horses. Although he knew next to nothing about saddles, the cinch seemed no more complicated than a belt.

And he was a man on a mission, determined to provide for his lover. In a relatively short time he'd pulled off both saddles and placed the blankets on the ground with the side that had touched the horses on the bottom.

Then he pulled the red-and-white-checker tablecloth out of the saddlebag containing the snacks. He thought they needed rest more than food right now. The makeshift bed finished, he returned for Caro and led her to the tree-shaded bower he'd prepared.

She didn't question or protest as he drew her down with him. After some maneuvering, they were settled on the nubby blankets, Caro lying with her back to him and her knees drawn up, Logan curled protectively around her.

Last of all he spread the tablecloth over both of them, stretched out his arm and urged her to use it as a pillow. She must have been too exhausted to argue, because she cuddled against him and fell fast asleep. Wrapping an arm around her waist, he held Caro close.

As he drifted off to sleep, Logan realized he'd never been happier in his life.

9

CARO WOKE UP TO THE SOUND of birds chirping in the branches over her head. For a moment she was totally disoriented and couldn't imagine where she was. Then she felt Logan's arm around her and his warm body pressed against her back.

Oh, yes. She'd ridden out here with this hunky, conflicted man and they'd been so desperate for sex that they'd done it up against a pine tree. She'd never been that wild and crazy with a guy, but Logan seemed to bring out all her hidden fantasies. No wonder. The arm draped around her was beautifully sculpted, and the rest of his body was the same.

But her reaction to him was about more than his physical attributes. He needed her. Through example, Grandma Bonnie had taught her the joy and satisfaction of being there for a person in need.

Logan was going through a dark period in his life, and he needed someone to help him deal with his demons. She could help. She'd never lost a career, but she'd lost her mother at the tender age of twelve.

She didn't kid herself that this was a lasting attraction. He'd figure out his next steps and be on his way. She would have served her purpose, that of being a bridge over troubled waters. She was okay with that.

Or mostly okay. The longer she was with him, the more

she began to dream. But he wasn't for her, and she knew it. He'd find a career that would put him in the limelight again, and he wouldn't find that career in Shoshone, Wyoming.

He nuzzled the back of her neck. "You awake?"

"Uh-huh."

"That was the last condom, I hate to say. I couldn't come up with a way to get more without causing a stir in the community. Something tells me that if I drove into town and bought a box, the word would be out before I was halfway back to the Last Chance turnoff."

"You're probably right. The only secretive way to get them is in the men's room at the Spirits and Spurs, and we know that machine is completely unreliable."

"Do you have the three-to-eleven shift tomorrow night?"

"Yes."

"Think I'll have to come by for a beer…and a few condoms from the machine."

She sighed. "Nice idea, but if you stay after closing, we might as well put up a billboard announcing that we're shacking up."

"Yeah, you're right. And ultimately, you're the one who'll have to deal with the gossip after I leave."

He was right, but the more Caro thought about it, the more she was ready to stand up for her right to have sex with Logan if she wanted to. She was a big girl. "You know what? I don't care about gossip."

"You don't?"

"People may suspect something's going on, anyway. Let's get it out in the open. I'll give Josie the courtesy of telling her tonight. I'll let her know that you and I want to spend quality time with each other, and neither of us is looking at it as a long-term commitment. I know she worries that I'll get hurt."

His arm tightened around her. "So do I."

"You can only hurt me if I allow it." She was glad they

were having this conversation when she wasn't looking at him. She'd have an easier time convincing him—and herself—if they weren't face-to-face.

"And you won't allow it."

"No. I'll let Josie know I'm going into this with my eyes wide open, and that I know you're destined for greater things than a quiet existence in Shoshone, Wyoming. She should be fine with it."

"I hope so."

"I'll make sure she is. The bottom line is, we can do whatever we want, as long as I don't ignore my obligations to Josie or Grandma Bonnie."

"Are you going to Jackson in the morning?"

"Yes—I always do."

"Let me go with you."

"Why would you want to?" Caro remembered how she'd thought about taking him so he could appreciate his own good fortune in comparison. She was a little surprised that he would suggest it himself, though.

"You're helping me with my problems and I'd like to help you with yours. Maybe if I met your grandmother, I'd have some ideas about how she might adjust to her new circumstances." He paused. "She's had the rug pulled out from under her, and I know what that feels like."

"True. I'd love for you to go." Caro hesitated. "If you come with me, would you be willing to tell everyone who you are? The residents would be so excited, especially some of the men."

His breath was warm on her shoulder. "I can do that. For you."

"You'd rather not, though."

"No, it's fine. If it would make those folks happy, then it's a small thing. The more I'm with you, the less the end of my career matters to me."

She squeezed his arm. "Good. Maybe the pain is fading a little bit."

"It fades totally when I'm deep inside you."

She smiled. "Don't be saying such things when we're out of condoms."

"You're right. Sorry about that." He released her and sat up. "We should get back. It won't be long until dinner."

Immediately she missed the warmth and closeness of lying on the blankets with him. It wasn't a particularly comfortable bed, but she'd cherish their time here. She sat up, too, and combed her hair back from her face. "I must look like a mess."

"Nope, you look terrific. But your lipstick is all gone."

"I brought more."

"Smart girl."

"Thanks. I try to plan ahead." Feeling slightly shy, she tucked the tablecloth around her as she stood. Logan didn't seem to have any problem walking around naked, but then he'd spent the past fifteen or twenty years in communal showers with the rest of the jocks.

He began pulling on his clothes. "I think Josie and Jack are supposed to be at dinner, so that will give you a chance to inform Josie about us, if you still want to."

"I do." Caro lifted her chin. Let the gossip begin. Logan needed her, and she needed him, at least for the short term. He would be here only a little while, and she hated the idea of wasting that precious time because she was worried about wagging tongues.

"You're absolutely sure you're okay with being open about our arrangement?"

"This kind of secret won't last long in Shoshone, so it's either be open or stop. I choose option A."

He grinned. "I like a woman who has her priorities straight." He fastened the snaps on his shirt.

"Can't help it. You're pretty potent, Carswell."

"I am? That's nice to hear." He tucked in his shirttail.

"It's true. I've never let any man have sex with me up against a tree."

"For the record, I've never had sex with a woman up against a tree, either." He buckled his belt and looked up. "It's a total first for me."

"Really?"

His grin was quick. "Really. And I'd appreciate it if you'd put some clothes on while I saddle up the horses. Otherwise I'm liable to suggest we find ways to have fun without a condom. I can think of a couple already."

So could she, and her body began to hum. "You're going to saddle up the horses?"

"Sure. Blanket, saddle, cinch. How tough can it be?"

She could just let him do it and find out for himself. If Destiny puffed out his belly when the cinch was being tightened, Logan would end up on the ground when the cinch became loose and the saddle rotated.

But she wasn't the type of person to let that happen to any greenhorn, let alone someone who already had a bad knee and a sore behind. "Once you tighten the cinch, wait until the horse lets out a breath, and tighten it some more. Put your knee against their ribs if you have to." She caught herself before saying *use your good knee*. "They'll try to fool you by swelling up with air."

He glanced at her as he adjusted his hat. "Thanks for the tip."

"You're welcome." She was struck by how much more comfortable Logan looked in those clothes than he had when she'd first met him. He even wore his hat with more confidence. "You're liable to turn into a cowboy yet." She waited for him to contradict her.

Instead he smiled. "Funny, but I think I could, at that. I survived falling off a horse, which has to be one of the tests."

"It is. And you climbed right back on, like any true cowboy would."

"Well, I was motivated to get into the woods ASAP." He waggled his eyebrows at her and she laughed. "But I guess what I'm trying to say is that I like this riding business. Too bad my home owners association won't let me keep a horse in my condo."

"It's not exactly cowboy country back there, is it?"

"Nope. Now get dressed. I'm going to show how proficient I am at saddling these two hay burners."

"Now you're even talking like a cowboy." She watched him work as she pulled on her clothes, and his movements weren't as smooth as a seasoned rider's would be, but he got the job done, making sure the cinches were tight around each of the horse's bellies.

When he finished, he turned to her with a boyish grin of pride. "How's that?"

"Excellent." She finger-combed her hair and dug in her pocket for her lipstick.

"Hang on. Don't do that yet." He walked over and drew her into his arms. "One more for the road."

"You want to kiss me?"

"Yes."

"But you know we can't have sex."

"Yes. So what?"

She gazed up at him and wondered if he realized the significance of that. A kiss that was part of foreplay was purely sexual. A kiss that wasn't foreplay was… She didn't want to put a name on what it was.

"Don't you want me to kiss you?"

"I do." And she didn't want to put a name on the yearning in her heart, either.

"Good, because I intend to." But when he leaned down to kiss her, his hat bumped against hers. "Now that's inconvenient."

"There's a trick to it." Her heart melted a little more the longer she was in his arms. "Tilt your hat back a little. Then I'll lean one way and you lean the opposite way. It's how a cowboy kisses a cowgirl."

"Is that so?" Angling his head, he followed her directions. When his lips almost touched hers, he paused. "Any more kissing tips I need to know?"

"No." Emotion flowed through her, warm and sweet. "You've mastered the rest of it."

"Not even close. But fortunately, I love to practice." His mouth found hers.

His kiss was familiar now, and she welcomed the velvet heat of it with heat of her own. Passion was there, as it had been from the beginning, but…this kiss was about more than passion. It brimmed over with joy and with caring and… She blocked the next word that came to her in a soft, seductive whisper.

But the word, and the feelings it brought with it, crept around the edges of her barricade. She couldn't ignore the way he was kissing her, because it was different from the other times. Whether he'd admitted it to himself or not, he cherished her.

And that could blossom into something neither of them were prepared to handle. Her heart aching, she pulled back. "If we keep this up, we'll be up against a tree in no time," she said.

It was an excuse. She wasn't worried that he'd back her against a tree and rip her clothes off. He hadn't telegraphed that kind of wild urgency this time. She was worried about something far more significant.

He cleared his throat. "Thanks for teaching me how to kiss like a cowboy."

"You're welcome." She brushed a piece of grass off her sleeve. "You handled it like a pro."

"I'm not so sure. I think we need to try it again."

She looked into his eyes. "Better not." She hoped he'd get the message without having to discuss it. Once they gave voice to the possibility that they might be falling for each other, it would become the elephant in the room and ruin whatever time they had left.

"Okay." He sounded reluctant, but he released her. "You're the boss."

She glanced up through the trees at the angle of the sun. "Besides, it's getting late."

"We didn't eat Mary Lou's snacks. I don't know her well, but I don't think she'd take kindly to us rejecting her food."

"What is it?"

"I don't know. Let's look." He walked over to Destiny and opened the saddlebag. "Six cookies. Four chocolate chip and two oatmeal and raisin. Plus a couple small bottles of water. She probably won't care if we drink the water or not. She didn't bottle it personally."

Caro laughed. "Chocolate chip is my favorite."

"Mine, too."

"So let's eat those and leave the oatmeal cookies for the birds."

"All right." He brought the plastic Ziploc bag over to where she stood under the shade of a tree. "Bon appétit."

She smiled at him as she took a cookie from the open bag he extended to her. "Here's another tip. Cowboys don't speak French."

"I don't speak it, either." He bit into a cookie. "That's about all I know, but I'll strike it from my vocabulary while I'm home on the range where the deer and the antelope play."

"Wise plan."

"So what would a cowboy say?"

"Oh, maybe 'tuck in' or if they were feeling long-winded, they might say 'let's tie on the old feedbag.'"

Logan gazed at her. "Chocolate chip." He touched the corner of his mouth.

"Here?" She wiped her face with the tip of her finger.

His eyes darkened. "No, here." He reached over and brushed the crumb away. "And here." He touched the other side of her mouth. "And…God, Caro…" Dropping the bag of cookies to the ground, he swept her back into his arms.

Both their hats fell off as his lips came down on hers with no thought given to angle or technique. His mouth was hungry, the thrust of his tongue possessive. He kissed her until they were both breathless.

Then he released her and stood back, his chest heaving. "Sorry, but I needed that. You're the most adorable chocolate chip cookie eater I've ever met."

She drew a shaky breath. "Thank you. That's not something a girl hears every day."

"I suppose not. But I actually want to thank you—for being here, for generously giving of yourself with no thought of getting anything in return."

He was falling for her. And she was falling for him, too, damn it. She'd been so involved with her grandmother that she'd forgotten what it was like to be desired by a wonderful man. He inspired a vision of a fuller, more satisfying life.

But he wasn't the man to give her that life. She attempted to get them both back on safer ground. "I get something in return. Orgasms."

"Yes, but—"

"Logan, we really need to start back. If you'll scatter the oatmeal cookies around for the birds, I'll put on my lipstick."

He gazed at her for a moment longer. "Yeah, it's getting late."

Too late, she thought as she somehow managed to put on lipstick with a hand that shook. She'd been determined to keep an emotional distance between them, but it was too late.

10

As they rode back to the ranch, Logan felt as if a hive of bees had taken up residence in his brain. In his baseball career he'd always been able to think strategically, both on the field and when planning various career moves. But ever since learning that his playing days were over, he'd lost that ability, or so it seemed.

He certainly wasn't being sensible about Caro. She was supposed to be a diversion, a safe haven for a few nights while he tried to figure out what to do with his life. Good sex— and she certainly represented that—had always been a way for him to relax and forget his problems. Good sex had never *become* the problem.

Okay, he admitted to himself, it wasn't the good sex that was a problem. It was the woman herself. He liked her way too much, and he wasn't in a position to like somebody too much, especially a woman who belonged, in all senses of the word, in Wyoming.

Even if he asked her to go back to Chicago with him, she wouldn't. Her grandmother was here, and so were her roots. She liked living in Shoshone, liked her job, liked to ride horses and spend time outdoors. He could tell that from the way she'd perked up the minute they'd headed down the trail.

So what the hell was he doing, courting her? It was an old-fashioned word, but it fit his behavior. He found himself complimenting her and kissing her for no reason. Actually, he did know the reason, and he should be worried about it.

The sad part was, he couldn't seem to help himself, couldn't seem to control his emotions when it came to Caro. He'd always been a very self-disciplined person with his eye on the prize. Now there was no prize to keep an eye on—except her, and she was completely out of reach.

Well, unless he wanted to go into the furniture business in Shoshone. Oh, yeah, that sounded like a barrel of fun. See what former Cubs star Logan Carswell is doing now? He's building furniture and selling it out of a little storefront in Shoshone, Wyoming. Pitiful.

But he'd be near Caro, and that almost made him consider it. Almost. But he couldn't imagine how a little furniture business would be enough for him. So he sold a few pieces and kept busy building more. So what? It didn't compare to making the game-winning out against the hometown rival Chicago White Sox.

His life used to matter, and now it didn't. Oh, sure, it mattered to his family and his friends, but not to the world in general. He used to thrill people with a good performance behind the plate. But now he didn't know what his role was supposed to be, and that was no time to fall head over heels for a woman. He couldn't trust his own feelings.

By the time they arrived at the barn, Emmett and the hands were busy feeding the horses. Both Caro and Logan offered to help unsaddle and brush Destiny and Cici, but Emmett seemed to think they were both needed up at the house.

"Big doings," Emmett said. "Sarah has a visitor, a guy who plans to buy some horses. He's also a baseball fan, so he's eager to meet you. Sarah asked me to send you both up to the house when you arrived."

Logan groaned inwardly. Just what he didn't need, some rabid fan who would want to talk about the joys of baseball. He could handle the old folks at the assisted living facility, maybe because their glory days were behind them, too. Other than that, though, he had no interest in reliving old plays.

But he knew Sarah would be happy about the prospect of more sales. Alex's PR must be paying off, and Logan would be an ungracious guest if he didn't try to humor this man. So he'd put on his best manners and be pleasant.

"I need to at least wash up a little," Caro said.

Emmett nodded. "Will the sink at the end of the barn do?"

"Sure."

"I'll come with you." Logan walked beside her, down the aisle between stalls where horses were munching away. It was a cozy atmosphere and he wished he could stay here instead of going up to the main house to socialize with whoever this man was.

As Caro washed her hands at the sink, she glanced at Logan. "You don't look especially happy."

"It's okay. You know I don't relish talking baseball, but if Sarah needs me to because this is a good customer, I'll do it."

"You're a good guy, Logan." Caro moved away from the sink to give him room while she dried her hands on a paper towel.

"Not really." He lowered his voice. "A good guy wouldn't be trying to find more ways to get into your bed."

"I didn't say you were a saint." She moved closer to him. "But you're good...and good in bed."

He chuckled. "You're not so bad yourself, Miss Davis."

One of the hands walked by, so they didn't say anything more until they were on their way up to the house. Sure enough, a shiny black king cab sat in the drive behind Caro's old pickup.

"Still planning to talk with Josie?" Logan asked.

"Yes."

"Then I guess you might want to mention that I'm following you home tonight."

She looked over at him. "You are?"

"Of course I am. Once you've said something to Josie, you won't be able to get rid of me. I'll spend the night with you and then we'll drive into Jackson together in the morning. Besides seeing your grandmother, we'll stop at a drugstore so I don't have to manhandle the condom machine at the Spirits and Spurs anymore."

She smiled at him. "I see you have it all worked out."

"I have the next twenty-four hours worked out. Beyond that, I'm still struggling."

"I didn't provide you with a plan B like I promised, did I? I was thinking about that while we rode home. How do you feel about becoming a sportscaster?"

He sighed.

"That sigh says it all. You don't want to."

He paused at the bottom of the steps and turned to her. "It's just that so many ex-players go into broadcasting. I don't know if I have the personality for it, either. Alex does, but he's not an athlete. Some combination of Alex's talent behind a microphone and my sports knowledge would be terrific, but we happen to be two different people."

"I think you'd be good at it. You obviously know the game and the players. And you'd look great on camera."

"Why, thank you, ma'am. You're probably biased, but I'll take that vote of confidence that I'm photogenic."

"It's not bias. I saw your picture dozens of times on the internet. The camera loves you."

"Yes, but would I love it back?" He shook his head. "It's a thought, and I shouldn't dismiss it. I know my agent is exploring that possibility. He wants me to capitalize on whatever fame I've achieved."

"And you should. You've worked hard for it."

He wondered if he'd ever met somebody so unselfish. Some women who had a wealthy man paying attention to them would be trying to convince him to settle down with them and make their lives easier. Logan was virtually certain that his money made no difference whatsoever to Caro. She just sincerely wanted him to be happy.

"I promise to think about the TV angle more seriously," he said. "It makes sense. I just have to get used to the idea."

"You'd be terrific. If you end up doing that, I might have to start watching sports on television."

Now there was a depressing thought—him stuck in a broadcast booth somewhere and Caro in Shoshone watching him on TV. It was a realistic scenario, but that didn't mean he had to like it. "Come on, gorgeous. Let's go inside and make nice with the man who's buying Last Chance ponies. Then we'll reward ourselves with some quality time under your homemade quilt."

"That sounds wonderful, but I just thought of something. If you're going to spend all that time with me, when are you going to work on Josie and Jack's cradle?"

"While you're tending bar, I'll come back here and work. It shouldn't take me that long, anyway. Besides, the longer I spend on the cradle, the longer I can stay at the ranch."

"Nice."

"Yeah, I agree." But he was no fool. He knew the longer he stayed at the ranch the deeper he'd get into this relationship. He should probably set a limit on his time here by booking a flight out. A smart man would do that.

Lately, though, he hadn't been acting very smart.

CARO FELT A LITTLE MUSSED and underdressed to be a dinner guest at the Last Chance, especially with a horse buyer in attendance. But she told herself that nobody would be paying attention to her, anyway. Logan would be the man of the hour.

She knew he would rise to the occasion. She'd seen him in action behind the bar, juggling martini shakers. He might not think he was a showman, but he had the makings of one.

He could be anything he wanted, really. He had the intelligence and coordination to master whatever he set out to do. She just hoped that whatever it was, he loved doing it. He deserved to be happy in his work.

As they walked into the living room of the ranch house, she admired the casual elegance of the place. Large Navajo rugs hung on the walls, and a wooden staircase spiraled up to the second floor. The furniture was large and leather, befitting a ranch. It was grouped in front of an immense rock fireplace, although no fire burned there on this warm August afternoon.

Sarah sat in one of the brown leather armchairs, and a tall, gray-haired man wearing a white cowboy shirt and obviously new jeans sat in a chair across the round coffee table from her. She held a glass of red wine, and he was drinking what looked like Scotch on the rocks.

Both she and the man stood when Caro and Logan walked in.

"There you are!" Sarah put down her glass and came forward. "Caro Davis and Logan Carswell, let me introduce Peter Beckett." She gestured to the man behind her.

He set down his drink and walked toward them. "Miss Davis, Mr. Carswell, it's a pleasure." He shook Caro's hand first, and then Logan's.

Caro appreciated that, considering how the guy's eyes lit up when he saw Logan. Next to him, she could fade into the background easily, so at least Peter Beckett had manners. He was nice looking, too, with kind blue eyes and a wonderful smile.

She'd guess he was probably in his sixties, and obviously very prosperous. His boots appeared to be custom made and his watch looked as if he could use it to contact James Bond if necessary. She hoped he'd bought a lot of horses and given the ranch a hunk of his money in return.

"What can I get each of you to drink?" Sarah hurried over to the liquor cabinet. "I have wine, beer, bourbon, Scotch, brandy…"

"Whatever wine you're having is fine with me," Caro said. She hoped wine wouldn't make her too loopy considering how little sleep and food she'd had today. She thought of the cookies she and Logan had scattered for the birds, and wished she'd eaten more of them.

"I'll take a beer, whatever kind you have," Logan said.

Sarah opened a door in the cabinet to reveal a small refrigerator. "Bud, then."

"That works."

"Go ahead and sit down. Have some chips and salsa."

Caro took her cue and positioned herself on the leather sofa near the chips. So long as she ate those, she shouldn't embarrass herself with one glass of wine.

Logan sat next to her, but not so close that anyone would think they were a couple. He turned toward Sarah's guest, who'd remained standing. "So, Mr. Beckett, do you live nearby?"

"Not too far away. About thirty miles. I have a place outside of Jackson. And call me Peter."

"Peter came to the open house we had in June," Sarah said as she brought over Caro's wine and Logan's beer, along with a couple cocktail napkins. "He didn't buy anything then, but I think he's ready to now."

"Absolutely." The man waited until Sarah was seated before levering his tall frame into the chair opposite her. "But that's not the only reason I'm here."

"Oh?" Logan took a sip of his beer.

Caro felt him tense and knew he was afraid that he was the other draw.

Peter swirled the ice cubes in his glass. "I'm trying to talk Sarah into going along with a new venture of mine."

"And I'm still thinking about it," Sarah said. "Peter's involved with a program to help troubled teens, boys mostly, and now that I have so much empty space in this big house, he's asked if I'd take some in and help provide a work experience for them."

"Of course, I'd pay for the privilege," Peter said. "My investments have worked out well and I can afford to underwrite this program. I thought about creating a ranch from scratch on the land I own, but here's one ready-made."

Logan gazed at Sarah. He'd been here only a few days, but he could see what a big change this would be. "So what do you think, Sarah?"

"Well, Archie and Nelsie named this place the Last Chance because it was their last chance to make a go of things during the Depression. That's been sort of a mantra around here ever since. This would be in keeping with that idea. I have to consult the boys, of course. I'll talk to Jack and Josie tonight when they come to dinner."

"But this place is so beautiful," Caro said. "I'd worry that the kids might—"

"They'd sign a contract before they ever set foot on the property," Peter said. "Coming here would be an incredible privilege, and one step out of line would mean the end of their stay. I've seen it work in other places."

"And I raised three active boys here." Sarah sipped her wine. "There's nothing delicate about this house. And we had a runaway teen girl here for a few years. Roni's married and off on the NASCAR circuit now, but she was trying to hot-wire one of the trucks when we asked her to stay. It's not like we don't have a precedent for this."

"It could be really great." Peter leaned forward, his glass held loosely between his big hands. "On top of that, when I heard you were here for a visit, Logan, I had another brain-storm."

Logan put down his beer. "What's that?"

"I know you're not playing anymore."

"No—no, I'm not."

Caro hoped she was the only one who heard the emotional undertones in that answer, emotion that Logan tried so des-perately to conceal. She held her breath, not sure what was coming next.

"I'm sure you have plans, lots of irons in the fire."

"A few."

Caro wanted desperately to touch Logan, to give him sup-port as he braved this through. "I'm certain the TV networks will want him," she said. "He'd make a great sportscaster."

"Yes, he would." Peter nodded. "And if you go that route, Logan, you probably can't do what I have in mind."

"Which is?"

"I'd love to have you help run the program each summer. Kids love their sports idols, and you would be worshipped by the boys. You could do team building with them. If Sarah agreed, we could lay out a ball field in one of the meadows. You'd be a tremendous asset to the program. Of course, I doubt I could pay what the networks could pay."

Logan picked up his beer but didn't drink. "I appreciate the offer, and money isn't really the issue, but—"

"You have other plans," Peter said. "More exciting plans. I understand completely. It was just a thought."

"It's not only that. You'd also want me to be a positive psychological influence on those kids and I'm not sure I would be."

"Nonsense. Of course you would. You've achieved so much, and I know you had to have a great deal of self-discipline to do that. You could pass that on to them."

Logan shook his head. "I don't know that I could. Your plan's a good one, but I'm not a guy who could inspire anyone right now."

Peter gazed at him in silence for several seconds. "It's too soon. I can see that now. Forgive an old guy for rushing his swing. I'm so excited about the project that I barrel ahead even when I should go slow." He shrugged. "Besides, I still have to talk this lovely lady and her three sons into going along with my zany plan."

"It's not zany," Sarah said, her cheeks pink. "I think Archie and Nelsie would have loved the idea."

Caro couldn't say for sure about that, because she hadn't known the two people who'd created the Last Chance Ranch. But Peter Beckett's project gave her a new perspective. Logan had turned down his offer, but mostly because his self-confidence wasn't in the best shape right now.

But he was improving in that area. She'd seen progress in the short time she'd been a part of his life. For the first time since laying eyes on Logan, Caro nursed a tiny flame of hope that he might not be out of reach, after all.

11

LOGAN HAD BEEN RELUCTANT to lay himself bare like that, but somebody with Peter Beckett's good heart deserved the truth and not some trumped-up excuse. He'd expected Beckett would want to talk baseball. He'd been unprepared for a job offer.

As the four of them sat in the living room talking about Beckett's plans for the program, Logan was glad he'd refused the offer. Maybe someday he'd feel that he was qualified to guide young kids, but not now, or in the near future. He was having enough trouble figuring out his own life, let alone helping some teenagers figure out theirs.

Jack and Josie arrived and were told about the project. Josie was immediately enthusiastic, while Jack, typically for him, apparently, was more reserved. The group moved from the living room down the hallway, through the large dining room that seated all the hands during lunch, and into the small family dining room.

"The kids could eat in the big room with the hands during lunch," Josie said as they took their seats at the table. "And then they could gather here for dinner."

"What about family dinners on Friday nights?" Jack asked. "When we have the whole family here, we fill the place."

"I know exactly what we'll do." Sarah's eyes were bright

as she looked over at Peter, seated to her left. "Friday nights will be an old-fashioned cowboy cookout down by the bunkhouse with the hands. I'm sure Watkins can handle that."

"Indeed, he could." The ranch's cook came through the door with platters of ribs. "And that would get him out of my hair for the time being."

Jack laughed. "Come on, Mary Lou. We all know you don't mind having Watkins around all that much."

Mary Lou rolled her eyes. "Depends. Sometimes he's a royal pain in the patoot."

Logan had talked a couple of times with the stocky wrangler, who sported an impressive handlebar mustache worthy of vintage baseball players. Logan had also heard the rumors that Watkins and Mary Lou were pretty tight. In fact, Watkins had been known to make regular nighttime visits to Mary Lou's apartment, located right off the kitchen.

"In any case," Sarah said, "we could put Watkins in charge of a cookout, which would free up the family dining room on Friday nights. I really like Peter's whole concept. I hope Nick and Gabe do, too."

Jack cleared his throat. "Hang on a minute, Mom. I haven't said I was in favor."

"Aren't you?"

Jack looked over at Peter. "I'd need to see some figures." Then he turned back to Sarah. "And what about Emmett's daughter, Emily? She's renting one of the upstairs bedrooms right now."

"Yes, she is, but unless I'm misreading the signs, she and Clay Whitaker will be married before next summer. She'll have moved out by then."

Jack picked up his fork. "We'd have to change the bedroom furniture, maybe put up some bunks." He glanced at Logan. "Built-ins make the most sense. If this is going to fly, we sure could use your carpentry skills."

"Well, I—"

"I'm afraid Logan's got other plans," Peter said.

Logan wasn't ready to be a project leader, but the bunk beds sounded like a fun thing to do, and he didn't want Peter speaking for him, either. "Depending on when you need them, I might be able to help with the bunks." He looked at Caro. Yes, he might have to return to Chicago soon, but the prospect of a future trip sounded good to him. Her quick smile told him she thought so, too, and his heart warmed.

"Excellent." Sarah beamed at Peter. "See how this is coming together?"

Logan thought something else might be coming together. According to Alex, Sarah had been a widow for almost two years, and Logan thought she was showing more than a friendly interest in Peter.

"So what does Mrs. Beckett think of the idea?" Josie asked.

Logan used his napkin to hide a smile. Count on Josie to cut to the chase.

"I'm sure she'd have loved the idea," Peter said. "She passed away three years ago."

Everybody around the table murmured their regrets, but glances darted with new interest to Sarah and Peter. It would be entertaining to stick around and see how this all turned out. Logan began to see the Last Chance as a continuing story, one that would never quite end, unlike his baseball career. He had to admit he was drawn to that aspect.

But he had more immediate concerns. Through some jockeying, Caro had arranged to sit next to Josie. Now they had their heads together, and Logan knew exactly what, or who, they were talking about. Josie kept looking at him, and he had to pretend not to notice.

Gradually the meal came to an end. Coffee and dessert were served and consumed. Chairs scraped back, and goodbyes started to circulate.

Logan glanced across the table at Caro, and she gave him a carefully disguised thumbs-up. Joy rushed through him and he fought the urge to suggest leaving immediately. Instead he lingered, waiting for the dining room to empty out.

Finally Josie made it around to his side of the table. "I've had an interesting conversation with Caro," she said in a low voice.

"And?"

"Just so you know, if you cause that girl any distress whatsoever, you'll answer to me."

He nodded. "Understood."

"She thinks you hung the moon, but I know better."

"Do you have to be so hard on me, Josie?"

"Not if you'll stick around and build cradles and bunk beds."

"That's not what you'd call a career path."

"No, but it beats wallowing in self-pity."

His gaze snapped to hers. "Is that what you think I'm doing?"

"I hope not, Logan. I sincerely hope not, both for your sake and Caro's." She patted him on the shoulder. "Be good to her. She's a special person."

"I know." His response was automatic, but he was still stuck on her "wallowing in self-pity" remark. That sounded a whole lot worse than trying to get his bearings, or searching for a new direction.

He was still considering that when Caro came to stand beside him.

"I think we're cleared to leave," she said. "Whatever vehicle you're borrowing, you should get it now if you're planning to follow me home."

"Caro, do you think I'm wallowing in self-pity?"

"Who told you that?"

"Josie."

Caro's response was a little slow in coming. "Well, don't forget that she's pregnant and hormonal."

"Right." But Caro hadn't really answered his question. Maybe she and everyone else on the ranch thought he *was* wallowing in self-pity. God, he hoped not. That was the last thing in the world he'd want to do.

The first thing, though, was to obtain a set of keys. He approached Jack. "Is there a truck I can drive for the time being?"

"Yeah. Josie already mentioned that you wanted to follow Caro into town tonight. Take the green Chevy. The keys are on the second hook from the right on the board hanging by the door."

"Thanks, Jack."

"Don't mention it. By the way, I spent a lot of nights in that apartment myself. There are shades tucked up under the valance of the curtains. I'd use them if I were you."

"Duly noted."

"And make sure they're all the way down, because they tend to flip back up a couple of inches and you'd be surprised what people can see."

"Good to know."

"Oh, and one other thing. The kitchen table isn't as sturdy as it looks."

CARO DROVE THROUGH THE night with the windows down and the radio up. Country tunes serenaded her as she kept checking her rearview mirror. She knew Logan was following her, but still she got a thrill every time she looked back and saw the headlights of his borrowed green Chevy truck.

Despite herself, she was entranced by the notion of the Last Chance Ranch. Until now, she hadn't heard how it got its name, and the optimism of that concept fit right in with her philosophy.

She understood why Sarah would be interested in Peter Beckett's idea. It blended perfectly with the ranch's mission. Selfishly, Caro wanted Logan to be interested in it, too.

But he wasn't, and he might never be. Once again she had to remind herself that she was welcoming him into her bed for the short term, and not because she thought he'd change his mind and stay forever. Josie had made it clear that Logan had always been very ambitious, and she predicted he'd eventually take a job in sports broadcasting because that was the kind of high-profile life he was used to.

Caro had listened carefully. Josie had known Logan ever since he was a neighbor kid in Chicago. The only person in Shoshone who would know Logan any better was Alex, and Alex was on his honeymoon and not due back for another week.

Still, Caro sensed there was more to Logan than pure ambition. He'd used ambition to get him to the big leagues, but that hadn't lasted. Maybe now he was ready to hook up with something less glamorous yet more likely to give him satisfaction for the rest of his life.

Caro thought this project of Peter's could be it, but she wasn't going to say so and risk poisoning the well. It was a decision that would have to come from Logan in his own time. It might never come.

Privately, though, Caro had decided to offer her services to the project, assuming that the Chance brothers gave it their stamp of approval. Initially, she could make quilts for all the bunk beds. A colorful quilt on each bed, handmade with love, might be the welcome that some of those kids needed.

But if the program ever expanded to include girls, she could teach them to quilt. She'd be willing to teach the boys, too, but teenaged boys living in cowboy country and searching for their identity might not go for quilting lessons. They might have girlfriends or mothers who would like one, though.

In any case, Caro wanted to be part of the Last Chance legacy. She hadn't appreciated that history before tonight. Up until now, the ranch had simply been the place where Josie lived now that she was married to Jack Chance. Sure, it was a landmark, but one that Caro had taken for granted the whole time she was growing up in Shoshone.

She approached the town limits and slowed down. It wasn't much of a town, really—two intersecting roads with one stoplight. When she reached the light, it turned red, as it usually did whenever a single vehicle arrived at the intersection of the highway and Main Street, no matter which direction they were traveling.

The Spirits and Spurs sat across the intersection. A person turning right on Main would pass all the major businesses, including a bank, a post office, a feed store, a small grocery and an ice cream parlor.

Elmer Crookshanks's gas station was across the intersection on the left. Last year Jack Chance had accused Elmer of rigging the light so that people had to stop and take notice of his gas station. Elmer had denied it, and the light continued to turn red more than seemed necessary, considering the lack of traffic.

It was a funky little town, and Caro loved it. Yes, she hoped to travel and see other places, but her heart would always be here. Now that she knew more about the Last Chance, she was even prouder of her little corner of the world.

Behind her, the Chevy's engine rumbled. She imagined Logan sitting in the driver's seat, waiting impatiently for the light to turn green so they could both cross the intersection. He might not know what he wanted out of life, but he knew what he wanted when it came to her, at least for the immediate future. Being desired with that kind of intensity was a thrill she'd never forget.

The light turned and she drove through the intersection,

with the Chevy right on her tail. She barely had time to park, pick up her hat from the seat and climb out of her truck before Logan was there, dragging her close. He must have left his hat in the truck, because he was no longer wearing it.

"That was the longest damned dinner and the longest damned drive and the longest damned red light." He kissed her quick and hard. "I'm so pumped I could carry you up those stairs, bad knee or not."

Heat sluiced through her veins. "But we have to go into the bar first."

He squeezed his eyes shut. "Right. How could I forget? Got your keys? I'd rather not parade through the bar itself if we can go in through the back."

"Right here." She held them up.

"Then lead me to the condom machine." Wrapping an arm around her waist, he guided her in the direction of the back door.

"If it doesn't work, I'll come in with you and see what I can do."

"That won't look right."

"Judging from the empty parking lot, the bar's not crowded right now, anyway. Nobody would notice." As they reached the back door she quickly unlocked it and stepped into Josie's office, which was also locked this time of night.

"But a guy should be able to obtain his own condoms." Logan walked in behind her. "Hey, it's dark in here." He slipped an arm around her waist and drew her back against him. Beneath his jeans he was ready for action. "Maybe we don't have to go upstairs, after all."

She couldn't resist nestling against him, but her words were as stern as she could manage, considering her level of excitement. "We're not having sex in Josie's office."

He pulled back her hair and kissed the curve of her neck

while he cupped her breast through the cotton of her shirt. "Or on your kitchen table, either."

"What?"

"Jack warned me it's not as sturdy as it looks." He raked his teeth gently over her skin as he fondled her breast. "I gather he and Josie found that out the hard way."

Caro moaned and leaned against him as she imagined making love on whatever available surface presented itself. "This is madness. We have to stop so you can get the condoms."

"I know." He continued to massage her breasts. "But I love touching you. I haven't been able to touch you for hours."

"I love touching you, too." She struggled for breath. "But… I'll be able to do that so much more…efficiently…once we're safely up in my apartment."

"You're so logical." He gave her one last squeeze before releasing her with obvious reluctance. "And so right. Give me a minute before you open that office door. I need to focus on some baseball stats."

She took a deep breath to compose herself. "I should go out and talk to Steve while you buy condoms. He might wonder what's going on if you come through the door of Josie's office all by yourself. Technically, you shouldn't have a key."

"In my current state, with all the blood drained south, I'm not sure I would have thought of that."

"I almost didn't. I was going to wait here in the dark until you came back." She walked over to Josie's desk and turned on the green glass lamp there. "Steve might wonder why we didn't turn on a light, too."

"Good thinking, once again." Logan heaved a sigh. "Okay, I've cataloged a list of every game-winning home run the previous season. I'm calmed down enough to walk out there."

"Want to stop for a drink?"

"No."

"So I'll just say that we wanted to check to make sure he's doing all right. You should walk over to the bar with me, in fact, just to be friendly. For all he knows, you're headed back to the ranch and need to make a quick trip to the bathroom before you make that drive."

"Steve doesn't strike me as the dim-witted type. I doubt he'll think I'm going back to the ranch if I walk in from the office with you." His heated glance touched every part of her. "Especially if you have a couple of snaps undone on your shirt."

"I do?" She looked down and quickly fastened them. "When did you do that?"

"Just now, I guess. It was so automatic I didn't realize what I was doing."

"And I was so aroused I didn't notice that you'd done it." She met his gaze. "I think we'd better get ourselves upstairs, and fast, but we need to look casual doing it."

"Fine, but don't expect me to juggle any martini shakers."

She laughed as she moved toward the door. "I won't. But before you leave town, I want you to teach me how." She was proud of herself for tossing out a carefree line that included a mention of his inevitable leaving. More comments like that would help her stay focused on reality.

"I don't like thinking about that."

Then don't go. But she wouldn't say that, because he'd made his position clear when he'd turned down Peter Beckett's offer.

Her hand on the knob, she turned back to him. "But you should keep it in mind, Logan. You will be leaving." By the time she unlocked the door and walked into the bar, she was much more in control of herself.

If she intended to play this game, she needed to be.

12

LOGAN FOLLOWED CARO out of the office and tried like hell to look as if he had no sexual interest in her whatsoever. He kept his distance, and gave his best impression of a nonchalant cowboy saunter as they approached the bar.

The room was empty except for Steve, who seemed delighted to see them. "Business is slow," he said. "I guess everybody partied hardy last night and now they're staying home."

"That happens," Caro said. "So you're feeling better?"

"Way better." He grinned. "Rough night, but it was over fairly fast, so I think it was food poisoning, after all. Did you do something fun with the time off?"

"Sure did. Logan and I went riding." She kept her attention firmly on Steve.

Logan appreciated that. If she'd looked at him, they both would have been swamped with memories of their afternoon together, and no doubt it would have shown on their faces.

"Nice." Steve glanced at Logan. "Have you been on a horse much?"

"Nope. I came off of this one today, but I'm none the worse for wear."

"Didn't reinjure your knee, I hope."

"Fortunately not. Hey, if you two will excuse me, I need to head back to the men's room."

Steve's eyes didn't flicker. "You bet. I just cleaned it. Nothing else to do."

"Thanks." Logan wove his way through the tables to the tiny hallway that led to both bathrooms. He had cash in his pocket, and with luck, the condom machine would decide to dispense condoms tonight.

But after five minutes of fiddling with it, he was still empty-handed. Because the bar was deserted except for Steve and Caro, he couldn't risk banging on the sides of it the way he had before. He was forced to walk back out and over to the bar.

"Still no customers, huh?" He glanced around. "Seems like a waste to keep the place open. How soon would you normally close?" If he could get rid of Steve, then he could manhandle that condom machine. Or maybe there was a key to it somewhere. He'd take the thing apart, if necessary.

Steve checked the Budweiser clock on the wall. "Another half hour or so. But you're right. It is a waste. Unless you two care to order something? It's on the house."

"No, thanks." Logan controlled his impatience. "I really should be leaving." *And going upstairs with this delicious woman.* "I'm not the person in charge around here, but I can't believe Josie would care if you locked up early."

"No, she probably wouldn't." Caro either sensed there had been a problem with the condom machine or was simply going along with his suggestion. "I can't call to ask, because I'm sure she's asleep by now. Knowing Josie, I think she'd want us to use our own judgment. There are no customers to offset the utility bill, so let's lock up."

"Sounds good to me," Steve said. "If you'll turn around the sign on the door, Caro, I'll close out the register and be on my way."

She started for the front door, but turned back toward Steve. "You know what? I can take care of it. You've been sick, and although you may feel better, I'll bet you could use the extra sleep."

Logan could have kissed her. Well, he'd wanted to do that, anyway, but he really had the urge now that she was on the get-rid-of-Steve bandwagon. "Yeah, we can handle everything," Logan said. "Take off, buddy." *And I mean that sincerely.*

Steve glanced at Logan, and his eyes registered a lightbulb moment. "I do believe I'll take you up on that. I'll just head on out the back door, then." As he passed Logan, he lowered his voice. "Hope you didn't need the condom dispenser, 'cause it's empty."

"Oh."

"Nobody got more in, either. I checked."

"Oh."

"Good luck, buddy."

"Thanks." Well, damn. Not only were there no condoms, but good old Steve knew what was going on. Logan had predicted he'd figure it out, anyway. Josie also knew, and so did Jack, and word would spread from there. Soon the whole town would know that Logan and Caro were lovers.

Until this moment, Logan hadn't fully understood the consequences of that. The town would know, and then he'd leave. Although Caro had said she was going into this with her eyes wide open, was she, really?

He wondered if she'd considered that a certain percentage of those who knew would assume she'd been the plaything of a famous man and then been dumped when he was tired of her. He'd experienced firsthand the sour feeling pity left behind, and he didn't want that for Caro. Without thinking this through, he'd set her up in the victim role. And he didn't know how to fix it.

She came up behind him and wrapped both arms around his middle, mimicking the way he'd held her earlier when they were in Josie's office. "Am I guessing right that the condom machine is a problem?"

"According to Steve, it's empty and nobody ordered more. He checked."

"I see."

Logan took hold of her hands and eased out of her grip so he could turn and face her. "And I owe you an apology."

She laughed. "For failing to acquire condoms? That's not your fault."

"No, not that." He took her by the shoulders and kneaded them gently. "For failing to realize that when I leave, a lot of people in this town will assume you've been dumped, no matter what either of us say."

"I don't—"

"You can claim not to care, but you deal with the population of Shoshone almost every day. Are you prepared for the pitying looks? The veiled allusions to the guy who broke your heart? The cracks about sports stars who go through women the way other people go through a package of Twinkies?"

"Like Twinkies? Really?"

"Well, *I* don't, but plenty of guys do. I mean, yeah, I've had a few one-night stands in my life, but generally I—hell, this isn't about me. It's about you living in a small town where the word will now be out about…about us."

"I knew that when I decided to tell Josie," she said quietly.

"I wish you'd said something. I'm from the big city, where nobody cares unless it's juicy enough to make the tabloids. I didn't stop to think what bringing it out in the open with Josie would do to your…not your reputation, exactly, but you will get those who think you've been done wrong."

Her smile was soft. "Then I'll tell them I kicked you to the curb."

"I hope you do! I hope you tell them that I begged you to let me stay, but I had a ton of bad habits that you couldn't tolerate anymore. Say that." He squeezed her shoulders. "Promise me you'll trash my rep after I'm gone."

"I can't do that. You're coming back to build bunk beds. You don't want people snickering behind your back when you're buying screws and nails and lumber and stuff."

"You're not taking this seriously at all, are you?"

"No."

"You should."

"I should not." She reached up and pinched his cheek. "Because they won't pity me. You're like a rock star, Logan!"

"Oh, for God's sake. I am not."

"You are in this tiny burg. The women will envy me and want to know if you're as good in bed as you look like you would be. I'll just smile and let them eat their hearts out. The men will figure I must be hot stuff if I attracted the attention of a professional ballplayer, even for a few nights. Don't worry about me, okay?"

"I can't help it. This is uncharted territory for me, coming into a small town and getting involved with you. I feel as if I have to protect you."

"Well, you *do,* which brings us back to the condom issue."

"I wasn't talking about that kind of protection."

"I am."

"So are we driving to Jackson to find a twenty-four-hour pharmacy?"

"We could. Or…" She moved closer and rubbed her hand over the fly of his jeans. "We can get creative."

His happy cock leaped to immediate attention. "Like how?"

"The bar is loaded with all sorts of interesting items. You should know. You used to be a bartender."

As the possibilities slowly unfolded in his fevered brain,

his body tightened in anticipation. "Are you suggesting we grab a few supplies and take them upstairs?"

"We'll have to figure out a way to ring them up and pay for them, but, yes, that's exactly what I'm suggesting."

"Whipped cream?"

"For starters. And flavored liqueurs."

His johnson began to ache. "I'm in."

"I thought you might be. Let's go raid the pantry."

Fifteen minutes later they'd locked up the bar and climbed the stairs with their purchases.

"This could be messy," he said.

"I plan on it." She moved around the kitchen and living room, lowering shades.

"I don't want to get anything on that handmade quilt."

She braced one palm on the kitchen counter as she tugged off her boots. "That's why we're going to do it in here, instead." She glanced at him. "Are you planning to get naked or not?"

"I am." He pulled up a kitchen chair and sat down to take off his boots and socks. "But I have dibs on the first round. I have plans for the butterscotch schnapps and the cherries."

"I have plans for the whipped cream."

He paused in the act of pulling off his second boot as his penis responded to that statement by swelling with enthusiasm. "I can only imagine, and once you start licking whipped cream off my cock, it'll be all over. That's why I'm going first."

"But you're so slow." She flicked off her bra and shucked her panties before walking over to him. "I'm finished and you're still mostly dressed."

"So I see." Reaching for her, he pulled her down to his lap. "I'm still a city boy who's not used to boots and jeans."

"I'll help you." She straddled him, nudging her damp curls against the ridge of his fly.

"Much more of that kind of help, and you won't need the whipped cream." He spanned her waist and slid both hands up and around until he was cradling her breasts. "Mmm." He stroked his thumbs over her tight nipples. "I might not need the butterscotch schnapps, either. Lift up a little bit for me."

Putting her feet on the floor, she rose up so that her nipples were even with his lips. "Like this?"

"You read my mind." Slowly he drew in one firm tip and rolled it between his tongue and the roof of his mouth. They had all night this time, and he intended to make the most of it…or as much as he could without condoms.

So he would feast on the wonders of her body, with garnish and without. As he showered attention on her breasts, her breathing grew shallow and she began to quiver. She had such an erotic nature. She might give him credit for being good in bed, but she was the most responsive woman he'd ever been with.

Her fingers dug into his shoulders as he licked and massaged, nibbled and sucked. On impulse he reached between her thighs and rubbed his thumb over her clit. Just like that, she climaxed, arching her back and gasping his name.

Kissing his way upward to her lips, he lowered her to his lap.

If only he could lower her onto his cock, which strained against his jeans.

Logan feathered kisses over her parted lips. "You're easy to please, Miss Caro," he murmured.

"Not…" She gulped for air. "Not always."

"No?" He stroked her sleek backside as she sat on his jeans-clad thighs.

"You…turn me on."

"That's good news." Logically, he should want to believe she was like this with any man, because then it would be easier to let her go. But his possessive male instinct roared with pleasure knowing that her reaction to him was unique.

She took a shaky breath and looked into his eyes. "I want your shirt off."

"Then take it off."

Sliding both hands into the open neck, she yanked, and the snaps popped all the way down. "There." She flattened her palms against his bare chest. "I haven't spent nearly enough time touching you, either."

He hoped he could take it while she did. Her slow massage was sexy as hell, especially when she leaned down and began to play with his nipples. He had to admit they were more sensitive to her touch than to any woman's before her.

He moaned and shifted her weight so that she wasn't bearing down on his increasingly interested pride and joy. She was getting him riled up with nothing more than a chest massage and some attention from her hot little mouth. Incredible though it might seem, she might be able to make him come like that.

But he wouldn't allow it. When she reached for his belt buckle, he stopped her. "Not yet."

"But I want to—"

"I know, and you will." He lifted her off his lap and stood. "But first…" He glanced around the kitchen, planning his next move. The table was out, according to Jack. But the kitchen counter was fair game. He approved of the rounded edge on the laminate. That should suit his purposes nicely.

"Here." He circled her waist with his hands and placed her on the counter, thanking all those sessions in the gym for the upper-body strength that allowed him to do it without dropping her. That would have put a real dent in the mood.

As it was, she seemed sort of impressed that he could swing her around like that. She gazed at him in obvious anticipation. "What now?"

"Butterscotch schnapps time." He pulled the bottle out of the bag, along with a jar of long-stemmed maraschino cherries. "Lean back against the cabinets while I mix up a little something special."

Putting her hands behind her, she relaxed against the oak cabinets while she watched him.

"You said I could get creative, right?"

"Uh-huh." She ran her tongue over her lips.

He fished some cherries out of the jar and laid them in the lid. "Every time I made a buttery nipple for a customer, I wanted to make a real one."

"That's why you wanted—"

"The butterscotch schnapps. Yep." He opened the bottle. "Hold still." Tilting it, he allowed a little to drip on each breast.

She shivered. "Cold."

"That's because you're so hot." Lovingly, he smoothed the schnapps over her nipples. As they tightened into hard little nubs, she closed her eyes and whimpered. "That feels sinfully good."

"You're not garnished yet." Picking up a cherry, he tied the stem around her nipple.

She gasped. "What are you…ohhh, wow…" She closed her eyes again. "Funky. I like it."

"Not done yet." He tied the other one securely. And then he began to lick and nibble, both her and the cherries.

"Ahh, Logan…" She arched toward him, offering her breasts, squirming against the counter as he tugged at the end of the cherry stems. Tunneling her fingers through his hair, she gripped his scalp and began to breathe faster.

At last he closed his lips over both nipple and cherry, pulling them into his mouth and squeezing them against his tongue. By the time he moved to her other breast, she was writhing against the laminate.

"Logan, I want…could you please…"

With one final caress, he moved back and picked up the schnapps bottle. "Yes. Now. Just open up a little…." He nudged her thighs apart and dripped the liqueur onto her brown curls, where it slid down into the pink treasure hiding beneath.

She moaned and opened even more for him, all hesitation gone in the flood of her need. Her trust and surrender were complete, a gift he prayed he was worthy to receive.

Crouching down, he tasted butterscotch and woman, mixed into a heady brew that drove him insane. He would need some relief soon, but first…first he would give her this. He didn't rush, even as the pounding of his blood and the pressure on his cock, and yes, the tension in his knee, begged him to hurry.

Instead he started with gentle movements of his tongue and an easy suction. But gradually he bore down, pushing her harder as her cries grew in intensity. He held her hips to keep her right where he wanted her, right where he could… there, that was the spot.

Her thighs began to tremble as she let out her breath in one long wail and came, bathing his tongue in her release. He held her and kissed her drenched curls as she sank back to the counter.

Taking his head in both hands, she urged him upward. "That was…"

He gasped as pain jabbed his knee.

"Oh, Logan. Your—"

"Not a word." He looked into her eyes. "Not one word."

"All right." She met his gaze. "Thank you."

He smiled. "You're welcome."

"Now it's your turn."

13

CARO CONVINCED LOGAN to move into the bathroom, where they could rinse off in her tub shower. She knew it would be a tight fit for him in there, but she didn't think he'd fit any better on her kitchen counter. She lit a couple candles for atmosphere and brought the can of whipped cream as she led him into their new venue.

But it wasn't until she finally had him stripped down that she noticed the large bruise on his backside. "Yikes, Logan. You hit the ground really hard, didn't you?"

"And I don't want to hear anything about that, either. Next thing I know, you'll decide I'm too feeble for the whipped cream treatment. I'm a professional athlete. I can take it."

She slid her hands up his powerful chest. "You're one tough guy, huh?"

"Yes." His lips curved in a smile. "And don't ever forget it."

"I won't, but I'm putting my fluffy bath mat in the tub before you sit in there." She positioned the mat at the end of the tub. "Climb in, big boy."

"Is it pink?" He peered at it suspiciously in the flickering candlelight. "It looks pink."

"It's salmon. Besides, when I'm through with you, you won't care if it's purple with green and yellow spots."

That made him laugh, and he stepped into the tub. "No doubt."

Once he was in, she surveyed the situation. There wasn't much room left for her. He was a bigger guy than she'd realized. "Can you put one foot out on the floor?"

"Like this?" He accomplished it easily, by bending his knee and angling his leg outside the tub.

"Perfect." Now she had a spot right where she needed to be, facing his impressive package. Once she completed this maneuver, she'd never be able to mix a drink that involved whipped cream without thinking of Logan.

She started to ask him if he was comfortable, but that was a silly question. Of course he wasn't. He had a bruise the size of a saucer on his fanny. His knee probably still hurt from crouching down to give her an orgasm to end all orgasms. He was the walking wounded, but she intended to make him forget that, at least for a little while.

Stepping into the tub with the whipped cream can in one hand, she lowered herself carefully to her knees. "Hold still," she said, copying his words on purpose. As if she'd been able to hold still once he'd started smearing butterscotch schnapps on her nipples.

"I don't think I could move if I wanted to. Your tub has me in a hammerlock."

"Good. Then you can't get away." She put her finger on the nozzle of the can and pointed it at his gloriously erect penis.

"I have no desire to—ah! That's cold!"

"You won't be cold for long." She decorated him with whipped cream from tip to base, and he flinched with each sweep of the spray can.

"Am I supposed to like this?"

"You will in a minute." She set the can outside the tub, leaned forward and began to clean him up. Oh, yes, this was fun. He tried to maintain his cool, but soon he was breathing hard and twitching with every swipe of her tongue.

The combination of salt and sweet was delicious, and she was tempted to spray him again, except she didn't think he'd last through another coating of whipped cream. Whenever she glanced up, his eyes were squeezed shut and his jaw was tightly clenched. He was desperately struggling not to come.

That desperation aroused her, too, and she realized that must have happened to him while he'd treated her to his revised version of a buttery nipple. He had more self-control than any man she'd met, but she was about to destroy what little he had left.

After taking care of the last smears of whipped cream on his quivering penis, she closed her mouth over the tip and slid down, taking him as deep into her throat as she could. His answering groan was her reward. Hollowing her cheeks, she drew back, caressing him with her tongue as she moved upward.

His voice was strained. "Devil woman."

She released him and blew across the velvet tip. "Yeah. Want more?"

"Yes."

With a smile, she enveloped him in her warm mouth once again, and this time she reached down and cupped his tight balls. Some more suction, a gentle massage, and he was hers. With a hoarse cry, he erupted, and she took all that he had to give.

He lay there, his massive chest heaving in the aftermath of his orgasm. With one last swallow, she released him and sat back to survey her handiwork.

He opened heavy-lidded eyes. "That was incredible."

"Glad you liked it."

"Is it okay if I stay like this forever?"

"Sure." It was easy to say—they both knew he wouldn't.

But for now, she'd live for the moment, and this particular moment was pretty doggone wonderful.

LOGAN DIDN'T BELIEVE they'd both fit in the shower at the same time, let alone have room for him to give her another orgasm. But apparently they were both inventive and reasonably agile, because that's how it worked out. Afterward, they dried each other off, gave in to exhaustion and crawled under Caro's quilt to sleep until dawn.

Morning came with the cry of a hawk as it wheeled through the brilliant Wyoming sky. Logan pulled Caro close and couldn't remember the last time he'd felt this good.

She snuggled against him. "What time is it?"

Lifting his head, he was able to make out the numbers on the digital clock on her nightstand. "Eight."

"*Eight?* Seriously?"

"Unless your clock's on the blink, it's eight."

"We have to get a move on." She wiggled out of his arms and climbed out of bed. "Grandma Bonnie expects me there by nine every morning."

Logan thought Caro needed to break Grandma Bonnie of that habit, but it wasn't his place to say. He'd offered to go with her to Jackson, and he couldn't very well start off by criticizing her handling of her grandmother.

He swung his feet out of bed. "We'll pick up breakfast on the way."

"There are usually doughnuts and coffee in the visitor's lounge. She'll want to go there, especially if she thinks people will be excited about seeing you."

He wasn't used to making do with coffee and doughnuts, but he didn't mention that, either. After a lifetime of eating foods that would create the peak performance he required for his job, he was in the habit of eating a decent breakfast even though he was no longer playing ball. But if Caro needed to be there at nine, and that meant coffee and doughnuts were the easy solution, he'd put up with that for one morning.

"You take first shower," he said. "I left an overnight bag in the truck. I'll go get it."

She went into the bathroom and tossed his jeans out before turning on the water. "You'll need these if you're going down to your truck."

Putting on jeans without briefs was a trick, but he managed it with great care. The shower was already running by the time he went outside, barefoot and shirtless, and started slowly down the steps. His knee was stiff, but it usually was in the morning. Considering the workout he'd given it yesterday, it could have been worse.

Maybe sex was good therapy for his knee. He smiled at that as he walked gingerly over to the Chevy, his bare feet coming in contact with a few sharp rocks along the way. In his haste to be with Caro, he'd left the truck unlocked, with the keys dangling from the ignition. Not cool.

His overnight bag was still on the seat, though, along with his hat. He doubted the crime rate was particularly high in Shoshone, Wyoming.

A guy in a battered old sedan that was probably some shade of brown under all the grime pulled over and rolled down his window. "Everything okay?"

Logan gave him a wave. "Fine, thanks."

"Don't often see shirtless, barefoot cowboys out on the street."

"I suppose not." Logan didn't consider the parking lot exactly "the street," but he should have realized that coming out here wearing only his jeans would add to any rumors circulating about his relationship with Caro. He didn't mind being described as a cowboy, though.

"I'm Elmer Crookshanks," the guy said. "Run the gas station across the street. If you need gas, I'm your guy."

"Thanks. I'll remember that."

"You're that baseball fella, aren't you?"

"Yes."

"Staying with Caro, I see."

"Uh, no, not exactly." Now Logan really regretted not bringing his overnight bag up last night.

"If you say so. Well, gotta go open the station. You take care, now."

"You, too." Logan felt like banging his head on the roof of the truck. He might as well have put up a billboard announcing he was sleeping with Caro. Now every person who stopped to buy gas from that scrawny little guy would get the word—"that baseball fella" had been parading around minus his boots and shirt, which had to mean he was fooling around with one of the local girls, namely Caro. Shit.

Logan didn't say anything about Elmer while he and Caro got ready to go to Jackson. He would eventually, because she needed to know in case it came back to bite her later on. Caro insisted on driving, and he was sure relieved that she didn't need any gas from Elmer's station before they left.

She looked extremely pretty this morning, with her glossy hair swept up in the ponytail he'd found so perky when he'd first met her. She wore a moss-green tank top and khaki shorts. He supposed that was because today she wasn't required to be a bartender or a cowgirl. Instead she was a granddaughter.

Country music had been playing on the radio when she'd switched on the engine, but now she turned it off.

"I don't care if you'd like to listen to that," he said.

"I'd rather talk to you. What did Elmer Crookshanks have to say?"

"Weren't you in the shower?"

"I made it a fast one. Then I came out to see if you were

back, and when I looked out the window, there you were, trapped by old Elmer."

"Without my boots and shirt, which I think telegraphed what we've been up to."

She looked at him, wide-eyed. "You think that telegraphed whipped cream and butterscotch schnapps?"

"Maybe not *specifically* what we've been up to, smart-ass. I like to think the whipped cream and butterscotch schnapps will be our little secret for at least the next fifty or sixty years."

"Sorry. I've already contacted the *Enquirer* and they want my story. Gonna pay me big bucks, too."

"Don't bother. Elmer Crookshanks will have the whole thing leaked by sundown, and the *Enquirer* isn't interested unless they get an exclusive."

"There goes my retirement fund."

"Seriously, Caro, I'm sorry I ran down there half-dressed and practically announced to the world that I've been in your bed all night. I should have figured out a different plan."

"As I keep telling you, it will only raise my stature in this community if everyone knows I've had *S-E-X* with the great Logan Carswell. Relax."

"You're not going to tell anyone about the whipped cream and butterscotch schnapps, though, right?"

She grinned. "I don't know. What's it worth to you?"

"Caro!"

"No, I'm not telling that, for heaven's sake. That was private. But as for everyone figuring out that you spent the night in my apartment with me, I don't give a flip. It was worth it."

"You're one special woman, Caro."

She gave him a quick smile. "I'd have to be to snag a hunk of burning love like you for a few nights."

He reached over and gave her knee a squeeze.

"Watch it. We don't have condoms yet."

"I know. And you're driving. The last thing we need is a fender bender because I was distracting you." He settled back in his seat. "So what do you think about this Peter Beckett?"

"His project, or him in general?" She reached for a pair of aviator sunglasses on the dashboard and put them on.

"Both, I guess." Logan knew he should be enjoying the scenery out the window, but he was more interested in the scenery inside the truck. Caro looked hot in that outfit and the sexy shades made her look even hotter.

"His project sounds fabulous. I've heard of programs like that, where teenagers go stay somewhere they have space to move around, and can interact with animals. It's supposedly very good therapy for them."

"I can see how it would be. And there would be plenty of adult supervision, with all the hands around to ride herd on them. Emmett told me that mucking out stalls was great therapy."

"I'll bet it is. I haven't had much opportunity, but I can imagine that you get down to basics when you're shoveling horse poop."

"I should probably try it."

She glanced at him, but her expression was hidden behind her shades. "You probably should."

He couldn't help wondering what else she thought he should do, like maybe accept Beckett's offer. She hadn't said so, but if she was so high on the idea, she must be thinking he was a fool to pass it up.

"Do you think I should consider working with Beckett?"

"Not if you don't want to."

"It's not that I don't want to. It's that I don't think my head's in the right place to be a help to those kids."

She didn't respond.

"Caro?"

"I don't know whether I should say anything or not, Logan.

This is your life, and you have to come to these decisions on your own."

"You're right, and I will, but something's going on in your head. I can tell. I'd like to know your opinion."

"You might not like what I have to say."

"So what? Do you think I can't take it?" When she hesitated, he finally realized what was going on. "You don't think I can take it."

"Alex warned us that you would probably be a little…fragile."

Logan blew out a breath. "Fragile." The word felt bitter on his tongue. He might be struggling, but he was never *fragile*.

"Well, is that so wrong? You just said your head wasn't in a good place to help those kids! Isn't that the same thing?"

"No! It just means I don't feel qualified to give anybody advice on how to live their lives at the moment, because I don't know how I'm going to live mine. Eventually I'll figure it out, but I'm not there yet."

She took a deep breath. "If you would get into something like Beckett's program, I'll bet it would help you as much as it would help the kids."

"That's not what Beckett is looking—"

"You don't really know what he wants from you, because you didn't give him a chance to discuss it."

"He said he wanted someone the kids could look up to, a role model. I don't see how I can be that when I'm essentially out of work."

"Logan, don't you see? Those kids don't need some super-successful dude who's never had a real problem telling them how to live. I'm sure they'd prefer somebody they can relate to. You're coming back from a hard knock. They'll understand that. They might even teach *you* something about how to recover."

"Ah." Logan stared out the windshield, but he still wasn't

seeing the Wyoming countryside. Instead he saw his dad's face as he'd crouched down in front of him during a Little League game when Logan had just struck out, ending any hopes for the team's victory. He'd been eight years old, and close to tears.

His father had taken him firmly by the shoulders. *Never let them see you sweat, son.* His father's words had shaped Logan's entire career, his entire life, come to think of it. He'd had highs and lows during the past twenty-five years, but nobody, by God, had ever seen him sweat.

In effect, Caro was suggesting a complete one-eighty. She was asking him to show the world, or at least these teenagers, that he was vulnerable, that he could be hurt, that he *had* been hurt. He wasn't sure he could do that.

"I was afraid you wouldn't like it," she said.

"It's not that." He glanced over at her. "What you're saying might be great advice for somebody else. I don't know that it would work for me."

She shrugged. "No biggie. It was just an idea."

But he thought it was more than that. It was a way that he could be with her. Although she would never point it out, any idiot could see how taking Beckett's offer would mean Caro could be part of his life. But unfortunately, she had the wrong man for the job.

14

CARO DROPPED THE SUBJECT of Peter Beckett's project after that and spent the rest of the drive pointing out places of interest. At last they pulled into the parking area beside the assisted living facility, only a few minutes later than Caro normally arrived there.

"Looks like a nice place," Logan said.

"It's a beautiful place. As you can see, they nestled it in among some tall pines, without clear-cutting the property. There are shady walking paths for the residents who are ambulatory, and bird feeders by the windows of those who aren't. The décor is cheerful and the food's good. I just wish my grandmother liked it."

"How long has she been here?"

"Six months."

"And she's eighty…what?"

"Eighty-three. She lived in her house in Shoshone for almost sixty of those years. She and my grandfather rented it at first, and then scraped together the money for a down payment. He'd died by the time I moved in as a kid, but it was obvious the house contained many memories of him."

"So it's not hard to understand why she's resistant to this place."

"No." Caro gazed at the one-story building with its hanging

pots of petunias and rockers on the front porch. "I get it, which is why I come to visit her every day. I know physically she's much better off here, but mentally…" Caro sighed.

"What are her health issues?"

"Osteoporosis, for one. She's already had several small fractures and she has to use a walker because her balance is bad. And she's diabetic, and arthritic, and has a heart condition. You know. The usual."

"I don't know. My grandparents on both sides are doing pretty well, judging by that laundry list."

"Then you're lucky." She wasn't surprised that his relatives would be healthy, considering what a fine specimen he was. She'd bet that poor health was considered a weakness in his family. "We'd better go in. I'm sure she's sitting there waiting impatiently for me."

Caro opened her door, but Logan, despite his bum knee, managed to round the hood of the truck in record time. "Nice manners, Mr. Carswell."

"Good thing I have them, too. I learned right away that Sarah Chance is a stickler for manners. I wouldn't have lasted long in her house acting like a clod, no matter how famous I am."

Caro accepted his guiding hand as she climbed down from the truck. Touching him was such a pleasure. She would miss that. "Do you think Sarah has a little bit of a crush on Peter Beckett?"

"Looked like it to me." Logan gave her hand a squeeze before releasing it. Then he closed the driver's side door. "I wonder if anybody else picked up on it."

"Oh, I'm sure they did. Sarah might not be ready to admit it to herself, though. Jonathan Chance cast a long shadow in this area. She might think a romance would be disloyal to his memory."

"That would be too bad, especially if she's attracted to Beckett."

"I guess we'll just have to wait and see." Or Caro would. Logan's interest in the matter would probably disappear once he returned to Chicago.

She walked with him up to the glass double doors that opened onto the visitor's lounge. Sure enough, Grandma Bonnie sat in a wingback chair facing the entrance, her walker at her side. Her short white hair was perfectly styled, her makeup carefully applied, and her slacks and white blouse spotless. She'd always been fastidious.

Several other residents sat in the lounge, too. More casually dressed and quite chatty, they were gathered around a couple of card tables playing games. Grandma Bonnie had never shown any interest in joining them.

But she was certainly interested in Caro's companion. Her eyes widened behind her rimless glasses and she gave Logan the once-over. Then she glanced at Caro, her expression alarmed. She obviously thought this man represented a threat to her routine.

Caro hurried over, Logan by her side. "Grandma, I'd like to introduce Alex Keller's friend, Logan Carswell. He came from Chicago for the wedding." She hadn't rehearsed what to say after that.

"But why did he come to Pine Grove with you?" Bonnie immediately asked.

Logan stepped forward. "Until a few months ago, I was a catcher for the Chicago Cubs," he said in a voice loud enough to carry to the other residents. "Caro thought some of the folks here would like to talk a little baseball."

"You mean *Carolyn.* I hate that nickname she uses now."

"I'd like to talk baseball!" A bald guy with black-framed glasses left the table where he'd been playing cards. "Are you Logan Carswell, the guy who got hurt last season?"

"That's me."

"Logan Carswell!" A portly man hobbled over with the help of his cane. "Right here at Pine Grove! I need to find me something you can autograph! My grandson will be over the moon. Hell, *I'll* be over the moon. I need two things you can autograph. Wait here. I'll be back."

Caro watched in fascination as a crowd gathered around Logan. In addition to asking for autographs, they plied him with coffee and doughnuts.

"Here." A stout little lady shoved a paperback at him. "You can autograph this."

Logan looked perplexed. "But I didn't write it."

"Doesn't matter. You can still autograph it."

"But—it's a romance novel."

"And you look like a romance hero to me, so…" She waved a ballpoint pen in his direction. "Just put your John Henry on the inside. I don't know who you are, but everybody else seems to think you're important, so what the hey. You're cute, which is what I like about you."

Logan sent Caro a helpless look before signing the inside of the paperback.

Caro worked hard not to laugh. At least her grandmother couldn't be worried that she'd brought Logan here because he was her new boyfriend. She'd brought Pine Grove a trophy, obviously. Everyone was thrilled.

Except Grandma Bonnie.

"I still don't understand what he's doing here," she murmured to Caro. "The wedding's over, isn't it?"

"Yes, it's over. Alex and Tyler have left on their honeymoon."

"I'll bet they had the reception at the Spirits and Spurs. If I still lived in Shoshone, I could have gone to it."

Caro didn't want to let her get started down that conversational path. "Let me get some coffee and doughnuts for us, too."

"Okay, I guess."

Caro used her waitressing skills to balance the coffee, napkins and a couple of doughnuts. She set everything on a small table next to her grandmother's chair. "Exciting news, Grandma. A guy named Peter Beckett wants to set up a summer camp for troubled teens at the Last Chance Ranch."

"That's nice." Her grandmother seemed more interested in the doughnut selection.

"If they do it, they'll build bunks in the upstairs bedrooms, so I was thinking I might make some quilts this winter for the beds and donate them to the effort."

Grandma Bonnie frowned. "I don't know how you'll have time, what with your job and coming to see me."

"I may not, but I'd like to do it. I think it would be so homey and comforting for them to walk in and see those handmade quilts on the beds, don't you?"

Her grandmother's face softened. "There's nothing quite like the look of a handmade quilt on a bed."

"No." Caro waited to see if the seed she'd planted would take root. "There isn't."

"I might be able to make a quilt or two this winter."

Caro wanted to shout for joy. "Could you? That would be wonderful, Grandma."

"What you really need to do for those poor children is let them take the quilt home when they leave. Now *that* would be something special. Of course, then you'd need a lot more quilts...."

"I suppose so." Caro wasn't sure where this was going, but she let her grandmother take the lead.

"You know, there's a lot of card playing around here."

For one terrible moment, Caro thought Grandma Bonnie

was slipping into dementia, because the comment had no connection to the topic.

"When what these people could be doing, instead, is cutting out quilt squares. In fact, some of the ladies might know a thing or two about making quilts, and if they don't, I'll teach them." Bonnie glanced up at Caro, and for the first time in six months, there was a gleam in her eyes. "What do you think?"

"I think it's brilliant. I have to make sure this project is on, for sure, and the minute I know, we'll get started."

"You mean it might not happen?" Her grandmother's sparkle disappeared.

"I'm virtually sure it will happen." Caro mentally crossed her fingers behind her back. "In fact, I'm so sure, I'll bring in some supplies tomorrow when I come, and a few extra pairs of scissors, so you can get this show on the road."

"But if it might not be needed, then—"

"It will be. I'm positive. We'll get started tomorrow morning. You can alert whoever is going to help. Even the guys."

"Of course I'll tell those men! Why, your grandpa used to cut out squares for me all the time. He was good at it, too."

Caro glanced over to the crowd that still surrounded Logan, and realized he'd likely be busy for the rest of the time they stayed. She'd have to tear him away from his admirers when it was time to leave.

"He seems like a nice young man," Grandma Bonnie said. "If he didn't live in Chicago, you might want to date him."

Covering her astonishment that her grandmother would suggest she get involved with someone, Caro turned back to her. "Well, he does live in Chicago, so that takes care of that."

"I guess it does. Now, we need to make a list of what you're bringing tomorrow. I'm sure I gave you my box of fabric scraps, but you might have to buy some material. Look for a sale."

"If I'm going fabric shopping in the morning, I might have to show up a little later than usual."

"That's fine." Grandma Bonnie waved a hand as if it made no difference, something she never would have done before. "We'll need extra thread, and needles, and cotton batting." She glanced at Caro. "Why aren't you writing this down?"

"Uh, I have no idea." Maybe because she was too busy gloating over this amazing turnaround. She'd left her purse under the seat of the truck, so she had nothing to write on, either. "Let me find some paper and a pen." Once she obtained those from one of the attendants, she sat on the floor at Grandma Bonnie's feet and made the list.

They had so much fun planning the quilting project that she forgot the time, and when she finally looked at her watch, she jumped up. "Logan and I need to go, Grandma, or I'll be late for my shift."

"All right." Bonnie didn't look nearly as sad to see her leave as she had on past visits. "If I think of anything more for the list, I'll call you."

"You do that." Caro leaned down and kissed her on the cheek. "See you tomorrow." Then she raised her voice. "Logan, I'm afraid we have to leave."

A chorus of disappointed groans rose from Logan's new fans, but he extricated himself with a graciousness that he'd probably perfected over the years. Then he walked over to her grandmother and crouched down beside her chair. "I'm glad I got a chance to meet you," he said. "Sorry we didn't get to talk more."

"That's okay. You can come back tomorrow." She smiled at him.

"You bet. I'd be glad to. You take care, now." He touched her hand and walked quickly over to the entrance, where Caro waited for him. "We're outta here," he said quietly. Then he waved enthusiastically and called out goodbyes to the residents before turning and practically pushing Caro out the door.

"Was it terrible, then?" she asked, as they returned to the truck.

"Not terrible." He opened her door for her and helped her in. "I could use an insulin shot after all those doughnuts, but it was kind of nice to talk with everyone."

"I'm glad. I'll get you some proper food when we're back at the Spirits and Spurs."

"Fine, but I'm not leaving Jackson without a box of condoms, and by my calculations, we just barely have time to buy some and still get you back to the Spirits and Spurs for the start of your shift. I was getting worried that we hadn't left yet."

She laughed. "You really do focus on your stated goal, don't you?"

"That's why they used to pay me the big bucks." He closed her door and jogged around to the passenger side. "I'm not asking you to speed," he said as he got in and fastened his seat belt. "But I wouldn't mind having you push the limit a little so we can be assured of that trip to the pharmacy."

"No worries." She started the truck and backed out of the parking lot. "I've made this run every day for six months. I know exactly where we'll find a drugstore."

"Every day for six months is a lot of visits."

"Yes, but I had a breakthrough today. At least I hope it'll be a breakthrough. I'm in trouble if Beckett doesn't set up his summer camp, but I think he will, whether it's at the Last Chance or not. Anyway, I told my grandmother I wanted to make quilts for the bunk beds, and now she wants to help me with that. She's planning to rope other residents in, too."

"Hey, that's terrific! I saw you two with your heads together. Here I'd come with you intending to offer suggestions for handling her situation, and then I got swept into the other business. Good thing you didn't need me to help."

"Turns out I didn't, but don't minimize your contribution. You made a lot of people happy today. They'll talk about this for months. Oh, and you don't have to come back tomorrow. You've done your stint."

"You know, I probably do need to come back. Right before we had to leave, a couple of the guys told me about some die-hard baseball fans who are bedridden and couldn't make it out to the visitors' lounge. I need to go around the building and see those fellows." He sounded almost eager to do it.

"All right, but you'll have to hit the fabric store with me beforehand. I've promised to come armed with quilting supplies, and tomorrow morning will be my first chance to go shopping for them. You'll be bored stiff," Caro warned.

"I doubt it." He chuckled. "Watching you fondle bolts of fabric may make me stiff, but I won't be bored."

"You really do have a one-track mind." But his teasing was having an effect on her libido, and buying condoms had become a priority with her, too. Putting on the turn signal, she waited for traffic to clear, then swerved into the parking lot of a drugstore. "Here you are, hotshot."

He released his seat belt and opened the door. "I'll be right back. Keep your motor running."

"Mine or the truck's?"

He grinned. "Both."

15

THE NEXT FEW DAYS FELL into a routine that Logan knew couldn't last. But he put off the inevitable by procrastinating making plane reservations. Eventually he'd do that, but he was having too damned much fun to rush into it.

Hot nights in Caro's bed were followed by visits to Pine Grove, where Logan had become the highlight of the day for most of the residents. Some wanted to hear baseball stories, but some were interested in his rehab from the knee injury. Without really meaning to, he'd inspired quite a few to resume their exercise programs.

At a staffer's request, he'd drawn up progress charts, which attracted the interest of even more residents. The facility's director ordered a box of Cubs caps, and those who met their goals got one signed by Logan. Between the exercise programs and Caro's quilting project, Pine Grove buzzed with activity every morning.

During Caro's shifts at the Spirits and Spurs, Logan spent time at the ranch. He worked on the cradle, but he took it slow, because once it was finished, he really should leave for Chicago. So he took breaks from that project to saddle a horse and practice his riding skills.

He also asked one of the hands to show him some roping basics. At this point all he could lasso was a post located behind the barn specifically for roping practice. Before he left he planned to try his luck with a horse or a cow.

He'd just successfully roped the post for the third time one afternoon when Jack came around the corner of the barn and headed toward him. Logan flipped the loop off the post and coiled the rope. "Hey, Jack."

Jack nodded toward the rope. "Not bad for a greenhorn."

"Thanks. The post tried like hell to get away, but I was faster."

He grinned. "Anybody who can rope a runaway post can hang his hat at the Last Chance anytime. Listen, I wanted to ask you something."

"If it's about the cradle, I'm close to finishing."

"It's not about that, but the cradle looks good. Josie's looking forward to having it for the baby."

"So what's up?"

Jack took off his hat and combed his fingers through his hair. "We've decided to give Beckett's idea a try, which means we'll need the bunks." He gazed at Logan. "Were you serious about building them?"

"Yep. Totally serious." Logan couldn't help smiling. The project sounded like fun and would give him an excuse to come back here. More importantly, though, the Pine Grove quilt project now had a guaranteed purpose. Caro would be so excited.

"Good to hear. We need to figure out a time frame. It makes sense to get all the supplies before the first snow, but I suppose you'd have some leeway as to when you did the work because it'll be all inside."

"Let me take a look at my schedule," Logan said automatically, even though he had no schedule.

"Yeah, I know you must have obligations in Chicago. Josie asked me the other day if you had mentioned when you were heading back there."

"Soon." Logan was willing to bet Josie was worried about Caro's reaction to his departure, whenever that might be. "I wanted to make sure I finished the cradle first."

"Right." Jack didn't say what they both knew—that Logan could have finished the cradle days ago.

"Has Caro said anything to you about the quilts?"

"Oh, yeah, she told Josie all about that. Josie drove into town a little while ago to give Caro the good news that the Beckett project is a go. I was designated to get a final word on whether you planned to build the bunks."

"I do." Disappointment took a little of the shine off his good mood. He'd looked forward to telling Caro himself.

"Beckett's willing to pay you, by the way."

Logan frowned. "I don't want money for it."

"I didn't think you would, either. A tax write-off is probably better for someone in your bracket. Beckett's filing the paperwork to make this a nonprofit program, so our tax guy is working out whether we should charge him for the use of the ranch or claim it as a write-off."

"I guess it's good to consider all the angles." Logan's accountant would probably appreciate it if he'd be more conscious of such things. But he'd never been in the habit of thinking that way. He'd offered to build the bunks because he liked the work and wanted to help, not because he could write it off his taxes.

"Yeah, but bottom line, this will be a good thing for everyone, especially the kids."

"Yeah." Logan refused to feel guilty that he hadn't agreed to help next summer. The idea of helping those kids still made him nervous. Besides, he wanted to keep his options open. A network deal might come through, or maybe some offer he hadn't even considered.

Jack settled his hat back on his head. "Whenever you're

ready, we can take some measurements, decide how much lumber to buy."

"Tomorrow afternoon?" This afternoon was fading fast and Logan planned to drive into town soon. Caro would still be working, but sometimes he got behind the bar and helped out. He felt like doing that tonight.

"Sure, tomorrow works. See you then." Jack started to leave, but turned back with a sigh. "Josie made me promise to ask something else."

Logan tensed. "What's that?"

"She heard that you refused Beckett's offer to work with the kids next summer, and I totally understand that. But Josie wants to know if you've changed your mind."

"No, I'm afraid not."

"I told her you wouldn't have. Just because you're helping Caro with the folks at Pine Grove doesn't mean—"

"You know about that?"

"Buddy, whether you want to be or not, you're a celebrity around here. Plus, as you may have noticed, we're a small town. Word gets out—always."

Logan slowly nodded. "I'm beginning to see that. But you'll have to tell Josie I'm still not interested in Beckett's project, other than building the bunks."

"I'll tell her. See you tomorrow."

"Right." Logan stared after Jack as he walked away. Josie might not understand it, but Pine Grove and Beckett's project were entirely different animals.

The Pine Grove situation had dropped into Logan's lap, and nobody had expected anything from him. Whatever good came out of his visits was a bonus. Beckett's project would be loaded with expectations, ones that Logan couldn't or wouldn't meet because he wasn't willing to bare his battered soul to a bunch of teenagers.

But now that Jack had brought up Pine Grove, Logan

worried that Caro might be thinking the same thing as Josie. She could be. The two women were friends and they talked. He didn't doubt they talked about him. He'd told Caro that he got a kick out of working with the folks at Pine Grove.

Damn. He should probably discuss that with her and make sure she wasn't building castles in the air. His chest tightened as he felt a trap closing around him. Caro could be expecting too much of him. He wasn't the guy for Beckett's project, no matter what she might think.

Time to get out of Dodge. He'd make a plane reservation before he went into town to see her. These past few days had been great, but if they were giving Caro false hope that he'd be a camp counselor to those teenagers, he needed to stop immediately.

Caro felt the usual rush of pleasure when Logan walked into the Spirits and Spurs around dinnertime. She wondered if he realized how much he looked like a real cowboy these days. He seemed completely at home in his hat, boots, jeans and Western shirt. Even his walk seemed to have changed.

Or maybe it was wishful thinking on her part. When Josie had come in earlier to deliver her great news about Beckett's project, she'd commented on how settled Logan seemed recently. He was taking his time with the cradle, which Josie thought was a sign he was in no hurry to leave.

Both Caro and Josie were impressed with Logan's work out at Pine Grove. Josie had mentioned it to Beckett and told him not to give up on the possibility of having Logan on board. Caro had been afraid to put that thought into words, but after Josie's comments today, she had allowed a tiny ray of hope to shine.

Her life had definitely taken a positive turn. Grandma Bonnie was a different person now that she had quilts to make and workers to supervise. Her former optimism had resurfaced. That left Caro free to pursue her own future, which might, just might, include the tall man walking toward the bar.

"Hey there, little lady." He slid onto a stool and smiled at her.

"Hey, there, cowboy." She smiled back, happier than she'd been in a long, long time. "Did you hear that the Chances are going ahead with Beckett's project?"

"Jack told me. I'll bet you're doing cartwheels."

"I am. I called Grandma Bonnie and she's planning to step up the effort. She wants a backlog of quilts so that there's no question that each kid can take one home. She hasn't been this excited about anything in months."

"That's terrific."

"Did Jack talk to you about the bunks?"

"He did. We'll work out the details tomorrow."

"Good. I—whoops, excuse me. Customers. Be right back."

"Feed me a hamburger and I'll come back there and help you finish out your shift," he called after her.

"You've got a deal." She put in an order for a hamburger the way Logan liked it, with mushrooms and Monterrey Jack cheese. After delivering drinks to the two men at the other end of the bar, she filled a mug with root beer for Logan and set it in front of him. "Speaking of your carpentry skills, how's the cradle coming along?"

"Almost done."

It wasn't quite the answer she'd expected after Josie's claim that he was dragging his feet so he could hang around. But she told herself he might be finishing the cradle so he could start on the bunk beds. "I'd love to see it. Maybe we could skip Pine Grove in the morning and take a trail ride instead. My grandmother adores you, so she should be okay with that."

"Sounds good."

"Then let's plan on it." She hurried off to fill another drink order, but her thoughts remained fixed on Logan. Maybe it was her imagination that he didn't seem as enthusiastic about the trail ride as she would have thought he'd be.

Then again, he might really like going to Pine Grove, or he could feel that the residents would be disappointed if he didn't show up. They would be, but he couldn't be expected to keep up his daily visits. She decided to discuss it later, when they were alone.

That time alone, whether they were in her apartment or driving to Jackson, had become precious. The sex every night was amazing, but it turned out she liked his company even when they both had all their clothes on. She didn't dare put a label on what she felt for him, but it no longer fell into the category of friendship.

Business was brisk now that the regular customers had recovered from the wedding reception and had returned to their usual habit of stopping by for a beer or two. Once Logan finished his hamburger and joined her behind the bar, the usual requests came in for some martini shaker juggling or the flaming drinks he was now famous for.

Logan certainly spiced up her work life, too. Although she'd asked him to teach her to bartend the way he did, tossing things around and lighting various types of cocktails on fire, she didn't really want to learn. She'd rather have him do guest appearances.

But as much fun as she had working with him, she was glad when closing time arrived. Logan handled the cleanup duties while she closed the register. After several nights of doing it, they'd perfected the system so they were done quickly and could head up to her apartment.

She felt like celebrating tonight. Thanks to Peter Beckett, her grandmother had a new lease on life and Logan would be around at least until he'd finished those bunk beds for the kids. The longer he stayed, the more he seemed to like it here. That had to be a good thing.

Once they were in her apartment, he drew her into his arms, as he always did. But instead of kissing her hello, he gazed into her eyes. "We need to talk."

She laughed to hide her sudden case of jitters. "That sounds ominous."

"Sorry. Didn't mean to be dramatic, but something Jack said today has been on my mind, and I decided you and I need to be sure we're on the same page."

"Okay." That didn't improve her jitters. "How about something to drink while we talk?" She slipped out of his arms, walked over to the kitchen area and pulled some white wine out of the refrigerator. "I'd like to toast the Chances for agreeing to Peter Beckett's proposition."

"We can do that."

She wasn't imagining it. He'd lost that carefree attitude he'd had only hours ago when they'd been together. But she'd offered wine and she'd serve wine.

Taking two goblets from the cupboard, she opened the bottle and poured them each about half full. She had a feeling this wouldn't be as much of a celebration as she'd hoped. "Here you go." She walked over and held out his glass. "To Peter Beckett's project."

He touched his glass to hers. "To Peter Beckett's project. And that's what I want to discuss."

But not in a good way, she guessed. "What about it?"

"From what Jack said, I think Josie still hopes I'll be a part of it, mostly because of my visits to Pine Grove."

Caro shrugged in an effort to be nonchalant, but her heart beat faster. "She might."

"Caro, one doesn't have anything to do with the other. I might be helping the residents to exercise more, but I'm not expected to turn their lives around. What I've done there is a little blip on the facility's radar screen. Beckett wants a tsunami wave of inspiration out of me."

"Hmm." Neither of them had touched their wine, and she decided to drink some of hers. Maybe then she wouldn't lose her temper. The wine slid down her throat, but instead of calming her, it seemed to add fuel to her fire.

He gazed at her. "I take it you don't agree?"

"No, I don't." She took a deep breath. "But we've been over this. You see the job Beckett offered one way, and I see it another."

"Yeah, I know. You imagine that the kids and I would somehow bond and help each other heal, but as the adult in the equation, I don't think that's a fair—"

"Have you any idea how you've blossomed ever since you've been trekking out to Pine Grove with me? You're not dwelling on your own problems, because you're focused on theirs. Being around those old folks takes you right out of yourself."

"Maybe so, but I still think that handling kids is a whole other deal. They're so young and impressionable that what you say to them can leave a lasting imprint. Hell, half the time the old people don't even hear what I say."

She took a shot in the dark. She might be going down for the count, anyway, so why not? "Did someone say something to you when you were young and impressionable?" His expression told her she'd hit the mark. "Who was it?"

"My father. And that's my whole point. Quite likely these kids won't have a father figure in their lives, so I'm liable to be it. I'd be in a position of authority, compounded by the glamour of my baseball career. I hate to think what weight they'd give anything I'd say to them."

"But don't you see? You've been through that experience, so you *won't* repeat it with them. You can tell them how that statement, whatever it was, affected you, and why you won't do those things to them."

He shook his head. "Once again you're asking the impossible. I'm not made that way. I'm not about to reveal the innermost workings of my—"

"Why the hell not? What good is it to go through these things if you're not willing to share your experiences? Listen, if you don't work with those kids, somebody else will, and it might be a guy who doesn't have half the understanding that you've obtained the hard way."

He blew out a breath, walked over to her kitchen counter and set his untouched glass of wine on it. "I can't be the man you want me to be, Caro. It would be great if I could, but I can't."

Adrenaline surged through her system, leaving her shaking. "You mean you won't."

"I guess that's another way of putting it." His expression was bleak. "So I was right. You hoped that the Pine Grove experience would soften me up for Beckett's plan."

"No! You make it sound as if I orchestrated that. Let's not forget that it was your idea to go out to Pine Grove in the first place. I admit I wanted you to go, and discover that there are people a lot worse off than you, but the suggestion to visit came from you, not from me."

He nodded. "You're right, it did. I saw you drowning under the weight of your grandmother's needs, and I thought you deserved better. But as it turns out, Peter Beckett deserves the credit for saving you, not me."

"You deserve credit for caring. Peter Beckett has no idea that his project threw a lifeline to me and my grandmother. You do." She swallowed a lump in her throat. She was going to lose him, and she knew it. But then, he'd never been hers in the first place.

"I do care, and that's why I made a plane reservation today. I'm leaving day after tomorrow."

The statement hit her like a blow to the stomach. "So soon?"

"I would have made it earlier, but that was the soonest they had available."

She looked at him through a haze of misery. "Are you that eager to get away from me, then?"

"No. Leaving you will be one of the hardest things I've ever done. But I don't plan to stay here, Caro. We both knew that. The longer I stick around, the worse it will hurt you. I've been selfish to stay as long as I have."

She shook her head and fought back the tears. "Like I said, all you've done is beef up my reputation as a hot chick. A girl can't complain about that."

His smile was so incredibly sad. "You are a hot chick. If anyone doubts it, have them call me."

Desperate, she grasped at straws. "What about the bunk beds? What about building them?"

He hesitated, as if he hadn't thought of that. "I'll...I'll donate some money to hire a carpenter. I'm sure there are a bunch of them in the Jackson Hole area. It doesn't have to be me wielding the hammer."

"Guess not." Oh, but she'd counted on that more than he would ever know.

"All things considered, I think I should drive back to the ranch tonight."

"I don't." She was pathetic, but she'd take whatever she could get.

"I do." He walked toward her, kissed her on the cheek and headed for the door.

"A kiss on the *cheek?* Is that the way a major league ballplayer ends things? That's the lamest breakup gesture I've ever seen, Carswell!" Yes, she was going a little crazy, and saying things she probably shouldn't, but then again, the love of her life had never walked out on her before.

He turned around and came back. "I'm going to miss you like hell, Caro Davis." Then he grabbed her and delivered a kiss that would have rocked her world if she hadn't been sobbing all through it.

Then he was gone, and she couldn't decide if she loved him so much she'd do anything to get him back, or hated him so much that she'd kill him if she had the chance. Either option would be a disaster, so she hoped he'd be in Chicago before she made up her mind.

16

LOGAN FELT LIKE SHIT. He was supposed to be a superior strategist on the field, but apparently off the field he was a total schmuck. He'd managed to take the most positive, optimistic woman he'd ever met and turn her into a sobbing wreck.

The memory of his parting with Caro haunted him as he finished up the cradle and packed to leave. He hadn't intended for their discussion to end with him dramatically stalking out the door, but once he'd realized how much he was hurting her, he hadn't seen an alternative. And as much as he wanted to talk to her again, that would only extend the misery, so he stayed away.

He also managed to avoid Josie and Jack, leaving the finished cradle on the workbench with a note. He had to borrow a suitcase from Sarah because he'd picked up so many pairs of jeans and Western shirts. He might never wear them again, but he took them, anyway.

He even went so far as to dress like a cowboy for the trip back to Chicago. Sarah drove him to the airport in Jackson, and it was a mostly silent trip. He wouldn't be coming back, so there wasn't much to say to each other. No doubt he'd let her down, but classy lady that she was, she took him to the airport, anyway.

In his jeans, white Western shirt, boots and hat, he wasn't

recognized as former Cubs catcher Logan Carswell as he stepped off the plane. He hadn't bothered to notify his family he was coming home, because he wasn't ready to discuss his recent trip with anybody. He took a cab back to his condo.

When he walked in, he hoped for a feeling of sanctuary and peace. Instead the condo just felt huge and sterile. He'd paid a professional to decorate the place, and she'd created a bachelor pad in black, white and gray, with a few touches of red. The furniture was modern, and the general effect, now that he looked at it with new eyes, was hideous.

He longed for gingham curtains and handmade quilts. He missed the noisy bar that smelled of smoke, beer and onions. Most of all, he missed Caro—her smile, her laughter, her ponytail that bounced when she walked.

But she was expensive. In order to have her, he'd have to sacrifice the image that he'd maintained of himself for twenty-five years. She didn't understand what she'd asked of him.

Soon after he carried his suitcase into his bedroom, which was no cozier than the rest of his condo, his home phone rang. His first thought was that it might be Caro, but then he remembered he'd never given her this number. When he picked up the receiver, his agent's name came up on the screen. He hesitated, and finally decided to answer.

"Where the hell have you been?" Derek sounded impatient, but that was par for the course with him. "I've been calling your cell all day, but all I got was your voice mail."

"I flew home today. Guess I forgot to turn my phone back on." He usually never forgot things like that, but he'd been a little distracted lately.

"Well, thank God you're back in town, because I have a fabulous deal for you. ESPN has offered a contract, and it's a good one. I think we can get them up a little more, but my advice is to take it once they bump the salary. They have big plans, and they're willing to put most of them in writing."

Logan realized he should be overjoyed with this news. Two weeks ago his career had been on the skids, but Derek had just found a way to put it back on track. Sometimes players became as well-known in the broadcast booth as on the field. This was a terrific break.

"I don't hear party horns and champagne corks in the background, Logan, old boy. Are you jet-lagged or what? This is *fabulous*. Most out-of-work players would give their right nut to have a deal like this. Do you read me?"

"Derek, it sounds great."

"Wow, try to contain your excitement, will you?"

"Sorry. I've spent the past week and a half in the boondocks." He felt disloyal saying that, but it was something Derek would understand. "I need some time to kick the shit off my boots. Then I'll be ready for—"

"You bought *boots?*"

"And a hat. It was a Western-themed wedding, so everyone was expected to dress the part."

"You can ditch all that now. You're going to be wearing ESPN polos and suits from this point on."

Logan had no intention of getting rid of the clothes he'd bought in Wyoming.

"So let me see if they'll go up some on the money, and then I'll get back to you."

"Sure, I guess." He heaved a sigh. "You know I don't need more money."

"*You* might not, but I do! My kid's decided to go to Harvard Law. That's gonna set me back. So let me wheel and deal. If they come up, are you in?"

He should be. Logic told him that he needed to take this deal while his name was still recognized. Another year or two, and they might forget who he was. It happened all the time.

"Let's see if they come up," Logan said. "Then we'll talk."

He was making no sense and he knew it. First he'd told Derek he didn't need the money, and now he wouldn't commit to the deal until he knew the bottom line.

Derek muttered something that sounded a lot like "temperamental sports stars," but his next words were cheerful and upbeat. "I'll get them up, Logan. Don't worry. I'll call you the minute I have a new offer."

"Thanks, Derek. You're working hard for me, and I appreciate that, man."

"I'm working hard for *us,* Logan. We're in this together, buddy."

No, they weren't, Logan thought as he disconnected the call. Oh, sure, there was a mutual financial benefit, but Logan had a different view of partnership after spending time with Caro. He clicked with her on so many levels.

They'd started off well, working together behind the bar without a hassle. Then…the sex. God, the sex. He'd never established such an instant rapport with any woman. Caro was the most perfect sexual partner he'd ever had.

But they complemented one another in other ways, too. He smiled as he remembered falling off during their trail ride. She'd come to his rescue by fetching his homeward-bound horse.

At Pine Grove, they'd worked in tandem, and because of their visits, the residents now had more reason to get up in the morning. They were making quilts and exercising with greater enthusiasm. Good things happened when Logan was with Caro.

Good things happened when he was with Caro. He stood in his silent apartment as that sentence bounced around his brain for several long seconds. *Good things happened when he was with Caro.*

How the hell had he missed that key point? She hadn't

actually said it, but he knew that if he accepted Beckett's proposition, she would be with him every step of the way.

Of course she hadn't said it. That wouldn't be her style. But if he asked her if she'd help him with the kids, she'd say yes. He knew that as surely as he knew that she loved him.

Yes, damn it, she *loved* him. He hadn't wanted to admit that she did, but he'd known it. And he loved her. Dear God, he was the biggest idiot of the century, because with Caro by his side, he could do anything. Her love would inspire him to be the man she believed he could be.

Without her, he would remain the out-of-work baseball player who never let anyone see him sweat. He might make it as a sportscaster or he might not. He might figure out how to be happy, but he wouldn't lay bets on it. With Caro around, it was a sure thing.

He glanced at his suitcase. Good thing he hadn't unpacked. He had another plane to catch.

THE PAST THREE NIGHTS the bar had been busy, but not overly so. Caro could have handled it alone, but Josie seemed determined to keep her company. Caro figured it was partly for moral support and partly to make sure Caro didn't accidentally poison the customers with some weird concoction.

Judging from everyone's concerned expressions when they looked at her, they expected her to crack under the strain. She'd be damned if she would. Logan had been right, though, and she'd been wrong. Instead of envying her for the fling she'd had, they pitied her for getting dumped at the end.

She'd thought about taking his suggestion and telling people she threw him out because of his bad hygiene and boring conversation. But Alex and Tyler were home from their honeymoon, and Caro didn't want to trash Alex's best friend with lies. Her real gripe about Logan—that he didn't love her enough—wasn't for public consumption.

He did love her, though. That last kiss had told her so. But not so much that he'd be willing to stay. That being the case, she was glad he was gone. She loved him enough that she'd follow him to the ends of the earth, even if it meant leaving Shoshone and Grandma Bonnie.

But he seemed to have a mild case of love, and that would never be enough for Caro. She required a full-blown, over-the-top, chronic case from a man.

"Caro, I think the mug's full."

She glanced down at the draft beer spilling over the top of the mug she'd been filling for a customer. Fortunately, it was running into the drainage area under the spigots, so it wasn't making a mess, but she was wasting beer.

She tilted the mug and dumped out a little more so she'd be able to wipe down the sides and hand it to the customer without slopping beer everywhere. "Sorry, Josie. You'd probably rather have me take the rest of the night off, but please don't. I'd rather be working than not."

"You're fine." Josie gave her a reassuring smile. "I've been there, kiddo, and staying busy is the best therapy there is. We can afford some spilled beer."

"Thanks." Caro swallowed a lump in her throat. Josie was the best. After delivering a few choice words concerning Mr. Logan Carswell, aka the Loser of the Century, she'd never mentioned him again. For that Caro was supremely grateful.

No point in talking it to death. Logan had made his choice, and that was the end of that. Alex hadn't brought up the subject, either, which Caro considered very wise. In Shoshone, Logan's popularity index had plummeted in the past three days.

Not so at Pine Grove, however, because none of those folks knew that Logan and Caro had been an item. They'd asked eagerly about him and had wanted to know when he'd be back.

She'd given them a vague answer because she couldn't bear to see their faces crumple with disappointment.

"Damn," Josie said under her breath. "I don't believe it."

"What?" Caro glanced up, and the glass she'd been holding slipped from her fingers and landed with a loud crack on the stainless steel counter.

Logan walked toward her, his expression tense.

Although Caro was speechless, Josie was not. "You have some nerve coming back, mister," she said. "There is not one thing you can say to excuse the way you treated my friend."

"I agree." Logan's voice was gruff with emotion. "I've behaved like an ass."

Josie nodded. "Well put. And unless you intend to grovel at her feet and beg her forgiveness, you can go right back out that door, because you're not welcome here."

"Josie!" Caro had never heard her talk that way to any customer, ever.

"Well, he's not. Logan and I go back a long way, but he's currently on my shit list. If I had a bouncer, I'd have him thrown out. Come to think of it, I could probably get a couple of cowboys to do it for me, gratis."

"Which is no more than I deserve," Logan said. "But I'm asking you to give me one minute to say something to Caro."

"Only if you say it while I'm standing right here. I no longer trust you not to make her cry."

By now Alex and Tyler had joined the curious crowd in the bar. Caro figured out that the newlyweds had probably driven to Jackson and picked Logan up at the airport. He couldn't have spent much time in Chicago if he was back this soon.

Her face felt hot with embarrassment. "Josie, maybe it would be better if Logan and I went—"

"Nope. I'm not letting him out of my sight." Josie looked at her watch. "Start talking, Logan. Make it fast and make it good. I'm timing you."

He swallowed and nodded in agreement before turning to Caro. "What my dad said that made such an impression on me was 'never let them see you sweat.' Well, I'm sweating now, and I don't care if you know it. I don't care if every damned person in the bar knows it."

Her heart squeezed. This had to be excruciating for him. But…sometimes excruciating was a good thing.

He cleared his throat. "I threw away a chance at happiness by leaving Shoshone and leaving you. I know forgiving me for treating you so horribly won't be easy, but I'm begging you to forgive me and let me come back."

Josie folded her arms. "That's a start. What else have you got?"

"A plan. I'm hoping Beckett can still use my services, because I can't think of a better job than working with kids at the Last Chance every summer. As for the winter, there's plenty to do at Pine Grove, and maybe Josie would consider letting me get behind the bar once in a while." He glanced at her. "Or not."

"I'll take it under advisement," Josie said. "Go on. There has to be more."

Logan ran a shaking hand over his face. "There is. Caro, I'd be the luckiest man on the planet if you'd consent to spend the rest of your life with me. With you by my side I can face anything. Including sweat."

Heart thudding, Caro opened her mouth to reply.

Josie got there first. "Are you talking about shacking up or marriage? Let's not have any of this vague language going on. Be precise, please."

Logan looked into Caro's eyes. Then he dropped to one knee. His bad knee. "Marriage," he said. "If you'll have me."

"Your knee! You shouldn't be—"

"You're probably right." He grimaced and staggered back to his feet. "But it seemed like the thing to do."

Josie nodded. "Nice gesture. Now what about kids?"

Caro stared at her. "You can't expect him to answer that in a crowd of people."

"Sure I can. He created this mess, so now he can clean it up. It's an important question. You're looking all dewy-eyed and gaga, so I'm afraid you'll say yes without finding out the important stuff."

"I'd love to have kids with you, Caro," Logan said. "If you want to."

She forgot all about the people standing around as she met his gaze. Her heart swelled with love for this brave man. "I do."

"That's great!" He beamed at her, and then his smile faded as he looked earnestly into her eyes. "I love you so much. Let me make you happy."

She didn't realize tears were running down her face until Josie glanced at her and threw up her hands. "See that? You made her cry, after all!"

Swiping at her cheeks, Caro forced words past her tight throat. "But these are good tears. I love you, too, Logan. And I can't think of a better life than being by your side, wherever you choose to be."

Joy glowed in the depths of his brown eyes. "I wouldn't ever ask you to leave Shoshone."

"You could, though." She sniffed. "You really could, Logan. It's not fair of me to expect you to stick around here, when you could—"

"I've already made that decision. ESPN wanted to hire me. I turned them down."

"You did?" Caro was beginning to believe in miracles.

"Yeah, I'm ready to leave those days in the past, where they belong. You're my future."

A sigh went up from the crowd. "That's beautiful," someone said.

Logan glanced over at Josie. "Is my time up yet?"

Josie was smiling. "It was up quite a while ago, but you were on a roll, so I gave you some overtime."

Caro looked at her. "Is there any chance that I could take my break, now?"

Josie laughed and hugged her. "Take the night off, kiddo. You've earned it. But if this big lug gives you any trouble, call me. I'll clean his clock, or better yet, get Jack to do it." She lifted the hinged portion of the bar and Caro ducked out.

As she walked toward Logan, she was aware that everyone continued to stand around watching the show. Logan would probably want to wait until they were alone before they sealed this moment with a kiss.

She took a deep breath as she reached him. "So, maybe we should—"

"I love you." Then he pulled her into his arms and kissed her thoroughly amid whoops and hollers from the crowd.

At last he released her and lifted his head. "Free drinks for everyone!" he called out. "I'm buying!"

The crowd surged around them, mobbing the bar.

Logan put his lips next to her ear. "Now's our chance to escape."

She struggled for breath. "But aren't you supposed to be buying?"

"I feel certain Josie will put it on my tab."

"So you want to go upstairs?"

"Uh-huh." He led her toward the door. "I've told you how much I love you, and now I want to show you."

She slipped out the door with him and nobody seemed to notice. Later, as they lay naked and sated from their lovemaking, she could still hear the party in full swing down below. "They're going to cost you a fortune."

"Nope. My fortune is right here." Moving over her again, he proceeded to show her how rich they were going to be for the rest of their lives.

Epilogue

JACK CHANCE COULDN'T imagine being happier. Until recently, his wife, Josie, had been a little bit on edge about Caro Davis, but that problem had been resolved last night when Logan had shown up and proposed.

Jack was glad of it. Josie had been threatening to take a hatchet to the cradle Logan had made, and Jack hated to see good carpentry ruined. He also hated to see his wife in a bad mood, and she'd been extremely cheerful when she'd arrived home after a long night at the bar.

As Jack sat in his dad's office the next morning, studying Beckett's plan in preparation for a discussion with the accountant, he smiled to himself. A cheerful Josie was a lusty Josie. They'd set the sheets on fire last night, and this morning Jack was thinking seriously of sending his wife flowers.

He'd have to order them from Jackson, but a motivated and well-paid florist should be able to deliver by dinnertime. That might earn Jack another roll in the hay tonight. He wasn't above a little bribery.

He was in the middle of checking the phone directory for a florist when Sarah walked into the office. "Someone's here to see you."

"Who?" He stood automatically. Sarah Chance had drilled manners into all three of her sons.

"His name's Wyatt Locke. Does that mean anything to you?"

Jack searched his memory. "No, but I'm not good with names. Did he say what it's about?"

"Just that it was private business. In fact, he's acting sort of…mysterious. I was sitting out on the porch with my coffee when he drove up in an SUV. He's not from around here, though. He asked for your dad, and when I said he'd passed away, this fellow seemed surprised. Then he asked for you."

"So where is he now?"

"I left him in the living room. Maybe I shouldn't have."

Jack rounded the desk and walked toward her. "I'm sure it's fine, Mom." He still got a kick out of the way her eyes sparkled when he called her that. A year ago he would have addressed her as Sarah, because of some stupid-ass idea that because he was her stepson, he didn't have the right to claim her as his mother.

"It probably is fine. I'll just go back to the porch and finish my coffee. If you need me, you know where I'll be."

"Thanks." He put his hands on her shoulders and leaned down to give her a kiss on the cheek. "By the way, I've been meaning to tell you that I approve of Peter Beckett."

She blinked. "You mean his project?"

"No, I don't mean his project. I've seen the way you look at him, and I just want you to know that I—"

"There's nothing to approve!" She flushed. "I don't know what you imagine you're seeing, but I'm simply being polite to the man. I was happily married to your father for almost thirty years, and I don't have any intention of—of…" Her face grew redder with each passing second.

Jack chuckled. "Then you might want to be a little less *polite,* because I think Peter has intentions."

"He most certainly does not. He's just being nice."

"Right." Still smiling, Jack gave her shoulders a squeeze.

"I guess I might as well see what this Wyatt Locke wants from me. Probably a donation to some cause or other."

"Could be. Just tell him we're putting all our financial support behind this teen program." Sarah headed back to her rocker on the front porch.

Making a mental note to order those flowers for Josie the minute this conversation was over, Jack walked into the living room. The visitor looked to be about the age of Jack's younger brothers, which put him under thirty. He was engrossed in examining the family photos arranged across the mantel, and didn't seem to be aware Jack had walked in.

Jack took a moment to try and place him, but nothing about the guy registered. He was at least Jack's height, and his sandy hair was cut short. Judging from his faded blue T-shirt, khaki shorts with extra pockets, and boots with some serious tread, he was a hiker.

"What can I do for you, Mr. Locke?"

The guy turned and his expression was difficult to read. He studied Jack for several seconds. "So you're Jack Chance."

"I take it we haven't met before?"

"Nope. I didn't even know you existed until a month ago."

Now there was a strange statement. Jack frowned. "Look, I don't mean to be rude, but I have a full schedule this morning, so could we please cut to the chase?"

Wyatt blew out a breath. "Sure. You might want to sit down while we have this conversation, however."

"I doubt there's any need for that." But uneasiness slithered up his spine.

"Up to you." Wyatt glanced at the ceiling. "Rafe is going to kill me for coming here, but I just thought..."

Impatience erased Jack's good manners. "Who the hell is Rafe? Could you just get to the point?"

Wyatt's eyes were a clear gray, almost silver, and he focused them intently on Jack. "Okay. Rafe is my twin brother.

We're from San Francisco, where our mother moved after she left Shoshone. She married Harlan Locke, who's our father."

Jack grabbed at the most salient piece of information in that barrage of words. "Your mother used to live here?"

"She used to live right here, as a matter of fact, in this house. Her name is Diana, and you look a hell of a lot like her. It startled me at first."

All the air left Jack's lungs. He stared at Wyatt. His mother had given birth again, and this time, apparently, she'd stuck around to raise her kids. All this time Jack had told himself that she'd left because she wasn't the motherly type. Apparently she was when she chose to be.

He'd thought he was over the pain of her abandonment. Between Sarah and Josie, he'd thought he'd healed. But Wyatt had just ripped that wound wide open. He swallowed. "Why are you here?"

"Mom and Dad got a divorce this year. I think he sensed that she was keeping some big secret from him, and he finally left in frustration. She got counseling and decided to tell us what she'd been hiding all these years. Turns out it was you."

Jack felt shaky, and wished he'd taken Wyatt's suggestion of sitting down. But he'd be damned if he'd do it now and show any weakness.

He cleared his throat. "So I'll ask again. Why are you here? If you expect me to roll out the red carpet, or give you a job, then I'm afraid you—"

"I don't want a damned thing. I guess Rafe was right, and this was a mistake. But I thought I should at least meet my half brother. Sorry to have taken up your time." He started for the door.

"Wait."

Wyatt glanced back, his stance wary.

"I need some time to get used to this."

Wyatt hesitated. "I suppose that's fair. Look, I don't want

you to think I came all this way just to lay this on you. I'm a wilderness guide. I took a bunch of folks on a trek through Yellowstone this past week."

Jack nodded. "I figured you for a hiker."

"And I figured you for a cowboy."

The mood lightened a little. Not much, but enough for Jack to consider this might not be totally bad news if Wyatt had a sense of humor. Jack admitted to being curious about these two guys. And Diana. He wouldn't call her his mother, but he wondered…lots of things.

He gazed at Wyatt. "So do you get down this way much?"

"It's my last trip to Wyoming this year, but I'll be back in June."

Jack let out his breath. That would give him plenty of time to get his head around this. "Maybe you could stop by when you come back."

"I'll think about it." Wyatt fixed that silver gaze on Jack. "You really do look like her. So does Rafe."

"So you're not identical twins?"

"Fraternal. He's four minutes older. People might not see much resemblance between you and me, but they'd know immediately you and Rafe were brothers. Doesn't matter, though. You'll probably never meet him. Well, so long, bro." Then he was gone.

Jack scrubbed his hands over his face. Hell of a way to start the day. At least he wouldn't have to think about the situation again until next June. Maybe Wyatt was so turned off that he wouldn't come back.

Jack wasn't sure whether he wanted him to or not.

* * * * *

NOTORIOUS

1

GIRLS! GIRLS! GIRLS!

The electronic message on the billboard over the Pussycat Lounge expanded against a background of cascading fireworks, then disintegrated as a new message took shape.

ON STAGE NOW!

Noah Garfield walked past the entrance to the bar, located two streets over from the Las Vegas Strip. Although he had no intention of entering the place, he wouldn't be a normal guy if he didn't spend a moment picturing topless women dancing inside the darkened interior. Sexual adventure seemed more wicked when it was offered at two in the afternoon.

And sexual adventure still made him think of Keely, even after ten years. He could hardly believe so much time had gone by since she'd shocked the good folks of Saguaro Junction, Arizona, by posing for the centerfold of *Macho* magazine. With no trouble at all he could still see her stretched out in all her nineteen-year-old glory, smiling at him and about half a million other guys. Born to be wild, that was Keely Branscom.

He'd love to know where she was now. Maybe married with three kids, although he had a hard time picturing that. More likely she was performing in a club exactly like the one he'd just passed. That wasn't so hard to imagine.

The bachelor party tonight would be at a similar kind of place, and Noah wasn't really looking forward to it. He didn't have a steady relationship with a woman like the other guys in the wedding party, which meant he was sexually on edge. It wasn't a good idea to watch a lot of seminaked women bobbing around when you were in that state.

The heels of his boots tapped out a steady rhythm as he continued on his way. The last time he was in this town for a pro rodeo about five years ago, he distinctly remembered a little neighborhood-type bar in this area. No dancers, no loud music, just cold beer and a couple of outdated slot machines.

Now he couldn't find it.

He'd counted on that little bar to be his hidey-hole over the weekend, whenever the festivities for his good buddy Brandon threatened to overwhelm him. He was glad, honored even, to be a groomsman—he really was. But Brandon and Jenny's engagement last fall had meant that Noah was the only one of his rodeo buddies who hadn't found himself a wife.

To top it off, his little brother, Jonas, had become engaged, and of all people, he'd picked Keely's sister, B.J. Noah wouldn't mind getting married. In fact, he would *love* getting married. But he'd been kept busy with the ranch, and Saguaro Junction wasn't exactly overrun with eligible females. Until recently, any that happened along had been instantly appropriated by Jonas.

Well, maybe now that Jonas was settling down, Noah would have the time and opportunity to find a wife of his own. But, in the meantime, here he was, smack-dab in the middle of Sin City at a time when he was feeling especially vulnerable to suggestions.

You could do just about anything you wanted to in this town, and that was way too much freedom for his taste. After only a few hours here he could already feel the sexual pull of the city, the urge to do things you'd never think of doing in your own hometown. It made him nervous.

Keely had affected him that way, all those years ago, and he'd wisely decided to steer clear of her. If he could just get that centerfold picture out of his mind, he'd be all set. But this was the sort of place to freshen that memory, not erase it.

At the next intersection he paused and glanced around at a passel of gift shops, liquor stores and pawnshops. No neighborhood bar. It had probably gone out of business. With a sigh he turned around to retrace his path to the hotel.

The hotel had several bars, but they were all too trendy, too noisy. He hungered for worn vinyl stools and a little country music. Someplace like the Roundup Saloon in Saguaro Junction.

It was a pitiful thing for a man of thirty-two to be homesick, but that's what he was. He wouldn't even mind mucking out stalls right now if he could be back on the ranch looking forward to a barbecue this evening and a sunset that would make your eyes water with its beauty. He loved that ranch the same way his daddy had, and his daddy before him. It was Garfield land, and Noah always felt better when his feet were planted on it.

He was so caught up in his daydreaming that he wasn't paying any attention to the other people on the sidewalk. It took him a while to realize that the redhead walking toward him looked a lot like Keely. But his mind was probably playing tricks on him, considering he'd just been thinking of her.

With his hat pulled low to shade his eyes, he could study her more closely without being caught at it. Yep, sure reminded him of Keely. The blue flowers decorating her dress looked sweet and innocent, but the dress itself, filmy and cut to midthigh, was anything but. The skirt flounced around her smooth legs with every step she took.

It was a mouthwatering dress, clingy enough to allow every curve to make itself known when she moved. It laced up over her breasts, and although the neckline didn't show much cleavage, the dress revealed a hell of a lot of leg. Bare, brightly painted toes peeked out of a pair of high-heeled sandals. Keely could wear high-heeled sandals like nobody else.

Of course, this *wasn't* Keely. But this woman could be her twin. Same full, pouty mouth; same determined chin; same "I Gotta Be Me" stride.

She wore sunglasses, so he couldn't see her eyes. The eyes would be the clincher. No other woman in the world had Keely's eyes. Some people said green was a soothing, cool color. Not on Keely. She could scorch a man's heart with one glance. A few thought the devil himself stoked that blaze, and it could well be. Looking into her eyes, a man might consider selling his soul.

The Keely look-alike paused outside the dance club and Noah paused, too. Of course she wasn't Keely, but now he had to be absolutely positive before he could walk on past.

She dug in her shoulder purse for something and came out with a small leather notebook. Flipping it open, she shoved her sunglasses to the top of her head while she studied whatever was written there. Snapping the notebook shut, she thrust it back into her purse and stepped toward the entrance.

"Excuse me." He moved toward her and came up with the first line he could think of. "Could you tell me what time it is?" Damn, she even *smelled* like Keely. She'd been partial to raspberry-scented body lotion.

Without looking at him, she glanced at her watch. Then she raised her head and gazed in his direction. "It's two-fif—" She stopped abruptly and stared at him.

He gasped and his heart began to hammer the way it always did in reaction to her. Those eyes. God, they were more potent than ever.

"Noah?" Her mouth gaped open. "Noah Garfield, is that you?"

"It's me." The shock of seeing her made his head buzz.

"Wow." She let out a breathless little laugh. "I can't believe this."

"*You* can't believe it? *I* can't believe it. I was just thinking about you and then bam, you showed up." Whoops. He shouldn't have said that.

"Really?" Her kiss-me-now mouth curved in a smile. Her lipstick was the color of a ripe peach, and she must have recently put it on, because it still had a gloss that made her mouth look wet. "After all these years? How flattering."

"Well, I—uh…" Damn it all, now he was blushing.

Her smile widened. "Couldn't be the sign flashing over our heads that reminded you of me, now, could it?"

As usual, she knew right where to press to make him squirm. "Now, Keely, that's the sort of thing best forgotten, don't you think?"

"It's obvious *you* haven't forgotten it." She reached out and patted his arm. "That's okay. It's not every day that the girl you used to chase around the stock tank decides to bare her all in a centerfold. Folks in Saguaro Junction aren't used to that kind of thing. I guess it would tend to stick in your mind."

"I think most people have forgotten about it." Not true. Mention Keely Branscom anywhere in town and eyebrows still rose. He struggled to get some purchase on the conversation. "So how've you been?" Now *there* was an original question.

"Fine."

"That's good." Another brilliant comment. He had to admit she looked fine. Saucy as all get-out, the way she'd always been. Judging from the way the dress fit, she hadn't put on an extra ounce in ten years.

"How about you?" she asked.

"I'm good." He wondered how she made her lipstick look like that, as if she'd just licked her lips. He shouldn't be looking at her mouth, but her eyes weren't any safer a place to rest his glance. Well, he could look lower, at her breasts rising and falling under the thin, flowery material. That wasn't such a good idea. Better concentrate on her mouth, even if it did remind him of the one time she'd kissed him.

"What brings you to Vegas?" she asked.

He had to stop and think. Oh, yeah, Brandon. "A friend of mine's getting married."

"Really? Anybody I know?"

"I don't think so. He's from Wyoming. We met up on the rodeo circuit a few years back. I don't think he ever made it to the ranch, but we've kept in touch."

"That's nice." For a split second she sounded a little wistful. Then that cocky tone of hers took over again. "So what's up with you, Noah? Found yourself a salt-of-the-earth ranching woman yet?"

"Nope." Once again she'd managed to hit a subject he was touchy about. "Been a little busy." He hesitated, not sure how much he wanted to reveal. After all, she'd been the one who'd decided to break off contact with everyone in Saguaro Junction, including her father and sister. But finally he decided to tell her some of the news. Couldn't hurt. "My dad died a couple of years ago."

"Oh. Oh, I'm sorry." She gazed up at him, her green eyes filled with sadness. "He was a nice man."

"Thanks. He was." He couldn't ever remember seeing sympathy in her eyes before. Defiance plenty of times, devilment nearly as often and, once, on a very memorable night, desire. Never this soft, endearing sympathy.

He'd always thought of her as being so tough, but maybe she wasn't. Ten years ago he hadn't allowed himself to see past her cheeky bravado. Life had been safer that way. But he was older now, and he wondered if he'd missed a few things about Keely. He should have tracked her down, just to make sure she was okay.

"So you and Jonas are running things?" she asked.

"Yeah." He could say that now. Six months ago he couldn't have, back when Jonas spent more time chasing women than chasing cows. But B.J. had settled Jonas down considerably. "That's another thing that's happened," he said. "Jonas will be getting married soon."

"Get outta here!" She grinned. "Shotgun?"

"Nope. He's marrying your sister."

Disbelief flashed in her eyes, but it was quickly replaced with a touching vulnerability. She glanced away. "Well." Her throat moved in a hard swallow before she looked up, her gaze guarded. "She always was sweet on him, but she's making a huge mistake."

"A few months ago I would have agreed with you, but you'd be surprised at how Jonas has changed. He's getting more responsible by the day."

"What a shame."

The old irritation that had always been a part of his conversations with Keely pricked him now. If everybody had Keely's carefree attitude toward life, the work would never get done. "*I* happen to be glad for him."

She gave him that saucy smile, the one that always warned him that a smart-ass remark was coming. "You would be," she said. "You were born old."

His jaw clenched. Keely had a real talent for getting under his skin. She always had—in every department. "Everybody has to grow up sometime. Even you."

"Not if I can help it. And as for B.J. and Jonas, they should have years ahead of them before they have to settle into some boring routine. But no, they're shackling themselves to each other and that blessed ranch. I hate to see it."

"Nobody asked you to." Now, that was a low blow and he hadn't meant to deliver it. But he couldn't take it back, and he didn't know how to smooth over what he'd just said.

Her eyes registered the hurt. "No, I guess nobody did." She slid her sunglasses back on, and when she spoke again her voice sounded more brittle than bright. "And I suppose my father's as crotchety as ever?"

He was touched that she was brave enough to ask about Arch. She and her father had fought bitterly all through her teenage years, and he'd practically thrown her out after the centerfold incident. He hadn't been serious about sending her away, but with her nineteen-year-old view of the world, she'd taken it seriously. Neither of them had been able to swallow their pride long enough to make the connection again.

"Arch is fine," he said gently, wanting to reassure her of that much, at least. "In perfect health."

"I'm not surprised," she said with a grimace, although she sounded relieved. "He wouldn't tolerate the presence of an infirmity." She straightened her shoulders. "Well, now that we're all caught up, I'd better be going. I have an appointment."

He'd nearly forgotten where they were standing. Before he'd stopped her she'd been about to go inside this dance club. He had a sinking sensation that he knew why. "An appointment?" he asked, trying to keep the question casual.

"Yes. An interview."

"Oh." His gut churned. A job interview. The centerfold picture flashed through his mind again and he knew without a shadow of a doubt that she was trying to get a job dancing on the stage in there. She planned to take off most of her clothes and twirl those little tassel gizmos for the men who patronized this club.

He eyed the entrance once more and noticed chipped paint around the door frame. The rock music coming from inside sounded more sinister than it had a moment ago, and he heard loud male laughter. He hoped this place was a step down from what she'd been doing before and not a step up. But whichever direction she was headed, it looked like the wrong road to him.

"Listen, I'm already late, but it's been fun seeing you," she said. "What a coincidence, huh? Take care of yourself, Noah." She turned toward the shadowy entrance.

Without taking time to think about it, he grabbed her arm. "Don't go in there."

She glanced up at him in surprise. "Why not?"

"There have to be better ways to make a living." His breath hitched. Her bare arm felt warm and smooth beneath his fingers. She had wonderful skin, he remembered now. And she was planning to show way too much of it to strangers.

With her free hand she pushed her sunglasses to the top of her head. Then she gazed at him as if fascinated by this turn of events. "What do you think I do for a living?"

"I'm…I'm not sure, and to tell the truth I'd rather not know. I'm just asking you not to go for that interview. I've been in places like this. I know how they expect the women to—"

"Do you, now?"

He released her arm as if her skin might burn him. "Damn it, Keely. You know what I'm talking about."

"I'm not sure I do. I'm still getting used to the concept of Noah Garfield in a topless bar. Did someone trick you into going in?"

"No!" The woman sure had a way of getting his goat. "I went in under my own steam. I'm not a saint."

A slow smile spread over those peach-colored lips. "Couldn't prove it by me."

"Look, Keely, I know we haven't always seen eye to eye

on things. Years ago you seemed determined to head in a certain direction, and you wouldn't listen to anybody who tried to talk you out of it. But I'm asking you right here, right now, to reconsider. Maybe you met me on this street for a reason. Maybe it's time to think about alternatives."

She folded her arms and looked at him. Mischief lurked in her eyes. "Let's make sure I understand. Instead of going inside and getting a job wiggling my ta-tas for the customers, you want me to reform and go into a more respectable line of work. Is that the gist of it?"

"You're making fun of me, but yes, that's the gist of it."

The gleam of devilment grew brighter. "You want to save me from myself."

"Aw, hell, Keely." He figured she was going to roast him for this attempt to do the right thing. "It's not that topless dancing is so terrible. I know you think I'm some sort of prude, but I'm not. And I understand that you've always wanted to kick the status quo in the butt. But isn't this getting a little old? I should think you'd have moved on to something else by now."

"I'm not even thirty!"

"Damn close."

"Ten whole months away, buster."

"See, it's the perfect time to make a change." He was thinking she looked years younger than thirty. Because they'd grown up together he knew exactly how old she was, but a stranger would think she was in her early twenties. No doubt her body would look good on stage for a long time to come, but he didn't intend to say that. He didn't even want to think that.

"And what sort of job should I do?" she asked, tapping the toe of her sandal against the pavement.

"I'm not sure." He rubbed the back of his neck. Now that

he'd jumped into this white-knight routine, he didn't know how to proceed. "Maybe we could kick around some ideas."

"And when could we do that? You have a wedding to attend, as I recall, and I need to make a living."

And there was the heart of the matter. If she was looking for a job, she was probably short on cash. He couldn't very well tell a woman like Keely to forget about the money she'd make dancing topless and take a job flipping burgers instead. She'd laugh in his face. He wasn't going to convert her to a different lifestyle during one conversation on the street corner.

He stalled, trying to think what to do. "How long have you been in Vegas?"

"Just got here yesterday."

"Okay." He thought quickly. One step at a time. "I understand the economic realities. You just came to town and you need a job, but could you hold off for the weekend so we could talk about it? I could cover your expenses for the next few days."

"You mean, pay for my room and board? I don't think so."

"Then how about this? Cancel your room reservation and move in with me for the weekend. Would that save you enough so you wouldn't have to work right away?"

"You want me to share your hotel room?" She eyed him with interest.

That look triggered a vivid memory. She'd kissed him with the passion of a woman that night in the barn, even at the tender age of sixteen. "Strictly as friends," he said quickly. "It's a minisuite. I'll take the couch and you can have the bed. This isn't a proposition, Keely."

"Are you sure?" The mischief had returned to her green eyes. "I realize you're not in the habit of kicking over the traces, but we're not in Saguaro Junction anymore. No one from back home has to hear about this. And we all know what a naughty girl I am."

Warmth flooded through him. She really had a knack for saying exactly what would bring a reaction. "That's the kind of thinking you need to get away from," he said. "Life is about more than sex." At the moment he couldn't think what else it was about, but he'd get his bearings again soon.

"Let me make sure I understand. You're inviting me to stay in your room for the weekend, but you have no intention of us fooling around. Instead, you're going to do some career counseling for me."

"That's right." Not that fooling around with Keely didn't hold some appeal. But she apparently thought that's all she was good for, and he didn't want to reinforce that notion.

She frowned in confusion. "I asked you if you had a wife back home and you said no. But is there a serious girlfriend? Because I can imagine you would be totally loyal once you committed yourself to somebody."

"No serious girlfriend." Come to think of it, he hadn't even had a date in months.

"Noah, are you gay?"

He nearly choked to death. As he was coughing and sputtering, he shook his head and gasped out his denial.

She ticked off her conclusions on the tips of her fingers. "You're not committed to anyone, you're not gay, and you don't want to have sex with me, even if no one back home would ever find out."

"That's right." He did want to have sex with her, always had, but that was a white lie he could live with.

"Then you surely must be a saint who has dropped down out of the sky to save me from my wicked ways. Okay, I accept."

He cleared his throat and tried to look more confident than he felt. "That's great." Now that she'd pointed out to him that only a saint could be expected to resist her, he'd begun to think this whole idea was doomed. But if he could somehow find the strength to keep his hands off her, then maybe she'd develop a new image of herself. And that was worth doing. After all, his brother was marrying her sister. She would be family soon.

"We should probably go pick up your stuff," he said. "Is your hotel far from here?"

She looked suddenly worried. "Uh, the thing is, they, um… lost my luggage. You know how that happens. I don't have any stuff."

"Oh." So it was worse than he thought. Obviously she was making up the story about lost luggage, so that must mean she was staying in some fleabag motel and didn't want him to know it. Worse yet, her belongings were pitiful enough to be embarrassing to her. As together as she looked now, the outfit she wore was probably the only decent thing she owned.

Knowing that fact renewed his resolve to pull her out of this nosedive she was in. "Okay, then!" he said with more heartiness than the situation called for. He sounded like a damn used-car salesman. He cleared his throat and tried again. "Let's walk on back to my hotel. Then I can advance you a little money if you want to go shopping for a few clothes later."

"We'll see about that. But before we leave here I want to duck inside and let them know I won't be keeping the appointment. I don't want a black mark beside my name, in case I need to come back someday."

"I'll go with you."

She smiled at him. "I'd rather you didn't."

"Why not?"

"In this neighborhood, if some guy is tagging around after a woman, looking like he's keeping track of her, people might think he's her pimp."

As he wondered how she'd become so knowledgeable about such things, ice water shot through his veins. "Keely, please tell me that you've never—"

"No. I've never. I may be a naughty girl, but I've never been that naughty."

He sighed with relief.

"Yet."

His muscles tensed all over again and he opened his mouth to deliver another warning.

Keely's musical laugh cut him off. "Relax. I'm kidding. You were around for the first nineteen years of my life. You should know by now how much I love to tease people. Especially people like you." She fluttered a hand at him. "Hold down the sidewalk. I'll be back before you know it."

He watched her walk through the entrance into the cave-like interior of the club. That Keely. She always could get him going.

Then he blinked as if coming out of a trance. *He had just arranged to spend the weekend sleeping in a hotel suite with Keely Branscom.*

What the hell had he been thinking? He'd arrived in this place feeling on edge and sexually deprived. Now he'd invited the sexiest woman he'd ever known to stay with him in extremely close quarters. Less than four hours into his Vegas stay, and the city had him right where it wanted him.

2

KEELY HAD MADE A CAREER of acting on impulse. This particular impulse—to play along with Noah's outrageous plan to save her—could be lots of fun, especially if she turned the tables and took him for a walk on the wild side, instead. So why this sudden attack of nerves?

Maybe she was still dealing with the news that her sister and Jonas were getting married. That situation would definitely take some getting used to. Yeah, it was the sudden word of their wedding that had her spooked.

Surely she wasn't still into Noah the way she had been at sixteen. And seducing him here in Vegas would be an awesome way to get revenge for the way he'd brusquely pushed her away at that tender age. But in order for that revenge to be sweet, she had to be certain she was completely over him. Well, she was. Of course she was.

Shaking off her uneasiness, she walked into the sparsely populated bar and glanced at the blond woman gyrating on the small stage. No, that wasn't the one. Her interview subject was a brunette.

"Would you like a table?" A thin man dressed in a white shirt and tight black pants appeared at her elbow.

"No, thanks. I'm Keely Branscom and I'm here to talk with Suzanne."

"Oh!" The man grew more animated. "You're the reporter from *Attitude!* She's in the back. Please sit down. I'll go get her."

Keely pulled out a chair at the nearest round cocktail table and sat. This might take longer than she figured. No doubt Noah would be outside having a conniption, thinking she was secretly filling out a job application. But she couldn't be rude and leave without speaking to Suzanne.

The sound system in the bar wasn't very good, but the blonde on the stage was an excellent dancer. Keely counted five men in the place, all of them with their attention glued to the stage. She'd love to believe they were admiring the skill of the performance, but after years of reporting on the guy/gal scene for *Attitude!,* she could reasonably conclude they were fixated on the dancer's chest instead of her footwork.

In general, a man's motivation was pretty simple, which was one reason she was so intrigued by Noah's offer to reform her. His motivation was more complex. She really believed he didn't intend for them to have sex. Well, he just might have to reevaluate that decision.

"Ms. Branscom?"

Keely glanced away from the stage and saw that a curvy brunette in purple spandex exercise gear stood next to the table. Keely pushed back her chair. "Suzanne?"

"That's me." Suzanne held out her hand.

Keely stood and shook her hand. She had to practically shout to be heard over the pounding music. "Please call me Keely. Listen, it turns out now isn't a very good time for me to do the interview, after all. I wonder if we could reschedule."

"I guess so." Suzanne raised her voice and leaned closer to Keely. "The only thing is, I have, like, this horrific exam coming up in my psych class, so I need to spend most of my free time, like, inhaling the textbook. And tonight I'm dancing."

"Right." Keely was glad they weren't conducting the interview like this. It would give her a headache in no time. She wasn't sure when she'd stopped loving loud music.

She quickly considered how to work around Suzanne's schedule and her own interesting situation with Noah. He'd probably have some wedding-related thing going on tonight, so she might be able to slip over here.

"Do you get a break tonight?" she asked.

"Sure." Suzanne raised her voice as the music's volume increased. "About ten-thirty!"

Keely had to shout, too. "Are you planning to study during your break?"

"Nah! I'll probably kick back! I only get about fifteen minutes!"

Blissfully, the music changed tempo and became softer. "If you're willing, I could do the interview then." Keely couldn't get over how young Suzanne looked. Yet she was twenty-two, three years older than Keely had been when she'd posed for the centerfold.

"Tonight would be cool, but are you sure that's enough time?"

"Maybe not, but we'll get a start, anyway."

Suzanne glanced over at the stage. "Joy, she'd like to be interviewed, too. She's not going to college, like me, but she's going to beauty school. Does that count?"

"Sure does. Anybody who's dancing to earn tuition fits into the article."

"Cool. That's her on stage now." Suzanne watched for a moment and unconsciously began to wiggle in time with the music. "She has some dynamite moves."

"Yes, she does."

"That guy over there in the black T-shirt is her boyfriend. I am, like, so jealous. He is totally hot."

"He is?" Keely could only locate one person in a black T-shirt, and he didn't look like anything special. For one thing, she was getting sick of shaved heads and multiple piercings. And baggy pants did nothing for her these days, either. Plus, he looked more like a kid than a man.

"Yeah, he's awesome." Suzanne gazed at him in rapture. "Totally."

Keely glanced from Suzanne to the kid and reminded herself that this was her magazine's target audience. She needed to do a better job of relating. "He is pretty cute," she said. Cute was as far as she would go. And cute didn't do it for her anymore, unfortunately.

But someone who did do it for her stood right outside, waiting. "Well, Suzanne, I'll see you tonight, then," she said.

"Maybe Joy can come by so you can talk to her, too."

"That would be great. Thanks." Keely shook hands with Suzanne and hurried outside.

Noah was lounging against the side of the building, but he looked wary, not relaxed. He straightened and walked toward her. "I was beginning to wonder if something happened."

"Sorry. It took a while to find the person I needed." She gazed at him with new appreciation. Now here was an example of hot. His clothes might not be trendy, but they were classic turn-ons, at least for her. She'd grown up admiring the way a pearl-buttoned western shirt defined a man's broad shoulders and how smooth-fitting jeans defined even more interesting parts of his anatomy.

Noah looked mighty fine in that department. For years she'd dreamed of exploring the wonders so lovingly cradled by his Wranglers. From all indications he had a body built for serious sinning. Consequently he'd been a worthy challenge ever since she'd hit puberty.

But as luck would have it, when she'd gone for the gold that night in the barn, he'd turned her down. He hadn't been particularly gentle about it, either. For three years she'd tried to get even with him for that rejection, taking every opportunity to taunt him with what he'd missed. He hadn't cracked.

But she'd learned a few things since then, and they'd be sharing a hotel suite. It just might be Samson and Delilah time.

"You know, I've been thinking…" he said, his voice sounding tight.

Uh-oh. She lifted her gaze to his face and tried to look innocent. "About what?" He must have caught her ogling. She'd have to be more careful not to overplay her hand. Some men loved being checked out. Apparently it made this particular man nervous. She slipped on her sunglasses to give herself more leeway.

"Why don't I see if I can get you a room on the same floor?" he said. "You'd probably be more comfortable with that."

Oh, he'd definitely caught her ogling. She had to take quick action. "No way, baby doll! I feel like enough of a charity case as it is! Tell you what, let's forget the whole thing."

"No, no. We're not going to forget the whole thing." He sighed. "Come on. The hotel's this way."

So he had a place on the Strip. She would have liked that, too, but the magazine had booked her at one of the less expensive places downtown. Maybe when he was otherwise occupied, she'd head over there and pick up a few things.

She fell into step beside him. "You know what your problem is? You think too much."

"Could be. But that's better than not thinking enough."

"Ah. That would be me you're referring to, wouldn't it?"

His mouth twitched with amusement. "I didn't mean just you."

"Oh, you probably did, but that's okay. I won't take offense. It you're talking levels of caution, on a scale of one to ten I'd be a minus fifteen."

He laughed.

"You, on the other hand, would be a plus thirty."

"You're exaggerating."

"No, I'm not!" She felt great walking down the street with Noah. Because she stood five-eight in her bare feet and had generous breasts, not many men could make her feel small and delicate. Noah had the height and breadth of shoulder to carry it off. Maybe it wasn't politically correct to enjoy that, but she did. She always had. *Always. Uh-oh. What if she wasn't over him?*

"If I'm so damn cautious," he said, "then why did I take up bull riding?"

"I thought about that. And it does indicate a streak of daring hiding in there somewhere." She had to be over him, she decided. After all, it had been years.

"See?" He looked pleased with himself. "I can be daring if I want."

"Yes, but you only have to maintain that daring for eight seconds or less. That's not a long time." She kept up the banter, but inside she was scanning for evidence, trying to decide if she was still hooked on Noah.

"Oh, yes, it is a long time. When you're in the heat of the action, eight seconds is an eternity. A lifetime."

"Really?"

"Really."

"Well, I sure hope that's not your attitude when you make love. If so, your lady friends must be *very* frustrated." There. If she could poke fun at him, then she was over him. Definitely.

He blushed. "We weren't talking about that."

"I was." That blush of his was so cute. The people she hung

out with in L.A. were all pretty jaded when it came to sexual innuendos. Finding a man who could blush when he talked about sex was refreshing. And arousing.

He tugged his hat down lower over his eyes. "Well, I wasn't thinking about that particular subject, and you know it."

But he was now, and that was her goal. If only she knew for certain she could pull off this caper without getting hurt herself. "The fact is, I have no idea what kind of lover you are, Noah. You're a conservative guy, so when you talk about eight seconds being an eternity, I can't help wondering if you think that's plenty of time for—"

"Of course it's not!" He was really red now.

She'd forgotten how adorable he could be when he was flustered. "Well, good. Glad to hear it. Because most women need a whole lot more than eight seconds to become thoroughly—"

"I'm aware of that! Now, could we please change the subject?"

"Sure. Be glad to." She used to love teasing him like this. She loved it still. Probably too much, and she'd be wise to walk away from this whole setup. But then she'd never know if she could succeed in breaching his defenses. She had to know, no matter what it might cost her. And she was tough. She'd picked up the pieces before and could do it again. Damn the torpedoes. Full speed ahead.

"Thanks." He sighed in apparent relief.

Little did he know there was no relief in sight. "Oh, there's a drugstore," she said. "Would you mind if we stopped in there before we get to the hotel? I need a few things, and I'm sure they're more expensive in the hotel shops."

"That's fine." He sounded grateful to be doing something as harmless as shopping. "I guess you would need a toothbrush and...other stuff."

"A big bottle of lotion, for one thing. I'd forgotten how

desert heat affects my skin. Back on the ranch I had to practically take a bath in lotion, remember?"

"Can't say as I do."

Liar. "Oh, sure you do. You even commented about it one
evening when I was on the front porch of Dad's house, slath-
ering it all over my legs and arms. You said if I kept that up
I'd slide right out of bed in the middle of the night."

"Mmm."

"My favorite is raspberry scented, but they might not have
that." She peeked at him as they walked through the door into
the air-conditioned store to see if any of what she'd said was
registering. He looked more than a little agitated.

Two years ago she'd done an article on scent as an arousal
factor. All the guys she'd interviewed rated scent very high,
and most of them fondly remembered how former lovers had
smelled like cinnamon, or lily of the valley, or in one instance,
chocolate. She was counting on Noah having the same response, and she'd used raspberry-scented lotion ever since
she'd turned fifteen. If she couldn't find any in the drugstore,
she'd smuggle over the bottle she had in her hotel room.

But raspberry lotion wasn't her primary target in the drugstore. She could hardly wait for the moment when Noah discovered what she planned to stock up on.

NOAH HAD BEEN IN TIGHT spots in his life and he'd always managed to come out okay. He clung to that hope as he followed
Keely around the store and tried not to think of the scent of
raspberries.

That scent had drawn him to her dad's porch on the night
she'd mentioned. Dressed in cutoffs and a halter top, she'd sta-
tioned herself on the creaky old porch swing with a bottle of
that damn lotion. To get near her, he'd made up some excuse
about checking the area for snakes.

Keely wasn't the type to run off screaming at the mention

of a snake, so while he'd swung a flashlight beam around and pretended to scout for rattlers, she'd nearly driven him crazy smoothing that creamy, fragrant stuff over her bare legs. They hadn't talked much, but he remembered crickets chirping and the rhythmic squeak of that swing, which could have passed for the sound of bedsprings. To this day he couldn't smell or taste raspberries without hearing that steady creak and seeing her hand slowly massaging the tender skin of her inner thigh.

That might have been the first time she'd discovered the stuff, but after that she'd used it constantly, trailing the scent of raspberries wherever she went. He'd come to dread that aroma, because it never failed to give him an erection, no matter how inappropriate the moment. More than once she'd glanced at his crotch and smiled, as if thrilled with her new power.

Then, a few weeks after she'd turned sixteen, she'd way-laid him in the barn. And she'd smelled exactly like a bowl of fresh raspberries. She'd tasted like that, too—juicy and moist, bursting with ripe sweetness.

He often wondered if she'd been a virgin then. If so, he'd bet she hadn't stayed one long after he'd turned her down. He'd probably given up the chance to be her first lover that night. Saying no hadn't been easy, considering she didn't look or act like any sixteen-year-old he'd known before or since.

But somehow in the midst of that hot, wet kiss, he'd remembered she *was* sixteen, and all the lust in the world wouldn't change that. He'd left the barn in a hurry, followed by the angry insults she'd hurled after him. At the time he'd thought she was furious. Now he wondered if she'd been more hurt than angry. He hadn't been particularly sensitive about ending the embrace.

Sensitivity hadn't been on his mind. Self-preservation had been all he could think about. God, how he'd wanted her. But giving in would have meant angering and disappointing two men he cared about—his father and hers.

Shortly after that he'd gone out on the rodeo circuit, figuring escape was the only answer. During his brief trips home over the next three years he'd noticed that Keely had gone overboard to become the sex symbol of Saguaro Junction. But innocent or wild, she turned him on like no one else. How ironic that he hadn't wanted to be her first lover, but later on he hadn't wanted to be the next one in line, either. With great difficulty he'd kept himself in check.

He was much older now and should have better control. But as he watched her scan the shelves looking for her raspberry lotion, he wondered if he'd changed at all where Keely was concerned.

All of a sudden she pounced on a bottle. "Look! Here it is!"

"Looks like it." He groaned to himself. *Wouldn't you know.*

"Okay, now a toothbrush." She moved quickly to that aisle and grabbed a red one. "What kind of toothpaste do you use?"

He told her.

"That'll be fine. We can share, if that's all right with you."

"Uh, sure." He was aware of another customer, a matronly woman, giving them both the once-over.

"Great. The hotel shampoo will do for a couple of days, but I'll have to buy deodorant. I don't want some bracing, manly smell on my body."

His mind spun wildly as he followed her to the antiperspirants. What in God's name had he been thinking, proposing this scheme? How was he supposed to keep a level head while they shared the same shower, the same sink, and squeezed from the same toothpaste tube?

Dark red hair bouncing around her shoulders, she stalked through the rest of the store as if looking for something.

And like an idiot, he had to ask. "Is there something else you need?"

"Condoms."

He choked. "Why?"

"I'm surprised you would say that. Really, Noah, I'm beginning to wonder what kind of sex life you have. Ah, there they are, the little devils. Here, hold my stuff for a minute so I can look these puppies over." She shoved her lotion, deodorant and toothbrush into his hands.

Panic swelled within him. "Look, you don't need those things. I'm telling you, we are not—"

"Oh, these aren't for *you.*"

"They're *not?*" The conversation had gone from bad to worse.

She studied the packages hanging on the display rack. "Not unless you change your mind."

"I won't, so let's just go, okay?" He glared at a teenage kid who was lingering nearby, obviously enjoying the show. The kid grinned and left. Noah lowered his voice. "Come on, Keely. Forget this stuff."

She ignored him. "These prices are really reasonable. Maybe I should stock up. You'd think men would look for inexpensive stores like this, but no. They like to be spontaneous, which usually means paying top dollar because they're in a rush. Or worse yet, suggesting we skip this step. Ha. As if."

He tried again. "All things considered, I don't think you really need to worry about—"

"I make it a habit to have some on hand in a couple of sizes, for emergencies. And we're here, after all. I really can't imagine a better bargain coming along anytime soon." She took a package from its hook and began reading. "'Ultra-comfort. Unique shape for more freedom.' I wonder what that means?"

"Keely."

"Noah," she mimicked. "Hmm. Maybe these are better." She unhooked another package. "It's so hard to know which ones are the best, with all these great descriptions—'shared sensation, enhanced pleasure, ultimate feeling.' Oh, look. Here's one with a larger tip, and then there's the ribbed kind. Which do you think is the best?" She turned to look at him, a package of condoms in each hand, and devilment shining from those green eyes.

He ground some more enamel off his back molars. "Keely Branscom, you are doing this on purpose."

"Of course I am! I always budget money for a package of condoms."

"You're trying to get me going, is what you're doing."

"From the way you're breathing, I'd say I've succeeded." She grinned. "I really am buying the condoms, Noah. At least two packages of extra-large. And I'm giving you a chance to tell me which kind you like."

His jaw was clenched so tight his teeth seemed welded together. *"We are not going to need them."*

"Maybe not. But that's the thing about condoms. The packages are small and they store well. And there could be a time when you will thank me for planning ahead. Now give me my stuff. It's time to check out." She took her items from him and sashayed down the aisle with her lotion, her deodorant, her toothbrush and two kinds of extra-large condoms.

She obviously expected him to be wearing them before the weekend was over. It was a classic case of damned if he did and damned if he didn't.

3

Keely had just laid her purchases on the checkout counter when her cell phone rang from deep inside her shoulder purse. *Damn*. She'd forgotten about it.

She wheeled away from the counter, startling the young male clerk. "Forgot something!" she called over her shoulder to Noah, who, fortunately, was trailing her by a few paces. She figured he was embarrassed for the clerk to notice that she was buying condoms so he'd hung back from approaching the counter. Good thing. Maybe he hadn't heard her cell phone.

It rang again as she made a mad dash for the aisle labeled Feminine Products. If Noah had been schizy about the condom display, he surely wouldn't follow her there. Once she was safely surrounded by rows of tampon and sanitary-napkin boxes, she dug in her purse and took out the phone.

When she put it to her ear she heard the familiar voice of her editor. "Keely, sweetheart. Good news."

"Hi, Carolyn," she murmured softly. Trust her editor to call at the exact wrong moment.

"Why are you whispering? Are you in a movie theater or something?"

"No, but I can't talk loud. Or long."

"That's okay. This will be quick. Remember you mentioned

expanding this article by interviewing some dancers in Reno, but I wasn't sure we should bother?"

"I remember, but can I call you back on this?" She glanced nervously behind her to make sure Noah wasn't there. "I—"

"I'll only be a sec. The publisher loves the Reno angle. I've lined up a couple of interview subjects for you there. You have a seven-forty flight out of Vegas on Monday morning. Got a pen? I'll give you the confirmation number."

"Carolyn, I—"

"Ready? Here it is." Carolyn rattled off the number.

Keely grabbed her notebook out of her purse and wrote down the number, but all the while she was thinking that this cell phone could blow her cover in no time this weekend. Carolyn expected her to keep the phone turned on while she was on assignment.

"Got it?" Carolyn asked.

"Got it, but Carolyn, you're fading out." Keely pressed the disconnect button a couple of times. "Carolyn? I think the phone's going on the blink. It's—" She broke off and ran the phone up and down the edge of a box several times, hoping the noise sounded like static. Then she put it back to her ear to gauge Carolyn's reaction.

"Keely? What's going on? Keely, can you hear me?"

"Barely," Keely whispered. *"I think it's—"* She dragged the phone around on the boxes some more before turning it off. Maybe she'd convinced Carolyn that the phone was dead. Keely buried it in the bottom of her purse again before heading back toward the checkout counter.

Looking extremely uneasy, Noah stood by the counter next to her items, which had been set aside while the clerk rang up another customer's purchases.

Keely smiled sweetly as she walked up to Noah. "Those prices weren't as reasonable, so I decided not to bother."

His eyes narrowed with suspicion. "What was that funny sawing noise?"

During her wild teen years, fast thinking had saved her more times than she could count. "I had an itch in the middle of my back. I used the corner of a box to scratch it." She gave a little wriggle. "All better."

He gulped. "Oh." His voice was strained as he attempted to sound casual. "That explains it."

Somehow she kept from laughing. One wriggle and he was gulping for air. She didn't remember him being so suggestible years ago. Apparently she had the advantage this time… so long as she kept her heart out of the equation.

"I can ring you up now, miss." The clerk, who couldn't have been more than eighteen, regarded her with adoration.

"Fabulous." She winked and sent him a high-wattage grin. "You have a very nice store here…" She paused to glance at his red plastic name tag. "Chad."

Chad grew as red as his name tag. "Thank you very much," he mumbled, and then he concentrated on punching the right numbers into the register. He had to clear his throat before he could tell her the amount. His gaze kept drifting to her chest and then he'd pull his eyes back with an obvious effort.

She opened her wallet and removed the money as quickly as she could. Her press pass was in there along with a gold card, but Noah would have had to be paying close attention to see either of them.

Chad took the money and handed over her change. "Do you, uh, live near here?" he asked eagerly. "I mean, would you like to be on our mailing list for…um…future sales?"

"Thanks, but I'm currently between addresses."

"Oh." Chad glanced over at Noah, then back at her, as if trying to decide if they were a couple. "Well, uh, feel free to stop in anytime. We always have specials."

"Thanks. I'll remember that." Picking up the plastic bag containing her purchases, she looked at Noah. "Ready?"

He gave a curt nod.

"Bye!" Chad called. "Come back anytime!"

She turned and smiled at him. "Bye."

Noah held the door for her as they left the store. Judging from the set of his jaw, she didn't think he was very happy. From all signs, he was a wee bit jealous—of a boy barely old enough to shave. Amazing.

Once upon a time she'd turned herself inside out trying to arouse Noah's jealousy, to no avail. Now it seemed that she'd done it with one hand tied behind her back. She decided to test the waters. "He was a nice kid," she said as they walked along the street.

"The way he was drooling I thought he might flood the store." Noah sounded quite irritated. "I think with a little more encouragement he would have asked you out, even though you're old enough to be his—"

"Big sister? He wasn't *that* much younger."

"Hell, he probably got his driver's license yesterday."

"He looked more like eighteen or nineteen to me. And by the way, men date women who are ten years younger than they are and nobody says boo."

He stared at her. "Don't tell me you're interested in him?"

She wasn't, not even slightly, but a jealous Noah was something she'd waited years to experience. She wanted to savor the feeling a little longer. "Well, he was very sweet, and he had the cutest dimple in his chin."

"You're putting me on."

"Okay, maybe I am. But, for the record, I don't think it would be the end of civilization if I happened to be interested in him. Some of my friends have deliberately taken younger lovers."

"Probably so they can lead them around by the nose."

Oh, this man had some things to learn, and she was just the gal to educate him. "I don't think that's the part of their anatomy they care about. A younger guy is usually so eager to please, and he generally has more…staying power."

Noah snorted. "Yeah, if you're into quantity instead of quality."

She pitched her voice lower, so it came out a sultry purr. "Quality can be taught. And young men are *so* coachable."

The sound that came from Noah bordered on a growl.

"What was that? I didn't quite understand you."

"Nothing."

She didn't think it was nothing. She thought it was the sound of a male animal whose masculinity had been challenged. From her experience, a man so challenged would be looking for opportunities to prove his prowess. Even if he hotly insisted otherwise.

Before long, Noah would beg to make love to her, and that would go a long way toward healing the hurt he'd inflicted, knowingly or not, when he'd rejected her sixteen-year-old advances. Maybe a few words of desperate need from him were all she needed to finally get him out of her system.

IT WAS ALL COMING BACK to him now. Not only had he been tortured with feelings of lust where Keely was concerned, he'd also been ready to kill every guy who so much as looked at her. Leaving Saguaro Junction to follow the rodeo circuit had kept him away from Keely, but it had also saved a lot of cowboys from having their jaws busted.

Apparently he hadn't changed in that regard, either. The drugstore clerk was a mere baby, but when his hormone-driven attention had settled on Keely's breasts, Noah had been ready to take the kid apart. He'd have to work on that reaction, because men weren't going to stop looking at Keely during the next three days. Men were *always* looking at Keely.

The worst part was that he couldn't understand where his protective instincts were coming from. Maybe because he'd grown up with Keely, he had some big-brother feelings going on, but she'd never acted like a shrinking violet in need of male protection. The males probably needed protection from Keely, when it came right down to it.

That might be the heart of the matter, he realized with sudden insight. He hadn't been willing to face that his childhood friend had become an extremely sexy woman. Every drooling guy who hung around emphasized the very thing he didn't want to admit, so the answer was to keep them away from her. Knowing that she'd never tolerate that kind of protectiveness had been one of his major frustrations in life. The safest course had been to stay away himself, which had the added benefit of protecting him from his own sexual feelings for her.

He should have continued on that course today. But he couldn't have left her at the topless bar, knowing she'd have a job in no time and be dancing there by tonight, probably. The way things were going, the bachelor party really would end up at that exact bar and he'd have to watch his buddies and a host of strangers ogling Keely. The centerfold spread had been torture enough, but at least it hadn't been firsthand torture.

"Where are you staying?" she asked as they arrived at the Strip and turned left.

"The Tahitian." He'd been floored by the prices, but he had to admit the rooms were nice.

"That new place? Cool! I've been meaning to check it out. The cliff-diver show is supposed to be awesome at night. And don't they have an actual beach with surf in the courtyard?"

"I guess. I haven't seen it yet."

"You haven't? Everybody talks about it—white sand, salt-water waves lapping at the shore, palm trees swaying—the whole nine yards. I guess your room must not look out on that, or you'd have noticed."

"Nope. Mine overlooks the parking lot." He had a vivid mental picture of Keely lying at the edge of that lapping surf, the foam curling over her naked breasts and licking at her smooth thighs. Oh, boy. He was in trouble. He'd been denying her sexuality for years, but denial wasn't working anymore.

"In fact, considering you're staying at such a premier resort," she said, "I'm surprised you didn't want to hang out right there and soak up the atmosphere instead of wandering around in the heat on a basically boring side street."

"Well, the thing is, I—"

"Noah Garfield, were you planning to actually go into that bar? Don't tell me that you're secretly a voyeur who pays to look at naked women?"

He winced as several people on the crowded sidewalk turned to stare at him. Taking Keely by the arm, he leaned down. "No, I am not a secret voyeur, but now several people in this city think I am." He released his grip on her arm before the soft warmth under his fingers gave him even more ideas.

"Sorry about that," she said. "You know I always tend to speak my mind."

"I do remember that. Obviously you haven't changed."

"Obviously you haven't, either. Still worried about what the neighbors think."

She was baiting him. He knew that, but still she got his dander up. He wondered if he had any chance at all of changing her attitude this weekend. Probably not, but he had to try. He'd keep reminding her of her roots and see if that helped the cause. "Where you and I come from, you'd better stay chummy with your neighbors if you expect to make it in the ranching business."

"Well, I have no interest in making it in the ranching business."

She scored another hit with that one. He loved his life as a rancher and took negative comments about it personally. "I think you made that perfectly clear when you took the deal with *Macho.*"

"You noticed that."

"Everybody noticed that." And that was the other big reason he'd better get his mind off the lovely body of Keely Branscom. He'd never been the kind of guy who could have sex for the hell of it. With him, a physical relationship with a woman needed to be going somewhere. With Keely, it could go nowhere. She didn't want what he could offer.

"Noah…about that centerfold…" She sounded hesitant, which was unusual for her.

Surprised at the sudden shift in her manner, he glanced over at her.

She cleared her throat. "It was my ticket out." Her gaze slipped up to his face, but her expression was disguised by her dark glasses. "Can you understand that?"

"Sort of." Frustrated by not being able to see her eyes, he faced forward again. "I mean, if you wanted to get out of Saguaro Junction, posing for that magazine sure worked like a charm. And I can see why the town might seem too conservative for you. But to cut yourself off completely…"

"It was easier that way."

"Maybe, but growing up there wasn't all bad, was it?"

"No, of course not."

"Don't you ever miss the place?" He decided not to talk about missing the people for now.

She didn't answer for a long while. "Sometimes," she murmured at last. "Yeah, sometimes I do."

She was full of surprises. He didn't think she'd admit to that so soon. Maybe he had a chance, after all. "Then why not come back and mend some fences?"

"I don't fit in there, Noah. I'm too much like my mother."

He barely remembered Keely's mother, who'd died from complications surrounding B.J.'s birth. But Arch had said his wife had loved the excitement of the city and had been bored by country living. "I didn't mean you had to move back. But would it kill you to visit?"

"Maybe." She smiled wistfully. "Although I have to say, this business of my little sister getting married has me thinking. You never did mention when the wedding was."

"Let's see. It's…two weeks from Saturday," he said with some shock. "I didn't realize it was getting so close, myself. And I still don't have a gift bought, either."

"That soon? Are you *sure* this isn't a shotgun affair?"

"Absolutely sure. Jonas is the one who is pushing to tie the knot."

"I'm amazed." Keely shook her head. "B.J. must have really changed."

"Not a whole lot. She's still a better ranch hand than most men. Better at some things than Jonas, to be honest."

"Then I don't get it. She's so not his type. He likes girlie girls, and B.J. is about as far from that as you can get."

"Maybe your sister has hidden depths."

"Maybe she does."

"One thing's for sure—Jonas thinks she's fascinating. And B.J.'s still the same riding, roping gal as always, but there is something sort of different about her. It's like she's in full bloom or something."

"See? She's pregnant!"

"No, she's not, but I can see you aren't going to take my word for it." He paused. "Guess you'll have to ask her yourself."

After a long moment, Keely sighed. "I understand what you're trying to do, Noah, and it's very sweet, but…too much water's gone over the dam, or under the bridge. At any rate, there's been a heck of a lot of water running. I don't think I'd be a welcome guest at the wedding."

"I wouldn't be so sure." Noah was taking a chance saying that. But he had a hunch Arch and B.J. would love it if Keely showed up. Besides, he didn't see how the gap in the family could get any wider, so he thought it was worth the risk to suggest she go.

KEELY WALKED ALONG SILENTLY beside Noah as they covered the last block before reaching the towering hotel that would magically transport them to the South Pacific. She was afraid to say too much more on the subject of her sister's wedding for fear Noah would figure out how much she longed to go back and see her father and sister. Maybe now her sister was old enough and experienced enough to understand what had happened all those years ago. Maybe they could be friends again.

Only two years apart, they had been friends once. Then Keely had launched into puberty like a rocket, leaving B.J. behind. Living on a ranch where the only other females were her boyish younger sister and the Garfields' housekeeper, Keely had found no one to help her through the confusing process of growing into a sexual person. She'd only had the dim memory of her mother to guide her, a mother who had apparently looked and acted just like her. Or so her father said.

Keely had developed early, B.J. late. And it had seemed to Keely that B.J. had tried to keep her tomboy image just to set her apart from her wild sister. Or maybe they'd split the parental influences between them, with B.J. becoming like Arch and Keely growing more and more like her mother. At any rate, B.J. had become the good daughter in their father's eyes, while Keely had continued to blaze a path toward bad-girl land.

But Jonas wouldn't be attracted to a woman who didn't

have a touch of naughtiness, so maybe B.J. wasn't Little Miss Innocent anymore. Maybe she wouldn't be as mystified by Keely now. Then again, maybe she would turn her back on her rebel sister, and that would be painful. Keely had a real aversion to pain.

In fact, she gravitated almost exclusively to pleasure and living in the present moment. The past couldn't be changed and the future was a guess, but for the moment she had Noah Garfield right where she wanted him at last. As they approached the Tahitian, a ripple of anticipation made her shiver with delight. He had found her hard to resist in a drugstore. Once she got him inside this tropical paradise, he'd be a goner.

Set a distance back from the street, the hotel beckoned visitors to approach by leading them through a man-made jungle misted with thousands of tiny jets and cooled with countless tumbling waterfalls. The air reverberated with exotic birdsong and the steady beat of native drums.

"What fun," Keely said as they joined the throng headed toward the entrance.

"I'd hate to get their water bill," Noah said.

"Oh, for heaven's sake. Can you do me a favor for the next three days and try not to think of practical things like that? You're going to ruin my fantasy if you insist on worrying about utility bills."

To her surprise, Noah laughed. "You're right," he said. "Vegas is over the top, and you might as well accept that from the git-go."

"Very *good*." She took off her sunglasses and slipped them into her purse as they approached a large clearing. "There's hope for you, cowboy. Maybe before the weekend is over, you—"

She forgot what she'd intended to say as the foliage gave way to a view of a granite cliff rising ten stories above them. "My God. They dive off this thing." She stood and gazed at the deep pool at the base of the cliff while she tried to imagine having the courage to hurl yourself into it from that height. "I definitely want to see this show tonight."

Noah glanced over at her. "I hope you don't mind watching it by yourself. I have a bachelor party I'm supposed to go to and it might run late."

That fit perfectly into her plans. She could squeeze in some interview time. "No problem," she said. "I'm good at amusing myself. But could we stop by the desk and get me a key to the room?"

"Oh. Sure." He sounded anything but sure.

"Would that make you uncomfortable?"

"No, no, of course not."

"You're worried that the people at the desk will think you picked up a call girl, aren't you? Just like Richard Gere picked up Julia Roberts in *Pretty Woman*." She thought that was a good image to plant in his mind.

He looked uneasy. "But I'm not—I mean, we're not—"

"Tell you what. I'm going to help you out, here. In that movie, he told everybody the girl was his niece. So let's say I'm your cousin."

"Nobody will believe that."

"Of course they won't, but they'll pretend to believe it, and that's good enough, right?"

"I think if we say that you're my cousin they'll know we're lying and be even more sure you're a call girl."

Keely smiled at him. "Okay, then what do you want to say? That I'm a wayward woman and you're trying to reform me? They'll believe that even less. I'd better be your cousin."

He gazed at the cliff before looking back at her. "Maybe we could share a key."

"I don't see how that would work, unless you want me to hang around outside the room waiting for you to come back tonight. I don't think that would be too good for your image, either."

"I guess not."

"Noah, we're in Vegas, Sin City. So what if you have your cousin staying in your room? That's probably one of the tamest situations they've seen around here in ages. I'll bet an hour ago they gave a guy *two* extra keys because he ran into his *twin* cousins. And remember that not a single person behind that desk is your neighbor. So you don't have to give a care what they think."

He gave her a wry grin. "Point made. Let's go get the key." But as he started toward the large entrance doors decorated in brass bamboo, he suddenly turned back and grabbed her arm. "Come this way," he said.

"Why?"

"Just go with it. Head back the way we came." He hustled her down the walk past the crowd of pedestrians.

"Noah, I don't understand what we're doing."

"I'll tell you in a minute. Come over here." He stepped into the landscaping and pulled her in with him.

Instantly she was spritzed from head to toe. "I don't think we're supposed to be walking on the—"

"Down behind this rock." He pulled her to a crouch behind a large lava rock.

"Noah, I'm getting soaked from all those misters spraying down. What on earth is the matter?"

"The groom." He took off his Stetson and peered up over the rock. "Brandon."

"Ah." She gazed at Noah's tense profile. Despite her complaining, the mist felt kind of good after the warmth of their walk. "So you're planning on keeping me a secret from the bridal party?"

"I hadn't thought about it until you started talking about

the extra key, but then I began thinking that it could be kind of awkward, trying to explain everything."

"Maybe you're right." Far from being insulted, she was delighted. One of her most popular magazine articles had dealt with secrecy in a relationship and how tantalizing the forbidden could become. She would love to be Noah's forbidden secret for the weekend. It would make her that much harder to resist.

"Here comes Brandon. Can you get down lower?"

"Sure." She got to her knees on the mossy ground and hunched down even more. The plants gave off a loamy, fertile scent that was quite exciting. And fortunately this wasn't *really* the tropics, so she didn't have to worry about putting her hand on an icky bug by accident.

Noah went down on his knees, too. Wrapping his arm around her, he pulled her in close.

Secrecy had all sorts of benefits, she decided as she snuggled against him. She'd only felt the hard press of his body once before and that had been wildly exciting. Yet he'd been a kid then, not much older than the drugstore clerk. She preferred this version. Maturity sat well on him—he had the solid strength and intriguing scent of a man in his prime. Their damp clothes seemed to melt against their bodies, giving the illusion of skin against skin. She could almost feel steam rising from where they were pressed together.

"I'm sorry you're getting all wet," he said softly.

"There are worse things." Like wanting to be kissed so bad she could hardly stand it. She studied his lower lip and longed to run her tongue along its length. She wondered if he'd moan the way he had the first time she'd kissed him years ago. And she wondered if he tasted more like a man than a boy. In order to find out, she needed him to tilt his face down toward hers, so she spoke his name. "Noah?"

Sure enough, he looked down at her. His eyes grew darker. "What?" he murmured.

"Lean closer," she whispered. "I need to tell you something."

His eyes grew darker still, and his lips parted as he drew near. "What?"

She slipped her hand behind his neck. "Jungle drums get me hot." Then she kissed him.

4

NOAH'S PROGRAM TO REFORM Keely was seriously off track. Not an hour into it and he was making out with her in the bushes. For the second time in his life he'd succumbed to the temptation of her mouth, but he'd had some idea he could deal with it this time. For some unknown reason, he'd expected a repeat of the kiss she'd given him as a sixteen-year-old. He'd sadly miscalculated.

Oh, she'd had plenty of passion back then, too, but she hadn't been quite sure what to do with it. Now, she'd learned. Good God, how she'd learned. The pressure of her mouth was light at first. Warm. Soft. Taunting him.

His first reaction was to move in and take control. He fought not to do that, because if he took control, he'd never know Keely's plans for this kiss. He had a strong feeling she had plans...and he grew dizzy with anticipation.

Gradually she increased the pressure, coaxing his lips apart. The gentle flick of her tongue was slow and lazy, seducing him by degrees. His head spun as the kiss grew deeper... and deeper yet.

He cupped the curve of her hip and reaction surged through him. Her thin dress was so damp from the mist that she might as well not have been wearing it. He flexed his fingers, tightening his hold a fraction, and heard the change in her breathing.

They should stop this. They really should. But she smelled like raspberries and tasted wicked and delicious, like the candy he'd swiped from the corner store when he was six. He'd eventually had to pay for that candy. He had a hunch he'd have to pay for this moment, too. Something so good always came with a price tag.

Her mouth was moist and hot against his, and the spot where his hand rested began to grow warm. He stroked her in a gentle, circular motion and felt her tremble beneath his palm.

The steady drumbeats coming from the sound system vibrated the steamy air around them, and his blood seemed to pump in the same rhythm as it gathered in a very predictable area. But no matter how hard he became or how much he ached, he felt safe from temptation—safe to explore her hot mouth and dream of her hot body without worrying they'd get totally carried away.

After all, they were in a public place. They were hidden from view, but not even Keely would dare go further when they were a dozen feet from a sidewalk full of people. Not even Keely would make love in broad daylight in the middle of the hotel's landscaping.

Then she guided his hand from her hip to her breast, and he wasn't so sure.

Time out! his mind warned. Too late. Natural reflexes took over as he touched one of Keely's perfect breasts for the first time. Although he'd tried to ignore her breasts ever since she'd turned twelve and they'd begun to show, he'd dreamed about them anyway, long before they'd been displayed in full color for the world to admire.

The magazine picture had only confirmed what he'd suspected—Keely's breasts were a national treasure, a living work of art. Only a dead man wouldn't squeeze that handful of heaven when it was offered. He groaned with the tactile pleasure of closing his hand around so much ripeness.

With a low, throaty chuckle she arched toward him. Maybe there was a note of victory in that chuckle, but he was too lost in the bliss of fondling her to care. Then the front of the dress loosened, and he vaguely realized she must have pulled at the laces, untying them. While his racing pulse was still reacting to that development, a soft pop filtered through his dazed state, and he felt the taut material of her bra go slack.

Framing his face in her smooth hands, she leaned away from his kiss. "Be my guest," she murmured.

This was a mistake. A definite mistake. But he couldn't not look. Slowly he let his gaze travel downward. Her breasts, kissed golden by the sun, lightly freckled as if dusted with nutmeg, spilled out of her dress. Of course this woman wouldn't wear anything when she decided to sunbathe. He imagined her lying on her back, warm and relaxed by the heat, her body glistening with oil, the scent of raspberries heavy in the air.

Moisture gathered in his mouth. He was so hungry for her. As he continued to look, heart pounding, the mist gathered in tiny droplets on her skin and her nipples tightened and darkened to a deep rose. His breath caught. This was a mistake. And he was going to make it.

Slipping a quivering hand under the velvet weight of one smooth breast, he leaned down to taste paradise.

Snip, snip, snip. Noah froze. The sound of hedge shears was unmistakable. And it was coming closer. *Snip, snip, SNIP.*

He released Keely instantly. "Cover up!" he whispered urgently, getting his feet back under him and clamping his hat back on his head.

With a lazy smile, she casually pulled the cups of her pale

blue bra over her breasts and snapped the front fastener. She seemed in no hurry whatsoever as she adjusted the straps.

The sounds of the gardener came even closer, yet Noah couldn't stop admiring her cleavage and wishing he had a little longer to enjoy it. But the guy would be upon them any minute. "Faster!" he urged.

"What's the matter?" Her eyes gleamed with mischief as she slowly pulled the laces of her dress closed. "Afraid of getting caught?"

He stared at her and realized that discovery didn't seem to bother her at all. Maybe once she'd taken off all her clothes for the camera, she'd discarded the concept of shame right along with her clothes. She possessed a freedom that he could only imagine. To his amazement he envied her. He was also incredibly turned on.

Here was a woman who wouldn't balk at *anything*.

Keely tied the laces of her dress at the same moment an olive-skinned man in khaki work clothes came around the boulder pushing a small wheelbarrow mounded with clippings, a pair of hedge shears resting on top of the cut greenery.

"Madre de Dios!" the man exclaimed. He nearly tripped over a giant fern as he backed up a step.

"We were just leaving," Noah said. He held out a hand to help Keely up and wished he looked as composed as she did. But he could feel the heat climbing up from his collar and he couldn't meet the gardener's shocked gaze.

Instead, he glanced at Keely, who was nonchalantly swishing bits of dirt from her shapely knees. She had never seemed more beautiful to him. The flush in her cheeks obviously came from pleasure, not shame. When she finished brushing herself off and peeked up at him, her eyes sparkled with remnants of desire.

He'd kissed off all that satiny peach lipstick, and her dress was rumpled, giving testimony to exactly what they'd been doing. Yes, he was embarrassed that they'd been discovered here, but in a way he was proud that he was the guy this gorgeous woman had been making out with.

While the gardener stared, Keely picked up her purse and the bag containing her drugstore purchases as calmly as if she were leaving a restaurant after a meal and the gardener was the busboy waiting to clear the table.

Noah thought of the boxes of condoms inside that bag and wondered what would have happened if the gardener hadn't come along. Noah suspected that if he'd been willing to make love to Keely's breasts, chances were he might have been coaxed to make love to the rest of her. The thought of the gardener coming upon them later and catching something even more involved made him break out in a cold sweat.

Swinging her purse strap over her shoulder, Keely flashed a winning smile at the gardener. *"Qué pasa, Jose?"*

For one startled moment Noah thought she might know the gardener, but then he glanced at the man's breast pocket and noticed the name embroidered on it.

Jose's shock and disapproval seemed to melt in the glow of Keely's smile. Slowly he grinned back and gave a little shrug. *"Nada, señorita."*

She winked at him. *"Bien. Adiós."* Then she picked her way carefully around the edge of the rock and headed for the sidewalk.

As Noah followed, he heard the gardener sigh with longing. Keely had made another conquest.

She was waiting for him at the edge of the sidewalk, and naturally she'd attracted a number of glances, both of the curious and of the lecherous kind. The way the damp dress clung to her was close to indecent and the moisture had turned her wavy hair into a mass of ringlets. She looked delicious.

When he stepped out from behind the foliage, several

people stared openly. He tried to act as if prowling around in the hotel landscaping was a perfectly normal thing to do.

"Dr. Livingston, I presume?" she said with a grin.

He figured he had to get things straightened out right away. "Keely, don't get the wrong idea. What happened back there was—"

"All my fault," she said. "I know. I was a bad girl." She didn't look particularly sorry about that.

Bad girl. Damn, but that phrase made his blood race. But he had to control those impulses from now on, or he might as well forget about his plan to rehabilitate her. "No, it wasn't all your fault. After all, I'm the one who dragged you back there in the first place. From now on, I don't intend on anything like that happening again. I just want you to know that." He looked into her eyes so he wouldn't be tempted to notice how the dress molded to her figure. Fortunately, sunlight filtered down to the sidewalk and the material was beginning to dry already.

"All right." She looked far from convinced.

"I mean it, Keely. No fooling around. We're going to get your résumé in shape."

"And I really appreciate that." She gave him a saucy look. "I'm just worried that my résumé's not very well suited to what you have in mind. But if you're willing to massage it a little, maybe there's hope. I'm looking forward to your input."

Heat flooded through him. "Stop that."

"Stop what?" She widened her eyes in innocence.

"You know perfectly well. Your choice of words. Like *massage* and *input*. You're trying to make me think about—" He realized the more he talked, the more aroused he was getting. "Never mind. Let's go in."

"Yes. Let's."

Noah clenched his jaw and started toward the entrance. He would do this. The object was to set Keely on the right path, while being careful not to amble down the wrong one himself. They were only talking about three days. Surely he could manage to keep his pants zipped for three days.

THREE DAYS IN A PLACE like this would give her plenty of time and opportunity to corrupt Noah, Keely thought as they walked through the glittering lobby toward the reservation desk. She didn't need to win the war in the first two hours. She should probably cool it.

All things considered, she shouldn't have allowed matters to proceed so quickly in the underbrush. A kiss would have been plenty for this stage of the game. A kiss would have been quite enough of a sampling, thank you very much. But no, she'd gone completely out of her mind.

Apparently all those years of wanting Noah had created a powerful backlog of needs. If dear Jose hadn't shown up she would have given away the farm right on the spot, behind a boulder in the front landscaping of the Tahitian. And despite what Noah thought of her shady past, that sort of stunt would be a first for her.

She wouldn't call it a bad idea, though. In fact, it was a pretty good idea. Extremely creative. But the timing was all wrong. Moving that fast, that soon, would have scared Noah to death, once he'd done the deed and come to his senses. She'd nearly blown her opportunity by overreacting. If she wasn't more careful, he might reconsider his weekend plan to save her.

And she so didn't want him to reconsider. After that kiss, if she were a pinball machine she'd be on tilt. The heavenly way his mouth had felt on hers had naturally made her think of how perfect his mouth would feel on her breasts. And she'd charged straight for that goal without thinking of the consequences, forgetting that she might be sacrificing a long-term gain for a short-term thrill.

Yet he was walking toward the reservation desk as if he still had every intention of asking for another key. Maybe after that last demonstration he was even more convinced that he had to save her. Maybe letting her impulses get the best of her hadn't been such a mistake, after all. Now he really believed she was bad, through and through. Eventually, he wouldn't be able to resist being bad with her.

Feeling better about the future of the weekend, she decided to cut him some slack. "Why don't I wait over by the potted palm?" she said. "That way you don't have to feel so uncomfortable about asking for the extra key because I won't be standing right beside you looking like your babe-for-the-night."

He glanced at her, a gleam in his eyes. Then he looked away, and when his gaze found hers again, the gleam was gone. "That's okay. After the incident with Jose, this will be a piece of cake."

"Really?" Now, this was an interesting development. She had the urge to dampen her finger and chalk up a point on an invisible scoreboard. In a very short time, she'd raised Noah's sexual daring a sizable notch. That was something to be proud of. At this rate, no telling what sort of adventures he might be willing to undertake by Sunday night. And though he'd tried to disguise it, she'd seen that gleam of desire when she'd mentioned being his babe-for-the-night.

Noah walked up to the desk, gave his name and asked for an extra key "for the lady."

Keely was majorly impressed. He hadn't even tried to pretend she was a relative.

"Certainly, sir." The desk clerk, a wholesome type of guy, didn't even blink as he called up Noah's account on the computer. But whatever he saw on the screen made his eyes widen. "Oh, boy. Good thing you stopped by the desk, Mr. Garfield. There's been a small problem with your room."

"What sort of problem?"

The clerk frowned at the screen. "I need to get the manager out here to talk with you. Excuse me a moment." He picked up a phone and punched in a number. "Mr. Garfield's at the desk. No, I don't think he's been up there yet. Right." He hung up the phone and turned to Noah. "Sorry for the inconvenience, sir. The manager will be right out."

Keely wondered if the delay, whatever was causing it, would make Noah more self-conscious about his request for a spare key. Apparently not, because he turned to her and shrugged.

"Mr. Garfield." A guy only slightly older than the desk clerk arrived and held out his hand over the counter. "I'm Martin Ames. Could we step down to the end of the counter for a moment? I need to inform you of our problem."

"Okay." Noah looked at Keely. "Let's go see what this is all about."

She hesitated. "Are you sure you want me to—"

"Yeah." He smiled and angled his head toward the end of the counter. "Come on."

"All right." *Congratulations, Noah,* she thought as she followed him. From all appearances he was bringing a call girl up to his room, but he didn't seem to care whether the staff assumed that or not. His friends were a different story, of course, but his reluctance there was understandable.

Ames came out from behind the counter and glanced pointedly at Keely before returning his gaze to Noah.

To Noah's credit, he made no effort to explain Keely's presence. "What seems to be the problem?" he asked.

The manager looked uncomfortable. "We're a new hotel, as I'm sure you know, and in the rush to get it open on time, apparently the hiring process wasn't…what I mean to say is, the screening of applicants might not have been quite thorough enough. At least in the housekeeping department."

"And you would be telling me all this because...?"

"One of the housekeepers vandalized your room."

Keely gasped.

"What?" Noah stared at the manager in obvious disbelief.

"It was a case of mistaken identity," Ames said quickly. "The woman's in custody, and we've learned from the police that she's mentally unbalanced. It seems she formed an imaginary attachment to one of our guests, and when her interest wasn't returned, she attempted revenge by damaging his room and its contents. That would be bad enough, but she became confused and hit your room by mistake."

"What about my stuff?" Noah asked.

"I'm afraid it's pretty well ruined. She took a knife to your clothes and suitcase and smashed your toiletries. The police took it for evidence, so I'm not sure how soon you can retrieve it. But from what I saw, there's not much point in getting your things back."

"My God." Noah shook his head.

"We take full responsibility, of course," Ames continued. "If you'll give us an estimate of what you lost we'll write you a check immediately. And of course we've moved you to a new room, and you won't be billed for your stay. If you should choose to move to a different hotel, we'll pay for that."

"No, I won't move. My friend is getting married here tomorrow night."

"Ah." Ames nodded. He seemed to be avoiding looking at Keely. "Then let me take you back to the desk and issue you a new key."

"Two keys," Noah said.

"Oh." The manager slid a glance over toward Keely. "Of course."

Keely could see that the discussion was drawing to a close. She was outraged on Noah's behalf. Her L.A. apartment had been vandalized once, and she knew the sick, violated feeling he was probably dealing with right now. Given the mental anguish, she didn't think a different room and some money to replace his belongings, some of which might be irreplace-able, was enough.

She cleared her throat. "Excuse me, but are you moving Mr. Garfield to another room that's similar to what he had?"

"Exactly like what he had," Ames said with a satisfied smile. "And there will be no charge, of course."

"I think he should be given a substantial upgrade," Keely said.

Ames blinked. "An upgrade?"

"Now, Keely," Noah said, "the same sort of room will be—"

"I don't think so," Keely cut in. "You've been traumatized, whether you're willing to admit that or not. And I'll bet your feelings about this hotel are very negative right now."

Noah gazed at her. "I wouldn't say I'm overjoyed with the place."

"See?" Keely turned to Ames. "I would suggest that you give Mr. Garfield an outstanding experience to take away with him, something that will at least partially cancel out the horrible thing that happened. I'm sure you have some luxury suites in this hotel. I would imagine at least one of them is vacant."

Ames straightened his tie and glanced toward Noah. "How do you feel about that, Mr. Garfield?"

Noah met Keely's gaze.

She lifted her eyebrows in a silent challenge. There was no doubt in her mind that he deserved this perk, but the Noah she remembered probably wouldn't have taken it. He would have scoffed at the idea of "luxury" accommodations, as if a rough-tough cowboy didn't need that kind of pampering. She'd love the chance to show him how wrong he could be.

Gradually a smile touched his lips. "I think the lady's absolutely right," he said. "Give us the best you can manage, Mr. Ames."

NOAH WOULD NEVER HAVE agreed to a fancy hotel room for himself. After all, he only planned to sleep in it, so extras would go to waste, as far as he was concerned. But he was glad to get the nicer room for Keely's sake. God only knew the type of place she'd been living in recently.

Besides, a bigger room meant they'd have more space to spread out. He imagined the suite might have two bathrooms and maybe extra sleeping arrangements. If he wasn't bumping into Keely every five seconds he might stand a better chance of keeping his vow not to make love to her.

Ames gave them a new key folder and directed them to a special elevator.

"I'm so glad you told him you wanted a better room," Keely said as they stepped into the mirrored elevator. Soft guitar music began to play as the brass doors slid shut.

Noah laughed. "I'm sure he didn't want to give it to me. These are the rooms they reserve for the high rollers."

"So what? If they're going to screw up and hire a psycho maid, then they can compensate the poor guy who gets his stuff trashed. I'm really sorry about that, Noah. Did you lose anything special?"

"I've been trying to remember exactly what I brought. I don't think any of it was that important." Noah was having a hard time concentrating on the vandalism incident when more potent subjects stood right in front of him. As he faced Keely in the elevator, the mirrored walls gave him many stimulating viewing options.

On the left and right walls he could admire her figure in profile—the impressive thrust of her breasts, the narrow waist, the long slender legs made even more sexy by the high-heeled sandals. The back wall of the elevator gave him a different perspective. When she shifted her weight, the blue flowered material of her dress quivered against her firm bottom and flounced against her thighs. There was something very enticing about the backs of her knees….

And without warning, he was imagining Keely naked in this elevator, surrounded by mirrors. He could see her lifting her arms over her head, stretching, turning this way and that, while the mirrors reflected every spectacular inch of her. His breathing grew shallow.

"…forget to give him that," Keely said.

"Hmm? What?" Noah felt his face heat as he realized he'd missed half of what she'd just said.

She smiled. "The list of what you had in the room. You need to make that up as soon as possible."

"Oh. Right."

Her green eyes began to sparkle. "Are you enjoying the mirrors?"

Everything he was thinking was apparently written on his face. "I was wondering how they keep them so clean," he fibbed. "You notice there are no smudge marks."

"Now that you mention it, they are very clean." Her eyes danced. "Mirrors can be a lot of fun. Ever made love in front of one?"

"No!" And suddenly that seemed like the only thing he wanted to do.

"Too bad," she said. "Well, there's still time."

Way too much time, he thought. *Especially this weekend.*

5

KEELY'S PULSE RACED with anticipation as she took the key card Noah handed her and slid it into the lock that opened the elevator doors to the hotel's exclusive top floor. Moments later she used the same key for the double doors leading into the suite.

Spending the weekend in a hotel room with Noah had seemed promising from the beginning. Now that they'd be surrounded by luxury, she was beyond excited. No doubt about it, she was her mother's daughter when it came to enjoying the finer things of life.

"I hear water running," Noah said. "I hope nobody left it on and overflowed the sink or something."

"Now that the psycho maid is in custody, I doubt it." She stepped inside the spacious entry and sighed in appreciation. A waterfall in the entry was a very good sign indeed. This one cascaded down a wall of lava rock into a shallow pool rimmed with lacy ferns. Colorful seashells lined the bottom of the pool. "There's your running water."

"I'll be damned."

"Or there's some of your water, at any rate. I think there's more." The gurgle of another water feature drifted through the arched doorway ahead. "Let's go see what else they've dreamed up."

Walking into the living area of the suite, she drew in a breath. Whoever had created this setting understood how fantasy worked. She would love describing this place to her girlfriends. They'd be green.

Automatically her journalistic training kicked in as she recorded details to take home. First of all, the walls resembled a rocky cliff face. Three separate waterfalls spilled down the rocks to gather in an actual, honest-to-goodness indoor stream that circled the room and flowed through an opening out onto a terrace. There it sluiced into a hot tub surrounded by rattan lounges and cocktail tables. She was speechless.

Inside, the designers had abandoned the idea of traditional furniture. A network of vines and splashes of red and pink flowers gave the impression of a jungle clearing. But this was a clearing with amenities. Velvet cushions in several sizes and shades of green lay in profusion on the smooth rock floor. Sand-colored concrete ledges mounded with more pillows created a raised seating area overlooking the stream. Pieces of driftwood topped with slabs of stone embedded with seashells served as end tables.

In order to get to the bedroom, she'd have to cross the stream on a bamboo footbridge. The concept was so cool that she hugged herself with delight. The bedroom would probably be awesome, too.

She walked over the tiny bridge and through another arched doorway into a haven of sheer white fabrics and romance. A white urn held waxy red anthuriums, but otherwise the room was so virginal-looking it slipped over the line to decadence. The huge canopied bed was draped with gauzy fabric and deep in pillows. Two overstuffed lounges, both slipcovered in white, sat in front of the floor-to-ceiling windows that repeated the view from the living area.

The simple elegance of the setting was a perfect contrast

to the lusty mating of bodies she had planned. Seduction was going to be so sweet in this room.

Through another arch she glimpsed a large bathroom that gleamed with white marble and gold fixtures. Oh, yes. Noah was so dead.

But where was he, anyway? Maybe he was standing transfixed in the middle of the living area, unable to believe his eyes. Crossing over the bridge again, she found the room empty. Apparently he'd bogged down in the hall for some reason.

"Noah?" she called. "What are you doing?"

"Trying to figure out how this wall-of-water thing works," he called back. "Do you think we have to turn it off at night? I've been looking for a switch, but I can't seem to find—"

"I don't think you have to worry about how to turn it off." She swallowed her laughter as she headed back toward the entry. He sounded so adorably earnest. Staying in a place like this with a man who'd never experienced luxuries would be a real kick. But she'd do well to remember how different their preferences were when it came to living arrangements.

Sure enough, he wore a frown of concentration as he surveyed the entryway walls, looking for the on/off switch. "All this water running with no way to control it makes me nervous," he said.

"That's because you live in the desert." She also thought anything unrestrained at the moment, water or lust, would get to him. "I'm sure they don't want us fiddling with their waterfall," she said. "And this is only the beginning, anyway. If running water makes you nervous, wait until you see the rest. Come on."

"Well, okay." He walked toward the arched doorway. "But I'd still feel better if I knew how to control the—" His eyes widened at his first glimpse of the suite's interior. "Oh…my… God."

She stood there with a silly grin as his startled gaze traveled from the waterfalls to the miniature creek to the glass wall looking out on the terrace with its exotic hot tub. Beyond the terrace lay the jeweled fantasy hotels along the Strip and the powerful thrust of the mountain range flanking the town. By day the view was impressive. By night it would beggar description.

And they were here because she'd spoken up. She was quite proud of herself. "A wee bit better than looking at the parking lot, wouldn't you say?"

He was obviously dumbstruck as he surveyed the room again, his attention lingering on the array of pillows and the footbridge leading into the bedroom.

She loved looking at him standing there, an Arizona cowpoke so delightfully out of place in the lush tropical setting. But get him out of those clothes and he'd fit in much better, at least for the weekend. Under those worn jeans and that faded chambray shirt was a body to die for, and soon it would be all hers to command. This unbelievable hotel suite would clinch her victory. A cowboy in paradise. What more could a girl ask for?

"I take it the bedroom's in there," he said.

Oh, yes. "Yes. It's a different style from this room, but it's still wonderful. And there's also an incredible bathroom, from what I could see. I didn't go all the way into the bedroom."

"And is that…all?"

She laughed in disbelief. "That isn't enough?"

"Don't get me wrong. I've never seen a place like this. It blows me away. But somehow I thought there would be more…space."

"The rooms are huge."

"I mean, more rooms."

"Ah." Now she understood. The more rooms, the less temptation. Oh, gee, too bad. "Sorry, but we seem to have an entry, a living room, a bedroom and a bathroom. And closets. Oh, and a terrace."

He looked out to the terrace. She could imagine the wheels turning as he tried to decide if he could sleep there, which was as far from the bedroom as he could hope to get and still be in the suite. She hated to tell him, but it wouldn't be far enough.

Finally he looked at her. "Do you like it?"

"Are you kidding?" She held out her hands and spun around on the smooth stone floor. "I *love* it!"

He smiled, although he still seemed a little on the nervous side. "Well, good. That's good."

"Don't you?"

"I…" He took off his hat and tapped it against his thigh. Then he ran his hand through his hair, combing it back from his forehead. "I don't know. It's so different. No couch, no chairs, no coffee table, no lamps. And where's the TV?"

If she had anything to say about it they wouldn't be watching any television this weekend, but he looked so uneasy she decided to find a TV for him. If imagining he'd be catching a ball game on the tube would ease his anxiety, then she was all in favor of locating the television set.

"I'll bet there's a TV somewhere." She figured the set was hidden, but a remote of some sort had to exist. Strolling into the room, she glanced around and finally found a remote-control unit lying on a rock ledge. "Here we are. 'Entertainment Center,'" she read from the list on the cover of the remote. When she pushed a button, precision motors whirred as a portion of one wall opened to reveal a giant screen.

Noah shook his head. "Amazing."

"Want me to turn it on?" She found the power button.

"No, that's okay."

"Let's make sure it works." Punching the button, she brought up a menu screen. Aha. Adult videos on Channel 14.

That might be worth checking out. She didn't want Noah to get *too* comfortable.

She pushed the numbers one and four on the numeric keypad. An incredible sound system filled the room with seductive music. *Naughty! Sassy! No Holds Barred!* flashed on the screen.

"Keely, don't—"

"I'm just testing the system."

"Come on, turn it off." He advanced toward her.

"In a second." As the preview began, she held the remote behind her back.

"Give it here." He reached around her.

"Not yet." She danced away from him.

"Now, you know we don't need to see this." He grabbed for the remote again.

She twirled out of reach. "Just the preview, okay?" She managed to sneak a peek at the screen. Wow. The people were so big. It seemed to make them more naked, somehow. She didn't think she'd ever seen a skin flick on a big-screen TV. And the music was awesome. Must be some primo speakers disguised in the rock walls.

He sounded a little desperate. "Look, I'm not going to wrestle you for it."

"Too bad. That could be fun." She noticed he kept looking at the screen, too, and his attempts to get the remote away from her had become halfhearted.

"Just turn off the video, okay?" he pleaded.

"Right after this part." When the woman dropped to her knees and unzipped the man's pants in obvious preparation for oral sex, the camera zoomed in. The man's penis nearly filled the screen. "Oh, now, see that? I'll bet you dollars-to-doughnuts a man directed this video. You can tell, because a male director always concentrates on fellatio, while a woman—"

"Keely, for God's sake!"

"It's true! If you've watched enough of these you'd have to pick up on it!"

"Well, I haven't, okay? Saguaro Junction doesn't exactly specialize in adult-video arcades!"

"Then you should be delighted to have this chance to see some," she said sweetly. "Whoops, is that a phone ringing somewhere?"

"It sure as hell is, and I'll bet it's Brandon. God, I was supposed to meet him at—" He checked his watch. "Ten minutes ago. A fitting for the tux." He scanned the area frantically. "Do you see anything in this jungle that resembles a phone, or should I go answer that trumpet-flower thing? That's where the ringing's coming from."

"I'm sure that's a flower." She moved the petals aside and saw nothing but lava rocks behind it.

"This is ridiculous. We can't even answer the—"

"Oh!" With sudden inspiration, she looked at the remote in her hand. "Here's a button marked Fax/phone. Let's see what happens if I push it."

His eyes widened in panic. "Don't! It might be a video phone or something."

"Okay, then take it." She thrust the remote at him. "You push those little buttons and I'll leave the room."

"And go where?" he asked, sounding even more agitated.

"To the bedroom." She winked at him. "Maybe I'll slip into something more comfortable."

"But you don't have any other clothes!" He sounded very worried.

She glanced over her shoulder. "I know." Then she crossed the footbridge with her best eye-catching walk. Poor Noah. When she decided to make her move, he wouldn't know what hit him.

With trembling hands Noah turned off the power to the big-screen TV, finally erasing the erotic images that had nearly driven him to do something he'd regret. Glancing uneasily toward the bedroom, afraid of what Keely might be up to in there, he pushed the button for the phone. Once again motors whirred as the rock wall parted and a shelf slid out, presenting him with a fax machine and a cordless phone.

Setting the remote on the shelf, Noah picked up the cordless and turned it on. "Hello?"

"Noah!" Brandon sounded relieved.

"Listen, I'm sorry I'm not down there like I'm supposed to be. There's been—"

"I heard about that. I dialed your room and couldn't get you, so the guys and I decided to go up there, because it's not like you to be late. That's when we found yellow crime-scene tape everywhere. Man, we went on a rampage, finally got ahold of the manager, Ames, and he told us what happened. I rescheduled the fittings for thirty minutes from now. Can you make that okay?"

"Sure. I could come down now if you want."

"They have another wedding party in the rental shop right now, but we can go have a beer if you want to. Or we could all come up there and see your new room. Is it pretty cool?"

"It's okay." Noah didn't want to describe it because his friends would be up in a heartbeat to check it out. "The usual."

"It must at least have a hot tub or something, right?"

"Well, yeah, it does." Noah picked up the remote to find out what else it controlled besides the TV and the fax/phone cabinet.

"Where? In the bedroom? Our honeymoon suite has a hot tub in the bedroom."

"Uh, it's on the terrace."

"The *terrace?* Damn it, son, we don't even *have* a terrace, let alone one big enough for a hot tub. What's your view like?"

"Um, you know—town, the mountains, stuff."

"I gotta see this. What's your number?"

"Well, I don't know if you can just come up. There's a special elevator." In his agitation Noah's thumb clamped down on one of the buttons on the remote. Another rock panel slid back to reveal a completely stocked wet bar backed by mirrored glass.

"A special elevator?" Brandon cried. "Shitfire, you're on the high-roller floor, aren't you? We are so coming up!"

Noah tried to close the panel over the wet bar and brushed against another button that activated the lighting system. "Listen, why don't I meet you in that bar that has all the tropical birds in it?" he said quickly as the colors bathing the room changed from cool blues and greens to purples, and finally to a very sexy red.

"You don't like tropical birds in your bars," Brandon said. "You told me that already."

"I think we should do it anyway, for the experience." The lights pulsed and glowed as they continued through their cycle. Orgy lights was all Noah could think as he watched them. "We'll get an umbrella drink," he said to Brandon. "I've been hankering for an umbrella drink."

"You have not." Brandon paused, letting the silence stretch between them. "Why don't you want us to see the room, bro?"

"You're right, you should see it," Noah said immediately. He couldn't risk hurting his friends' feelings. "You need to come up and see this room. Matter of fact, maybe we should switch rooms, you and me. After all, you're the bridegroom."

"You were afraid I'd be jealous because your room's cooler than mine, weren't you?"

"Well…" It was as good an excuse as any.

"Don't worry about it. And I appreciate the offer to switch, but I don't want to do that. Jenny told me she loves the idea of a hot tub in the bedroom, so we can go in it naked and fool around. I already have that picture in my mind and I'm really looking forward to it."

"I'll bet." And thanks to Brandon, Noah had a picture in his mind of fooling around with Keely in the hot tub.

"The thing is, I don't think she'd feel the same way about a hot tub on a terrace. She's kinda timid about things like that, getting naked outside and all."

Keely wasn't the least bit timid, Noah thought. She'd be willing to make love on that balcony. Now, if only he could forget that for the next three days, he'd be all set. But he didn't suppose he would, short of getting amnesia.

"Besides," Brandon said, "you earned this room, with all you went through. Are you gonna buy new clothes here, or do you want to borrow some things from us? I'm close to your size, and so's Clint."

"I hate shopping for clothes."

"Then just take the money and wait until you get home. We'll bring some things up when we come. Now, how do we get there?"

"I'm not sure. You can ride the elevator, but then you need a room key to get the door to open. I—oh, wait a minute. Maybe I do know how to do this." He glanced down at the remote and found a button marked Elevator. "Take the executive elevator. When you get to the top, I can open the doors from here. Go on into the hall, and it's the first set of double doors to your left."

"This is unbelievable. You're probably in the same damn room Garth Brooks stayed in when he played the Tahitian last month."

"I don't know about that." But Noah had no trouble imagining celebrities in this room. No trouble at all. And he wondered where a celebrity would stash his secret sweetie, if he had one.

"Okay, we'll be up there in a few minutes, after we grab some clothes for you."

"Great. Bye." Noah hung up the phone and headed quickly toward the bedroom. "Keely? Keely, the guys are coming up here. We need to figure out what to do."

She wasn't in the bedroom, but her dress and underwear were. She'd tossed them across the end of the white bed like pale blue warning flags.

He screeched to a stop. "Keely?"

"In here. I felt like taking a bath."

"Oh." He looked warily toward the bathroom. A heavenly scent drifted toward him, and he heard the sound of soft splashing, although he couldn't see what was going on, thank goodness. But he could imagine her lolling around in a bubble bath, with foam only partially concealing her golden skin, and her breasts bobbing on the surface of the water. Maybe imagination was more seductive than actually seeing her in the tub, but he wasn't going to take the chance on looking at the real thing.

"So your friends are coming up to the suite?"

"Yeah." He tried not to sound as panicked as he felt. "In just a few minutes."

"No problem." She splashed around some more and water gurgled, as if going down the drain. "I'll hide in the closet."

"Naked?" He didn't know why it mattered, but the thought of her hiding naked in the closet was ten times more anxiety-producing than if she put on clothes first.

She laughed and appeared in the doorway wearing a large white towel, her hair caught up in a loose topknot. "Naked in the closet. Now, that creates a real mental picture, doesn't it?"

He gulped. She'd wrapped the towel around her and tucked the end between her breasts. One flick of a wrist, either his or hers, and it would fall at her feet.

"There are two robes in that closet," she said. "I checked."

"I'll get one for you!" He nearly tripped in his eagerness to get to the closet. Of course the sliding door was mirrored, and the bed was perfectly reflected in it. Of course.

He pulled the terry-cloth robe from its hanger, rattling all the hangers on the rod in his haste to get her covered up. Then he turned.

"Thank you," she said, and let the towel drop.

Sweet Lord in heaven. He clutched the bathrobe and tried to remember how to breathe. No wonder people had been willing to pay for a glimpse of such beauty. Women with a body like hers had toppled empires, so maybe he'd be forgiven if he couldn't stop looking at her.

The fantasy atmosphere in the room must be getting to him. As he gazed at her, he started zoning out on weird thoughts of Keely making love to the sun, allowing it to kiss her skin until her body was golden and dusted with freckles. He thought of her lying under the sun being licked by tongues of flame until she was wet and eager.

She would be easy to arouse. He knew that from her response earlier this afternoon, and from the rapid, shallow way she was breathing now. Her nipples darkened and puckered, inviting him to linger in appreciation of her full breasts. Not long ago he'd touched, but he hadn't tasted.

Now he could. Now he could kneel before her and kiss the soft skin of her belly. He could explore lower, parting her auburn curls with his tongue until he reached…heaven. And then he could hear her cry of release, a sound he'd only imagined in his dreams. Then he would seek his own release from the hard, grinding pressure building relentlessly within him.

"The robe?" she asked softly.

He glanced at the robe, then back at her. If he didn't activate the elevator doors, his friends wouldn't be able to get onto this floor. He and Keely could be totally, completely alone for as long as they wanted to be, for as long as it took for him to satisfy this unbearable craving. His mouth grew moist as the possibilities beckoned to him.

"Now's not the time," Keely said, her voice gentle.

His voice rasped in his throat. "Why not?"

"You need to get fitted for your tux in a few minutes. I was only giving you a sneak preview." She reached over and took the robe from him. "We have all weekend, Noah."

While he watched, his body trembling with the urge to have her, she slid her arms into the sleeves of the bathrobe. The motion jiggled her breasts and he groaned. The robe gaped open a moment as she adjusted the collar, and her hourglass figure was perfectly framed by the white terry lapels. That view was even more erotic than when she'd worn nothing at all.

Then she overlapped the lapels and tied the belt, eliminating his view. But like a bolt of lightning, the image of her perfect body was burned into his retina.

6

AFTER NOAH LEFT THE room looking shell-shocked, Keely gathered up her clothes, purse and the drugstore bag before stepping into the closet. Sitting on the floor, she slid the door shut, leaned against the wall and closed her eyes. A smile tugged at her mouth. What a great moment that had been.

She hadn't planned to drop the towel, but it had started to slip as he'd turned to grab a robe from the closet. Rather than fumbling with her towel like a self-conscious virgin, she'd let it go.

Impulse had turned out to be more effective than inspiration. Although she wasn't about to let him ignore his wedding duties, she wouldn't mind having him think about her in the process. He would certainly think about her now.

Taking a bath had also been an impulse, but once she'd seen that huge tub, she'd looked at her somewhat grimy knees and decided to indulge in a quick soak while Noah dealt with his phone call. Yes, all in all her impulses were leading her in the right direction.

Rummaging through the drugstore bag, she took out her raspberry lotion, released the plunger and filled her palm with some creamy lotion. No reason to waste the time she was trapped in here.

Excited male voices filtered into her little hideaway. Noah's friends had arrived and were obviously impressed with the setup. She listened to them rave while she smoothed lotion over her legs. God, she loved this scent, and it seemed to be amplified by her confined quarters.

"We should have the bachelor party here, guys!" one of Noah's friends said. "I feel an orgy coming on."

"You always feel an orgy coming on," said another. "But it won't work, Clint, old buddy."

"Why not? It's perfect. It's decadent. It's—"

"And what about the entertainment, Einstein?"

Keely figured their idea of "entertainment" involved women wearing next to nothing and dancing around wildy for their benefit. She pumped another helping of lotion into her cupped hand.

"We could import the entertainment, couldn't we?" said the guy who was apparently named Clint. "This is Vegas! Girls, girls, girls!"

Then the conversation became a jumble of suggestions and countersuggestions. Keely pulled a foot into her lap and rubbed lotion into her sole and between her toes. She loved wearing sandals in the summer, but she had to keep massaging lotion into her feet every day to keep them smooth, plus she indulged in regular pedicures. She could just imagine what her ranch-foreman father would think of that extravagance.

While she applied lotion, she tried to guess how many men were out there besides Noah. She finally identified three. One was Brandon, the groom. Then there was Clint, who seemed to be the idea man, and a third person named Greg, who sounded like the joker of the group.

"I don't care if you want to use the place," Noah said at last, "but personally, I think it'll be a lot of extra trouble to bring in the entertainment."

Keely wondered what he'd do if she popped out of the

closet and offered to take care of that for the boys. Have a heart attack, most likely. It was a fun concept, though. Noah was such a sitting duck for stunts like that. She'd have to be careful not to overdo it just because it was so easy to shock the pants off of him—literally. She rubbed lotion on her other foot.

"Noah's right," said Brandon from the living room. He seemed to be the organizer. "Maybe we can just come back here to hang out afterward and drink ourselves silly."

Now, that could put a real crimp in her plans. She wondered if Noah would come up with something to kill that idea. After all, she had just given him a dramatic glimpse of what he could look forward to once they were alone tonight.

"That would be okay, I guess," Noah said.

Keely grimaced. He must be having another attack of conscience and wanted some built-in safeguards to keep him from acting on his urges. Corrupting Noah wasn't going to be quite as easy as she'd first thought.

She untied the robe and slipped her arms out of the sleeves so she could put lotion on her upper body. As she smoothed it over her breasts she thought of Noah's calloused hands caressing her. She was looking forward to a repeat of that experience.

"Then let's plan on coming back here," Brandon said. "We'll start the evening at that topless bar we picked out and then head back to the hotel. Oh, and these are the clothes Clint and I came up with for you, Noah. Two pairs of jeans and three shirts."

"You're sure you guys don't need them?" Noah asked.

Keely cupped her breasts and closed her eyes. She wanted to hear that voice of his murmuring in her ear. Soon. She'd figure out how to get rid of his friends tonight.

"I always pack too many clothes," Clint said. "Besides,

Sharon and me are gonna be enjoying that saltwater beach. I bought some bathing trunks, and—"

"Trunks, my ass!" Greg chortled. "You bought yourself a Speedo, boy. You are into the Vegas lifestyle, big time!"

Clint laughed. "Why not? Hell, I can wear those cowboy duds anytime. This weekend I'm gonna be a beach bum."

Keely wouldn't mind seeing Noah in a bathing suit, come to think of it. She might have to include a shopping trip in her evening plans.

"And you make a great beach bum, old buddy," Brandon said. "Listen, we need to get down to the tux-rental place."

"I have to hand it to you, Brandon, for staging this shindig in a Vegas hotel," Clint said. "Tux rental, bridal shop, florist, chapel and reception hall, everything together in one building. When Sharon and I got married we ran all over the damn place."

"I remember," Brandon said. "I ran all over the damn place with you, and Greg and Tina's wedding was no better."

"Tell me about it," Greg said.

"Okay, guys. We gotta boogie," Brandon said again, sounding a little more impatient.

"Can't we see the bedroom and bathroom first?" Greg asked.

"If we make it quick." Brandon said. Footsteps sounded over the bamboo footbridge. "I'd love to know what this room goes for per night."

The closet was getting a little warm, Keely thought. Or maybe she was heating up the space with her lusty thoughts about Noah in a bathing suit.

"They don't charge for these kinds of rooms," Greg said, the sound of his voice coming closer. "The guys who stay here are the ones who fly in by private jet and drop thousands at the tables. Something you clowns can only dream about."

"Excuse me?" Clint said. "I did pretty good in the casino last night."

"Oh, you were awesome," Greg said. "That bucket of nickels sure impressed Tina and me. Any minute now they'll roll out the red carpet for a big spender like you."

"At least I had a bucket of nickels, while a certain cowboy I could mention had a whole lot of nothing in his bucket," Clint said.

Keely decided against putting the robe back on for fear she'd start sweating. She leaned her bare back against the wall, which was smooth and cool. Ah, that was better.

"Wow, will you look at this bedroom?" Brandon said. "It even smells good in here. Like raspberries."

She smothered a giggle.

"And the crime of it all is that Noah is staying solo in this layout," Greg said. "Hey, Noah, maybe you should look around tonight and see if there's anybody worth bringing back for the weekend."

Sitting up straighter, she listened for his response.

"I don't think so," Noah said.

She relaxed back against the wall.

"What do you mean, *you don't think so?*" Clint said. "This is Vegas, cowboy. Vegas girls. You're the only one of us who's free to sample. We were counting on you to perform for the group so we can get some secondhand thrills."

"I guess you'll have to get your thrills someplace else," Noah said. "I'm not in the mood."

Liar, liar, pants on fire, Keely chanted softly to herself.

"How can you not be in the mood?" Greg said. "This place cries out for a hot interlude with a temporary babe."

"Yeah," Clint added, "and you didn't exactly avoid that kind of experience when you were on the rodeo circuit."

Keely blinked. Noah had hot interludes on the rodeo circuit? That didn't fit her picture of him at all. Although the idea of him getting it on with another woman made her pea-green with jealousy, she was dying to know the details.

"Yeah, I remember a certain lady in Cheyenne," Brandon said. "You two were holed up in that motel room for forty-eight hours at least. And there was that little gal in San Antone, the barrel racer. And then at the Pendleton Roundup, you—"

"Never mind," Noah said, sounding very tense. "No point in dredging up ancient history."

"Well, damn." Greg sighed. "Obviously our buddy Noah is over the hill."

"I am not! I just—"

"The facts speak for themselves," Greg continued. "We need a moment of silence, boys, for the late, great Noah Garfield. The guy's in Vegas and he can't get it up."

"Maybe he's not dead yet," Brandon said. "Maybe staying in this passion pit will inspire him to regain his former glory."

"God, you would think so, wouldn't you?" Greg agreed. "Look at that bed. It's criminal to sleep alone in that bed. And right across from that great bed, you've got mirrors on the closet doors." He sighed again. "I had mirror sex once. It was great."

"You had sex with a mirror? Are we talking self-gratification for the Gregster?" Clint asked, laughing.

"*No,* I had sex with a woman in front of a mirror, lame-brain. And no, it wasn't with Tina, so I'd appreciate keeping this discussion between us."

"Always is," Brandon said. "Listen, y'all take your bathroom tour and then we're outta here. Time's getting short."

"Wow." Clint's voice echoed slightly in the tiled bathroom. "That tub's big enough for six *Playboy* bunnies. And look at this! Suds in the tub! Noah, did you just take a bubble bath?"

Keely clapped a hand over her mouth. She'd forgotten that somebody might notice that.

"A bubble bath?" Greg said. "Noah Garfield? This I gotta see. Oh my God. Looks like somebody took a bubble bath. Come to think of it, there was a towel on the bedroom floor. So the evidence mounts that a bubble bath was indeed taken. And the occupants of this suite are Noah Garfield, and…well, *nobody,* so the incriminating finger points to you, old buddy."

"Gotta be Noah," Brandon said, laughing. "No wonder you didn't want us up here, bro. Did you hide your rubber ducky? I don't see it anywhere."

The laughter grew louder and the comments more crude.

Finally Noah's voice rose above the hubbub. "You morons should try a good soak in the tub once in a while," he said. "Clears the mind."

"It wrinkles your privates, is what it does!" Greg said. "Maybe that's your problem, son. Too many bubble baths. Only good time to take a bath is when you have somebody in there with you. I can't see the advantage in sitting there by yourself. Well, unless you're into that." More laughter followed.

"This has been most edifying," Brandon said, "but we really have to leave. Want me to put these clothes in your closet, bro?"

Keely froze. Then she fumbled around frantically as she tried to put her arms in the sleeves of her robe without making any noise. She couldn't seem to find the armholes.

"You can just leave them on the bed," Noah said quickly.

Keely tried harder, but the robe was hopelessly twisted.

"The shirts are on hangers," Brandon said. "I might as well—"

"Okay, then I'll do it," Noah said.

Keely sagged against the closet wall with relief.

"Sheesh. You always were a bossy son of a gun," Brandon said. "Here."

"Thanks. I appreciate the loan of the clothes."

Keely held herself very still as the closet door slid partly open. She found herself staring up at Noah's crotch as he blocked the opening with his body. She had the biggest urge to whisper *peek a boo* and give him a little tickle on the zipper of his fly, but she controlled herself.

His gaze flicked down to where she sat, and she waggled her fingers at him. His quick gasp told her he'd noticed that she'd slipped out of the robe. No doubt he thought she'd done it on purpose to torment him, but this time she was innocent. Well, sort of innocent.

Abruptly he hooked the hangers over the rod and shoved the door closed so hard she was afraid he'd crack the mirror.

"Boy, that raspberry smell sure is strong," Clint said. "They must have hung one of those sachet doo-dads in the closet."

"Must have," Noah said. "Come on, let's go."

She waited until there was nothing but silence outside the closet door before she shoved it open and crawled out, leaving the bathrobe in a heap on the closet floor. Grinning, she stood and stretched, all the while wondering what Noah was thinking about right now. Naked women in closets, most likely. The cool air felt great on her skin, and she decided that this suite was made for walking around naked. She crossed the footbridge into the living room.

So Noah had been a wild man out on the rodeo circuit. That made her mission to corrupt him even more important. He'd moved home to the ranch, shouldered all those responsibilities and lost his spark. It was encouraging to know that he used to have a spark. And she was just the girl to rekindle it.

This hotel suite was the very place to light such a fire, she thought as she surveyed the cushions spread everywhere. But she needed some more ammunition. Originally she'd planned a quick trip to her hotel to get the rest of her clothes, but they weren't naughty enough for what she had in mind. This hotel would undoubtedly have a couple of shops that would be perfect for the occasion, and she could pick up Noah's bathing suit at the same time. But first she had to find out if Noah had thought to leave her a key.

They hadn't had time to discuss where he'd put the extra one. Considering his condition after she'd dropped her towel, he wouldn't have been able to focus on such matters, anyway. But she hoped he'd thought of it before he left.

Ten minutes later, she stood gazing out the sliding doors to the terrace and fanning herself absently with the empty key folder. The key wasn't anywhere. He'd probably taken both keys without thinking about it. Or maybe he had thought about it and didn't want her venturing out yet. Either way, she didn't intend to let the lack of a key stop her. She'd simply have to go find him.

Until she went shopping she'd have to make do with the dress she had, but she longed for fresh underwear after that nice bath. Finally she decided to rinse out her panties and dry them with the hair dryer. She could skip the bra. After all, she was in Vegas, as Noah's friends had pointed out more than once.

She touched up her makeup with supplies she kept in her purse, put on her slightly damp panties and pulled her dress over her head. Then she released her hair from its topknot and finger-combed it into place. Time to go find the Romeo of the Rodeo Circuit.

SHE'D ENDED UP NAKED in the closet, after all, Noah thought as he stood in the tux-rental shop and buttoned the vest he'd be wearing as a groomsman. Now all he could think about was how she'd looked. He should have guessed she'd be in there putting on her raspberry lotion.

When he'd opened the closet door he'd been hit with a double whammy, a naked Keely and the overwhelming scent of raspberries. How he'd managed to close the door and walk out of the bedroom as if he were a sane person, he'd never know. He could still see her there in the dusky interior of that closet, smiling at him and wiggling her fingers in greeting.

She was a devil woman. And she wanted to tempt him the way she'd tempted others before him, but it wasn't going to work, damn it. Somewhere he'd find the strength to resist and demonstrate to her that at least one man valued her for something besides sex. He would show her there was another path she could take and that her spectacular body didn't have to dictate her future.

But he'd have to be careful. He'd nearly cracked when she'd dropped that towel. If he were completely honest with himself, she'd been the one to call a halt, not him. If she'd given him even the slightest encouragement, he would have aborted his plan and been all over her. He knew it and he suspected she knew it, too.

That damn raspberry lotion wasn't helping, either. He couldn't very well tell her not to use it if that's what she liked. And he wouldn't want to be responsible for the dry air damaging that soft skin. That satiny, golden, sweetly freckled...

"Yo, Garfield!" Brandon clapped him on the back. "Just two more buttons and you'll have that vest together. Work with me, man. Button, buttonhole. That's it. I think you've got it now."

Noah's neck grew warm with embarrassment. No telling how long he'd been standing there staring off into space. "Can't a guy take a moment?" he said. "These weddings are big medicine. I've got some deep thinking to do."

Brandon laughed. "That sounds like my line. Anyway, you'll have plenty of thinking time later, when we all have a beer in our hands. Right now we have to find out if your monkey suit fits. Here's the coat."

Noah stuck his arms in the coat Brandon held for him. "Why does everybody always get rigged up like this for weddings?" he asked.

"Because it gets the women hot," Greg said as he adjusted the lapels of his coat. "Right, Brandon?"

"So I've heard."

"It's true." Clint checked out his reflection in the three-way mirror. "Chicks can't resist a guy in tie and tails."

"If you say so. You all could pass for city slickers, if that's what you're after." Noah grinned as he watched his three friends walk around in their rented finery. Looking at them now, nobody would guess that Clint and Brandon were two of the finest bareback riders in the country and that Greg could rope and tie a steer faster than almost anyone on the circuit.

Clint and Brandon were as close as brothers, but they'd never pass for biological brothers. Clint was tall and blond and Brandon was short and dark-haired. Greg, a freckle-faced red-head, had developed a slight beer belly now that he'd reached his thirties, but he was strong as an ox.

"I think I look like a high roller," Greg said, sucking in his stomach. "Maybe this getup will convince somebody to give me a suite on your floor, Noah."

"This from a guy who bombed out on nickel slots," Clint said.

Immediately Greg wanted to debate the possibility of a system for playing slots. Noah tried to concentrate on the conversation, but Greg's mention of the suite had derailed him. Once again all he could think about was Keely.

He could even smell raspberries. Amazing how a scent could stay with you like that, even when the source was…

Wait a minute. He turned toward the door of the tux shop and, sure enough, Keely had just walked inside.

She didn't look at him. His heart raced as he wondered what she was up to. If she'd meant to blow his cover, she would have come right over and greeted him. Instead, she wandered around the shop gazing at the displays, while his three friends stared openmouthed at her.

He couldn't blame them. With her tousled hair and short, flirty dress, she was a traffic stopper, all right.

The clerk hurried up to her. "May I help you with something?"

She turned her high-wattage smile on him. "I'm getting ideas."

Noah would bet the ranch on that one.

The clerk nodded happily. "When is the happy occasion?"

Keely's glance flicked ever-so-slightly in Noah's direction. "Soon." Then her attention swung back to Noah with more purpose. "And, you know, that's quite a bit like what I had in mind, right there."

Noah forced himself to breathe normally as she came toward him. He didn't have to look to know that his buddies were watching intently.

Her green eyes held that sparkle of devilment that was pure Keely. "*Very* nice," she said, giving him the once-over. "Would you turn around, please, so I can see how it looks in back?"

He really didn't have a choice. He turned.

"Yes," she murmured. "Exactly what I'm looking for."

He faced her again and hoped the red in his face didn't clash too much with the dove-gray coat. "I need to get changed." He winced at the obvious catch in his voice.

"Thank you for letting me look." The corners of her mouth tilted up. "The *key* is in the fit of the trousers, don't you think?"

She was torturing him and she knew it. He heard muffled laughter coming from the back of the shop where his friends had gathered to observe the action. No doubt they thought he was being picked up, assuming he was willing to be picked up.

"We think of ourselves as the premier tux shop in town," the clerk said, puffing out his chest with pride.

"And accessibility certainly is a *key* factor in that," Keely said. "Accessibility and availability are the *keys* to success in any venture, in my opinion."

"Absolutely," agreed the clerk.

Noah was afraid he'd sweat through this outfit if he stood there much longer listening to her sexy comments. "If you'll excuse me, I'll go take this off," he said.

"Now, there's something else I need to know," Keely said. "Do your dressing rooms have *keys?*"

Noah nearly came unglued. He couldn't look at the clerk. "I'll be in the back," he said. And if Keely followed him into the dressing room and tried anything, he'd…well, he'd do something. He wasn't sure what. At the moment the idea of Keely in the dressing room with him was causing a problem with the fit of his trousers, and he had to get away from her.

"I'll bet that man is a *key* player in whatever he does," she commented as he hurried toward the short hallway leading to the dressing rooms.

"I couldn't tell you," the clerk said. "Now, how many tuxedos will you be requiring for your event?"

Noah didn't pause to hear her answer.

"Told you the monkey suit works," Greg said in an undertone as Noah barreled past his friends without looking at them. Then all the guys just about killed themselves laughing.

Noah went into the dressing room where he'd left his clothes and closed the door firmly. Sure enough, there was a lock and he twisted it shut. She was not going to seduce him in the tux-shop dressing room, damn it, not even if it would be about the most risky, exciting thing he'd ever experienced in his life. His fingers trembled as he started taking off the rental clothes.

A soft knock sounded at the door.

"Busy!" Noah called out.

Loud male laughter greeted his statement, along with various comments about his lack of sex drive.

He walked over and opened the door to find his friends grinning at him. "What you think was happening was not happening," he said.

More laughter.

"We know that," Greg said with a chuckle. "The lady was trying to score, but nothing was happening. Garfield, have you lost your mind?"

"Or some other significant body part?" Clint added. "That woman was *hot,* and she was coming on to you, and you acted like some damn virgin!"

Brandon shook his head sadly. "This is not the Noah Garfield we've come to admire."

"She's nuts, is what she is," Noah said. "Did you hear her? She wanted to know if the dressing rooms had *keys,* for crying out loud."

"Yeah, she sure did." Greg sighed and looked longingly into the distance. "A woman with imagination is a beautiful thing. In one of these dressing rooms you could have three-way-mirror sex, not to mention sex in a forbidden place."

"These monkey suits are dynamite." Clint said. "She was pulled right in, and what a catch! I'll bet she's a dancer." He waggled his eyebrows. "You know, a *dancer?*"

"And she picked you right out, bro," Brandon said. "Did you hear her say she thinks you're a *key* player?"

And finally Noah got it. Keely wasn't here to sneak into

a dressing room with him and have three-way-mirror sex. He felt almost sad that her motivation hadn't been naughty, after all. She'd been trying to tell him she needed the extra key. Apparently, in his agitation, he'd left the suite with both of them.

She probably needed some money, too, if she planned to do a little shopping this afternoon. He'd left her pretty much high and dry up there. Well, high, anyway. Nothing was dry about that suite.

Greg peered around the corner into the shop. "She's still out there. You might be able to salvage this situation if you go talk to her."

"Okay, I'll get dressed and go talk to her," Noah said. "But I'm not having sex in one of these dressing rooms, and that's final."

7

KEELY WASN'T SURE WHETHER or not all her signals about keys would get through Noah's sexual fog. No matter how many times she vowed not to tease him, she continued to do it. He was such a delicious target, and each time she scored a hit, the painful memory of his rejection all those years ago faded a little more. She'd give anything for a snapshot of his face when she'd asked if the dressing rooms had keys.

Another of her features for *Attitude!* had dealt with unusual places to have sex, and dressing rooms had been one of them. She'd never personally tried it, though. In fact, she hadn't personally tried many of the adventures she wrote about in the magazine. This weekend seemed tailor-made for those kinds of adventures.

Getting a glimpse of Noah in a tux had doubled her determination. What a babe magnet. With those baby browns of his and that killer physique, he could well have left a trail of broken hearts on the rodeo circuit. But now he was stuck in Saguaro Junction, and she knew from experience that the action was skimpy around those parts. She'd give him a vacation from the deadly-dull social life of a small town.

But she really needed the extra suite key in order to keep this operation smooth. If Noah took off with his buddies before slipping her the key, she might have to try something more blatant. She didn't want him leaving for the evening while she was locked out. Yes, she could always go back to her own hotel if necessary, but it wasn't exactly next door.

As she continued to talk to the clerk about her imaginary "big event," she heard laughter from the dressing-room area and figured Noah's buddies were giving him a hard time. Those guys were a kick, a goofy bunch she'd like to make friends with if the situation were different. She'd matched up the voices with the bodies, so she'd pretty much tagged each one of them.

Greg was the redhead with the cute little belly. The tall blonde with the all-American good looks had to be Clint, and then there was Brandon the bridegroom—short, dark and adorable. Too bad his life would be over in a couple of days, once he'd tied the knot.

Both Clint and Greg already wore wedding rings. Poor guys. This bachelor party might be their only chance to break away from the tedium of their constricted lives. No wonder they wanted dancing girls tonight and hoped Noah would act out their fantasies this weekend.

And speaking of the fantasy man, he was strolling out of the dressing room, his arms full of rental clothes. He handed the stuff to the clerk who took it toward the counter, then headed in her direction. Thank goodness. He'd figured out her code.

"Nice to see you again, cowboy," she said.

"Sorry to be so dense." He held out his hand. "Here," he said, keeping his hand closed over the key. "The guys think you're propositioning me, by the way."

"I am." She took what was in his hand and realized money had been folded around the key. "You don't have to give me this." She slipped the key into her purse and tried to give him back the money.

"You need some clothes, right? For God's sake, put that

away. And don't move to the right or left. If you stay right where you are, I'm blocking their view of you, so they won't see what we're doing."

"Really?" She lifted both eyebrows and ran her tongue over her lips. "So what do you wanna do?"

His mouth twitched, as if he might be holding back a laugh. "Nothing, okay?" he said in a low voice. "Now get rid of that money."

"All right." She tucked the money down the front of her dress. Fortunately, the lace-up bodice gave her some cleavage, even without wearing a bra. The gesture would have lost impact if the bills had fallen through her dress to the floor.

"Keely."

"Noah, you're so funny. From what I heard, your rep could use some polishing. This little conversation we're having could do your image a world of good if you put the right spin on it. In fact, I don't know why we're keeping secrets from these guys. They seem like an open-minded bunch to me."

"I can tell you where their minds are. Listen, they want to come up to the suite after the bachelor party tonight. I didn't know how to tell them they couldn't, but I'll have to figure out some way to keep them from doing that. You can't very well spend the night in the closet."

"Oh, I don't know." She winked at him. "I had a good time in there."

His face reddened.

"But I have to admit that after a while it did get pretty hot."

"Keely, is it possible for you to talk about something besides sex?"

"Sure, but what fun is that?" She chuckled at his pained expression. "Look, why don't we just tell your friends that you're being a good Samaritan and helping me find a new and less interesting career?"

"Because they wouldn't believe it. If they knew you were

staying with me, they'd leap to one conclusion and one conclusion only. We'd never be able to convince them otherwise."

"Would that be so terrible? Apparently you're no stranger to the wild-weekend concept."

He frowned. "So you heard all that."

"Clear as a bell."

"I want you to know I cared about those women. It wasn't the way they made it sound."

She would rather have heard that the women meant nothing to him. "Noah, I'm the last person in the world who would judge you for enjoying a little healthy sex. And your friends won't, either."

His frown deepened. "I don't want them thinking that about you."

"Why not?"

"Because…because we grew up together, damn it, and I don't like it when guys think those things about you."

"Noah, what they're thinking, that I'd be fun in bed, has some basis in fact. I'm not that kid you grew up with. Not anymore."

He flushed an even darker color of red. "I don't care," he said, sounding a bit like a kid himself. "Nothing's going to happen between us."

She chose to let her smile answer that one.

"It's not! I forgot myself a couple of times, but I won't forget myself again."

"If you say so." She continued to smile at him.

"I do, and that's that." He crossed his arms over his chest. "I'm going to find some way to keep the guys from coming up to the suite tonight. I don't know how, but I'll think of something. Now, please go buy some clothes. And work on your résumé. Tonight we'll go over it and come up with some ideas."

"Sounds promising."

He blew out a breath in obvious exasperation. "You don't think I can pull this off, do you?"

She managed to control a burst of laughter. "What an interesting, and very Freudian, choice of words." She drew a slow circle on his arm with one finger and watched the material of his shirt quiver as the muscles in his forearm bunched. "Forgive me for not understanding why you can't give me job counseling *and* a really good time in that suite. I'm not your sister, Noah. I never was." She looked up at him, enjoying the darkening storm in his eyes. "So why does it have to be black and white, either-or?"

He opened his mouth as if to answer her, then hesitated, apparently reconsidering what he'd been about to say. "Because we need to focus on your job situation," he finally muttered.

She didn't think that was all of it. "You've never heard of multitasking?"

"I—"

"Or could it be that you're a coward?" she murmured.

"What do I have to be afraid of?"

"Letting go. Letting go of your old image of me, letting go of your old image of yourself."

"That's ridiculous."

"You're right," she said. "Absolutely ridiculous. Well, I must be off. I really do need to buy clothes, especially underwear. I realized when I started to dress to come down here that I didn't have anything clean, and I really hate to put on previously worn underwear after a bath."

His attention drifted to her breasts and he swallowed. "So what did you do?"

"I'll bet you can tell if you look closely. It's cool in this shop, which is making my nipples—"

"I can see that." He sounded hoarse. Slowly his gaze lifted

to her face. "Are you—" He cleared his throat. "Are you tell-ing me you don't have anything on under that dress?"

"I'll let you figure that out. See you around, cowboy." She turned and sashayed out of the shop, giving her hips an extra twitch because she knew he was watching the movement of her skirt and picturing her naked under it. And if she knew men at all, he was drooling.

She thought he might as well give in now, because the outcome of this weekend was a foregone conclusion. But he was a stubborn sort and it looked as if he had quite a bit more fight left in him. Come to think of it, she was enjoying the challenge. His resistance would make his final surrender that much sweeter.

In the meantime, she'd look for a few outfits that would guarantee success. Before she left for Reno Monday morning she'd return Noah's money, but in the meantime she'd pretend to use it to buy new clothes.

Spying a racy-lingerie shop, she headed for it. Between shopping for clothes and interviewing Suzanne and Joy over at the topless bar tonight, she'd be a busy lady. And then there was the cliff-diving show. She didn't want to leave the Ta-hitian without seeing that at least once. Considering that the weekend could get a tad complicated, she should probably try to see the cliff divers tonight before Noah returned.

MANY HOURS LATER NOAH headed back to the hotel on foot with his three friends and several of the male wedding guests. They were a happy, slightly drunk bunch of guys, with the exception of Noah. He'd gone easy on the beer, knowing he had some tricky maneuvers ahead of him.

First of all he had to convince his buddies not to turn his suite into party central without offending them. Assuming he accomplished that, he had to spend the night with Keely without making love to her. That feat alone required him to stay stone-cold sober.

For about the millionth time, their last conversation played in his head. When she'd asked him why sex couldn't be a part of this weekend, he'd come close to giving his white-knight speech, the one in which he promised to show her that at least one man on the planet wasn't after her body. Maybe that would boost her self-esteem enough that she'd have the courage to try a career that didn't depend on sex appeal.

But he wasn't sure how she'd take that kind of statement. After all, he was implying that she was too insecure to consider any job that didn't trade on her physical attributes. He hadn't wanted to take a chance on insulting her when they'd have no chance to talk it out. Besides, she'd probably laugh at him. So far he'd done a damn poor job of ignoring her body.

He planned to improve for her sake. Of course it was for her sake. Her suggestion that he was a coward, that he was afraid of letting go, of admitting that she was a desirable woman, was pure hogwash. He was perfectly capable of letting go with her or any woman and then getting control of himself again. On the rodeo circuit he'd proved that more than once.

But he'd never really tested himself with Keely. A part of him didn't want to know that she was a spectacular lover. Childhood friends weren't supposed to turn into spectacular lovers, especially when they were as far out of reach as Keely.

As the men navigated the busy sidewalk along the Strip, most everyone in the group was singing, or trying to sing "Let Me Entertain You" from *Gypsy.* Apparently the topless dancers had inspired them. They could afford to be inspired, Noah thought. Not a one of them had the sexual challenge that waited for him once he was alone again with Keely.

He'd never been so sexually frustrated in his life, or so un-likely to have that frustration eased soon, unless he wanted to abandon his principles. None of the strippers at the bar had been half as beautiful as Keely, but they'd kept his mind firmly on the subject of sex with every bump and grind.

Brandon slung a friendly arm around Noah's neck. "Hey, you bull-riding son of a gun. I'm glad you could tear yourself away from that ranch long enough to see me get hitched. I know how much that place means to you and how you hate to leave it."

Noah grinned at him. "Anything for you." Brandon was about as plowed as a bridegroom should be on the night before his wedding, Noah decided. He was plenty loose, but not falling-down drunk.

"Y'know that plan we had, all of us goin' up to your place for the rest of the evening?"

"Yeah," Noah said. "And the thing is—"

"I know what the thing is," Brandon said with a chuckle. "We all do. We were gonna pretend we were goin' up there so we could watch you squirm, but back at the bar we had a confab and decided not to torture you. So relax. We'll close out the night in the bird bar so you can have a little R and R upstairs."

Noah stared at him. "I don't have the foggiest idea what you're talking about."

Brandon smiled. "The woman in the tux shop, buddy. That's what I'm talkin' about."

"I told her I wasn't interested." Which, in a manner of speaking, was true.

"Uh-huh. And that's why you gave her a key? And money?"

"What makes you think I did that?" He was sure he'd blocked their view of the transaction with his body.

"There's this cute little security camera in the shop. We watched the action on the monitor."

Noah groaned.

"And we're happy for you, buddy. You're carrying on the tradition for those of us who are no longer able. Way to go, bro." He gave Noah's neck a squeeze and released him.

"Brandon, listen, I—"

"Enjoy the bachelor life while you can, Noah, old pal." With a wink, Brandon turned away and made a megaphone of his hands. "Hey, you guys!" he shouted. "If we get a move on, we can make it for the last cliff-diving show of the night!"

Noah sighed. He hadn't a clue how to respond. Nobody who saw him give a key and money to a woman who looked like Keely would believe that was an innocent arrangement. But it would be, damn it. And somehow he'd find a way to explain that to the guys. But he might as well forget trying until tomorrow.

"Yeah, come on." Greg flicked an imaginary rope over the group. "Get along, little doggies. Let's go see the diving."

"Aw, what's the big deal?" Clint said. "It's just some guy showing off."

"No, it's a guy and a gal," Brandon said. "They're supposed to be star-crossed lovers or something. There's a whole story that goes along with it. It's a pretty cool show. Jenny and I watched it last night."

"So is the gal topless?" Clint asked. "I'm not interested unless I can see her ti—"

"They're diving, you sex maniac." Greg whacked him on the shoulder. "The dive takes about one second. You wouldn't see anything, anyway." He chuckled as he glanced over at Noah. "You're under no obligation to stay for the show, lover boy."

"But I want to see the show," Noah insisted.

"Sure you do," Greg said with a smirk. "And then you want to go play bingo, and after that you'll be ready to get steak and eggs at the coffee shop. No chance. Don't try to kid a kidder, buddy."

"I do want to see the show."

"Then you're drunker than I thought," Greg said. "Come on, then."

Noah followed his friends as they mingled with the crowd heading for the cliff and diving pool. On the way he walked past the large rock where he'd kissed Keely that afternoon. The misty jungle atmosphere and the wildly beating drums rekindled a vivid memory and created all kinds of dangerous sensations in his body. The longer he put off going up to the suite, the better. "In fact, I'm going to the bird bar with you guys," he said over the sound of the drums.

Clint snorted. "The hell you are! You get your fanny up to that room and do your duty. You owe it to us, now that we're out of the game."

Noah decided it was pointless to argue. Tomorrow he'd straighten everything out. Somehow.

"Look!" Greg said. "There they are, ready to dive!"

Glancing up, Noah saw an olive-skinned couple in scanty swimsuits standing at the edge of the cliff. Each wore a lei and a crown of flowers. Torchlight glinted off their burnished bodies as they held hands and gazed into each other's eyes. Then they embraced, bodies writhing in passion.

Great, Noah thought. More suggestive behavior to stoke him up.

Then two warrior types came from either side of the cliff and pulled the couple apart. As the drumbeats softened, a gentle woman's voice described a Polynesian version of Romeo and Juliet—lovers from warring families who were forbidden to marry.

As the narration continued, the couple pantomimed begging for permission. Finally, according to the narrator, the father of each family agreed to a test of the couple's devotion. If the lovers could survive a leap from the great cliff called Nooki-Nooki, they would be allowed to wed.

"And I thought Jenny's dad was a hard sell," Brandon murmured.

Clint elbowed Noah in the ribs. "A cliff called Nooki-Nooki. That's where you're gonna hang out tonight, cowboy."

"Oh, ease up on him," Greg said. "From the way he's acting, you can tell he's out of practice. If you keep after him he's liable to develop a case of performance anxiety."

Clint hooked an arm around Noah's shoulder. "It's like riding a bicycle, buddy. Once you hop on, I promise you'll remember what to do."

"I appreciate the advice," Noah said. The conversation was not helping his state of mind. "Now, are you two going to watch this dive or stand around flapping your gums and miss the whole thing?"

"Guess we might as well watch it," Greg said, turning toward the cliff. "But God knows what you're doing here, Garfield, when you could be upstairs doing the horizontal hokeypokey with a woman who could be Julia Roberts's twin sister."

Personally Noah thought Keely was better looking than Julia Roberts. As the drumbeats swelled to a crescendo, he scanned the crowd. She'd said she wanted to watch this show. His pulse rate quickened at the idea that she could be here in the crowd, maybe only a few feet away.

And then he saw her.

She stood about fifty feet from them, her face lifted as she watched the couple at the top of the cliff. And she'd been clothes shopping. But if Noah had hoped for outfits that wouldn't stir him to new heights of lust, he was out of luck.

Her new dress was pale green and strapless. He couldn't for the life of him figure out how it stayed up. From the appreciative glances Keely was collecting, several men in the crowd were hoping it *wouldn't* stay up. The slinky material hugged her hips and ended at the middle of her golden thighs.

With Keely standing there looking as delicious as a frozen daiquiri, Noah couldn't imagine how any male in the area could concentrate on the divers. He certainly couldn't. When the splash came he didn't even glance over at the pool.

"That was amazing," Clint said. "And now our friend Noah can—oh, will you look at that?"

"What?" Noah quickly swung his gaze to meet Clint's, but he knew he was dead. Clint had caught him gawking at Keely.

Clint grinned at Noah. "Spotted her, did you? Hey, guys, Noah's sweetheart, ten o'clock. And raise your heat shields, boys. This gal's hotter than the space shuttle on reentry."

Greg whistled low through his teeth. "Wouldn't you love to find that prize at the bottom of your Crackerjack box?"

Brandon chuckled. "And if you two are real good to me, I promise not to tell Sharon and Tina what you just said."

Noah definitely didn't appreciate his friends ogling Keely. In fact, he hated it. It might be hopeless, but he had to take a stab at setting the record straight. "Look, I know what you guys all think about her, but here's the truth. She's between jobs and short on money. I offered her a place to crash for the weekend while she decides what to do. We're not going to have sex."

His friends nearly split a gut laughing.

"Yeah, right," Clint said as he wiped tears from his eyes. "I'll tell you what, old buddy. If you spend the weekend with that woman and don't have sex, I'll give you all my leather-bound issues of *Hustler* and see if I can locate a hotline for Dr. Ruth, because you obviously need serious therapy."

"It's true," Noah insisted. "She's…well, I knew her a few years ago. She's like a sister to me." That lie didn't come easily.

"A sister," Brandon said, his tone skeptical.

"Yeah, a sister," Noah repeated. Maybe if he said it often enough even he'd believe it. "We grew up together."

"No kidding?" Greg seemed impressed. "Then you picked the right place to grow up. Nobody I grew up with turned out like her."

"So she's really a friend?" Brandon asked. "Then you should bring her to the wedding, man."

"Uh, I don't think that's a good idea." He'd begun to look at this weekend as sort of a surgical strike—do a good deed and then get the hell out of the area. The only way he could deal with the temptation Keely provided was to keep her isolated from the rest of his life.

"I think that's a *great* idea," Clint said. "Let's go ask her right now before she leaves. What's her name?"

"Keely," Noah said. "But don't ask her. I don't think she'd feel comfortable about coming."

"That's not the impression I get from the lady," Greg said. "She looks like the kind of person who'd be comfortable *anywhere*." He waggled his eyebrows.

"See, that's why I don't want her to come to the wedding," Noah said. "You guys would be tripping over your tongues, and your wives would get mad, and it would ruin the whole event."

"You let us worry about that," Clint said. "Come on. Let's go see Keely and invite her to the wedding."

"Back off, Clint." Noah hated when situations got out of control, and that seemed to be happening a lot lately. "If anybody's going to ask her, I will."

Brandon grinned. "A little territorial, are we?"

"No, I'm not." A guy who became territorial about Keely had nothing but heartache ahead. But the feelings churning through him were too damn familiar. That protective streak that had caused him so much trouble many years ago hadn't died the way he'd hoped it had.

"So you'll ask her," Brandon prompted.

Noah felt trapped. If he didn't agree to ask Keely they wouldn't believe that she was an old friend. "Okay, I'll ask her, but don't expect to see her there. She's not a fan of weddings."

"Then she's gorgeous *and* unusual," Greg said. "Noah, you've picked a winner this time around. Lots of great sex with no commitment required is a helluva combo, my friend."

"We're not having sex, damn it."

"Hey, buddy," Clint said. "I think the woman you're not having sex with might be heading back up to that lust chamber you call a hotel room."

Noah glanced over toward the place where Keely had been standing. Sure enough, she was walking away, and nobody made an exit like Keely. She'd perfected that walk by the time she'd turned sixteen, and it caused grown men to whimper like babies.

"Ay, chihuahua," Clint moaned, right on cue.

"I can't look," Brandon said. "I have to keep my thoughts pure for Jenny."

"Well, I'm looking," Greg said. "That's what I call poetry in motion. In fact, I feel a poem coming on. I'll call it 'Ode to Keely's A—'"

"Never mind the odes, Shakespeare," Noah said.

"So," Brandon said, a knowing smile on his face. "Are you gonna go up to your suite or hang out with us?"

"The thing is, I have to go over Keely's résumé tonight."

"Her résumé?" Greg chortled. "I can't believe you said that with a straight face."

"I can't believe you're still standing here," Clint said. "Go handle that résumé, buddy."

"I really am helping her figure out a game plan for her career." Noah edged away from his friends. "I know you don't believe me, but that's exactly what we'll be doing."

His friends all nodded as if they were convinced he was a nutcase they needed to humor. They probably didn't believe that Keely was a childhood friend, either.

"Really," he said.

Clint gave him a thumbs-up. "See you in the morning, stud."

8
_____

KEELY WAS IN A FUNKY mood as she rode to the top floor of the hotel in the brass and glass mirrored elevator. She'd seen Noah and his buddies at the cliff-diving show and she knew they'd seen her. No doubt they were still trying to talk Noah into hooking up with her for the night.

But they weren't encouraging him because they thought she was a nice girl. Quite the opposite. Normally she'd take satisfaction in their view of her. She'd been thumbing her nose at stuffy convention for so many years that it was second nature to her now. Her strapless dress was designed to raise eyebrows and she'd bought it for the purpose of making Noah's eyes bug out. She was reasonably sure it had.

But lately the thrill of shocking and titillating people was wearing thin. Difficult as it was to admit, she was growing tired of always being the bad girl, the rebel, the outsider. Interviewing Suzanne and Joy had been like taking a trip back in time to attitudes she'd held dear when she'd posed for the centerfold.

In those days she'd dared anybody to stop her from doing what she wanted, when she wanted. If baring her body could get her where she wanted to go, then she'd take her clothes off with pride, and to hell with anyone who disapproved.

Suzanne and Joy felt the same way about dancing topless to earn college tuition.

Keely applauded their gutsy decision and wasn't sorry she'd made a similar one so many years ago. The money had helped her get a journalism degree and the moxie she'd shown in posing had influenced Carolyn to hire her at *Attitude!* Because of that centerfold, she'd left Saguaro Junction far behind, which had been her goal.

She'd snagged the trendy apartment in L.A., mingled with the cool people, had all the sexual freedom she could want. She wouldn't trade her life for anything, and yet at the moment she felt restless and out of sorts, wishing for something she couldn't identify.

Using her key, she activated the elevator doors and stepped onto the lush, jewel-toned carpeting of the hallway. She needed to shake off this mood if she expected to seduce Noah tonight. But as she walked to the suite and went inside, the falling water in the entry reminded her of the cliff divers. Maybe the show was to blame for her weird thoughts.

For all its sappiness, the narration had touched something in her. It was only an imaginary story, but still she wondered what it would be like to love somebody so much that you'd risk your life to be with them. She'd never taken a relationship with a man that seriously.

Maybe she wasn't capable of such deep passion. Maybe she didn't want to be capable of it. Passion that intense had tremendous power to wound. Or to trap. Like her mother had been trapped in Saguaro Junction. Her father had admitted that his wife had been unhappy on the ranch, and more than once he'd said that Keely was just like her. Keely had no intention of making her mother's mistake and letting love coax her into a life she wasn't suited for.

But while she'd watched Noah and his friends from the corner of her eye and thought of the occasion that had brought them all together, she'd felt a moment of…could it be envy? Surely not. She didn't want any part of that white-lace-and-promises routine. Let other women turn into Betty Crocker if they thought it would satisfy them. Her sister, B.J., was welcome to that role, but she had no intention of becoming an apron-wearing, muffin-baking, floor-scrubbing drudge.

Still, loving someone so much you'd jump off a ten-story cliff for them—now, that would be something to experience. Once upon a time, as they said in fairy tales, she'd imagined herself that much in love with Noah. But at sixteen every emotion had been hung with heavy drama, each moment carried the weight of life and death. Noah had rejected her, and guess what? She'd survived just fine. Okay, so she'd leaped at the chance for revenge, but that didn't mean she still had a thing for him.

And he wouldn't reject her this weekend. Not with what she had planned.

Now that he'd viewed her slinky green dress, she could move on to the next item in her shopping bag. Walking over the footbridge into the bedroom, she nudged off her sandals and shimmied out of the dress.

In moments she'd slipped on the black thong bikini she'd bought. She'd considered greeting Noah naked, but there was still the chance that his buddies would come back to the suite with him. Besides, minimal coverage often played with a man's mind more than complete nudity. She'd done an article on the subject three years ago.

Come to think of it, over the years she'd gathered plenty of ammunition on the most effective ways to seduce a man. And that's why Noah was going down.

She'd explored all the options of the remote earlier in the evening. Taking it from the ledge, she turned on the colored-light show, the adult movie channel and the hot tub, which was nicely positioned for viewing the giant screen. She clicked through the movie options and chose one called *Playmates in Paradise.* That should start his engines.

The well-stocked bar included some excellent champagne. She filled the ice bucket, opened the champagne and settled it into the ice. Wrapping a bar towel around the whole arrangement, she carried the bucket and two crystal flutes out to the terrace. After retrieving the remote and placing it within reach of the tub, she poured herself a glass of champagne and climbed into the bubbling water.

Easing down onto a molded seat, she glanced to her left and there was the glittering Strip stretching toward the downtown area where her hotel was located. If she turned her head in the opposite direction, she could watch three busty women get naked with one well-endowed surfer.

Keely took a sip of champagne and watched the movie action for a while. Stimulated by bubbles and the erotic behavior on the screen, she began to really look forward to Noah's arrival. The movie was fairly classy, yet here was yet another film directed by a man. A woman would have reversed the equation. Keely had never made love with more than one partner at a time. In real life it might be very confusing and she wasn't sure she'd like it, but she didn't mind including that scenario in her fantasy life.

Then the man who'd played several roles in her fantasy life walked into the living room. He glanced out to the terrace and then looked at the screen.

Keely picked up the remote and muted the sound of the movie. "I'm relaxing," she said. "Unwinding from a long, busy day. How was your bachelor party?"

He cleared his throat. "Okay. Listen, Keely, it's…uh, perfectly obvious what you have in mind here, but I have no intention of—"

"Oh, I *know* that," she said. "You don't plan to have sex with me, right?"

"Right." He sounded hoarse.

"Well, don't worry about it. I can take care of myself." Her natural talent for improvising kicked in. "In fact, that's what I was doing just now, before you arrived. The movie got me in the mood, and then the jets in this terrific hot tub did the rest. Somebody knew exactly how to position the nozzles. It's the best design I've ever experienced." There. That should turn his crank.

He stared at her and swallowed hard. "Oh."

"It seemed a shame to let all this go to waste." She took another sip of champagne to keep from grinning in triumph. "I admire your principles and all, but the mood of this suite really gets me hot. I needed to blow off some steam. Now I'm all mellow and ready to brainstorm my career options. Did you know that a good orgasm can make you think more clearly?"

"I…never heard that."

She'd never heard it either, but it made sense, considering how sex improved a person's circulation. Maybe that would be a good subject for a future magazine article. "Well, next time you have a particularly big problem to work through," she said, "you could try masturbating first and see if you don't come up with a solution afterward."

He coughed and gazed out at the city lights. "Right."

"So how about it? Shall we brainstorm in the hot tub?"

He glanced at the movie again. "With that going on? I don't think so."

"Sorry. I forgot it was still on." She clicked the remote and turned the movie off. She figured it had served its purpose of putting him in the right groove, but she didn't want him to be distracted from the real thing by a filmed version.

"Thanks." He seemed relieved that the film wasn't playing anymore.

"You should try this hot tub," she said. "I mean, think

about it. How many chances will you have to sit in a hot tub on a terrace overlooking the Las Vegas Strip? Psycho maids who break into your room and destroy your stuff don't come along every day, you know."

He glanced around the terrace and back at the hot tub. "Okay, maybe I will try it."

"Good. I promise we'll talk about my career options." She tried not to look overconfident. Once he was in the bubbles with her he was so going to be seduced.

"I'll go put on my—" He paused in the act of starting toward the bedroom. "I don't have a suit."

"I thought of that."

He sent a piercing glance in her direction. "And before you suggest it, I'm not going in without one."

"I didn't think you would. When I was shopping for mine I realized you wouldn't have one, either. In fact, I realized you wouldn't have underwear. I took the liberty of picking up a few things for you. I estimated you have a thirty-four waist. Is that close enough?"

"I guess so, but you didn't have to go buying me underwear." His cheeks turned the color of brick.

"What were you planning to do about that?"

"I, uh, hadn't thought about it."

"Well, now you don't have to." She took another swallow of champagne. "You'll find everything lying on the bed."

"Okay." Looking very uneasy, he turned and walked into the living room, over the footbridge and into the bedroom.

She figured in about five seconds she'd get a reaction. It only took four.

"Keely, this underwear is way too small!" he bellowed. "And it's *colored*."

"It's not too small if you're a thirty-four waist," she called back. "It stretches. And don't you get tired of wearing white all the time?"

"No."

"Well, this is Vegas, Noah. It's tough to find boring underwear in a resort boutique. I did the best I could."

Silence. "I guess I can make do with these for the weekend," he said at last.

"Good."

"I mean, it's not like anybody will see them."

Except me. She smiled and finished off her champagne.

"Where's the bathing suit?"

"On your—uh, on the pillow." Earlier in the evening she'd
turned down the bed and draped his skimpy suit over one
of the pillows. The suit was black, to match hers, and she'd
enjoyed the way it looked against the fine white linen pil-
lowcase. But she'd known it would look even better cupping
Noah's generous equipment.

Reaching for the ice bucket, she took out the champagne
bottle, poured another glass for herself and filled Noah's flute.
The party was about to begin.

She knew he'd found the suit when he began to laugh.

"I double dare you," she called out, surprising herself with
the same phrase she'd used to taunt him when they were kids.
And he'd risen to the bait every time except one, and they
hadn't really been kids anymore by then. On that hot summer
night when she'd double dared him to make love to her, he
hadn't taken the dare.

For one panicky moment she wondered if that iron will
would assert itself again. She couldn't let that happen. A flash
of insight told her that success had become very important to
her, maybe too important. But it was too late to worry about
that now.

"It's that or come in naked," she said. "The underwear
won't work. It becomes transparent when it's wet."

When he didn't reply, she tried to think of more induce-
ments. "If you go back home and tell Jonas you stayed in a

room with a hot tub on the terrace overlooking all of Las Vegas and you didn't sit in it even once, you'll never hear the end of it. You don't have to mention me at all. Just tell him you were sitting there sipping good champagne and enjoying the view. That will drive him nuts. He—" She stopped speaking. She nearly stopped breathing. Noah stood in the doorway wearing the suit.

Dear God, the boy she remembered had become a man. And what a man. The women in that skin flick could have their pretty-boy blond surfer with his carefully shaved chest. She'd take this broad-shouldered cowboy with chest hair the color of burnt sugar. No gym had shaped this body. He'd earned those muscles and scars during years of riding and roping.

As her gaze traveled over him, she was filled with gratitude that he'd agreed to wear the suit. She was virtually certain few women had seen him like this—all that masculine beauty punctuated by a coal-black exclamation point outlining the most intriguing aspect of his physique.

Thanks to his talkative friends, she knew that on the rodeo circuit he hadn't been shy about using his considerable endowments to give pleasure to the women he'd met. And now fate had given her a chance to discover his talents before he chose a proper ranch wife and settled down to a life of dull married sex.

She couldn't remember the last time the sight of a nearly naked man had left her speechless with yearning. Finally she forced herself to say something. "C-come in. The water's perfect." She couldn't help the stutter. He was so magnificent she couldn't think straight.

"And we're going to talk about your career."

"Of course." She'd agree to talk about Einstein's theory of relativity if he'd just get in the hot tub with her.

"I guess we have to talk somewhere. And you're right. If

Jonas finds out I didn't take advantage of the stuff in this suite, he'll carry on something fierce." He walked over to the tub and climbed the steps. "But that's not why I'm doing this."

She gazed up at him and wondered if she'd died and gone to heaven. Talk about a great camera angle. She swallowed. "So why are you?"

"Because I figured out that I wanted to. It's been awhile since I did something just because I wanted to." He stepped down into the swirling water.

"Oh." It was the most she could manage as the bubbles inched up his body. When he finally sat across from her she had to work not to whimper because her view had been obliterated by the damn water.

"This feels good." He leaned back against the edge of the tub and closed his eyes. "Damn good."

She almost groaned out loud. She could imagine something else that would feel damn good, but she didn't want to scare him off right when he was beginning to relax and enjoy what came his way. "I guess the ranch is quite a responsibility," she said.

"Don't you know it." He opened his eyes and glanced over at the view of the Strip. "I truly love that place, and I don't begrudge all that I put into running it, but I haven't had a vacation since I took over two years ago."

"Then it's about time." She handed him the champagne flute. "Here. This goes with the view."

He took the delicate crystal, his hand brushing hers, his gaze holding hers for a precious moment. "Thanks. I guess it does." Then he cleared his throat and took a drink of the champagne. "It tastes expensive."

"It is." She leaned over and lifted the bar towel to show him the bottle.

He shook his head. "I'll have to take your word for it.

Looking at the brand won't tell me anything. I'm not into champagne." He took another swallow. "But this isn't bad for being a girlie drink."

"I'm glad you like it, because once you open a bottle this pricey, it's criminal not to finish it off." She didn't want him to get drunk, but she wouldn't mind having him loosen up a little more.

He rolled the stem of the flute between his fingers. "Why do I have the feeling that you want to sit here and drink champagne instead of talk about your career plans?"

"There you go again, setting us up for either-or. We can do both. I think talking about career plans while drinking expensive champagne is a great idea."

"Okay, then let's start by you telling me what jobs you've had since you left the ranch."

She'd thought about this and was ready for the question. "I've waited tables, taken on some light secretarial work. Then there was the telephone soliciting."

He nearly dropped his flute. "Telephone *what?*"

Excellent. His mind was firmly in the gutter. "I made cold calls for a carpet-cleaning company," she said.

"Oh. That kind of soliciting."

"What did you think I meant? Phone sex?"

"No! Of course not. I mean—" He paused to gulp some more champagne. "Hell, never mind. Carpet cleaning. Okay. What else?"

"Let me put a head on that for you." She lifted the bottle from the ice bucket and waited until he held out his glass.

He hesitated.

"You said it yourself. It's a girlie drink. Not much punch to it."

"Yeah, you're right." He extended his glass so she could fill it again. "So, what else have you done?"

"A little bartending."

He nodded. "What else?"

She adjusted the straps on her bathing-suit top for no reason other than to jiggle her breasts and make him notice. "You probably don't want to know *all* the jobs I've had," she murmured.

As she'd planned, his gaze drifted to the twin triangles of black material that barely covered her nipples. "Maybe not," he said, a thread of huskiness winding through his voice. "How did the…uh…carpet-cleaning job work out?" Bringing his attention back to her face appeared to take great effort.

"Not too bad. People seemed to respond to my voice on the telephone. Want to hear my sales pitch?"

"Sure." He took another big swallow of champagne.

"I think I can remember it. Let me concentrate for a second." Keely really had spent about a week calling for a carpet cleaner, and she'd had such bad luck in the first day that she'd modified the phone message they'd given her without telling them. Then her calls had been wildly successful as long as she'd talked to the man of the house. But when the president of the company had discovered what she'd been saying, he'd fired her. The man had completely lacked a sense of humor.

"Here goes," she said, holding his gaze across the foaming water and lowering her voice to a sultry purr. "'Hey, there, big guy. Can we talk dirty? Dirty carpets, that is. Your carpet needs your attention, it craves your attention. It deserves to be stroked firmly, massaged and caressed until it ripples beneath your hand, and then, my friend, it needs to be washed clean and…sucked…thoroughly and completely, until it springs up, aroused to its full…potential. How soon would you like this done…to your carpet?'"

During her recitation Noah's breathing had become labored and his gaze turbulent.

She wasn't completely calm, herself. If he didn't make a

move soon, she was going to be in bad shape. "So," she said, smiling brightly, "what do you think? Do I have any talent for sales?"

"I think…" He paused and cleared the huskiness from his throat. "I think you need to go to bed."

Her pulse raced with anticipation. "And you will…?"

"Not."

Damn. "But you want to," she murmured, willing to bet a year's salary that beneath the foaming water he was completely erect.

The muscles in his jaw worked. "Yes. I want to."

And so did she. So very, very much. She was going crazy with the wanting. "Noah, what could it possibly hurt? We're two free, consenting adults. Both of us are dying to consent. I don't understand why we can't go into that bedroom and have a wonderful time. For that matter—" she slipped the straps of her bathing-suit top off her shoulders "—we could begin the fun right here."

"Keely, don't."

"Don't what? Enjoy the movement of the water against my skin?" Putting down her champagne flute, she unhooked her top and allowed it to float away. A girl could only hold herself back for so long before she cracked. She wiggled out of her bottoms and they floated to the surface, too.

"You know what I mean," he said in a tight voice.

"Yes, and you know what I need." Cupping her breasts, she rose to her knees on the bench seat so that the foaming surface tickled and played with her nipples until they were taut with desire. "This feels good, Noah. Do you think it's wrong for me to like it?"

Never taking his gaze from her breasts, he shook his head.

"And right above this bench there's a water jet. If I position myself just right, I can enjoy that, too." She found the pulsing stream and tilted her pelvis back. There. Mmm. It wasn't Noah's touch, but he still seemed to have scruples. "Is that wrong?"

His tortured gaze held hers. "No," he said, his voice rasping low in his throat.

"I want you, Noah." The pulsing water worked quickly on her already aroused body. Her breathing grew shallow and her heart pounded with excitement. She'd never dared so much in front of any man, but now that she'd begun this little exhibition she found that it packed its own kind of thrill.

She could tell he was going insane watching her. Good. He deserved to go insane.

"Yes, I really want you," she whispered. "But if I can't have what I want…" She closed her eyes and ran her tongue over her lips. "I'll take what I can…get." As the tremors of her orgasm overtook her, she squeezed her nipples hard and gasped with pleasure. Knowing he had watched every second intensified the sensation more than she would have believed. Breathing hard, she leaned back against the edge of the tub.

Slowly she opened her eyes and looked at him.

He was destroyed. She'd never seen anybody in such agony in her life.

Taking a long, shaky breath, she braced a hand on the side of the tub and coaxed her rubbery legs to support her as she stood. "Well, that sure was fun," she said. "You really should have come along." Retrieving the two pieces of her suit, she climbed out of the tub and walked dripping and naked into the living room and over the footbridge.

9

NOAH HAD NEVER EXPERIENCED anything like the rush of watching Keely making love to the hot-tub jets. And the fact that she'd deliberately done it while he was sitting there totally fried his circuits. If he'd come upon her when she hadn't known he was there—well, that would have been wild enough. But she'd *chosen* to have him see this, knowing full well how much he wanted her. She'd hoped he'd break.

He would not break. In this charged moment he couldn't remember the reason, exactly, but he knew control was very important.

Until Keely had snuggled up to that water nozzle, he'd thought he understood sexual frustration. He'd kidded himself that he was strong enough to deal with it, no matter what the temptation. But the frustrations he'd lived with in the past were small change compared to the gut-wrenching, groin-pounding urges that shook him now. Keely had pushed him into unknown territory.

The water churned around him, teasing him, taunting him with liquid fingers that had brought Keely relief while he remained in straining agony. A jet of water gurgled against his back, suggesting possibilities, beckoning him to follow Keely's lead. Beneath that scrap of material some idiot designer called a bathing suit he swelled until it seemed the tiny garment couldn't hold him any longer.

In a wild frenzy he reached beneath the water and ripped it away, tearing the seams in his eagerness to be rid of the restraint. His penis surged free. With a moan of surrender he stood and turned toward the rippling stream of water.

Hands braced against the edge of the hot tub, he eased his rigid flesh into the outer swirl of the pulsing jet. Oh, God. This wouldn't take long. The lights of the Strip blurred into a river of color as his climax crept ever nearer.

Finally, holding back a groan with clenched teeth, he gripped the edge of the tub and shuddered as the milky evidence of his passion rose and merged with the bubbling water. Struggling for each breath, he let his head sag between his still tense shoulders.

"Nice going," she said softly from the doorway behind him.

He refused to turn around. "Go away," he whispered hoarsely.

"I will. I only came back out to bring you a robe, so you wouldn't get chilled."

His laugh sounded like a rusty saw against a fence post. Chilled. Never in a million years.

"I'm leaving it here on a chair."

Still he didn't turn around. No telling what she was wearing, or not wearing. And if he looked at her, he would want her again as much as before. The picture of her making love to the jet of water was too fresh for him to even think of blotting it out of his mind.

"That little teaser of relief won't be enough, you know," she murmured. "At least, it wasn't for me. You're such an endearingly stubborn man, Noah. But if you decide to bend that iron will of yours, I'll be in the bedroom. We could have a very good time."

He wondered if she'd have a very good time without him. Once again he tried to remember why he shouldn't make love to her. He was positive he'd had a good reason, back when he could think. And because he knew that eventually he'd be able to think again, he was determined to wait out this period of insanity.

When he heard nothing more from the vicinity of the doorway, he cautiously looked over his shoulder. She wasn't there. Climbing out of the tub he felt shaky as a new foal. Sure enough, a white terry robe lay across one of the rattan patio chairs.

He picked it up but couldn't seem to make himself put it on. All his nerve endings felt tender, as if the slightest contact would send shock waves through his system. On some level he realized that he was standing naked on a terrace within view of several high-rise hotels. Naked and still partially erect.

His nakedness didn't seem like the most critical issue. As long as he stayed out on the terrace and Keely stayed in the bedroom, he might be able to quiet the roaring in his ears long enough to reason this through. He spread the white terry robe open on the cushioned rattan chair and eased down on it. God, his skin felt sensitive, as if he could feel each individual loop of the plush terry caressing his butt and his balls.

Gingerly he leaned back in the chair and gazed out at the sparkling, churning kaleidoscope that was Las Vegas. The combination of this city and Keely Branscom would corrupt any guy with a pulse.

But he had to resist, anyway. He didn't like to think of himself as the kind of man who would meet a childhood friend and promptly jump into bed with her even if she invited him. His brother, Jonas, was a different story. But Noah had taken his older-brother role seriously. His mother had told him to set a good example for Jonas and he'd tried to do that. He'd tried especially hard after his mother died, for her sake.

But it hadn't worked that way in the motherless Branscom household. In that case, the younger one, B.J., had turned out to be the responsible kid and Keely, the oldest, had been hell-bent-for-leather from the beginning.

Maybe it had nothing to do with circumstances and everything to do with personality. Keely and Jonas were cut from the same cloth. Noah was extremely grateful that he was here instead of Jonas, because if she'd made Jonas the same offer she'd made him, Jonas would have grabbed it. Well, maybe not now that he seemed to be in love for the first time in his life.

And maybe not ever, come to think of it. Jonas hadn't talked about wanting to get Keely alone and have some fun. She was about the only woman he hadn't gone after, though. Noah and his father had lived in constant fear that Jonas would get all the county's eligible girls pregnant. It was a miracle that no one had come to the ranch insisting that she carried Jonas's baby.

The issue of birth control aside, Noah couldn't claim much success with Jonas's personal development. Maybe little brothers were programmed to be contrary. At any rate, B.J. seemed to be accomplishing what he'd failed to do—Jonas was finally becoming a grown-up.

Noah wondered if that had anything to do with his own restlessness lately. He wasn't required to model good behavior anymore. Or maybe it was simply Keely getting under his skin the way she'd always done and bringing out the devil in him. Maybe it was time to admit he'd always been a little afraid of her, because when she was around his control began to slip.

And maybe it was time for him to let go, at least for a weekend, but he had the wrong woman for that. Keely didn't need a man who was ready to let go, no matter what she said. She needed a man who would be steady and responsible, a man who would guide her to make some better decisions.

That was what he'd been trying to remember—keeping his hands off Keely was for her sake, not his.

A cool desert breeze drifted across the terrace. It blew gently over his body, drying the drops of water that still clung to the hairs of his chest and groin. He considered putting on the robe, but the night air felt too good. And there was a certain forbidden thrill sitting here under the stars without a stitch on.

There was nothing really wrong with it. He was on his own private terrace where he should have the right to do this if he wanted. Anyone who wanted to spy on him would need a pair of binoculars to see anything.

And yet a sense of freedom and sexual excitement washed over him as he sat there naked gazing out at the city bustling around him. He wondered if Keely had felt that excitement and freedom when she'd posed nude for *Macho* magazine. The more he thought about it, the more he believed that might have been the attraction, maybe even more than the money.

Today when she'd unfastened her clothes so that he could touch her breasts as they kissed behind the boulder, she'd seemed to relish taking that risk. He'd never met a woman more willing to celebrate the wonders of her body without shame than Keely. And encouraged by her, he longed to take a few sexual risks, himself.

But he liked to think he knew where to draw the line. From all indications, Keely didn't. If he hadn't come along, she'd be bumping and grinding in some bar like the one he'd visited tonight with his buddies.

He hated the thought of that. Keely had more to her than a gorgeous body and an uninhibited attitude. She was creative, funny, brave and endlessly optimistic. There had to be a career that would make the most of those qualities—a safe career that wouldn't put her in the path of drunken, sexually aroused men every night of her life.

He had approximately forty-eight hours to come up with suggestions for her. And part of that time he'd be tied up with the wedding, so he didn't have the entire forty-eight hours. He'd forgotten to ask her whether she wanted to go to the wedding. Oh, hell, she probably wouldn't be interested. So he'd take care of his wedding duties by himself, and use the remaining time to discuss job options with Keely.

Daylight would help him stay on the subject. Coming upon this scene tonight had nearly eliminated his defenses, but in the morning he'd be in better shape to handle her constantly seductive behavior.

Curving his spine, Noah scooted lower in the chair and laid his head against the back cushion. He needed to get some sleep. Tomorrow promised to be one very busy day.

As Keely lay against the soft cotton sheets and listened for Noah's approach, she finally decided he planned to spend the night on the terrace. If she were scoring this battle of wills, she'd say they were about even. Maybe she hadn't gotten him into a condom yet, but he'd worn the sexy bathing suit she'd picked out and he'd given in to the seduction of the water jets.

Oh, how he'd given in. She'd watched him lean toward that pleasure and a rush of moisture had dampened her silk bikini underwear. When he'd come, she'd nearly climaxed, herself. She'd never watched a man masturbate before, except in X-rated movies. For that matter, she'd never allowed a man to watch her do the same thing. Noah might think that tonight's demonstration was commonplace for her, but it was a real first.

Of course, she'd never met a man who could sit in a hot tub with her and keep his hands to himself. When she'd begun her game with the jets she'd assumed that eventually Noah would get into the act. His continued resistance had left her no choice except to follow through. It seemed the more Noah held back, the more she dared. She'd discovered she liked this dynamic.

But she wouldn't want it to go on for the entire weekend. No, at some point she wanted him to become the aggressor. And he would. He'd already made some strides in that direction.

Although still aroused, she was beginning to get sleepy, too. She'd had a long and fascinating day. Tomorrow promised to be even more fascinating. Cuddling into a premium goose-down pillow, she drifted to sleep.

A RINGING TELEPHONE woke her the next morning. Fuzzy from sleep and sexy dreams, she blinked and tried to find a phone. The room had nothing so ordinary as a bedside table with a phone on it. Finally she remembered seeing one hanging over the tub. It looked like a seashell, but she'd noticed that it was plastic, and a place like this wouldn't have a plastic seashell on the wall. She'd lifted it and discovered that, sure enough, it was a phone.

Heading for the bathroom, she took the pink shell from the wall and pulled out the retractable antenna before punching the connect button. She cleared the sleep from her throat and put the shell to her ear, half expecting to hear the sound of surf. "Hello?"

"Keely, this is Brandon! Listen, sorry to disturb you two, but Jenny needs to know for certain if you're coming to the wedding. She wants to make sure she has enough leis."

"The wedding?" She combed her hair back from her face and glanced in the mirror to find Noah standing in the bathroom doorway wearing the white robe and looking dangerously sexy and unshaven.

Turning, she faced him. "I didn't know I was invited," she told Brandon.

"Noah didn't ask you? Oh, well, he probably has a lot of things on his mind." There was a thread of laughter running through Brandon's voice. "You are definitely invited. Noah says you grew up together."

"We did." She noticed Noah's attention on the thrust of her breasts under the white silk of her tank top. Looking him straight in the eye, she slipped her hand under the top. "He's like a brother to me." Slowly she caressed herself.

Noah sucked in a breath.

"That's what he was trying to tell us. Anyway, can you make it tonight?"

"I'd love to." She watched the desire build in Noah's dark eyes as she continued to stroke her skin. She was getting pretty excited, herself. "What time?"

"Seven. Oh, and there's a short rehearsal at eleven and a rehearsal lunch. You're welcome to come to that, too. We had to compress things because we're cramming it all into one weekend. I'm glad you'll be there!"

"So am I. Do you want to talk to Noah?"

"Is he available?"

"I'm not sure. I'll check." She took the phone from her ear. "Are you available?" she murmured.

He made a sound low in his throat.

"I'll take that as a yes." With a smile, she handed him the seashell phone. "Think I'll hit the shower." She peeled off her tank top as she walked toward the glass enclosure. When she glanced back to see if Noah was still there, he'd left the room.

He didn't reappear while she showered, washed and dried her hair, and put on her next killer outfit, stretch capris and a halter top that left her midriff bare.

When she was dressed she followed the scent of coffee to

the living room and discovered him there with a cup in his hand and a room-service tray on one of the driftwood-and-stone end tables.

He glanced at her outfit and sighed. "Not gonna let up on me, are you?"

She laughed at the pitiful resignation in his voice. "Noah, I am going to have you before this weekend is over. You know it and I know it, so you might as well give in and get it over with."

He put down his cup and stood. "And I'm telling you that you're wrong. I intend to prove to you that there's at least one guy out there—namely me—who is interested in you without needing to have your body as part of the arrangement."

She had to admit the concept was touching. Doomed to fail, but touching, anyway. "And what will that accomplish?"

He took a deep breath. "Now, don't take this wrong, but I'm hoping it will convince you to do something with your life that doesn't involve sex or the suggestion of sex."

"I see." So he was determined to sacrifice himself so that she'd get her head screwed on straight. And touching or not, his attitude was also pretty damn superior. He thought he knew what was good for her. She simply had to foil his plan, if only to make him a little more humble. Noah had a lot of good points, but humility wasn't one of them.

"I ordered up a few things." He gestured toward the tray. "Help yourself while I shave and shower. We need to leave for the rehearsal in twenty minutes."

She gazed at him. Maybe tomorrow morning she'd find out what his beard felt like against her skin while he kissed her all over. No use trying to organize such a maneuver now and make him late for the rehearsal.

"How are you going to shave?" she asked, remembering that he hadn't replaced any of his toiletries.

He picked up a small zippered pouch from beside the

breakfast tray and started toward the footbridge. "I asked them to send up the basics so I could shave and brush my teeth."

"You'd have been welcome to borrow my toothbrush." She held her ground and made him walk around her to get to the footbridge. "Once a guy's had his tongue in my mouth, sharing a toothbrush doesn't seem like a big deal."

"That won't be happening again," he muttered as he stomped over the bridge.

"Pity. You're very good with your tongue when it comes to kissing. I was hoping to find out if you're as talented when you use it elsewhere."

His groan as he went into the bedroom made her smile.

IF NOAH HAD EXPECTED any awkwardness between Keely and his friends, he'd been mistaken. During the rehearsal and the lunch that followed, Keely seemed to be getting along well with everyone. She made a special effort to charm both Brandon's and Jenny's parents and he remembered something he'd forgotten about Keely—she could talk to literally anyone.

The meal was served at a long table at the hotel's trendy Coral Reef restaurant, where the waitresses dressed in tight scuba gear and the menu included mostly fish. In the hubbub of getting seated, Noah was separated from Keely, who ended up at the opposite end of the table. His position allowed him to observe her technique for drawing people out. No question about it—she had quite a talent for that.

Once the food arrived, Clint's wife, Sharon, squeezed lemon juice on her tuna and accidentally shot some down Keely's front. Keely laughed and patted her chest, spreading the drops around. "Squirt some more over here. I've always wanted to smell like a freshly waxed table."

Sharon grinned. "You know, so have I," she said, and baptized herself, too.

Suddenly lemon wedges were at a premium as everybody started spraying juice around. Keely gave as good as she got, never for a minute seeming to consider that she barely knew these people she was tagging with streams of juice. It turned into a raucous lunch, and before it was over, Keely was as much a part of the group as if she'd been around for years.

And for all the seductive moves she'd made when they were alone, in public she acted like Noah's kid sister. In fact, she behaved as if sex was the farthest thing from her mind. A few suggestive jokes made their way around the long luncheon table, but none of them started with Keely. She laughed along with everyone else, but she didn't take the opportunity to send him one of those smoldering looks he'd been getting whenever they were alone.

In some ways he was a little disappointed about that. He had to admit that having Keely come on to him all the time had been damn good for his ego. He found himself becoming impatient for the lunch to end so he could have her to himself again. They'd discuss her job possibilities, of course. He'd realized that whatever she did should include interacting with people. Her small-town background and outgoing personality made her naturally good with people.

He was going through some options in his mind and anticipating a return to the suite with Keely when Jenny shot down his plans.

Standing, she turned to Keely. "Barb, Sharon, Tina and I have appointments for a manicure and pedicure at the hotel salon," Jenny said. "You have to come with us and tell us every embarrassing story you can remember about Noah. And if you want a manicure and pedicure, I'm sure the salon can squeeze in one more person. We've monopolized them for the afternoon, anyway."

"Sounds great," Keely said with a smile as she left the table and headed out with the women. Almost as an afterthought she turned and waggled her fingers at Noah. "See you later, big guy."

"What a terrific person she is," Brandon said after the women had left. "But I don't get this platonic thing you two have going."

"Yeah," Clint said. "You have to work yourself past that one, buddy. I realize you two grew up together, but the point is, you did grow up. And so did she."

Greg sighed wistfully. "Did she ever." Then he glanced down the table at the two dads sitting there. "I mean that in the most respectful way. I'm crazy about my wife."

Jenny's father chuckled. "We're all crazy about our wives. But when a woman like Keely comes along, you'd have to be dead not to notice her."

"Amen to that," Brandon's dad said. "I keep thinking she looks familiar, somehow. Has she been in commercials or something like that?"

"Not that I know of," Noah said. But that was another idea to add to his list of career choices. He wondered if Keely had ever tried to break into television.

"I know what you mean about her looking familiar," Clint chimed in. "I've had the feeling I've seen her before, too."

Noah didn't want any of the men to keep following that line of thought. "Maybe it's because she looks like Julia Roberts," he said.

"Well, she does, but that's not why," Brandon's father said. "I could swear I've seen her before. Even the name sounds like one I've heard. Give me some time. Before the weekend is over I'll make the connection."

Noah sincerely hoped not. Now was not the time for anyone to remember seeing Keely with a staple in her navel.

"Hey, who's ready to hit the beach?" Brandon asked, and the party started to break up.

As the men all prepared to leave the restaurant, Clint

nudged Noah in the ribs and spoke in an undertone. "I hope before the weekend is over you'll be able to make a connection, too, buddy. And I'm not talking about a mental connection, either."

10

KEELY COULDN'T REMEMBER the last time she'd hung out with married women, and apparently she'd been guilty of some stereotyping. Jenny, Barb, Sharon and Tina didn't remotely resemble Betty Crocker. Instead of trading recipes, these women wanted to trade sexual fantasies as they sat around taking turns having their toenails and fingernails buffed and polished.

"We spent the afternoon exchanging fantasies before Tina and Greg's wedding last year," Jenny explained to Keely. The bride sat with both feet in sudsy, whirling water in preparation for her pedicure. "And we all promised to do it again at my wedding. It's a lot more fun than having a surprise stripper, and we all get to play."

Keely nodded. "I like it."

"It's up to you if you want to tell us one of yours," Jenny added. "You can think about whether you want to or not while you're listening. Okay, here's mine."

Trying not to let her mouth drop open, Keely heard Jenny—a blonde with innocent-looking blue eyes—describe her fantasy of being carried off by a sheikh and sold into sexual bondage. While Josette buffed and massaged Jenny's feet with some sort of tangy-scented herbal cream, Jenny provided details of what the bondage would involve. When she was finished, everyone, including Keely, applauded.

"Me, next!" Tina said, raising the hand that had recently been tipped with Mango Madness. "Ooh, I love this one I came up with. Here goes." An olive-skinned Italian beauty, Tina sketched a scene in which she commanded male slaves to do her bidding. And she had an impressive list of duties for them to perform.

Keely joined in the applause for this one too and wondered if she'd forever associate the bracing smell of nail polish with women's sexual daydreams. She wished she could take notes. An article on female fantasies might be an excellent project for *Attitude!* magazine.

Then Sharon, a well-rounded brunette, detailed a fantasy that involved making love to a handsome stranger in the back of a moving limousine. Sharon was followed in the rotation by Barb, a tall woman with black hair. Barb wanted to be rescued from a burning house while wearing a negligee and then afterward to have sex with each of the gorgeous firemen as an expression of her gratitude.

"Do you want to tell us one?" Jenny asked, turning to Keely after Barb had finished and collected her applause. "You don't have to, but it's fun."

"I can see that." Keely was rethinking her assumption that marriage dried up your sexual imagination. As the only single woman there, she felt obligated to hold up her end of the game. "How's this? I am a beautiful queen, and my page is in love with me but he dares not show it because of his lowly station. I figure out that he's in love with me, so I begin subtly coming on to him."

"Oh, that's good," Jenny said. "And slowly he begins to crack."

"Right," Keely said. "And, being a normal man, eventually he can't help himself and he has to have me, but he knows he could be killed for it. So he risks his life to make love to me. At night. In the throne room. And it's raining outside." She found herself getting into the fantasy.

"And of course you tolerate it," Sharon said, her dimples flashing.

"Well, yeah," Keely replied. "I mean, the guy is hung like a horse."

Jenny laughed. "Naturally. And you don't have him killed."

"No, I only threaten it if he doesn't do his level best to please me. Night after night after night."

"Excellent!" Tina said. "He either produces multiple orgasms, or off with his head!"

By this time both manicurists were begging to add their fantasies to the collection, and then everyone decided they needed a second round.

Keely managed to come up with a second fantasy, but she loved the first one far more. And it wouldn't take a degree in psychology to figure out why, either. Oh, yes. Noah's ultimate surrender to his desire would be sweet.

"So, Keely, what was it like growing up with Noah?" Jenny asked as the women sat in the salon letting their fingernails and toenails dry.

Keely thought about that as she admired her fingers and toes tipped with Lotus Blossom Pink. "Well, his younger brother, Jonas, and I were the ones who always got into trouble, and Noah had to bail us out so we wouldn't get busted. Like the time Jonas and I took the tractor for a joyride before either of us knew how to drive it. We ended up in a ditch, of course, and broke some part or other. Noah used his dad's truck to pull the tractor out and then told his dad that he'd put the tractor in the ditch, not me and Jonas."

"I can picture Noah doing that." Tina wiggled her toes. "He seems like the protective type. So were you two ever involved?"

"Uh, not really."

"She's blushing!" Jenny said. "Dish, girl!"

Keely couldn't believe that she'd given herself away like that. "It was only kid stuff. You know, down by the barn. Nothing ever came of it."

Tina glanced at Keely. "I think something could come of it now. If you're interested, that is. He looks at you like a chocoholic would look at a box of Godiva."

Jenny laughed. "I'll bet all the guys do when they think we don't notice. That's a killer bod you have there, chick."

Keely felt her blush deepen. "Oh, this old thing. I've had it for ages."

"You wear it well," Tina said with a nod. "And I still say Noah's interested. I mean, *really* interested."

"Yeah, but he doesn't want to be," Keely said before she could stop herself.

Sharon's brown eyes opened wide. "Why ever not?"

Keely sighed. She hadn't meant to say even that much, but these women had a way of making her forget to guard her words. "He might be sexually interested, but he doesn't want to act on that because nothing could ever come of it and he can't just walk away from me when it's over. My dad and sister still work for him, and his brother is marrying my sister. So it's complicated."

"Back up a minute," Jenny said. "Why couldn't anything ever come of it?"

"Because." She paused and glanced around at these funny, intelligent women, all of them probably living out in the sticks somewhere with their cowboy husbands. "Don't take this wrong. I think you guys are fantastic. But I'm not the type to be a ranch wife."

Jenny burst out laughing. "Oh, yeah. The ranch wife. That wholesome woman who never wears makeup and brings in fresh eggs from the chicken coop every morning."

Tina joined in the laughter. "Oh, yeah, her. The one who bakes all her own bread and whips up gingham curtains for every blessed window in the house. Oh, and she makes table-cloths and napkins, too, to match the curtains."

"Don't forget putting up the preserves and making the quilts," Sharon added with a grin. "And helping with the branding in the spring and the roundup in the fall."

"And in between times she drives all over the countryside doctoring the sick and cheering the infirm," Barb said.

Jenny glanced at Keely, her blue eyes twinkling. "That's the one you're thinking of, right? Martha Stewart in boots and spurs?"

"I guess. I mean, maybe your picture is a little extreme, but that's about the size of it."

"Well, the thing is, that ranch woman—" Jenny winked at her sister and two friends. "Hit it, girls."

"She's so last century!" the women shouted in unison.

"Long live the new ranch wife!" Jenny shouted, punching a fist in the air. "She gets pedicures!"

"She serves fast food!" Barb raised her own fist.

"She shops at Nordstrom's!" Tina waved a fist in the air.

"She hires a cleaning service!" Sharon put both fists in the air and leaped up to dance around the salon, Rocky-style.

Keely laughed in delight. "Good for you. I'm impressed. Obviously you all have it together. But you've never lived in Saguaro Junction."

"I don't think the place matters," Jenny said. "Women everywhere are changing. It's the millennium, and drudges are out of fashion. Hey, if a woman *likes* doing some of that, great. But you can live on a ranch and still have lots of the goodies of life. I don't plan on going anywhere *near* a chicken coop. Times have changed."

Keely still had trouble picturing such liberation on the

Twin Boulders Ranch. "Somebody ought to tell that to Noah Garfield."

"Yep," Jenny agreed. "And I think you're just the gal to do it."

The salon party broke up after that. Keely excused herself so that she could use the second half of the afternoon to finish up the interviews for her magazine article. Because she didn't have time to conduct them in person, she had to risk using her cell phone. To make sure she wouldn't be caught doing that, she walked to the hotel next door and found a relatively quiet nook in the coffee shop.

On the way out of the hotel she passed a boutique that displayed a stunning dress in the window. Realizing that she needed something a bit more dressy for the wedding, she went inside. While trying it on, she gazed at herself in the mirror. Was this the image of the new, liberated ranch wife? Could a ranch wife be someone who'd posed nude for a men's magazine?

Of course not. And she had no business thinking like that, anyway. No matter how the image had changed, it still involved the tedium of marriage, that boring institution that sucked the life right out of a sexual relationship, right? But the women she'd met today didn't seem to be sucked dry. They were juicy ladies. And getting into bed with Noah every night didn't sound like such a bad deal, either.

Yeah, like he'd ask her to consider that option. The man didn't want to let himself climb into bed with her tonight, let alone for the rest of his life.

But he *would* go to bed with her tonight. She turned in front of the mirror. Definitely.

NOAH BOUGHT HIMSELF a pair of shorts so he could spend the afternoon playing volleyball on the resort's sand court with the guys. Throwing himself into the physical activity felt great. Maybe if he played hard enough, maybe if he spent the whole afternoon getting hot, sweaty and tired, he'd be too exhausted to be tempted by Keely in the suite tonight after the wedding.

He didn't go back to the suite until he had to change into his tux. Bracing himself for Keely to be parading around in something sexy or in nothing at all, he discovered she wasn't even there.

While he was taking his shower and getting dressed, he expected her to show up at any moment. Eventually his curiosity turned to irritation. She'd been invited to this wedding, and she'd damn sure better not be late. Then his irritation changed to concern. What if she'd gone back to the topless bar and taken that job, after all?

When he'd seen her last she was headed off toward the hotel's salon, but maybe she'd ducked out of that. He almost called Greg and Tina's room to find out if Tina knew where Keely might be. But he didn't really want to do that.

Standing in front of the bathroom mirror, he struggled with his bow tie. In the few times he'd ever worn a tux, he'd never really learned how to tie the damn thing. With a growl of frustration, he pulled it loose and started over.

A second before Keely spoke, he smelled her raspberry lotion. Instantly his groin tightened.

"Need some help, cowboy?"

He looked in the mirror and she was reflected there, leaning casually in the wide arch separating the bedroom and the bathroom.

Her purse was slung over her shoulder and a shopping bag dangled from her hand. She looked as if she'd been outside— her hair was tousled and her cheeks were pink from the heat. She was also breathing fast, despite her relaxed pose against the doorway. The crocheted halter top she wore quivered with each breath she took, and he wondered if she'd hurried up here because she was running late or because she was eager to see him again.

"That bow tie seems to be getting the better of you," she said. "Don't you have to be down there in a few minutes?"

"Yep." He met her gaze in the mirror and weighed the risk of having her help him tie it. "Are you going to have time to get ready?"

"Sure. I have at least a half hour more than you do. I'll get dressed after you leave. But you can't go with your tie looking like that." She put down her purse and her shopping bag and came toward him. "Turn around and let me see what I can do."

He assumed she'd learned the skill from hanging out with guys who regularly wore these monkey suits. Knowing Keely, she might be planning to turn this into a very seductive operation. Filled with misgivings, he faced her. "How was the manicure session?"

"Lotus Blossom Pink." She held up both hands to show him her nails.

They were covered in a pearly color that reminded him of the inside of a seashell. Or the inside curve of her ear. Or the inside of…places he'd do well not to think about. Damn, but she smelled good.

She stepped closer and took the ends of the bow tie in her pink-tipped fingers. "Now hold still," she murmured.

Oh, he'd hold still. He didn't dare move a muscle. He just hoped that involuntary reactions wouldn't take over. Some things he couldn't control.

Staring at a point over her head, he tried to block out all sensation, but he wasn't having much luck. He was very much aware of the light, whispery sound of her breathing, the brush of her fingers and the scent of raspberries. If she leaned forward a fraction, her breasts would touch the front of his white pleated shirt. He clenched his hands at his sides.

"Shoot," she muttered.

He glanced down and knew immediately that was a mistake. Keely could be the most provocative, tempting woman in the world when she tried. But right now, to his complete amazement, she wasn't trying. And he discovered she could be just as irresistible when she didn't try.

All her concentration was on his tie, and she'd tucked her tongue into the corner of her mouth while she worked. Apparently she didn't know much more about this process than he did, but she'd been willing to jump in and help. He found that endearing.

Frowning fiercely, she pulled the tie this way and that.

"Want me to try again?" he asked.

"No, I'm going to get it. I'm just out of practice."

That meant she hadn't been doing this favor for any man recently. Noah was glad to hear it.

"There!" She stepped back with a huge smile of triumph. "I did it!"

A lump of emotion stuck in his throat. He remembered seeing that expression on her face when she was nine years old. As a self-important twelve-year-old he'd been teaching her how to rope her horse as the gelding circled them in the corral. When she'd finally settled her loop over her horse's head, she'd given him that exact grin.

Her grin had turned to surprise when the rope had tightened and jerked her off her feet. He'd forgotten to tell her what to do after she'd roped the horse. Her skinned hands and knees were all his fault that day, and he'd blamed himself for weeks.

He'd been worried about resisting Keely when she turned on her sexual charm, but he might have an even tougher time resisting her when she reminded him of the eager, happy little kid she used to be.

"You look very nice, Noah," she said softly. There was no

taunt in her green eyes this time. Her compliment was simply and sincerely given as if she had no ulterior motive.

He was lost. "Keely." He gripped her arms, his fingers registering the warmth and smoothness of her skin.

Awareness blazed in her eyes. "You have to go," she said, her voice husky.

"I have to kiss you first."

"Noah—"

"I have to." He settled his mouth over hers with a groan of relief. Yes. How he'd needed this kiss, ached for it. Yet it was a different kind of ache from the one he'd had the night before. There was a sexual edge to this longing, but it was more about cherishing her than making frenzied love to her. It was the kind of ache that scared the hell out of him.

Ah, the joys of Keely's mouth—lips plump against his, responding, moistening, parting to let him stroke his tongue inside. His grip on her arms tightened, his fingers massaged that silky skin. And before he knew it, he'd slid both hands to her neck and untied her halter top.

And then...then he went a little crazy, filling both hands with her magnificent breasts, kissing his way over her jaw and down her throat. Braced against the edge of the counter, he leaned down and claimed his prize.

He grew dizzy from the pure pleasure of her breast in his mouth.

And she tunneled her fingers through his hair and held him close. "Noah..." she said, gasping out his name. "You have to...leave."

Oh, no. He couldn't leave now. Not when he'd found heaven.

"You...should go."

With a murmur of protest he lifted his mouth and caressed one wet, erect nipple with his thumb while he moved to dampen the other with his tongue. Men had died for less reward than this. He could barely believe he was really cupping the weight of her beautiful breasts. Squeezing them with trembling fingers, he gave thanks for his good fortune as he tasted and tasted again, his mind numbed by the wonder of what was happening. The sensations bombarding him made his head buzz and his ears ring.

And ring, and ring. Wow, that was some sensation, like a…telephone.

Keely backed away from his embrace. "Sorry," she mumbled.

Dazed, he stared at her as she went over to get her purse and then proceeded to dig through it. A man could go crazy watching uncovered breasts like hers quiver. Finally she pulled a cell phone from the bottom of her purse.

A cell phone?

She pushed a button and shoved the phone back in her purse. Then she glanced up at him. "You'd better go," she murmured.

"What—" He paused to clear his throat. "What was that?"

"Nothing."

"You have a cell phone?"

"Yes."

"Why?" He couldn't fit the cell phone in with her supposed rootless living style. Topless dancers moving from city to city didn't have cell phones. Or did they?

"It's for work," she said.

Everything clicked into place for him. "Keely, are you a call girl?"

"No, I'm not."

He should have guessed she'd deny it, both now and the first time he'd asked her. What had he expected her to do, confess such a thing? "You are, aren't you? And you were afraid to tell me."

"No, really. I—"

"It's okay." He couldn't blame her, not when every time he looked at her he wanted to take her to bed. After years of getting that reaction from men, she might have become convinced that was what she was born to do. "It's not your fault that men want you," he said. "Hell, look at me. I can't keep my hands off you, and I promised myself I would."

"Noah, I'm telling you I'm not a call girl."

"And I'm telling you that I understand. We'll work around it."

She threw up both hands. "Okay, believe what you want. But right now, you'd better get downstairs." She stood. Her halter top had fallen until it was draped around her waist, but she made no move to retie it around her neck.

"Yeah, I'd better get going." But he couldn't seem to stop looking at her. Light from the overhead fixture in the bathroom picked up the sheen of moisture on her breasts, moisture left there by his eager mouth. God help him, he wanted more.

A call girl. That made it even more important that he not make love to her. She needed a completely platonic relationship with him if she had a prayer of changing her life. And so far he'd completely bombed out on the platonic thing.

Gazing at him, she pulled the halter top off over her head and shook out her hair. "Unless you want a quickie before you go. On the house."

"No!" He backed toward the door, while his whole body screamed with frustration. "Listen, I should never have kissed you. I should never have gone beyond kissing you." But, oh, God, was it fantastic. He could still taste her on his tongue. "Tomorrow we'll map out a job strategy. I'm thinking something in sales."

She arched her eyebrows. "Because I already have sales experience, you mean? I guess that makes sense. If I can sell my body, I can sell widgets."

"That's not what I meant!"

"I must not be very good at selling my body, though." She kicked off her sandals and began to peel off her capris. "I've offered it to you several times now and you keep turning me down."

His heart thudded in his chest as he watched her take off the last of her clothes. A quiver of need passed through him. "It's very, very hard."

She laughed and glanced at his crotch. "I can see that."

"Hey! I didn't mean—"

"Men have told me all sorts of lies, Noah, but all I have to do is look at the fly of their pants and I know exactly what they're thinking. It's like those witching sticks some people use to find water. Men get around me and—boing!—that witching stick points right in my direction." The devilish gleam was back in her eyes when she met his gaze. "If you decide you want to drill for water, come and see me. I'll give you a special rate."

It took incredible willpower for him to turn away from a very naked, very tempting Keely and walk out of the suite. Somehow he did it.

11

NOAH WENT THROUGH THE motions of seating people in the rows of white folding chairs on the grassy courtyard where the wedding would be held, but his thoughts were still back in the suite with Keely. He'd been stupid not to see the truth immediately. The interview she'd been going to in the topless bar might have been with some sort of Las Vegas madam. Or worse yet, a pimp. The thought made him shudder.

Well, he was going to save her from that kind of life, just the way Richard Gere had saved Julia Roberts in *Pretty Woman*. Except Richard Gere had hired Julia Roberts for sex in the first place, so that had been part of the deal from the beginning.

If you decide you want to drill for water, she'd said, her skin flushed with desire, her eyes issuing a definite invitation. Was he a total fool to be so chained to his principles? Probably. His friends would certainly say so. Keely would certainly say so.

Then something else occurred to him. In her chosen profession as a hired lover, she wouldn't go to bed with a man because she wanted him. Having sex because she wanted to might be a real treat for her, a vacation from the same-ol', same-ol'.

Now, there was a dangerous concept. If he truly believed

that, he could start thinking that he'd be doing her a favor, giving her a chance for some mutual satisfaction for a change. That might be the only motivation he'd need to send him over the edge.

Then Keely appeared and he wondered if he hadn't toppled over the edge some time ago.

If he hadn't, this latest dress of hers would do the trick. A rush of possessiveness heated his skin as if he'd just opened an oven door, and he hurried over so that he'd be the one to escort her to her seat.

She smiled as he approached. The smile was sly and seductive, and it put the final touch on a picture designed to bring him to his knees. She'd tamed her wild curls, pinning them on top of her head for a regal, sophisticated look. But it wasn't any less sexy than the tousled style she usually wore. Maybe it was even more sexy, because he could imagine the fun of mussing her up.

Rhinestone earrings and a small rhinestone-trimmed shoulder purse sparkled in the light from the tiki torches surrounding the courtyard. But the fit of her dress was the real showstopper. It shimmered over her body like mercury, outlining her hourglass figure to perfection. Made of an iridescent material, it rippled and flashed like a hologram with her every movement.

Although the dress had a high-necked collar, a diamond-shaped cutout beneath the collar showed an impressive amount of cleavage. And the back of the dress was nonexistent except for that little band of a collar. Beneath it was a spectacular view of supple, golden skin sweeping down to her waist.

Her skirt was ankle length, but a slit up the side ran to midthigh. Another few inches and it would graze the edge of her panties. That was assuming she wore any tonight. She had a wicked gleam in her eyes, so absolutely anything was possible.

Pulse racing, he offered his arm. When she slipped her hand through and moved in close, he took a deep breath and nearly zoned out on raspberry lotion. "Where do you want to sit?" he asked.

"On your lap," she murmured.

"Keely." He thought his heart would pound right out of his chest.

"Is that a yes or a no?" She flashed him another of her I-dare-you smiles.

"You're outrageous."

"And you're turned on. I'll bet your witching stick is twitching. I'll bet you're picturing all the possibilities right now."

"Pretty sure of yourself, aren't you?" And she had a right to be. She was dead-on accurate about the state of his mind and his body.

"It's a safe bet that you'll be thinking about me straddling you instead of listening to the ceremony. And speaking of that, I'll sit on the groom's side of the aisle. He asked me to the wedding, after all."

Taking another deep breath, Noah escorted her to the seats on the right side of the aisle.

"And I can tell you're just dying to know, so I'll end the suspense. I'm not wearing panties. They ruined the line of the dress and it was too hot for panty hose. You can think about that while you're standing at the altar trying not to look my way."

Swallowing hard, he halted near a row of chairs with a vacant seat. He noticed that most of the men in the vicinity had their attention firmly fixed on Keely. He lowered his voice. "Are you planning to throw out lines like that all night?"

"I'm only trying to live up to your expectations, Noah. Do you like the dress?"

"It's…um…tight."

"Well, that's on purpose, because if it was too loose you'd be able to see right down the front." She drew closer and dropped her voice to a low purr. "I'm not wearing a bra, either."

He struggled for his next breath.

She ran her index finger along his sleeve. "Does looking at me in this dress make you hot?"

He cleared his throat.

"I'll take that as an affirmative. Besides, I know it does. I can tell by the way you're breathing, sort of rough, like a car that needs to be tuned. I'd be glad to give you a tune-up, Noah."

"You'd better take your seat."

"Guess so." She squeezed his arm briefly before turning toward the row of chairs. Then she glanced over her shoulder. "See you later, big guy," she murmured, puckering her lips in a phantom kiss.

Moments later he took his place at the altar with the other groomsmen. As the minister led Jenny and Brandon through their vows, he tried to pay attention to the ceremony. After all, that was the reason he was here—to witness his buddy getting married.

But instead, he spent the entire ceremony exactly as Keely had predicted he would. He tried not to look at her, but he couldn't help it. And every time his attention strayed in her direction, he thought about how little separated him from her naked body. Only one tight, silvery dress. A dress with no back and a slit up the side. Once the collar was unfastened, she'd be bare to the waist. And if they were alone, he could easily push aside that skirt….

KEELY BECAME MORE CAUGHT up in the ceremony than she'd expected to be. She'd meant to concentrate on Noah and complete the seduction she'd started with her entrance. Instead, she found herself listening to the words of the ceremony, and for some stupid reason they were making her cry.

She blinked back her tears. Maybe B.J.'s upcoming wedding was hitting her harder than she wanted to admit. When she thought of B.J. getting married without her being there, her stomach felt hollow. Years ago they'd talked about being maid of honor for each other. It had been a given. She wondered if B.J. had chosen her friend Sally for that job.

Discarding that depressing subject, Keely focused on Brandon and Jenny. They seemed so damn happy, as if they didn't mind a bit that they were severely narrowing their options with this move. Keely had always believed in keeping her options open. Any man who had dared mention the "M" word had been dropped.

By keeping her options open, she'd remained free to fly to Paris if she wanted, free to party wherever the music was the hottest, free to sleep with a gorgeous hunk who suddenly appeared on her radar. Jenny was giving up those options. And yet the life that Jenny had chosen didn't seem so bad at this moment, and all of Keely's options seemed to have lost their luster.

It was Noah's fault. Seeing him again had stirred up those childish dreams of living with one man—Noah Garfield— for the rest of her life. No other guy had ever inspired those dreams, and when Noah had rejected her, she'd decided it was a stupid idea in the first place.

And it was still stupid. Jenny and her friends might think the world had changed enough to allow a woman like Keely to live happily ever after in Saguaro Junction, but Keely, who'd inherited her mother's craving for excitement, knew better.

So did Noah, which was why he'd never consider her as his life companion.

Life companion. God, did Noah have that written all over him. Any woman fantasizing about a man who could see her through all the joys and sorrows fate could dish out would recognize Noah as the real deal. He made her mouth water as he stood up there in his tux. He made her yearn for things that were beyond her reach. But early on she'd taken a clear-eyed inventory of herself, and now she had to have the courage to accept who she was…and who she wasn't.

In the meantime, however, she could have one weekend of lovemaking. Another woman would be lucky enough to have him for a lifetime, but Keely had been allowed this weekend and she intended to make the most of it.

She was aware that the dynamics between them had changed since she'd accidentally left her cell phone on and he'd assumed that a cell phone meant she was a call girl. She wasn't sure exactly what was going on in that fertile brain of his, but she had the definite feeling that his resistance to her was weakening. It could be the effect of the dress, of course, but she thought something else was happening.

Whatever it was, she wouldn't question it. If thinking she was a call girl allowed him to let go and make love to her, then she'd let him think she was a call girl. She didn't care how he perceived her, so long as the end result was hours and hours of wild sex. And then they would part. It was the only way this could end.

She blinked back another rush of tears. Damn. Maybe one of the reasons she hated weddings was that they always made her cry.

"OH, MAN, WILL YOU look at that." Clint handed Noah one of the two piña coladas he'd brought over from the bar before turning to face the action—Keely doing the limbo in her tight, silver dress. "Tell me you're not letting that go to waste."

Noah took a cooling sip of his coconut-flavored drink, hoping the icy concoction would quench the fire in his belly. Or better yet, maybe the rum would short-circuit his brain. But the drink seemed to have no effect whatsoever and he was still in agony as he gazed at Keely sliding under the pole, her body moving rhythmically to the beat of the music and the clapping hands urging her on. "You have a one-track mind, son," he told Clint, although the comment applied to him, too.

"Every other track gets shut down when a woman built like Keely does the limbo," Clint said. "Any man with breath left in his body would respond to a sight like that. But you're the only guy here with a chance of acting on that impulse. I just need to know you're up to the job, so to speak."

"You might need to know, but you're not gonna know." Noah kept his tone casual, disguising the fierce emotions that had gripped him from the moment the luau reception had begun and Keely had made it clear that she planned to party.

When Keely partied, sexual sparks flew in all directions. She'd drawn the attention of every man in attendance, with the possible exception of Brandon, who was understandably preoccupied with his new bride. For a solid two hours Noah had fought his own sexual bonfire. At the same time he'd tried to stamp out the smaller blazes of jealousy whenever he caught a man looking at Keely the way Clint was doing right now.

"I guess you don't really have to tell me anything." Clint kept his gaze on Keely while he took another swallow of his piña colada. "It's a foregone conclusion that something's gonna happen between you two."

Noah had pretty much concluded the same thing, but he wasn't happy about it. He should be stronger, nobler, wiser.

Then he'd be able to keep his hands off Keely and be in a better moral position to help her turn her life around.

But he'd been forced to admit his own weakness and her greater strength. Before much longer, she would get her way. He couldn't hold out anymore. He'd tried to justify it as a pleasure that Keely deserved, after all those times when she'd only been doing her job. As a justification it didn't work very well. In his heart he knew that this would be about his needs, not hers.

By the time he'd finished his piña colada Keely had won the limbo contest, adding her prize to the one she'd picked up for taking first place in the hula contest. She turned in Noah's direction and blew him a kiss.

Clint chuckled. "Like I said, a foregone conclusion. At lunch I wasn't sure about the chemistry, but tonight she's on your trail, buddy." He clapped Noah on the back. "How does it feel to be the envy of every guy here?"

"Just wonderful."

"Funny, but you don't look as happy as I would expect you to. Is there a problem?"

Noah looked at his friend. Clint had no idea how many problems were connected to this situation, but Noah wasn't going to enlighten him. Instead, he grinned. "Clint, Keely's a woman. Of course there will be problems."

Clint nodded. "Point taken." He glanced at Noah's empty glass. "I think we need a refill. Let's—"

"Ladies and gentlemen," Greg crooned into a wireless microphone, "may I have your attention, please."

"Damn, but he loves that mike," Clint said. "I think he believes he's the next David Letterman."

"Don't complain," Noah said. "Better him as the emcee than either one of us."

"True."

Greg glanced around at the crowd. "It's now time to play

a special version of that old favorite, musical chairs, better known in this case as musical laps!"

Noah remembered having fun playing the game at Greg's wedding. The guys sat in a circle and the women moved around the circle ready to grab a lap when the music ended. But Keely hadn't been a part of the game a year ago. He didn't want Keely sitting on any lap but his.

"Finally something I can do," Clint said. "Come on, Noah. Grab yourself a chair."

He was going to hate this. Really hate it. He picked up a chair and set it beside Clint's. Greg organized the women, making sure there was one less man in the circle than there were women walking around it. To the melody of "Ukelele Lady," the women started to move around the group of seated men.

Whenever Keely passed Noah, she slowed down and gave him a secret smile. Then he watched helplessly as she cruised by with that killer walk of hers. The music stopped.

Amid breathless squeals from the contestants, Keely settled quickly in another man's lap. Noah didn't know him, but that didn't matter. He hated his guts.

Sharon plopped down in Noah's lap. "Hi, cutie," she said, turning to smile at him. "Having a good time?"

"Sure." He unclenched his jaw and smiled back. "How about you?"

"I'm having a great time watching you watch Keely. I've never seen you with that look on your face."

"It's indigestion. I should never have eaten that poi junk."

"Uh-huh. Indigestion and lovesickness look about the same on a man. I can see where I could get confused."

"You're confused, all right." Lovesickness? He'd better not be coming down with that disease. Catching it from a woman like Keely could be fatal.

Greg commanded the microphone again. "Okay, ladies, that's enough lap dancing for this round. On your feet."

Sharon slid off Noah's lap. "We all like her, you know," she said.

He played dumb. "Who?"

She rolled her eyes and glanced at her husband sitting next to him. "Did you find out anything interesting?"

"He's not talking," Clint said. "I did my best, but—"

"We have to eliminate a lap," Greg said. "Clint, come on out of there."

"Aw, *man,*" Clint grumbled as his wife began to laugh. "I never get to have any fun." Muttering to himself he hauled his chair off to the side and Greg started the music again.

Once again Keely passed by Noah, her hips swaying in time to the music. He ground his teeth and suffered. The tune continued and she approached for the second time, still wearing that secret little smile. When the music abruptly ended, Noah reacted without thinking. Grabbing her around the waist, he pulled her down to his lap.

"Oof!" she gasped, startled.

Heat climbed up from Noah's starched tux collar. He really hadn't meant to do that. On the other hand, he was very glad to have that silky silver bottom planted firmly on his lap instead of another guy's. Maybe a little too glad. In fact, a certain part of him was getting way too glad.

"I want a ruling on that!" Jenny, the woman left with no lap, stomped over to Noah and Keely. She attempted to look disapproving, but a grin was trying to break through. "I think that was some kind of interference on Noah's part." She turned to Greg. "And possible collusion on Keely's part. How would you call it?"

Greg nodded soberly. "Definitely a lap violation, and possibly a moving violation, as well."

"I'm innocent, Mr. Judge, sir," Keely snuggled down a little deeper.

"It's all my fault," Noah said. And his automatic reaction had also been a mistake. Not only had he telegraphed his feelings to everyone in the immediate vicinity, he wasn't going to be able to hide his erection if Keely didn't stop shifting her weight around.

"I say they're both guilty as sin," Jenny said, her lips twitching with laughter. "Throw the book at 'em."

Greg's eyes twinkled as he stroked his chin. "The bride has spoken, and tonight she's the law around here. I'm afraid I have to eliminate both of you from the competition."

"Sounds fair, right, Keely?" Noah stood immediately, hauling Keely up with him.

"If you say so," she said cheerfully.

He released her and backed away, hoping to hell nobody would notice the bulge in his pants.

"No hard feelings?" Jenny asked, winking at him.

"Uh, no." He just knew she'd used the word *hard* on purpose, and no doubt his face was pink as a flamingo.

"Then I have a favor to ask," Jenny said. "Would you two please go find the caterer and ask her to bring out some more fresh pineapple for the buffet table? I noticed we're running low. Just go behind the waterfall and straight down the hallway to the end and you'll find her. Her name's Julie Osaka."

"Uh, okay," Noah said, not sure he should venture anywhere with Keely at the moment.

"Let me get my purse," Keely said.

"All right." He couldn't very well order her to stay at the reception, so he waited until she'd retrieved her purse before he headed toward the waterfall at a brisk pace.

"Are we going to jog all the way to the caterer's office?" she asked, hurrying after him.

"Can't have Jenny running out of fresh pineapple."

"Okay, but if the two of us arrive in her office panting like racehorses, no telling what the caterer will think we've been up to."

He realized he was overreacting, besides behaving like an uncivilized jerk. He slowed down. They were going in search of the caterer. Surely he could keep his act together for a simple errand like that. "Sorry." He held the glass door open for her.

"That's better." She linked her arm through his as they strolled down a carpeted hallway. Then she glanced up at him. "All that work to get your bow tie together, and you've spent the whole reception with it hanging loose and your collar unbuttoned."

"I was hot." He quickly backpedaled. "I mean, warm. The night's very warm."

She slipped in closer so that the side of her breast nudged his arm. "Actually, I think a guy looks sexy with his tie undone. It's a tease, like the first stage of undressing."

"Hmm." He didn't dare try to carry on a conversation. Even though they were strolling at a leisurely pace now, he had trouble breathing normally. The most outrageous ideas stampeded through his fevered brain. She was wearing nothing more than that dress. All he needed was a dark corner. Surely there was one of those nearby. He'd already noticed a couple of places where the hallway branched off. God, he was depraved. And she'd done that to him.

A trim woman with Asian features came out of a doorway and started toward them.

When she was close enough for Noah to read her name tag, he realized they'd been lucky enough to run into the caterer. "Excuse me," he said. "We're from the wedding party, and the bride asked if you could see about putting out more fresh pineapple."

The caterer smiled. "Of course. You can't have a decent

luau without plenty of fresh pineapple. I was just heading down there to check on things. I'll stop by the kitchen and take care of that first. Anything else?"

"That should do it," Noah said.

"So the reception's going well?"

"It's lovely," Keely said. "Everyone's having a great time."

"Good. Then I'll let you get back to the party." The caterer headed down one of the side hallways.

Keely gazed up at him. "Mission accomplished."

"Right." He looked into her green eyes and found heat simmering there. The accessibility she'd built into that dress was driving him wild. "Now we can go back."

"Right." She ran her tongue over her lower lip. "Would you mind if I stopped by the powder room first?"

"I'm...not sure where it is." His heart pounded. He didn't think the powder room was what she had in mind, but he couldn't be positive.

"I'm not sure, either. We can explore." She tugged on his arm, leading him back down the hallway. Then she turned right down another long hallway that ended in a bank of windows looking out on a tropical atrium. "Maybe this way."

He didn't think so. The doors they passed looked like offices to him. At this time of night, no one was working in them. But maybe there was a rest room down here, and maybe that's really what Keely hoped to find.

As they neared the end of the hallway, he couldn't see any door marked Women. But he did notice the hallway widened at the end. Two private nooks on either side had been turned into conversation areas, and they each contained two armchairs, an end table and a potted palm. Probably a place for the office employees to take a short break.

His pulse quickened. Behind that chair. Up against the wall. It was the darkest corner he was likely to get. He doubted anyone came down this hallway at night. His mouth grew moist, his penis hard. No. This was insane.

He cleared his throat. "Nothing's here."

Keely eyed the two shadowy nooks. Then she glanced at Noah. "Pretty deserted spot, isn't it?"

"We need to get back," he said, his voice hoarse.

"We will." She tossed her purse on one of the chairs before turning to face him. Then she took the ends of his bow tie in her fingers. "In a little bit." Slowly she drew him closer until a bare inch was left between them.

He could feel the heat of her body and smell the scent of raspberries mixed with a more basic, musky aroma of excited woman. She'd been taunting him with this possibility all night. He'd never done something like this, never been driven to try. But then no woman had ever announced to him at the beginning of an evening that she wasn't wearing underwear.

Something within him snapped. With a groan he pushed her past the chair and into the corner of the tiny nook. With one hand he held her head while he plundered her mouth. With the other he found the slit in her skirt and reached inside. He encountered lace panties. He'd been had.

He gripped her lace-covered bottom and lifted his mouth from hers. "You're wearing panties," he said, breathing hard.

"Am I? I must have forgotten," she murmured.

"You were bluffing."

"I was teasing."

"I call it bluffing, and lady, I'm calling your bluff." He looked into her eyes as he reached down and grabbed a section of her skirt in each fist. Then he yanked it up over her hips and bunched it around her waist.

Her eyes burned with green fire. "Right here?"

"Right here." He held the skirt high while he used his free hand to pull down that underwear she'd promised she wasn't wearing. Then he slipped his hand between her legs and his mind reeled. She was drenched.

"Do you...have a condom?" she asked, her voice ragged.

"No," he whispered, allowing her skirt to ripple down around his wrist while he continued to caress her.

Her eyes fluttered closed and she began to pant. "We... need...one."

"Well, maybe you should have thought of that. You're the one who bought two boxes," he murmured before he claimed her mouth in another searing kiss.

12

NOT MUCH OF KEELY'S BRAIN was functioning, but she had to admit Noah was right. She *should* have thought of condoms. But she hadn't, and now…now he was driving her insane, using his fingers and thumb to create mind-altering pleasure. In a matter of seconds she'd lost all control of the situation.

Sensation rocketed through her, making her thighs quiver and her breasts tingle. Her nipples grew hard and thrust against the material of her dress. Oh. Yes. There.

She clutched his shoulders and arched toward him, craving more, craving deeper. If he chose to take her now, she wouldn't have the will to resist him. If he kept caressing her like this, she might beg him to take her, condom or no condom.

The birth control problem needed attention before it was too late. "Noah," she said, gasping. "We can't…" She couldn't think, let alone talk. "If we don't have a condom, then we can't…"

He lifted his mouth from hers while his fingers continued to work their magic. "I know we can't," he murmured. "So first you, then me. We'll take care of each other. Deal?"

"Deal," she said with a sigh as her legs turned to rubber.

And what a deal. He'd found the perfect rhythm to make her writhe in helpless abandon as her body throbbed and yearned for climax. He would give it to her fast, and that was fine. She wanted it fast.

Then, at the moment when she balanced on the very brink of ecstasy, he slowed the movement of his hand and gentled the pressure of his thumb. He slid his fingers out and teased her with a light, butterfly touch. Slipped slowly in again, then withdrew. Circled his thumb right where it would have the most effect, then stopped.

She whimpered against his mouth.

He lifted his lips a fraction from hers. His voice was rough and untamed. "I've decided I want more. Unhook your collar."

She trembled and fought for breath. She'd unleashed the wild man in Noah. "If I let go of you, I'll fall down."

He wrapped his arm more firmly around her waist. "Now you can let go." He nibbled at her lower lip. "I want that collar undone. And the way I feel right now, I might rip it."

Her hands shook as she reached back to unfasten the collar.

He brushed his mouth against hers. "I love it when you put your hands behind your head and push your breasts toward me like that." He continued to stroke her in a lazy way, just enough to keep her at a fevered pitch.

Oh, yes, Noah had made the transition from nice guy to rogue. She was quivering too much to manage the hooks. "I can't do it."

"I think you can."

"Then be still," she pleaded. He paused for a beat, and she unfastened the hooks. "There."

"Now pull the material down." He stroked her again with that easy rhythm, deceptively easy.

She was close. Very close. But it seemed he wanted her nearly naked when the moment arrived. Shaking with tension and the excitement of undressing in this barely concealed corner, she peeled away the top part of the dress and let it hang at her waist.

His breath was hot and sweet on her face. "Now put your hands behind your head again," he murmured.

She reached back and laced her fingers together, cradling her head in her hands. Her breasts lifted.

He leaned back slightly and looked down. A guttural sound of pure male satisfaction rumbled in his throat. Then his lust-filled gaze met hers. "Are you afraid?" he asked softly. "Afraid someone will see us? Hear us?"

"Sure." Her voice quivered. "That's part of the thrill."

His eyes darkened and his whole body began to shake. "Yeah," he said. "Yeah, it is. I didn't know. This is so good." With a soft moan he nuzzled her throat. "So good." He quickened the movement of his fingers, circled his thumb over her aching flashpoint.

"Yes. Oh, *yes.*"

"You're going to come soon," he said hoarsely.

She began to pant. "I...am."

His hot mouth trailed down the slope of her breast. "If you make noise...."

"I won't," she whispered.

Slowing the rhythm of his fingers, he drew a moist circle around her nipple with his tongue. "You're sure?" he asked, his breath whispering over her breast. "It's going to be good."

"Yes, I'm sure." She moaned softly. "Make me come, Noah. Please make me come."

Lightly, ever so lightly, his tongue flicked against her taut nipple. Slowly at first, then more quickly. And his thumb, centered over her trigger point, mimicked the flicking motion. Faster, and faster still, connecting two charged points, arcing tension between them...tightening...vibrating... faster, faster, faster—*now.*

She clenched her jaw to keep from crying out as spasms shook her. Stroking rhythmically with his fingers, he closed his mouth over her breast and sucked in deeply, then released the pressure, sucked in and released. The liquid sound of his sucking followed the beat of her orgasm, and each tug on her breast became part of her climax as he drew on her again and again.

Her throat ached with silent moans of release—blissful, perfect release.

His hand movement slowed, then stopped, but his fingers were still buried deep. With one soft kiss on the very tip of her throbbing nipple, he straightened and eased his fingers free.

Gradually opening her eyes, she gazed into his—heavy-lidded with passion, and smoldering, still smoldering. She cupped his face in both hands. "Thank you," she murmured.

"You're welcome." He lifted a damp finger and traced the outline of her lips. "I want to taste your secrets," he whispered before covering her mouth with his.

He kissed her thoroughly, sharing the musky tang of her climax and stirring the embers of her desire. Unbelievably, she began to want again. But this time her needs had a different focus.

Reaching between them, she stroked his crotch and found the metal clasp of his zipper. As she pulled it down, he shuddered. She slid her hand inside, cupping the warm weight of him, tight and near to bursting, barely contained in the skimpy briefs she'd bought yesterday.

Such foresight. The soft cotton gave way easily to her quick tug, and in no time she had her hand around his big, beautiful penis.

He gasped in reaction, lifting his head to look into her eyes.

Meeting his darkened gaze, she closed her fingers around the base of his shaft. Then she stroked upward until she encountered his most vulnerable spot. Lingering there, she absorbed the tremors that shook him each time her fingers made contact. Then she stroked down again and eased back up to torture him some more.

His eyes burned hot and hungry and his voice rasped in the stillness. "You're driving me crazy."

"I hope so." She rubbed her thumb over the moisture-slick tip and he closed his eyes with a groan. She knew what he longed for, but she wanted him to ask. It was so much more exciting that way. "Tell me, Noah, what else can I do for you?"

His eyes opened, and unchecked passion flamed there. He stared at her, and his chest heaved with his struggle to breathe. "I want you on your knees," he whispered hoarsely. "I want your mouth on me."

She loved playing with fire, loved taunting him as he'd taunted her. "Will you make noise?"

He gasped again as she brushed a finger where she discovered he could feel it most. "No."

"You're sure?"

"Yes." His voice cracked. "Please, Keely."

Dizzy from the thrill of her own sexual power, she sank to her knees. At first she used her tongue to explore and caress him until he was trembling so violently that he braced both hands against the wall. As she anticipated the moment to come, as she imagined him anticipating it, desire spiraled tighter within her.

By the time she took his straining penis in her mouth, her frenzy matched his. His climax came quickly, and as she swallowed his warm, salty essence, she throbbed with unmet needs. She wanted everything this man had to offer. And she would get it. The night was young.

NOAH HAD NO IDEA HOW much time went by before he gathered the strength to put his clothes back together and help Keely with hers. He felt like the victim of a shipwreck. Probably resembled one, too.

He touched her cheek with a still-trembling hand. "Incredible," he said, gazing into her eyes.

"Yeah," she said softly. She was totally mussed and outrageously sexy-looking, all tousled and pink. Her hairdo had self-destructed and her lipstick was MIA. Just thinking about how her lipstick had gotten smeared was getting him worked up again, so he'd be better off not thinking about it.

A slow smile of satisfaction tilted those kiss-swollen lips of hers. "So you liked taking a little risk?"

He looked into her green, devilish eyes. She'd won. "Yes, I did."

"Want more?"

Yes, he wanted more. More of whatever she could dish out. "I think you know the answer to that."

"I do." She stroked a finger over his lower lip. "But it pleases me to hear you say it."

He caught her hand and licked the crevice between each finger. "Do you want me to tell you I'm your slave?"

"Are you?" She sounded a little breathless.

"Looks that way." And he wanted a chance to turn the tables.

"What about the luau? And your friends? Shouldn't we go back?"

He studied her and searched for some diplomatic way to describe her rumpled condition. "I guess we should. For a while longer. But you might need to do a little repair work first."

"Oh." She touched a hand to her hair. "Right."

"We never did find a bathroom."

"No, but the window should make a good enough mirror."

"Yeah." Reluctantly he stepped aside and let her out of their private corner. He felt like claiming a chunk of plaster or a section of carpet as a souvenir for one of the peak experiences of his life. "You weren't really looking for the bathroom, were you?"

She turned from pinning up her hair, and with her arms up like that, she was so inviting, so completely feminine. "No, I wasn't," she said.

"Didn't think so."

She looked in the window's reflection again and continued doing her hair. "You didn't believe for one minute I was looking for the bathroom, did you?"

"I was hoping you weren't," he admitted. "I was hoping you were looking for a dark corner, the same as me."

"It's so great to be on the same page for once."

Right now he wouldn't mind being on the same bed. But first they had to get back to the luau and put in an appearance. He glanced down to make sure his fly was completely zipped, and there, plain as could be on the dove-gray material, was a lipstick mark. "Damn," he mumbled, trying to scrape it off with his fingernail. It wasn't working.

"What's the matter?" She turned from the window, her lipstick tube in one hand. Then she began to giggle.

"I'm glad you think it's funny. Lipstick on my collar is one thing, but I don't really want to walk into the luau with lipstick on my fly."

"Stop rubbing it. You'll only make it worse." She grinned at him. "I have something to take care of your problem." She capped her lipstick tube and dropped it back inside her purse.

"Like what?" He had learned to be suspicious of a smiling Keely Branscom.

"This." She produced a small packet and ripped it open.

He was immediately aroused and ready to destroy the work she'd put into her hair and makeup. "You said you didn't have one."

"I usually tuck one in my purse." She pulled out a small, white square from the packet.

He imagined that she'd forgotten about it in the heat of the moment, but he was confused by the configuration of the condom in her hand. "They make them *square* and *white?* How does that work?"

"I'll show you." She sat in the chair. "Come on over here."

He couldn't believe she was being so nonchalant about it. Her casual attitude excited him even more. "While you're in the chair?" They would be way more visible in that chair than they had been in the corner. But if she was willing to try, he was more than willing.

"Sure. That puts me at the right level."

He'd heard about making love with the woman in a chair, her legs spread over the arms, and he'd always meant to try it. But he hadn't expected the chair to be at the end of an open hallway in a public building. He quivered with expectation as he walked toward her.

She gazed at his fly and glanced up, amusement in her eyes. "Looking forward to this, are we?"

"You'd better believe it."

"This should be very interesting." She used the white square to rub the spot where the lipstick was.

He jumped back. "What in hell are you doing?"

"Getting your stain out. What did you think I was going to do?"

"I thought that white thing was a condom!"

She looked at the moist square and began to laugh.

"Well, it comes in the same kind of package!"

"Yes," she said, grinning at him. "Yes, it does. But this is a laundry aid. You use it to take out stains when you aren't near a washing machine. I think it would be totally useless for birth control."

He stared at her, unable to process this practical streak in a woman who seemed focused only on sexual experiences. "So how come you remembered to bring that and not a condom?"

"Because I thought we'd be at the luau the whole time. I guess I was more concerned about ruining my dress than getting pregnant." Laughter danced in her eyes. "Do you want me to work on that lipstick mark or not?"

"You'd better give me that thing. If you do it, I'm liable to end up with more lipstick on here, not less."

"I can control myself."

"That may well be, but I think we've established that I can't."

"I see." Gazing at him, she rubbed the towelette lazily back and forth between her fingers. "Then I guess you'd better do it."

"Stop that."

"You don't really want me to stop," she said softly. "You love being sexually on edge. You thought we were going to make love in this chair and you were ready to try, even with the danger of someone coming down the hallway and catching us at it. You crave the adventure, don't you?"

"Maybe. But I crave chocolate cake, too. That doesn't mean it's good for me."

"Well, there are several differences between me and chocolate cake." She lowered her voice to a seductive murmur. "And some similarities. I'm smooth and creamy, but I won't clog your arteries. And if you think you crave chocolate cake, wait until you've tasted me."

Amazing how he could stand there, not ten minutes after an unbelievable orgasm, and feel as if he could do it all again. "Give me that towel thing," he said. "The sooner we get back to the luau, the sooner we can leave."

"Now there's a plan." She handed him the towelette. "But I should warn you that someone could still come along. Would you rather they caught you rubbing your crotch, or me doing it?"

"No one's going to see a thing." He walked over to the

atrium window, keeping his back to the hallway. Then he started scrubbing at the spot on his fly.

She came to stand beside him and continued to fiddle with her hair as she looked at her reflection in the window. "I'll bet that doesn't feel as good as it might if I did it."

"Cut it out, Keely. I'm trying to clean this spot off without getting a major hard-on."

She lowered her voice again. "Looks like you're having difficulties with that. Have you ever allowed a woman to watch while you touched yourself?"

"No." Damn, but she had a way of thinking that turned him on. "And I'm not doing it now, either."

"We could save that for later. Did you like watching me in the hot tub?"

"Yes."

"I liked watching you, too. But you didn't know I was there. Next time, I want you to know."

He stopped rubbing the spot. If he kept it up while she was talking that way, he would lose control. "I guess that's good enough. Let's go back."

"Okay."

As they started back down the hall, he wadded up the towelette and tossed it in the planter on his way by. Then he took her hand, just to prove he could touch her without going crazy. It wasn't easy to keep the level down to hand-holding, but he would manage because he enjoyed the warmth of the connection.

"That was something," she said. "Really something."

"You've probably done stuff like that before." He shouldn't even ask, knowing he wouldn't like the answer.

"No, not really."

"You haven't?" He glanced at her in surprise.

"I only imagined doing it. I never did it for real."

"What do you know." As they continued down the hall,

he smiled to himself. Without realizing it, he'd made one of Keely's sexual fantasies come true. That was pretty cool. "And no one saw anything," he said, feeling damn smug about that, too.

"Well, not for the first part, anyway."

He tensed. "What do you mean?"

"Nobody caught us when we were in the corner, at least."

"Nobody saw me sponging my fly, either!"

"Maybe not."

"What do you mean, *maybe not?*"

"The janitor standing on the other side of the atrium might not have been able to see what you were doing."

He came unglued. "There was a janitor standing on the other side of the atrium? Why didn't you say something?"

"Because you were almost done." She chuckled. "And I didn't think having you freak out and spin around would do anything to change his opinion of what you were up to. So I just smiled at him. He smiled back."

Noah groaned. "Great. First the gardener catches us making out in the bushes, and now there's a janitor who thinks I'm some sort of weirdo who stands around playing with himself. Just great."

"Noah, if you're going to enjoy the weekend, you need to remember something."

"What?"

"What other people think of you is none of your business."

He sighed. She was right, of course, as long as they were here in the big city. But he had a lot of Saguaro Junction in him and, back home, such things mattered. And he was about to rejoin his buddies, people he would continue to see for years to come. He hoped that by the time they reached the party, his erection would be gone and the wet spot from the towelette would be dry. If not, he'd have to throw a cold drink on his lap to take care of both problems.

"How soon do you think we can leave?" she asked as she walked beside him.

"We should stay until Jenny and Brandon head up to their honeymoon suite." His imagination filled with a picture of Keely lying naked in the middle of a pile of green pillows. "I hope to God that's soon."

13

KEELY HAD NO SOONER rejoined the party than Jenny, Tina, Sharon and Barb pounced on her and dragged her away from Noah.

"Something happened, didn't it?" Tina said, her dark Italian eyes sparkling. "You were gone a *very* long time."

"And that was the plan," Jenny said. "Brilliant of me to send you off together, if I do say so myself."

"After the way he pulled you down on his lap during the game, I knew things were progressing nicely." Sharon grinned. "So here's what I think. You two have known each other since you were kids, right?"

"That's right," Keely said.

"Then it's fate, you two meeting like this in Vegas," Sharon continued. "I've seen Noah with a lot of women, and I've never seen him so totally preoccupied with any of them. I'll bet he's been pining away for you all these years without realizing it."

"Oh, I doubt it." Didn't she just wish, but she'd be a fool to let herself believe that. Maybe she had a sexual hold on Noah right now, but that was the extent of it. "We're having fun being together this weekend, but that's all."

"I think there's more to it," Tina said. "You have that certain glow whenever you're with him, too. And—"

A roar of male laughter cut off whatever else Tina had meant to say. They all looked over at the crowd of guys standing by the bar. Noah held an empty glass in his hand, and from the looks of things, he'd spilled the contents of it down the front of his tux, including his pants.

Keely couldn't help smiling. She had a pretty good idea that he'd done it on purpose for camouflage. Apparently his friends thought so, too.

"Lame, totally lame!" Clint chortled. "Nobody thinks that was an accident, buddy."

Brandon clapped him on the shoulder. "Just give it up and admit there was frisky business going on while you and Keely were AWOL, and you came back with a little evidence on your clothes. It's happened to the best of us. Even me."

"Yeah," Greg said. "Shirts buttoned up wrong, underwear on inside out, suspicious wet spots—we've seen it all. Come on, 'fess up."

Keely didn't mind the good-natured teasing because it meant that Noah's friends had accepted her. But she wasn't sure how Noah would take it. He hadn't intended to include her in this event, yet she'd accepted Brandon's invitation, anyway. Then she'd become chummy with the women in the bridal party, and then she'd dressed for the wedding in an outfit to drive him wild. Now he was suffering the consequences of her actions.

To her surprise and relief, he grinned. "What are you guys, nooky narcs?"

"Hell, no," Greg said. "I hope you *did* do the nasty. We made bets on it, and I want my money."

"You should know better than to bet on an outcome you'll never learn," Noah said. He glanced in Keely's direction. "I don't intend to satisfy your curiosity or settle your bet. Unlike you morons, we have too much class, right, darlin'?"

"Right," she called over to him. Thank heavens he wasn't

furious with her. She'd only meant to have some fun, not make him uncomfortable. Obviously he wasn't upset if he'd call her darlin' in front of everyone. She couldn't help feeling warm and special, and for one tender moment she imagined what it would be like to be his darlin' for more than a weekend. But she wouldn't be, and she needed to cool it around his friends so she wouldn't embarrass him any further.

"I was all set to claim my money on circumstantial evidence," Greg grumbled, "until you threw a piña colada all over Exhibit A."

"I'm willing to testify to what I saw before that suspicious event," Clint said.

"Yeah, me, too," Brandon added.

As the men started to wrangle about what they'd seen or hadn't seen, and the size and position of the spot, Jenny looked at her girlfriends and lowered her voice. "I think it's time to give those monkeys something else to think about before they mess up this budding relationship. They're starting to get a little crude."

"Agreed," Sharon said.

"It's not a budding relationship," Keely said.

Jenny smiled at her. "Sometimes the people in a budding relationship are the last ones to pick up on what's happening." Then she raised her voice. "Garter toss, guys! The bride has spoken!"

Brandon snapped to attention so quickly that Keely laughed. "That's impressive, Jenny."

Jenny grinned at her as Brandon started over toward them. "Oh, we came to an agreement. I get to be the boss during the ceremony and the reception. He gets to be the boss all during the wedding-night playtime. It works out."

"I'll bet it does." Keely saw the glow of love in Brandon's eyes as he took Jenny's hand.

They laughed and leaned against each other as they walked

toward the center of the reception area where Greg had already placed a chair for Jenny to prop her foot on. During the removal of the garter, both Jenny and Brandon joked with the guests, but most of their teasing was directed at each other.

They'll have fun being married.

The thought zoomed through Keely's mind, startling her. She'd never considered that marriage and fun belonged in the same sentence. She hadn't had all that many examples to go by, but most of the marriages she'd known had seemed extremely boring and restrictive compared to the excitement of the single life. Both her father and Noah's father had been widowed fairly young, and neither of them had chosen to remarry, so she'd concluded that they must not have enjoyed matrimony all that much. From all reports, her mother hadn't, either.

In high school the parents of her friends had never seemed to have anything resembling fun. Mostly they'd spent time trying to spoil any fun their kids had wanted to have. A few of her high-school friends had acted interested in the concept of marriage and some had even gone through with it, but once she'd relocated to L.A., nobody in her city-girl circle had considered it an option until after they felt too old to party.

But Jenny and Brandon gave a new dimension to her concept of marriage. For that matter, so did the others—Tina and Greg, Clint and Sharon.

In Keely's world committed couples were unusual. In this gathering they were the norm. For the first time in years she felt out of step. That would be cured once she left this group and returned to her own life, of course, but she was strangely reluctant to do that. She'd been given a different perspective and she wasn't quite ready to shut the door on that.

But the door might be shut for her. She didn't fit into this cozy scene. She never had and she was foolish to think she ever would. These people accepted her as a childhood friend of Noah's because that's all they knew about her. True, she wasn't as wild and racy as Noah imagined, but she was definitely a bad girl compared to Jenny and her friends. She doubted that any of them had ever posed for a centerfold.

A cheer went up from the assembled guests as Brandon held the garter aloft. He started to throw it toward the small knot of bachelors clustered by the bar, a group that included Noah, but Jenny caught his arm. Then she pulled him closer to whisper in his ear.

He straightened and turned toward the bar. "The bride wants to change the routine, and I'm sworn to give her absolute power during the ceremony and reception. If she wants the routine changed, then it'll be changed. There will be no throwing of the garter."

The bachelors looked relieved, even Noah, and here Keely had thought he was more than ready to catch a garter and be the next man in his group to walk down the aisle. But the married men weren't having any of it and they started complaining.

"Hold it." Brandon raised both hands. "I'm not going to *throw* the garter, but we can't let a perfectly good wedding garter go to waste. One of you single guys needs to end up with it. Jenny has asked that in this case I *bestow* the garter, so we don't leave the results to chance. It seems she has a particular person in mind."

Keely had a funny feeling in the pit of her stomach. Oh, well. It was only a silly superstition, anyway.

Brandon twirled the garter around his index finger as he walked toward the bachelors who were watching him nervously. Sure enough, Brandon stopped in front of Noah. "Sir Noah, you are hereby dubbed the keeper of the wedding garter. Cupid's got you in his sights, son."

Noah made some effort to protest, but in the end, with the

not-so-gentle help of his friends, he was wearing the garter as an armband. He avoided Keely's gaze.

Of course, he wouldn't give her soulful looks, she thought. He wanted only one thing from her, and he didn't need a wedding ring to get it. That was fine, because she only wanted one thing from him, too. That was her story and she was sticking to it.

Greg turned on the microphone again and took charge of the proceedings. "And now for the throwing of the bridal bouquet," he announced.

That was her cue to duck out, Keely decided. No way was she catching that thing, especially after Brandon had tagged Noah with the garter. Maybe it was only a superstition and meant nothing, but she didn't care to test it. If she ever did get married, it wouldn't be to a man like Noah who lived in Saguaro Junction. These friends of Noah's had made marriage look more attractive to her than it had in the past, but she was still a country mile away from the altar.

As she edged over to the sidelines, Tina caught her arm. "Where do you think you're going?"

"I, uh, need to go to the—"

"You can wait." Sharon grabbed her other arm.

"But—"

"Let's go, girl." Barb grabbed her waist from behind and pushed.

"Hey, wait a minute!" Keely tried to pull away from them as they tugged her over to an area where a small group of single women stood. A very small group. Four, besides her. Those were terrible odds.

"We have our instructions," Tina said. "Bride's orders."

Keely struggled in vain. "Look, I like all of you heaps and heaps, but you're about to be my new ex-best friends. I don't want to play this game."

"It's the hand of fate." Sharon gripped harder and kept pulling.

"Fate is a hell of a lot stronger than she used to be!" Keely tried her best to get away, but these were three determined women. "Have you girls been working out?"

"Oh, we rodeo from time to time," Tina said. "It's rough on the nails, but good for the ego."

"Rodeo? I thought you were all about Nordstrom's!"

"Those two interests aren't mutually exclusive, chick," Sharon said.

"Incoming!" Jenny yelled and sailed the bouquet in the air.

"We're on it!" called Sharon. "Excuse us, ladies," she said to the hopefuls standing nearby on the grass.

"What on earth are you doing?" She hadn't wrestled with females like this since she was eight, and finally the episode became funny. She began to laugh as Tina, Sharon and Barb shoved her over to the spot where the bouquet was coming down.

It hit her on the head, and while she giggled helplessly, Tina and Sharon made sure the bouquet fell neatly into her arms. Then they released her, leaving her standing alone with a sweet-smelling bouquet clutched in both hands. She'd never held a bridal bouquet before, and damned if the experience wasn't turning her to mush. But she couldn't get all sentimental and let Noah in for even more teasing.

Jenny turned, a huge grin on her face. "That should do it." Then she walked over and exchanged high fives with her girl-friends before turning to the deejay. "Music, maestro, if you please. It's time for the owner of the garter and the owner of the bouquet to dance."

Keely knew she should refuse to do it, but instead she stood as if rooted in the grass while Noah slowly walked over to her and took her hand. "Sorry," she murmured as he led her to the circle of smooth concrete that served as a dance floor.

"About what?" He swung her into his arms as the deejay played a waltz.

"Catching the bouquet." She rested it on his shoulder and gazed at the cluster of orchids and roses so that she wouldn't have to look at Noah. He waltzed very well, which surprised her. There were many things she didn't know about him, apparently.

"It appears you didn't have much choice about catching it."

"I shouldn't be here in the first place. From the beginning, you didn't want me to be part of this wedding, but I had to be my usual obstinate self and accept the invitation from Brandon. Now here you are, dancing with me in front of all your friends."

"I don't mind."

She figured he was just being nice. She could tell from the way he was dancing with her, keeping a good three inches' distance between them, that he didn't want to give anybody ideas about their relationship. "I know they're all trying to be matchmakers," she said, "but you don't have to worry. I told them this was a fun weekend, but that was all there was to it."

"You did, huh?"

"Yes," she said firmly. "So don't think I'm going to embarrass you out here by trying to snuggle closer or anything. I won't do that."

"I would love you to snuggle closer," he said. "But I have piña colada down the front of my tux and it's sticky stuff. I'd hate to get it all over that dress. I doubt if you have enough little white packets to take care of that."

She glanced up at him in surprise. "That's why you're keeping a space between us?"

"That's the only reason, darlin'." His brown eyes were warm as he looked down at her. "And that distance is killing me."

"Really?" Her heart lifted, and she couldn't help smiling. He wasn't embarrassed by being made a public spectacle with her. "Then to heck with the dress. I've never danced with you before, Noah. Let's make it count." She slid in tight.

Immediately cheers and catcalls erupted from the crowd.

"Maybe that was a mistake," she murmured, and started to back away.

Noah tightened his grip, holding her fast. "Uh-uh. I'm not giving up this sensation. Ignore them. Dance with me, Keely."

She took a deep breath. "All right." Meeting his gaze, she moved sensuously to the music, allowing her body to meld perfectly with his.

He sighed. "Yeah, like that. Sweet."

Oh, how they danced. The boisterous comments of their audience faded in the wonder of how perfectly they fit together and how easily they moved over the dance floor, as if they'd been practicing for years.

The corner of Noah's mouth tilted. "We should have tried this before."

"Who knew?"

"I think I did." His gaze heated. "I think I've always known how we'd fit."

Her breath caught. "They say that dancing like this is a lot like making love."

"Yes, they do." The flame burned brighter in his eyes. "And if this endless party ever winds down, I plan to test that theory. I wish we could leave right now."

Her blood pounded through her veins. "Me, too."

"Damn, that's the end of the song. With luck, the piña colada has glued us together and we'll be forced to leave the party to get unstuck."

Keely backed out of his embrace easily. "No such luck. Must be the material of this dress. I guess it repels everything."

Noah laughed. "Except me. I—"

"Miss November!" cried a hearty male voice near Keely's shoulder. "I finally figured it out!"

Horrified, she turned toward Brandon's father, Elmer. "Excuse me?"

"You're Miss November!" The festivities and a generous amount of liquor were prompting Elmer to speak much louder than usual. He beamed at her as if sharing the most wonderful news. "*Macho* magazine, right? I can't remember the exact year, but I sure remember how you looked, lying on that Thanksgiving table with all the food, and your—"

"You must have me confused with someone else." Keely glanced around and prayed nobody else had heard the exchange.

"Hey, Elmer." Noah hooked an arm around Elmer's shoulders. "Speaking of food, let's go get some of that wedding cake before it's all gone."

"No, thanks," Elmer said, ignoring him and focusing intently on Keely. "Listen, I'm sure it was you. I even remember the name Keely. I was going through a bit of a midlife crisis in those days, and so *Macho* was very appealing to me. I told my wife it beat running out and having an affair." He laughed and winked at her. "Good excuse, huh?"

"I'm flattered that you think I look like a centerfold," Keely said. "But you have the wrong girl." She glanced pleadingly at Noah, hoping he'd support her denial.

But for some reason he didn't. Instead, he turned his palms up as if to say he was out of ideas other than to continue distracting Elmer. Once again he tried to steer the older man gently away. "You look like a guy who could use another drink, Elmer," he said.

"Not yet," Elmer said. "First I want an autograph." He fumbled in his pocket. "I have one of the wedding napkins in here, which my wife insisted I take for a souvenir. Keely, would you sign it for me? And put *Miss November* on it, too? I still have that magazine in a box in the basement. Gosh, I wish I had it here right now so you could sign your picture!"

She wasn't going to talk him out of it. If she refused to go along with him, he might get louder and more insistent. At last she took the napkin and ballpoint pen he held out to her. "Okay, I'm Miss November," she said.

"I knew it! Here, use my back so you can write on that thing." He turned around.

"I try to maintain a low profile, Elmer, so I'd appreciate you keeping the information to yourself," she said as she braced the napkin on his back and signed her name. Considering how tipsy the guy was, she didn't think there was much chance of his keeping a secret, but at least she'd try.

"I think you should be proud of it!"

"Well, thank you, but not everyone agrees with you." She handed him the napkin. Too bad her father wasn't proud of her. But maybe Elmer wouldn't be, either, if she happened to be his daughter instead of a relative stranger he'd met at a wedding.

She didn't kid herself that everyone at the reception would be as thrilled as Brandon's father was to discover a centerfold in their midst. She'd found that out the hard way from her friends and neighbors in Saguaro Junction, and she didn't want to let herself in for the same kind of humiliation at this shindig.

Elmer gazed at the signature. "Keely Branscom. That's the name, all right." He looked up, and his gaze traveled over her from head to toe. "Yep, it's you, all right."

"Time for a drink, Elmer!" Noah grabbed him forcefully by the arm and propelled him toward the bar.

"Hey, is it true?" A young guy Keely hadn't met came over to her. "I heard him say you were in *Macho* magazine." He looked very hopeful.

Keely glanced toward the bar. Noah was trying desperately to keep Elmer under control, but the older man had still managed to sneak his napkin out of his pocket to let people look at it. In seconds she'd be the center of attention, taking the limelight away from the bride and causing herself and Noah all kinds of embarrassment.

She'd overstayed her welcome. How she'd looked forward to spending the night and the next day with Noah, but she'd be the subject of so much curiosity that she could only be an embarrassment to Noah now. Better for her to just disappear. A quick trip up to the suite to pick up her purse, and she could be gone.

The shock of such an abrupt ending to the weekend left her feeling numb. She hoped the numbness would last, acting as a painkiller at least until she made it out of the hotel.

"So, is it true?" the eager young man asked again.

"Yes," she said. "And if you'll stay right here, I'll run upstairs and get you an autographed picture."

"Just your face? Or…the rest?"

"The full monty."

"Cool!"

She looked in Noah's direction again, and luck was with her. He was so busy trying to keep Elmer corralled that he hadn't noticed she had more problems. He wouldn't see her leave.

"Stay here," she said to the guy. "I'll be right back." Then she hurried away toward the lobby to catch the elevator that would take her to the top floor.

14

NOAH NOTICED KEELY HAD attracted unwanted attention. He could tell from her harried expression that she wasn't happy dealing with the young stud who had cornered her. But it took him a minute to excuse himself from Elmer, and by the time he'd gone to her rescue, she'd disappeared. The young guy she'd been talking to was standing in the same spot, though, looking expectant.

Noah went over to him. "The woman in the silver dress. Where did she go?"

The kid glanced around and lowered his voice. "I don't know if I should say. She might not want me to."

Noah gripped his shoulder, exerting firm pressure. "I suggest you tell me, and tell me now."

"Hey! Who are you, her boyfriend?"

"Yes." The answer slipped right out, and he discovered he liked the sound of it. "Yes, I am."

The kid looked him over, as if measuring a rival. "I'd like to hear that from her."

Noah felt a stab of compassion for the kid, who was obviously awestruck by Keely. And the boy had no chance with her, first of all because Noah wouldn't give him one, and second because Keely hadn't looked enthralled with the guy, either.

He lightened his grip on the kid's shoulder. "Look, I think she was upset when she left, so I need to find her. I'd appreciate your help."

"She wasn't upset. She went upstairs to get me an autographed picture."

"I'm sorry to have to tell you, but there aren't any autographed pictures." At least Noah hoped there weren't.

"Oh, *man.* Then why did she say she was going to get one?"

"So she could cut out," Noah said.

"Why would she do that?"

"I think she was a little uncomfortable about being recognized."

"No kidding?" The kid thought that over. "I guess it could be a bummer." He shrugged. "Personally I think it would be cool to be famous, but I guess everybody's different."

"Yep, everybody is. And thanks for the info. I'll go see if I can smooth things over with her." He left the kid and looked around for Jenny and Brandon to let them know he was ducking out.

Maybe Keely had gone up to the suite and would wait for him there, but then again maybe she wouldn't. She'd looked pretty upset about being identified as Miss November, and he'd been caught flat-footed, not sure how to respond, so she might be upset with him, too.

She'd obviously wanted him to help her deny the whole thing, and the words had been on the tip of his tongue. But then he'd realized he couldn't win this one. If he helped her convince Elmer and everyone else that she wasn't a centerfold, it would be like denying that she'd ever done it, as if he was ashamed of her for posing.

And he'd never, ever been that. Frustrated, worried and confused—definitely. He hadn't known how to deal with the grown-up version of the little girl he'd been so close to, and so he'd only made things worse. But he'd never been ashamed of Keely Branscom.

He wasn't about to do anything that would give her that impression, either. But he could also understand why she wouldn't want the entire crowd at this reception to know her background, so he'd worked to keep Elmer toned down. It had been like trying to get shaving cream back in the can.

Well, now Keely was gone, and he felt a great urgency to follow her and find out her intentions. He didn't want her to disappear from his life and he was afraid that might be what she had in mind. Besides, nothing had been settled about her career, and she might go right back to dancing in topless bars, or worse. That possibility was no longer acceptable.

Locating Brandon and Jenny, he walked quickly over to them. "Listen, I need to—"

"Was Keely a centerfold for *Macho?*" Brandon asked. "My dad got her signature, and he swears—"

"She was, a long time ago," Noah said quietly.

"Get outta here!" Brandon said. "That's outrageous."

"She really was?" Jenny said. "Wow. A celebrity guest. That's cool."

"The thing is, I'm afraid she's a little embarrassed that your dad recognized her," Noah said.

"Oh, she shouldn't be!" Jenny looked concerned. "I think it's fabulous. I'm not surprised, either. Anyone could look at her and know she has the body for it." She glanced around. "Where did she go? I need to tell her that she has nothing to be embarrassed about."

"I think she left and went up to the suite," Noah said.

"You mean because of being recognized?" Jenny asked.

"I think so."

Jenny picked up her skirts. "I'm going straight to a house phone so I can call her and tell her to get her butt back down here. Leaving the party like she's in disgrace or something is plain ridiculous."

Brandon put a restraining hand on her arm. "Maybe not so ridiculous, Jen. I can't guarantee that every single person here will be open-minded about it. Can you?"

Jenny paused, a frown on her face. "I really hate to think that any of our guests would cause her a problem."

"But they might," Noah said, reluctantly agreeing with Brandon. "She's dealt with small-mindedness before, when the magazine hit the stands in Saguaro Junction ten years ago. I'm sure she doesn't want to put up with more of the same tonight, and I can't blame her."

"Okay." Jenny sighed. "You may have a point, and I'd feel terrible if somebody insulted her. So I'll call her and tell her that everyone in the bridal party is thrilled to have met Miss November. I know I can speak for all of us on that score. We've loved getting to know her. She's a kick."

"Go ahead and call if you want," Noah said, "but I'll bet she won't answer the phone. Listen, I was planning to stay here at the reception until you two headed up to your honeymoon suite, but I think I should check on Keely. If I know her, she might have decided to get out of Dodge."

"Oh!" Jenny's eyes widened. "You mean leave the hotel?"

"It's possible."

"Then go! Right now!"

Noah hesitated. "I don't know if I'll be back down before you leave, and tomorrow morning you have that early flight to Hawaii, so I might not see you again this weekend."

"Don't give that another thought." Jenny's eyes sparkled. "Your job right now is to convince Keely to stay. And I know you have what it takes."

Brandon clutched his chest in pretended shock. "You *do?* How could you know that?"

"By talking to his girlfriends." Jenny smacked her new

husband on the arm. "Now stop goofing around and let this man go. We're still at the reception part of this shindig, which means I'm fully in charge."

"Right." Brandon winked at Noah.

"I wish you both the best." Noah gave Jenny a hug. He stuck out his hand to Brandon, but ended up giving him a hug, too. "I'll be in touch."

"You bet," Brandon said. "I want to know how this turns out."

So did he, Noah thought as he sprinted toward the elevators.

Before he boarded the one that would take him to the top floor, he quickly scanned the lobby in case she'd already made it back down and was on her way out. He didn't see her. She wouldn't have left without going back to the suite, he reasoned. Her cell phone was up there, for one thing.

When the elevator opened, he half expected to see her in it. But the glass-and-brass cubicle was empty. All the way to the top floor he tried to decide what to say to her. He was beginning to realize that his original impulse to save her from herself had developed into something much more complicated. Now he was trying to figure out how to save her and also keep her in his life.

And that was plain crazy. They were from two different worlds now, and they certainly had different outlooks. She was a city girl who was glad to have escaped small-town life. He planned to spend the rest of his days on the Twin Boulders Ranch. His father had handed him the sacred trust of running the place, and he intended to pass the land on to his children one day.

Although Keely didn't think much of the institution of marriage, he wanted a wife and babies, and he wasn't getting any younger. Brandon's wedding made him sharply aware of that.

So he had no business chasing after Keely, who didn't fit in with his plans at all. Oh, but she fit perfectly when he was holding her. And the fit wasn't only sexual, either. Whenever he thought about Keely, he felt a sense of connection so strong that he couldn't imagine letting her disappear again.

Yet he had no clue what form a relationship might take at this point, or if she'd even agree that a relationship was a good idea, considering their differences. That's why they needed more time together, to work on those problems. And if they were destined to part, then he wanted to make love to her in that good old-fashioned, horizontal way at least once before they said goodbye. He thought they both owed themselves that much.

He had to convince her to stay, and if words wouldn't do it, then he'd try the physical approach. Of course, there was always the chance she hadn't planned to leave at all. As he walked down the hall toward the suite's double doors, he remembered the scene she'd prepared for him the night before—the hot tub, the skimpy bathing suit, skin flicks on the big-screen TV, champagne in the ice bucket.

Maybe she'd had a setup like that in mind when she'd left the party. Heart pounding, he slid his key into the lock and opened the suite door. "Keely?" he called, loud enough to be heard over the sound of the fountain in the entryway.

No answer.

She might be lying seductively on the pillows in the living room…naked. His body surged with desire as he walked into the empty living room, lit only with soft indirect fixtures. "Keely?"

Still no answer.

She wasn't in the hot tub or on the balcony, but a light glowed from the bedroom. Maybe she was waiting for him in that big, white bed. The image quickened his step and his pulse. He called her name again as he crossed the footbridge.

She wasn't in the bed, either, and he had a bad feeling when he noticed a neat stack of twenty-dollar bills lying on the white sheets. He didn't stop to count the money, but he guessed it was the same amount he'd given her the day before to buy clothes.

When he didn't find her in the bathroom, he could think of only one other place she might be hiding to surprise him. She might be lying in the closet as a joke, mimicking the way she'd tucked herself in there yesterday when his buddies had visited the suite.

But the closet was empty, too.

"Keely!" He knew in his heart she wasn't anywhere in the suite. He could feel her absence, had felt it from the minute he'd stepped inside the door. The electric excitement she carried with her everywhere was missing from these rooms. But he shouted her name, anyway, in a hopeless attempt to vent some of his frustration.

The only response was the gurgling of the stream in the living room.

Damn it! Where the hell had she gone?

She couldn't be far away, he decided, hurrying back over the footbridge and through the living room. He hoped that she hadn't caught a cab somewhere, that she'd be on foot. The Saturday-night crowds would be heavy, but she wouldn't be hard to spot in that silver dress. A woman like her wouldn't be hard to spot no matter what she had on, but if she'd made it up here and back down to the lobby before he left the party, then she hadn't taken time to change.

He would find her. Damn it all, he would find her.

KEELY HAD GUESSED NOAH would come after her once he noticed she was gone. After all, they'd had a pretty good time in that hallway, and once a gal had whistled a tune on a guy's piccolo, he usually wanted an encore. She wished she could give him one, because she'd truly enjoyed that first performance.

But it wasn't in the cards, as they said in Sin City. And if her heart was aching worse than she'd ever remembered, well, she'd have to get over it. Noah wasn't the right guy for her. Never had been and never would be.

Even he knew that, but chances were he wouldn't let her run away, so if she wanted to escape, she'd have to be smart about it. Consequently, when Noah hurried past the hotel's tropical garden on his way to the street, she watched him from behind the large lava boulder where they'd kissed the day before.

God, he was gorgeous. His mussed hair and rumpled tux only made him more adorable. And he was coming after her. Well, that was a picture to carry with her—Noah Garfield trying to chase her down. Years from now she'd probably still get a thrill thinking of this tall, broad-shouldered cowboy combing the streets of Vegas looking for her.

But it would be better for all concerned if he didn't find her.

Surrounded by dense foliage and night shadows, she crouched behind the boulder and waited for him to pass. Instead, he paused to stare at the lava rock. He couldn't possibly see her. The shadows were too deep. Yet her heart pounded frantically as she wondered if he'd somehow sensed she was there.

They'd played a lot of hide-and-seek as kids, and in those days she'd secretly wanted him to find her. Even at the tender age of seven, she'd felt a curl of excitement in her stomach when Noah was hunting for her. As he'd drawn near, she used to let him know her position with a slight rustle or faint cough. She'd squealed whenever he found her, as if she hadn't been hoping for that to happen all along.

Maybe she wanted him to find her now, too. Maybe she'd

chosen the boulder hoping that he'd look there. She held her breath and waited.

He gazed in her direction for another tension-filled moment. Then, with a shake of his head, he continued down the walkway toward the street.

She let out her breath with a sigh of disappointment. She'd outsmarted him. Damn it. So now that she had, it was time to continue with her plan.

Creeping out from behind the boulder, she ignored the puzzled glances from other pedestrians and focused on Noah walking ahead of her. Fortunately, his height and his gray tux made him easy to see. She kept him in sight all the way to the busy street.

He hesitated, looking right and left, studying the crowds. Finally he chose to turn left. Which way he went didn't matter to Keely, but she had to know so that she could head in the opposite direction. Once she had about four blocks between them, she hailed a cab and gave the driver the address of her hotel downtown.

The route took them along the Strip in the same direction Noah was walking, and soon she spotted him striding down the street and scanning the crowds on both sides. She pressed her lips together, determined that she wouldn't ask the cab-driver to let her out.

Although she longed to be with Noah again, she'd only be buying a little more time and a little more loving. The ending would be the same. Better to deal with the pain when it was manageable than to take a chance on getting hurt worse than she'd bargained for.

Blinking back tears, she settled deeper into the back seat of the cab as the driver maneuvered through the heavy traffic. Once they'd passed the point where she'd seen Noah moving along the sidewalk, she turned to look through the back window, but she couldn't pick him out of the crowd. Their little sexual adventure had come to an end.

NOAH WALKED TO THE POINT of exhaustion before he finally dragged himself back to the Tahitian. He believed Keely was still in Vegas, but he finally admitted to himself that finding her would be tougher than he'd first thought. And he was sick of walking the streets in a tux that smelled like overripe piña coladas.

Once back in the suite he went quickly into the bedroom and stripped down to the briefs Keely had bought him the day before. He thought about that first night and her open, generous invitation to make love. He'd been the noble fool who'd resisted her with no concept of what he was throwing away. He'd wasted hours trying to prove his superior morality, while he was living in the same suite with a goddess.

What a dope he was. If he hadn't been such a stiff-necked jerk in the beginning, he might have established a bond between them by now, one she wouldn't feel so free to break. He couldn't let her slip through his fingers, and he wouldn't.

But first he needed a few minutes of rest. Just a few. He stretched out on the big empty bed and figured on staying there a maximum of thirty minutes. Then he'd go back out and look some more.

Many hours later he awoke with a start to find sunlight streaming into the room. He glanced at his watch and groaned. Nearly noon.

Leaping out of bed, he showered and shaved in record time. While he dressed in jeans and one of Clint's denim shirts, he figured out where he had to start his search, where he would have gone the night before if he'd taken time to think about it.

Not long afterward he walked into the Pussycat Lounge.

"I'm looking for Keely Branscom," he told the thin guy who offered to show him to a table.

"Keely? I don't think she's coming by today, but I can check with Suzanne after her number's over, if you'd like to have a seat."

Bingo. Anxiety and anticipation churned in his stomach. She wasn't coming by today, the guy had said. That didn't sound as if she'd landed a job here. He hoped to hell it didn't mean she picked up clients at the Pussycat.

But at least he'd found a link to her. That was the main thing. And once they'd connected again, she wasn't going back to whatever it was she was doing. He'd be better off if he didn't think too much about what that might be.

Rock music from a faulty sound system blared and crackled as a brunette with large breasts shimmied topless for half a dozen customers scattered throughout the bar. She must be Suzanne, he decided. No doubt the dance was supposed to be arousing, but he was so eager to find out about Keely that he just wanted it to be over.

Finally it was, and the brunette sauntered backstage while the men in the bar whistled and called for her to come back for an encore. Noah hoped she wouldn't decide to perform one.

Fortunately she didn't. Moments later she walked toward Noah's table wearing an oversize T-shirt to cover what passed as a costume. When she sat down across from him, her gaze and manner were direct. "Brad said you were looking for Keely. What for?"

He'd expected that. "We grew up together," he said. "I heard she was in town, so I'd like a chance to see her."

Suzanne didn't seem totally convinced. "So where's home?"

"Saguaro Junction, Arizona. Her dad's the foreman on the ranch I own with my brother, Jonas."

Her expression softened a little. "She mentioned Saguaro Junction to me, so I guess you could be legit. You look pretty honest to me."

"Thanks. I don't mean her any harm."

"Probably not. But women like Keely and me have to be careful, you know? Guys can become, like, obsessed with us."

His gut clenched as he thought of the nutcases Keely might attract if she continued on her present course. "I'm sure that's true."

"I guess there's no harm in telling you where she's staying, though." She gave him the name of a midpriced hotel downtown.

"Oh," he said, unable to hide his surprise. The hotel wasn't the best Las Vegas had to offer but it wasn't the worst, either. He'd braced himself for some sleazy dive in a bad part of town.

Suzanne smiled. "I know. I was surprised, too. You'd think *Attitude!* magazine would put out the bucks for someplace a little glitzier, huh?"

"*Attitude!* magazine?" Noah's thoughts scrambled. The only magazine he'd ever connected to Keely was *Macho*. He'd vaguely heard of the other one, and thought it was for twenty-something women, although he wasn't absolutely sure about that.

"Wait a minute." Suzanne's eyes narrowed. "You sound surprised, like you didn't even know she's working for them. If you're such a good friend, how could you not know that?"

The information hit him like a microblast, and he struggled to come up with an answer. "We've been out of touch." *She worked for a magazine. She'd let him believe that she was a call girl, and she was a reporter for a women's magazine. She hadn't needed saving at all, and she'd played him for a fool.*

Suzanne stood. "In that case, she might not want to see you. What did you say your name was?"

"Noah. Noah Garfield." *Noah "the idiot" Garfield.*

"Noah." She backed away from the table. "I'm going to call her and warn her you're on your way. I shouldn't have told you where she is, but at least they have good security at that hotel."

"You don't have to warn her." He felt completely betrayed. Sure, at first he'd thought this weekend would be an isolated event, but then…then he'd started to care about her. He'd thought they were building something between them, and all the while she'd been laughing at him. "She has nothing to fear from me."

"So you say. I'm going to call her, anyway. I should have done that in the first place." Suzanne hurried away.

Noah left the bar and stood in the sunlit street trying to get his bearings. As the shock began to wear off, anger moved in. She'd been toying with him, amused with his white-knight routine, determined to corrupt the man who was trying to save her.

And she'd succeeded beyond her wildest dreams. He would dare anything now. He wondered if she could handle that. Maybe it was time to find out. As long as Suzanne was going to announce his visit, he might as well make it. He wouldn't want to disappoint a lady.

But he might make her wait a while, wait and wonder what he planned to do. He'd grab some breakfast. Something told him he was going to need his strength.

15

CAUGHT.

Keely thanked Suzanne for calling and slowly hung up the phone. Then she began to pace her small hotel room while her stomach did flip-flops. Childhood lessons kicked in, telling her that being found out this way, with Noah learning the truth from a stranger, was much worse than if she'd confessed, herself. If she'd told him the truth when her cell phone had rung while they were in the suite's bathroom, then he might have been able to laugh about the situation...eventually.

But when he'd assumed the worst—that she used the phone to turn tricks—she'd let him believe that, figuring it served him right for leaping to conclusions.

She'd still been into revenge at that stage. The sixteen-year-old who'd been rejected that night in the barn had wanted her payback. But now, after a sleepless night of missing Noah, she realized what she'd done to herself. The game had turned serious, and she'd fallen in love with him. Or, to be brutally honest with herself, she'd never fallen *out* of love with him. He'd been the only man she'd wanted for so long, and apparently he still was.

Ever since she'd left the Tahitian, she'd tried to talk herself out of being in love with him. When she couldn't sleep, she'd switched on her laptop and started her article, hoping that work would keep her from aching so badly. The laptop was still on, and she'd typed and retyped the first paragraph, but mostly she'd sat staring at the screen and thinking about Noah.

Perhaps most irritating of all was the stupid X-rated screensaver that flashed on automatically whenever she stopped typing for a while. Talk about rubbing salt in her wounds. If only she had aquarium fish swimming on that screen.

But she didn't have fish. Instead, a little naked cartoon woman chased a naked cartoon man, shoved him down and hopped on top of him. After some vigorous movement she jumped off, the man leaped to his feet and chased her down for more of the same. The cycle continued endlessly. A girlfriend who was into computers had created it for her as a joke.

This morning she wasn't laughing.

What a bummer of a weekend. For a few sweet hours she'd had Noah wrapped around her little finger. But that was history. Suzanne had said he looked stunned by the news that she was a reporter. Keely could just imagine. But once he recovered, he would be furious. He might leave Vegas without trying to see her, but she doubted it. No, he'd come to her hotel to give her a piece of his mind, and then he would leave, cussing her all the way back to Saguaro Junction.

She wondered if he'd tell her father, B.J. or Jonas about this. Probably not, considering the sexual nature of their encounter. But if she'd secretly been considering going home for B.J.'s wedding, she could kiss that idea goodbye. Even if Noah didn't say anything to the others, the tension she'd create on the ranch by reappearing would ruin B.J.'s wedding day, and Keely wasn't about to do that.

As she continued to pace she wondered how best to handle the confrontation with Noah. She could avoid it altogether by checking out of the hotel and moving to another one. She could even head for the airport and try to snag a flight to Reno this afternoon instead of going in the morning.

But that seemed cowardly. At nineteen she hadn't had the guts to face the music after her centerfold had appeared in *Macho* and she'd run away to L.A. Ten years later, she liked to believe she had more courage. Besides, what difference did it make if Noah yelled at her? It wasn't as if they had a future together or anything.

So she'd stay and wait for him to arrive. Because of the scene she anticipated, she'd better invite him up to the room. Dealing with his fury would be difficult enough without also putting on a show for every person in the lobby or the hotel coffee shop.

If he'd taken a cab downtown, he could be here any minute. Her room was trashed, the bed unmade and the covers tossed aside during her hopeless attempt to sleep. A couple of towels lay on the floor from a long shower that had done nothing to relax her. She thought of making the bed and picking up the area, but that seemed way too anal.

Then she glanced down at her outfit—her favorite knit tank top, the old white one she wore for writing because it was soft as a baby's bottom, and yellow gingham stretch capris, also a writing favorite because, for some reason, she always felt more creative wearing them.

Her clothes hadn't helped her write so far this morning. Neither had a big pot of room-service coffee. With Noah on the way, she might as well give up.

She thought about changing clothes now that she didn't intend to work on her article anymore. But she had no idea what to wear for a fight. And she was sure that's what they were about to have.

Maybe she should put on makeup, too, except that she didn't want to look as if she was coming on to him and make him even angrier. He couldn't very well think she was being seductive if she met him looking like this—barefoot, no makeup and her hair pulled into a ponytail. Maybe that was exactly the look she needed for a fight. In this outfit, she felt stripped to the basic, with her gloves off. Lean and mean, ready for anything.

She'd done an article on fair fighting for couples and the suggestions had sounded perfectly reasonable at the time. Now, as adrenaline poured through her system, the suggestions sounded ridiculous. To heck with fair fighting. Time to line up her defense. This whole thing wouldn't have happened if he hadn't assumed she was looking for a job dancing topless and pompously tried to save her. Just who did he think he was, anyway?

Yeah, no wonder she'd decided to teach him a thing or two. He'd been asking for it, behaving as if he had the corner on right living. Who made him in charge of the world? Suppose she had been a topless dancer and had loved her job? What right did he have passing judgment on her choice of career?

Okay, she was geared up for this donnybrook now. Let him come. And speaking of that, where the hell was he? Traffic wouldn't be that heavy right now, and if he'd come straight to her hotel from the Pussycat Lounge, he'd be here.

So he hadn't come straight to her hotel. That was a depressing thought. The only thing worse than having this fight with Noah would be not having it. She couldn't believe he'd go back to Arizona without telling her what he thought of her behavior. He'd want to have the last word. Wouldn't he?

When another half hour passed and her phone hadn't rung, she was nearly ready to stomp over to the Tahitian and find out what was keeping him. Damn it, he'd stirred her up and then left her to wear a path in the carpet. Surely he wouldn't track her down and then drop the whole matter. That would be so diabolical, so unlike Noah's direct approach to things.

She was ready to scream with frustration by the time the

phone finally rang. She snatched it up and uttered a curt greeting.

"Keely, darlin'," Noah drawled, "you sound upset."

"Where have you been?"

He chuckled. "Not far away. Just having a bite to eat in the coffee shop of your hotel."

She couldn't figure it out. He should be yelling, and he was *chuckling*. She was the one yelling. "How can you sit down there and *eat* at a time like this?"

"I was hungry." He sounded lazy and content…almost. But there was a subtle thread of tension underneath that casual tone.

Her heartbeat slid into a faster tempo. The years had made a few changes in Noah's behavior, apparently, because he wasn't reacting the way she'd thought he would. She had to believe he was full out furious, and yet he sounded loose and in control. All she had to go on was that hint of tension, which she might be imagining because she expected it to be there. "I guess…I guess you should come up so we can talk about this."

"That would be fine. But I don't want to interrupt your work."

His voice tickled up and down her spine, making her shiver. "I'm not working."

"Then maybe you're doing research."

"No." Maybe it was his location holding him back. He didn't want to yell at her while he was using the house phone in the lobby. Made sense.

"Then maybe you're testing the suggestions you made in your latest article," he said smoothly.

"Excuse me?" She was so nervous about this coming fight that she could barely remember her name, let alone what she'd written for the last issue.

"I picked up one of your magazines in the gift shop and,

sure enough, there was an article by you. I read it while I was eating. Learned quite a bit about multiple orgasms."

She swallowed. "Oh."

"The way I understand it, self-gratification is a big part of women learning how to have them." He might have been discussing cattle prices, from the nonchalant way he said it. "I thought you might be practicing."

If she didn't know better, she'd think he was sexually teasing her the way she'd teased him earlier in the weekend. But that didn't seem like Noah, especially now, when he was so angry. She wished he'd start yelling at her, because then she'd know what to do. She'd figured out her side of the argument. But he wasn't playing this according to her script and she was having trouble keeping her balance with the conversation.

She cleared her throat. "Noah, what's your point?"

"It seems I underestimated you, Keely. You have a lot more talents than I was giving you credit for. I'm here to apologize for reading you so wrong."

"You *are?*" Now she was thrown completely off-kilter.

"Absolutely. I'd like to make that apology in person, if you'll give me your room number."

Maybe they were going to discuss this like two mature adults. No passion. Damn it, that didn't feel right, but if that was his approach, she had to go along. You couldn't fight with someone if they wouldn't fight back, and it was up to him to strike the first verbal blow.

She cleared her throat, determined to take the high road, too. "Noah, I should apologize, too, for leading you astray."

He laughed. "You certainly did lead me astray, darlin'."

Her skin flushed hot. And that sexy laugh rolled through her, doing all kinds of mischief. If only he didn't have a sexy laugh. And a sexy voice. And a sexy mouth. "Actually, I meant for *misleading* you about my occupation."

"No apology necessary. There was a certain thrill involved,

thinking that you were a bad girl. You taught me a lot about fantasies, Keely. I'm grateful for that."

"Oh." She rubbed her temple, which was beginning to throb with the promise of a headache. She'd introduced him to fantasy and now he'd probably use that knowledge to enrich his life with somebody else. She'd been *useful*. Triple bummer. "I see," she said. "That's very...nice."

"Give me your room number. I think it would be better to say these things to each other face-to-face."

If they were going to have a civilized discussion, she could just as easily meet him in the lobby, but she wasn't really dressed for that. She gave him her room number.

"Thanks. I'll be right there."

She hung up the phone, totally confused. She'd expected him to blow sky-high on the phone, then demand her room number so he could yell at her some more in person. Instead, he was apologizing. Thanking her for introducing him to some fantasy concepts. *Getting ready for a kiss-off speech.*

Oh, Lord, that was it. Thanks for the memories. It's been a lot of fun. Bye.

She felt sick to her stomach. This was the speech she'd been trying to avoid ever since they'd met in front of the Pussycat and he'd indicated he wanted to save her. She'd figured if she called the shots, she could make the speech instead of him and protect her heart at least a little.

Even leaving the Tahitian hadn't been all bad, because she'd been the one saying a silent goodbye. If Noah had stormed up to her room and raged at her before stomping out, that wouldn't have been all bad either. Passion was never bad. Instead, he planned to deliver a calm, rational kiss-off speech. He sure knew how to hurt a girl.

When he knocked on the door, she jumped and her heart began to pound. Well, she'd grown up in the years they'd been apart, too. She would simply beat him to the punch.

Somewhere, she'd dredge up a few chuckles of her own as she told him what a fun and frivolous time she'd had this weekend. Years from now she'd be able to look back and laugh at how crazy they'd been, she'd tell him.

She opened the door with a smile. Forced, yes, but a smile, damn it. The smile wavered.

He stood there looking better than any man had a right to look, especially after the weekend they'd had. "Hello, Keely," he said quietly.

She glanced away. She'd never pull this off if she spent any time staring into those warm brown eyes. "Well, we certainly did it up this weekend, didn't we?" She stepped aside to let him in. "I also need to thank you for sharing that suite with me. As you can see, I don't have much in the way of fountains and hot tubs in here."

Noah walked into the room and glanced around. "It'll do."

She closed the door and leaned against it while she contemplated his choice of words. She watched as he took off his Stetson and laid it brim-side up on the table where her computer sat, still switched on. "Do for what?" she asked warily.

Without answering, he glanced at the computer, pulled out the chair she'd been sitting in and settled into it. He gazed at the screen for several seconds. "Some screensaver you have here," he said. "Puts my shooting stars all to shame."

"Why don't I turn that thing off?" She shouldn't be surprised that he used a computer at the ranch. Saguaro Junction was small and conservative, but that didn't mean the town was filled with hicks.

He leaned back in the chair and glanced at her. "Why turn it off? I'm not embarrassed, and you certainly shouldn't be, considering how daring you are."

She shrugged, not willing to admit that the stupid little screensaver reminded her of what she'd never experience with Noah. "Well, I'm not embarrassed, but for the record, I don't use that screensaver on my office computer. It's strictly for private use on my laptop."

He gazed at her. "You're really destroying my image of you, Keely. First I find out you're not a call girl, not even a topless dancer, and now you tell me you don't have X-rated screensavers on your office computer. Next you'll be telling me that you've never had a multiple orgasm, despite writing a whole article about it."

She drew in a quick breath and her pulse hammered. Man, she'd never expected that comment, and what was worse, he was dead-on. After writing the article, she'd meant to experiment a little, but then she just…hadn't. There were many sexual adventures she'd written about, fantasized about and ultimately retreated from. It was one of her well-kept secrets.

Her weekend with Noah had seemed like the perfect time to be brave. Here was a man who thought she would dare anything, and she'd felt the thrill of living up to her reputation for once. It had been liberating and wonderful, and…safe. Maybe that was why she'd cut loose. She could be as wild as she wanted to be with Noah because she'd trusted him to keep her safe.

Pushing back the chair, he stood. "Did I touch a nerve, Keely?"

She laughed, hoping she sounded amused and not nervous. "Are you kidding? You know what kind of woman I am, Noah. I have no rules, no limits. A free spirit, that's me."

"I thought so, too." He came closer, a gleam of purpose in his eyes. "But I'm beginning to wonder if I know you at all."

She backed up. He looked more intimidating now and a muscle twitched in his jaw. This was what she'd expected from him in the first place. She dredged up her carefully conceived arguments. "I'm sorry I tricked you, Noah, but it's your own fault."

"Is that right?" He advanced another step.

"I told you I was going into the Pussycat for an interview. You're the one who jumped to the conclusion that it was a job interview." She had nowhere to go. Her butt was pressed against the top drawer of a low-slung dresser and she gripped the edge for balance. Lifting her chin, she tried to stare him down. She wasn't afraid that he'd physically attack her, but by deliberately invading her space he was making her very uncomfortable and...yes...aroused.

She didn't want him to know that.

"When you realized what I was thinking, you could have corrected me," he said easily. But there was nothing easy about the look in his eyes.

"And I might have, if you hadn't offered to help me mend my wicked ways! Do you have any concept of how arrogant that offer was?"

He gazed at her, his eyes dark and intense. "You know, I think I do."

She blinked. Just when she was getting up to speed, he threw marbles under her feet. "You do?"

"Yeah. And maybe I deserved everything you dished out."

"Really?" She scrambled to regroup. "Right! You sure did!" She tried to breathe normally, but he was so very close, almost touching her. Her nostrils flared as she caught the scent of him. That alone was enough to get her juices flowing. "There you were, acting so high and mighty, like you were above it all, some sort of Eliot Ness of the sex world. I had to knock you off your perch and show you that you were corruptible like everybody else."

"You did a good job." He paused and the light of challenge sparkled in his eyes. "For an amateur."

"Amateur?" she yelped. Then she realized he was trying to undermine her credibility, which would give him more power. She couldn't let him get away with that. "Amateur, my G-string. You're talking to Miss November, buster. And what about all the articles on sex I've written in the past six years? When it comes to erotic fantasies, I know what I'm talking about!"

"Oh, I believe you." He'd closed the small gap between them and now he braced a hand on either side of her and leaned down until his face was inches from hers. His tone remained conversational. "I just wonder how much practical experience you've had—other than this weekend, that is."

Her heart thundered. She wanted him to think she was five times more experienced than he was so she could keep control of the situation. But she didn't feel in control. She wanted him to make wild, crazy love to her, and that wasn't good, because she figured he had a different plan.

Too late she realized she stood braced against the dresser with her legs slightly apart. She was too open, too vulnerable. And, oh, God, too wet. Yet if she moved to close her legs, that would tip him off that she was falling prey to his sexual game.

"Have you ever had a multiple orgasm, Keely?" he asked softly.

She could barely breathe. "None of your beeswax."

His lips twitched in amusement. "What did you say?"

"I said none of your business."

"No, you didn't." He grinned. "You said 'none of your beeswax,' just like you used to say when you were nine years old and I caught you trying to sneak sugar cubes to the horses."

"I'm not nine years old anymore."

His grin faded and heat blazed in his eyes. "I'm well aware of that." He stepped neatly between her legs and settled his erection against her crotch. "Painfully aware of that."

She swallowed a gasp. He felt way too good there. "I know where you're going with this," she said.

He pressed forward slightly and his gaze held hers. "Do you?"

She tried to keep the tremble from her voice, tried not to get lost in those dark eyes. "You want to get me worked up, and then you're going to walk out of here without doing anything, to punish me for fooling you."

"That's not a bad idea. There's only one flaw in it. Walking out of here without doing anything would punish me, too. On the way over I decided that I've suffered enough this weekend trying to hold back and be noble. I intend to leave here a very satisfied man."

She was light-headed with desire, but she fought the urge to give in. She might be in love with him, but he obviously didn't feel that way about her. In the end, he still planned to leave. "I won't let you use me for sex and then discard me."

His tone was low and intimate, and his eyes burned with an unholy fire. "Why not? Isn't that what you had in mind for me?" He nudged her with the ridge of his fly.

Sensation zinged from that tender spot between her legs to the tips of her toes and fingers. "No, I—"

"I think the big-city girl wanted some fun with the small-town boy." He nudged her again. "I think you wanted to play at being a really hot babe, a sex-driven bad girl, with a guy from back home who didn't know any different. Yeah, I think you wanted to use me for sex and then discard me. I think that's exactly what you wanted. I think you might even have been hoping for some of those multiple orgasms you've never had. Only, the plan got interrupted because somebody recognized you."

"You don't know anything about it! For your information, I—" She stopped speaking abruptly when she realized the trap she was in. The only way she could convince him that she wasn't a sexual predator was to admit she'd been in love with him for most of her life, and her weakness for him had motivated her more than anything else. She'd wanted one weekend to remember. But she wasn't about to give him that information and be hurt even worse than she had been at sixteen.

"Cat got your tongue?" he murmured, rubbing his fly back and forth, coaxing a response from her.

"Okay, you're right!" She was beginning to quiver all over, so she talked fast to hide it. "When you were determined to save me, I decided to turn the tables and have some fun with you for the weekend. Only the weekend. Then it would be over between us." *Because that's what you would want.* "If that qualifies as using you for sex, then I'm guilty. So shoot me."

"I had something else in mind. Did you get enough this weekend?"

She knew what he meant, but she just tightened her jaw and stared at him, refusing to answer.

"Let me put it another way. You're a liberated, fantasy-minded gal who likes good sex with no strings attached, right?"

She gripped the edge of the dresser so hard her fingers ached. "Yes."

"Then, darlin', you're going to love what happens next."

16

Noah had found out the truth and it wasn't pretty. If he'd been entertaining the faint hope that Keely had some deeper emotion going on, that she had more than sex on her mind and would like to continue their relationship somehow, that hope had been crushed. She obviously saw this weekend as a one-time experience.

Okay, if that's the way things were, he'd make it a hell of an experience. He'd stuffed more condoms in his pocket than he imagined ever needing, but as he stood there breathing in the scent of raspberries, he wondered if he'd brought enough. Time to get that first urgent need taken care of. Then he'd be able to experiment a little. Or a lot.

Maybe in the back of his mind he hoped he could love her so hard and long that he would break through that protective shell of hers and make her care about him. He might be kidding himself about that, but even if he didn't succeed, he'd have a terrific time trying.

He looked into her green eyes and found desire mixed with uneasiness. Good. He wanted her to be uneasy. He was planning to turn her inside out once he took the edge off his own needs.

"We'll start with the basics and work up from there." He hooked his thumbs inside the waistband of her pants and before she could react, he'd dragged them, along with her underwear, down past her knees.

She drew in a sharp breath, but whether she was shocked or delighted, he wasn't sure.

"Kick them off," he said as he unbuckled his belt.

Her eyes sparked green fire. "You seem so determined to run this show. Let's see if you can make me."

"Love to." Using the strength and sure-handedness that had won him ribbons on the rodeo circuit, he lifted her to the glossy surface of the dresser. As he'd calculated, it was the perfect height. Holding her there with the fingers of one hand splayed over her firm bottom, he slid two fingers of his other hand deep inside her. His penis throbbed as he probed her slick heat.

She moaned and squeezed her eyes shut.

"Are you going to kick them off?" he asked softly as he stroked her.

"Oooh, yes," she whispered, keeping her eyes closed.

"Glad to hear it." He eased his fingers free and unfastened his jeans.

Opening her eyes, she held his gaze as she braced her hands behind her on the dresser and kicked the pants and underwear to the floor. "Done."

"I'm nearly there." He was shaking, but he managed to rip the condom package open, shove down his briefs and roll the latex over his rigid penis.

He even made small talk. "In case you're wondering, this is the ribbed kind." His heart pounded like a jackhammer as he cupped her bottom in both hands and pulled her to the edge of the dresser. "I hope you like it." Then he entered her in one smooth stroke. He nearly passed out from the relief of finally being inside her.

Her gasp this time was all about pleasure. He could see it reflected in her eyes and the delicate wild-raspberry flush of her skin. Without mascara darkening her eyelashes, and her hair in that ponytail, she looked young, almost too young to have a man planted firmly between her thighs.

"Ribs...are good," she said.

"I'll...I'll make a...note of it." His breath hissed out between clenched teeth as he fought to keep from coming instantly. She wasn't too young, he reminded himself. She might not be as sophisticated as she'd led him to believe, but she was old enough to know exactly what she was doing.

And she felt so damn good. He should have known that he and Keely would be a perfect fit. He should have known that once he'd connected to her in this basic way he'd feel a surge of possessiveness so strong that he doubted he'd be able to leave his heart out of the equation.

Too late to reconsider. It was done. He was deep inside her, and very soon he would seek the release he had to have or go crazy. But first he wanted to burn this moment into his memory. Standing very still so he wouldn't climax while he looked at her, he let his gaze drift to her mouth.

He'd thought nothing could be sexier than the sheen of freshly applied lipstick on her sensuous mouth, but he'd been wrong. Her bare lips, naturally rosy and parted with desire, tempted him beyond belief. He remembered what that mouth could do, had done in the hallway of the hotel. Just thinking about that would take him past the point of no return. And he didn't want to go there yet.

Instead, he was going to look. His gaze traveled over the golden skin of her throat as he listened to the sexy, liquid sound as she swallowed in air. More memories rose, memories of losing control and listening to that same sweet sound as she'd taken all he had to give.

His climax hovered ever nearer as he savored the view of her breasts, plump as honeydews beneath her tank top. It pleased him to leave them covered this time and watch the snug white cotton pucker over her erect nipples. Then his glance dipped lower, past the hem of her tank top to red-gold curls surrounding the spot where his penis was buried to the hilt.

He tested his control by easing slowly out and sinking deep again, all the while absorbing the sight of that perfect connection. And he nearly came apart from the visual high that gave him.

Balanced on the knife's edge of release, he looked into her eyes. "This one's for me."

She sucked in a breath. "Go for it."

Tightening his grip, he felt the muscles of her buttocks contract beneath his fingers. With a groan of anticipation, he began to thrust. Oh, yes. Deeper and faster.

Her breasts jiggled from the impact. His excitement ratcheted up a notch, watching them shake faster and faster the quicker he pumped. Oh, damn, this was good.

Panting, she wrapped her legs around his hips and threw her head back.

He listened to her soft but urgent moans and knew she was close, but he couldn't wait, couldn't make sure she'd take off with him. Not this time. She'd have lots of turns later.

But now…now…the world tipped and he plunged forward with a moan wrenched from deep in his chest. Spasms ripped through him as he poured himself into her tight warmth. Fireworks exploded in his head and his knees began to buckle.

"Noah! Please!"

Her desperation broke through the song of joy bubbling through his body. He'd meant to be selfish this time, but he couldn't leave her writhing in frustration. Trembling with the aftershocks of his own climax, he sank to his knees, rested her thighs on his shoulders and pressed his open mouth right where he knew she needed him to be.

In no time she arched away from the dresser with a wild

cry. And as he listened to her breathless words of gratitude, he decided to settle in.

But she seemed to have other ideas as she struggled weakly, as if to get away. "You…were right." She gasped for breath. "I've never…I don't think I can…."

He ignored her and kept going.

"Noah…you don't have to prove any—" She gasped and her thighs began to quiver.

A fierce sense of pride surged through him. Ah, she tasted so good, and he was going to give her something no man ever had.

She moaned. "Oh…my. I've never… I think maybe… oh…oh…*my!*" Words became unintelligible whimpers as she arched like a bow once again.

He thought he had the combination now, was pretty sure he'd found the right rhythm and the right pressure, but he needed one more run to lock it in. Loving every second, he took her up a third time as she laughed and shrieked and called him a genius.

At last he stood, lifted her quaking body from the dresser and carried her to the unmade bed. Considerate of her not to have had the maid come in yet. Keely was limp as a wet mop when he settled her on the bed. While he shucked his clothes and tossed his remaining condoms on the bedside table, he enjoyed basking in her satisfied expression. As for him, he was already erect, already wanted her again. But he could wait.

KEELY WONDERED HOW MANY women had made the mistake of thinking that sex this good must mean that Noah was in love with them. She *felt* loved, even though she kept reminding herself that all he wanted was one action-packed weekend with her, and then it was *adiós, muchachas.*

Still, he sure made her feel cherished when he looked at her like that, his brown eyes warm and appreciative.

She was pretty darned appreciative, herself. She glanced at his stiff penis. "I'd be happy to return the favor."

"Maybe later. Considering the difference between guys and gals, I want to pace myself." He walked to the bedside telephone and picked up the receiver.

"What are you doing?"

"Ordering up some food."

"Food?" It was the last thing she'd expected him to suggest, considering he'd just had breakfast. She, on the other hand, was starving.

"Yeah, food." He grinned at her. "I tried to eat before I came up here but I didn't get much down. I'm willing to bet you haven't had anything either. And, right now, I'm damn hungry. How about you?"

"I could eat."

"Good." He punched in the number for room service and looked over at her. "How about a couple of club sandwiches and some fresh fruit?"

"Sure." Anything sounded good. And suddenly she realized that this was what a honeymoon would be like—making love and ordering room service afterward. But she had no honeymoon in her immediate future and she'd do well to remember that.

Noah placed the order and hung up the phone. Then he sat down on the bed beside her. "One of us has more clothes on than the other." He reached for the hem of her tank top.

"Wait." She placed her hands over his. "Won't we have to be dressed when the food arrives?"

"Will we?" His eyes sparkled.

"Yes. Taking a chance in a deserted hallway at night is one thing. Stripping down and inviting the room-service waiter in is beyond where I want to go."

"Okay. We'll put on clothes again. But I'll bet they won't show up for at least twenty minutes, and I want to see your breasts. Kiss your breasts. I'm crazy about your breasts. And look at that. They're crazy about me, too." He leaned down and gently bit one of the nipples that had stiffened under his gaze.

She sighed with pleasure.

"They want out," he murmured, moving to catch the other nipple between his teeth.

"Maybe so." She offered no resistance as he pushed her top up. She wanted to feel his hot mouth against her skin.

He licked and nibbled until, despite the satisfaction he'd given her not long ago, she began to ache for him again.

"Tell me a secret fantasy." He covered her breasts with tiny kisses. "Something you've never done. Something we could do in this room."

She didn't have to think very long about it, especially considering the sensual daze he'd put her in by stroking and lapping at her breasts. "To be tied up," she murmured. "Gently and considerately, of course. And then teased to distraction."

"You wouldn't be scared of me doing that?"

"Not with you." Her blood heated just thinking about it. "I'd be safe with you."

"Yeah, you'd be safe." He rolled her nipple against his tongue. "Let's do it."

"After room service."

"Before."

"Before?"

"Now." In a split second he'd pinned her to the mattress with his body and skimmed her tank top over her head, bringing her arms up with it.

Her wrists seemed tangled in the material and she tried to free them. "I'm stuck."

He raised up on one elbow and looked down at her with a satisfied smile. "I know."

Then she realized he was holding her wrists with his free hand. "Wait a minute! You can't just do it! I have to let you!"

He shook his head. "Way too tame for a woman like you."

"Tame was what I had in mind!" She tried to wiggle out from under him.

"Sorry." He held her still with the weight of his body while he twisted the material of her top and looped one armhole over the bedpost. Then he slipped the scrunchie from her ponytail and wound that around her wrists for good measure.

That was about the time she remembered she'd just invited a cowboy who bull-dogged cattle for a living to play bondage games with her. She might be in over her head. "Noah, seriously, room service will be here any minute. Let me go."

"Nope. This is fun." As he slid downward he grasped one ankle.

"Stop it!" She tried kicking with her free foot, but with both hands tied above her head and one ankle in his grasp, she couldn't get any leverage. "Noah! I'll scream!"

"I imagine the folks in the neighboring rooms will only think you're having another amazing orgasm, which, eventually, is what will happen if you're a good girl." Holding her ankle firmly in one hand, he picked up a corner of the sheet, put it between his teeth and ripped away a strip of it.

"You're destroying hotel property!"

"I'll pay them for the sheet." He moved to the other side of the bed to repeat the process and there she was, neatly tied, hand and foot, naked on the bed. He surveyed his work. "Nice. Very, very nice. Are you comfy?"

"Well, you didn't hurt me or anything, if that's what you mean, but I didn't mean for you to do it like this." She was panting, both from the struggle and—she had to admit it— from excitement. He'd tied her up while promising her an amazing orgasm. And he'd been quick, but gentle. None of her muscles were stretched too tight and, God, she felt sexy. A fantasy didn't get much better than that.

And yet she still felt honor-bound to complain. "I was picturing velvet ropes or silk scarves."

"You got any velvet ropes or silk scarves?"

"Well, no. Even so, you could have led up to it and taken it slower."

"You don't lead up to a stunt like this. That's boring." His smile was positively wicked as his gaze traveled over her. "And, don't worry, we'll take it slow. Now."

A shiver of anticipation ran down her spine. "My, how you've changed since Friday afternoon."

"That's where you're wrong. I've had my fantasies, the same as you." He walked slowly around the bed, eyeing her from every angle. "This is one we share."

She didn't dare ask him if she was the woman he'd fantasized about. If she hadn't been, she didn't want to know. Besides, if she hadn't been his fantasy woman before this weekend, she would be after this.

Taking his gaze from her briefly, he reached down and picked up his briefs. They didn't fit very well over his erection.

"I didn't hear anybody at the door," she said.

"Nobody's there yet."

"Then why—"

"I want to be ready." He stepped into his jeans and winced as he zipped them. "Talk about bondage." Then he walked casually over to the bed and sat on the edge of the mattress.

Her pulse raced at the look in his eyes. An involuntary shudder of excitement ran through her as the fact of her vulnerability finally penetrated. She was totally at his mercy. Did she trust him that much? Yes and no. Yes, that he wouldn't hurt her. No, that he wouldn't drive her beyond all her limits and strip away all her defenses. And that was where the thrill of danger came in.

"Cold?"

She shook her head.

"I didn't think so." Reaching down to her ankle, he trailed a finger along the inside of her calf, then continued up the tender skin of her inner thigh, drawing closer, closer, closer... and stopping. Holding her gaze, he brushed his knuckles lightly over her damp curls and she discovered how incredibly sensitive she was as she responded with a rush of moisture.

"You smell so good," he murmured. Boldly he slid a finger in deep, drew it out and licked it. "And you taste even better."

She wanted more...much more. But he'd promised to take it slow. She wondered if she'd survive the wait.

"Remember finger paints?" he asked.

Her chest was tight with anticipation, her answer breathy. "Yes."

"Let's pretend this is a jar of finger paint." He slipped two fingers back into her. "And I'm going to paint a beautiful picture on your soft body. You're so wet I should be able to create quite a masterpiece."

Delicious heat poured through her, flushing her skin and making her entire body tingle. "You're going to torture me, aren't you?"

He circled her breast with his damp fingers. "Yes, darlin', I am. And you're going to love it."

As an erotic tease, it was world-class. He stroked every part of her body with the musky liquid of her passion, always returning to the wellspring to caress her into panting readiness again. Yet he'd only stay long enough to make her whimper, never long enough to give her the climax that soon became her entire focus.

And just as she was ready to offer him anything if he'd

only give her that precious release, a knock at the door announced room service had arrived.

Noah leaned down and brushed his lips over hers. "Our food's here."

She gasped for breath. "Who cares? Noah, I need—"

"Soon." He climbed from the bed. "Be right there!" he called to the bellman.

"What do you mean, you'll *be right there?* Noah, don't open that door!"

"Don't panic," he murmured. Then he reached for the quilted bedspread that had fallen to the floor and pulled it carefully up to her chin.

"What—what are you doing?"

"Completing your fantasy." He propped two pillows under her head and arranged two more to disguise the fact that her hands were bound. "I've been paying attention, Keely. I'm going to turn us both on like we've never been turned on in our lives."

"H-how?"

"The waiter's going to come in and leave our food while you're lying there totally naked and aroused under that bedspread, unable to move, and by the time he's left the tray and I've paid the bill and he's gone, you're going to be hotter than you've ever been in your life, because it's so risky. Better than the hallway."

"Oh, Noah." She thought her heart would pound out of her chest. But in a secret, hidden part of her mind she suspected he was right.

"Trust me?"

"O-okay."

He walked over and opened the door.

The waiter came in, and after one quick look at Keely in the bed, he bustled about his task of setting down the tray.

Noah pretended to ignore her, too, as he took his time paying the bellman and walking him to the door.

It was the wildest feeling she'd ever had, knowing that the minute the bellman was gone Noah would whip off the bedspread and make love to her.

Her body throbbed with unreleased tension as she watched Noah open the door, let the guy walk out, close the door again and carefully lock it.

Then he turned and nearly tore off his jeans and briefs. The condom went on in record time. Then he yanked off the bedspread and released Keely's restraints before moving between her thighs and plunging deep. Her orgasm came instantly, rocking her with the most powerful contractions she'd ever felt. She clung to Noah as his frenzied cries of release blended with hers.

Gradually the world stopped spinning as they lay sweaty and entwined, gasping for breath.

Noah chuckled. Keely started to smile. And before they knew it, they were clutching each other and howling with laughter.

"Can you believe we did that?" Noah asked.

"No! You are really crazy!"

"You started the whole thing." He propped himself up on an elbow and looked down at her, a grin on his face.

"You mean the hallway?"

"No, I mean behind that lava rock! My imagination has been in overdrive ever since."

"I was trying to corrupt you."

"It worked. Man, did it ever work. I am never going to forget this weekend."

She felt a pain in the general region of her heart. If only he'd said he would never forget her. She managed a smile. "Me neither."

17

NOAH WAS GLAD HE'D ORDERED the fruit to go along with the sandwiches. With a willing woman like Keely, a guy could find all kinds of interesting things to do with fruit. He'd turned her into quite a fruit cocktail before he'd finished. And in the process she'd become a real fan of multiple orgasms.

Then she'd become creative with the mayo she'd scraped off her club sandwich and he'd gladly served as her private bedroom deli. He might not have been able to do the multiple-orgasm thing like she could, but the climax she'd given him had almost killed him.

All in all, it was the most excellent meal he'd ever had—best food, best atmosphere, best company.

He wondered why he'd never tried eating naked with a woman before. You could save a bundle on napkins. If either of you happened to drip, the other gladly licked it off. Personally he'd made an effort to be messy and he figured she had, too.

With all the interruptions, their lunch had taken quite a while. He realized just how long when he had to switch on a light to see Keely better. At the same time he glanced at the numbers on the digital bedside clock. Damn. His plane left in two short hours.

"Why the frown?" she asked, snuggling into the pillows. "Indigestion?"

"No." He settled down next to her and cupped her breast, rubbing her nipple to erectness with his thumb. "It's just that I can't stay much longer."

Her green eyes flashed with alarm. "Really?"

"My plane leaves tonight."

"Miss it."

"Can't."

She reached down and circled his penis with her hand. "Are you quite sure about that?"

He closed his eyes as she stroked and tickled him into aching readiness in no time at all. In the past forty-eight hours he'd become like his bulls when they were in the same pen with a heifer in heat. He couldn't get enough.

But he'd promised Jonas he'd be home tonight. Because of his promise, Jonas and B.J. had left the ranch that afternoon bound for Phoenix to check out wedding decorations. They'd planned to stay in Phoenix a couple of days and Noah needed to be at the ranch to take care of business while they were gone. Several matters demanded his attention, and he intended to keep his word to be back on time.

Keely scooted down and placed a kiss on the tip of his penis. "I'm sure you could get a plane in the morning." Then she used her tongue to add more fuel to her argument.

His breathing roughened and his voice grew husky with a passion that seemed to have no end. "Keep that up and I'll be able to fly there without a plane."

"I want you to stay with me tonight," she murmured as she nibbled her way from base to tip.

"There's nothing I want more. But I can't. I—" He drew in a sharp breath as she took him fully into her mouth and applied gentle suction. "But you have amazing powers of persuasion." By all rights he shouldn't be getting hard again, but damned if he wasn't. If he didn't stop her, she'd make him come, and he didn't want to spend the last orgasm he would share with her in that way.

Ah, but she gave him such pleasure. Reluctantly he combed his fingers through her hair and cradled her head, drawing her slowly away, bringing her tender mouth up to meet his. "Time for one of those little raincoats," he murmured between light kisses. "I want to be inside you this time."

"Okay," she said in a breathy, excited voice as she met his teasing kisses with ones of her own. "We can try a new position."

"I had in mind something boring. Hang on a sec." He turned over and grabbed a condom packet from the bedside table.

"Boring?" She smiled at him. "Here, let me put that on."

"I thought you'd never ask." He gave her the condom and she made a big production of unrolling it over his totally recharged penis. He loved her careful attention and tried not to think about this being the last time he'd feel her hands on him.

"I don't see how anything we do in this bed could be boring." She gave one last little tug on the latex. Then she cupped his balls and massaged them gently as she glanced up at him. "Not considering what we have to work with."

He couldn't believe he was so hot for her again, but she seemed to know instinctively how to touch him to turn him into a raging maniac. "Then you wouldn't mind the plain old missionary position?"

She gazed into his eyes. "You mean no props, no unique location, no thrill of discovery?"

"That's right." He searched her eyes for the emotion he wanted to find. "Just you and me."

"Scary."

"I know. Think you can handle it?" There. He thought he saw the visual clue he was seeking, but then it was gone again.

"I don't know." She looked nervous.

"Let's try it." He eased her to her back and braced his hands beside her shoulders as he moved between her thighs.

She ran her hands lightly down his back and paused as her fingers encountered the ridge of a small scar. "How did I miss this?" she asked softly. Slowly she traced the ridge with her forefinger.

"You couldn't have discovered everything. It's only been a weekend."

Regret flashed in her eyes. "That's right."

He gazed down at her, memorizing what he saw. This was his last chance to awaken real emotion in her. If he failed, he would never see her this way again.

Her tousled hair fanned out against the white pillow in waves of dark red, the color of desire. His glance raked over her, from her flushed cheeks to her passion-darkened nipples, from her flat belly to the red-gold curls between her thighs. A shell-pink treasure beckoned to him, peeking out from beneath those soft curls.

He focused on her face again—full lips parted, nostrils flared, green eyes dark with secrets. He held her gaze and moved his hips forward, easing partway in, adjusting to her heat so he could build his control.

"That feels so good," she murmured.

"Nothing like it." And he wasn't talking about sex in general, either. He'd never experienced anything to compare with making love to Keely. He was beginning to understand how rare this connection was...for him. But he didn't know how rare it was for her. Not yet.

Taking a deep breath, he pushed home. Slowly a flame grew in her eyes, a flame that warmed his soul. Maybe they had a chance. But he wasn't putting anything on the line by speaking about it. Instead, he'd talk around the problem. "Just so you know, I'm not going for the multiples this time."

"Okay." She swallowed and tried another smile, but it faltered. "Back to basics?"

"Yeah."

"You're leaving after this, aren't you?"

"Yeah."

Her grip tightened on his back and she closed her eyes. "I thought so," she whispered, her voice choked.

"Keely, open your eyes."

She shook her head.

"Please."

Her lashes fluttered upward, and her eyes glistened with tears.

Those tears hit him like a fist in the gut. "You're crying," he said, his throat raw.

Her voice was tight. "I think I have something in my eye."

"Bull. You don't want this to end any more than I do."

"It has to end." Her voice quivered. "I can't go back."

His heart sank. "To the ranch?"

"To the ranch, to my family, to my old life, to anything."

She didn't think he was worth the sacrifice. He could beg her to change her mind. And then what? Convince her to live a life she didn't want because he couldn't imagine giving her up? No.

"I guess this is it, then," he said.

"Yes, this is it."

"Well, you'd better hang on, sweetheart, because it's gonna be one hell of a goodbye." He began slowly, making each stroke count, and even her tears couldn't put out the flame in her eyes. "You know this is about more than sex," he murmured.

She didn't reply, but the flame burned brighter.

"It's about more than games and thrills." He increased the

pace, building that flame. She cared about him, damn it. He could see that she did. "It's about more than orgasms."

Tears dribbled from the corners of her eyes, and her gasps sounded almost like sobs, but she kept her eyes open and her gaze locked with his.

"But if I can't give you anything else, at least I can give you that." Shifting his angle slightly, he came in high and tight, stroking relentlessly now, drawing broken cries of pleasure from her lips. "Good, isn't it?"

"Yes!" she cried, helpless in her need.

"The best, right?"

"Yes, oh...*yes*." She met him thrust for thrust.

"Even just the basics."

Her fingers dug into his back. "I love...the basics," she said, panting.

His heart wept. She'd nearly said it. "I love...the basics, too," he murmured.

"Oh, Noah...Noah...now!"

As she tightened around him and pushed upward, he spiraled out of control with a groan of surrender—to his passion, to Keely, to a future that would not include this flame-haired woman. Shuddering, he held her close and gulped back a sob of frustration. It was over.

KEELY STAYED IN BED, cocooned in the covers while Noah dressed. Part of the time she watched him and part of the time she closed her eyes and battled tears. The gutsy move would be to get up and put her clothes on, too, but she couldn't bear to leave the haven they'd shared for so many hours. She wanted to stay here for as long as his scent remained in the sheets.

They'd had lots of sex in this room, but they'd only made love once, this last time. That cataclysmic event had nearly destroyed her. Their love, unspoken but real, was incredibly beautiful and absolutely hopeless.

Oh, if they could live their days in this room, if they never had to put on the clothes that branded each of them with the roles they'd chosen, then they might be able to make a go of their relationship. He'd just proved to her that they'd crossed into a whole other realm, one in which the mating of bodies was overshadowed by the joining of souls.

But they couldn't live in this room, and he was already dressed in the clothes of his chosen profession. Buckling his belt, he went in search of his hat. He was headed back to his ranch, and she had a story to finish for the magazine. In the real world they'd make each other miserable. She had to let him go.

He might think he wanted her around, but good sex had muddled his brain. Maybe, in the hot flush of desire, he'd imagined that he could mold her into the kind of rural woman he needed by his side. She, on the other hand, had never even considered asking Noah to become a city man.

As if he ever could. He stood in the middle of the hotel room smoothing the brim of his black hat, his long legs tucked into denim, his broad shoulders covered in soft chambray. He might own a computer and understand the principles of investing in the stock market, but in his heart he was a cowboy.

And she loved him that way. She wouldn't urbanize Noah even if she had the power.

He looked at her for a long moment. "I'll stop by the desk and settle up with them about the sheet."

She propped herself up against the headboard while holding the bedspread over her breasts. They'd dared everything with each other, and yet nudity seemed inappropriate now. "What are you going to say?"

A faint smile touched his mouth, the mouth she would

never kiss again. "I'll tell them we each took a strip of it for a souvenir."

"That's an idea."

He pulled a rolled strip of white material out of his back pocket and showed it to her. "I thought so."

She stared at the piece of sheet he'd carefully preserved and meant to take home with him. For some reason, that sentimental gesture got to her more than anything else, and she swallowed several times, praying she wouldn't break down.

"I have to go," he said softly.

She nodded, not trusting herself to speak.

"I'd better not kiss you goodbye, or I'll never leave."

She cleared her throat. "Okay." She clutched the bedspread and tried to breathe normally.

He walked toward the door.

In that moment she imagined how a condemned person must feel in the last few seconds of life. She'd known heaven today. In less than a minute she'd know hell.

Perhaps she could make things easier for herself if she looked away while he twisted open the dead bolt and reached for the doorknob. But instead, she watched every move, cherishing each second that he remained.

He turned the knob and opened the door. She braced herself. Then, slowly, he closed the door again and faced her. Her heart thundered with new hope, even though she couldn't imagine that he'd found a solution.

"At least come to B.J. and Jonas's wedding," he said.

Her heart twisted with agony. The wedding. Of course. What had she expected, that he'd fall to his knees and declare he couldn't live without her? That only happened in the movies. Somehow she managed to speak around the lump in her throat. "I'd only cause problems."

He shook his head. "I really think B.J. would love to have you there, and so would Arch."

She didn't know where she found the reserves to discuss this with him, but she dug deep and came up with a reasonably coherent response. "I haven't spoken to either of them for ten years. I can't just waltz in there in the middle of B.J.'s big day. That wouldn't be fair to anyone." And loving Noah as she did, she'd want to touch him, hold him, make love to him. Knowing that she couldn't would be torture.

"All right," he said quietly. "What if I mentioned to them that I ran into you and—"

She started. "Noah, you can't be planning to tell them what we—"

"No. I wouldn't do that, Keely. What we've done this weekend is our own private business."

"Thank you." The panic quieted in her chest. Noah had been a safe choice for adventure because he would never endanger her, physically or mentally. She knew that, but he'd given her a scare for a moment.

"Would you like to be at the wedding?" he asked.

Such a complicated question. But in the end, when she considered that her baby sister was getting married, that it was a day that could never be repeated, there was only one answer. "Yes."

"Then let me mention that I saw you. I'm sure they'll want you there, but I can drop you a line and let you know for sure, so there's no doubt that they're expecting you."

"There's another issue." She held his gaze, her heart thumping. "We both agree there's no future for us, right?"

His expression was guarded. "That's what you said."

"It's what I believe." She ran a tongue over her dry lips. "So how will that be, if I come back to the ranch for a couple of days? Can we handle that?"

His glance settled briefly on her mouth and heat flickered in his eyes. Then he looked away and cleared his throat. "Looks like we'll have to, for B.J. and Jonas's sake. Like you said, we don't want to take the focus off their big day." He faced her again and his chest heaved. "If you can deal with it, then I can."

She had no idea if she could or not. "Like you said, we'll have to. For the sake of the people we love." And she included him in that category.

"Right."

"Thank you for suggesting that I go," she said, meaning every word. "Assuming B.J. and Dad want me, it's the right thing to do. After all, B.J. and Jonas will probably have kids someday."

"Yeah, they probably will." His response was rich with longing.

Of course, he wanted children, she thought with a pang of regret. She hadn't ever considered kids, but if she could have one who called Noah daddy, that would be…special. Talk about a daydream. "I'll want to see my nieces and nephews," she said, "so I need to get past this awkwardness with B.J. and Dad, and the sooner I do that, the better."

He nodded. Then he stood there gazing at her until the air seemed to crackle between them.

She wondered what he'd do if she flung back the covers and opened her arms. From the look in his eyes, he'd miss his plane. But he didn't really want to do that.

So she would help him. "You need to go," she murmured.

He closed his eyes. "Keely—"

"Go, damn it! I can only be noble for so long!"

Without another word he left, closing the door carefully behind him. The automatic lock clicked into place.

She lost track of time as she sat staring at the closed door, willing him to knock and ask to be let back in. She stayed rigid and motionless until her head pounded and her eyes stung. But no knock came. He'd accepted her decision to end this amazingly beautiful connection between them.

The words she'd never spoken aloud rose in her throat, demanding to be free. "I love you, Noah," she whispered hoarsely into the silence.

KEELY DIDN'T WANT HIS love. Noah struggled with that knowledge as the plane left Las Vegas. In spite of everything, he'd been about to tell her that he loved her, but she'd cut him off, as if she didn't want him to make the mistake of declaring his feelings and saying things he couldn't take back.

Maybe she even loved him a little bit, too. He would have sworn that was love he'd seen in her eyes toward the end of their precious time together. But loving a guy like him would only tie her down, so she'd do her best to get over it. He wondered how well she'd succeed. As for him, there was a hole in his heart big enough to drive a truck through.

Suggesting that she come to the wedding had been a desperate attempt to maintain a tie with her. He suspected that B.J. and Arch would be thrilled to have her come home for the big day, and Jonas would be happy about it, too. Noah was more than willing to do them a favor, but his motives were purely selfish. Keely might not want his love, but the closer he came to Arizona, the less he was prepared to accept that as a final decision.

Still, he knew there were rough times ahead, and he was glad he'd arranged to get Keely back on Twin Boulders soil, where he was thoroughly grounded. In order to perform a miracle and coax Keely into his life, he needed all his strength, and he drew that strength from the land where he was born.

Yet he had to be careful that he didn't overpower her and force her into a life she didn't want. He was counting on the fact that she might not know what she wanted, or more precisely, what she needed. She'd convinced herself that she couldn't possibly fit in at the ranch, but he wanted to see that for himself.

Maybe she was right. Maybe when he looked at her and visualized her surrounded by their children, he was experiencing hallucinations brought on by the greatest sex he'd ever known. But after making love to Keely the way he had that last time, he couldn't imagine anyone else as his mate or the mother of his kids. A few other times in his life when he'd been sexually involved with a woman, even thought himself in love, he'd tried to picture that woman pregnant with his baby. The image had never come into focus.

But now…now it was clear as a bell. He could feel himself thrusting deep inside Keely and spilling his seed. Then, in a few weeks, they'd share the joy of knowing that she'd conceived. He could picture her eyes lighting up at the moment they knew for sure. Her body would grow round and ripe, sensuous in a new way. The image brought a rush of anticipation. Then the hour would come when she would give birth, and he would hold the child they'd created, the baby who was a visible sign of their passion….

He must be going crazy. Only a crazy man would fantasize about making a woman pregnant when she didn't want to admit that she loved him and certainly didn't want him to tell her of his love. Only a crazy man would think he had enough imagination, enough moves, enough love to satisfy a wild child like Keely Branscom.

But Noah would give ten years of his life for a chance to prove that he was the only man fit for the job.

18

"I'VE DECIDED WE NEED a piece on cyber-infidelity. The angle I had in mind was 'Are you cheating with an online lover?'" Carolyn clicked her ballpoint pen repetitively as she glanced at her editorial staff seated around the conference table. "Keely, why don't you see what you can do with that?"

Keely nodded automatically. She didn't want the assignment, but she'd take that up with Carolyn later. One of the younger writers might really get into the topic, but it didn't do a thing for Keely.

Although five days had gone by since she'd made love to Noah, her body still hummed with memories. After being touched like that, she had zero interest in the subject of cybersex. The idea of screen-to-screen hanky-panky paled next to being in the same bed with a man like Noah, skin-to-skin.

As the meeting droned on, she evaluated the other story assignments Carolyn handed out in case one of them would work as a potential trade. Unfortunately, they all sounded like a major yawn. She probably needed more caffeine.

Or more sleep. Sleep would be a good thing. Sleep had not been her friend since leaving Vegas. She gazed out the office window. Maybe the air quality was dragging her down. L.A. had been suffering through a major inversion the last couple of days and the air was the color and odor of dirty gym socks.

A day at the beach catching those California rays and she'd be right as rain. Sure she would. Like hell she would. She missed the guy, missed him like crazy.

She wondered how long she'd feel the effects of her weekend with Noah. Anyone would think she'd broken off a five-year relationship the way she was moping around the office and her apartment. Nothing interested her, with the exception of one brief shopping trip when she'd bought a dress to wear to B.J.'s wedding. She might have been premature in that purchase, because for some reason Noah's letter giving her the all-clear signal hadn't arrived yet. The absence of that letter nagged at her constantly.

She'd realized several hours after he'd left that she hadn't given him her home address, so she'd begun worrying that he wouldn't think to send the letter to her office. If he'd thought of doing that, she wondered if he'd know to look inside the magazine's cover for the address. Not everyone realized that the publisher could be reached at—

"Keely? Yo, Keely!"

She glanced up with a start and discovered everyone at the conference table smirking at her, including Carolyn.

"We've all taken bets," Carolyn said, "and most of us, myself included, think you met some hunk in either Vegas or Reno, which explains why you've been so whacked since you came back. Care to enlighten us?"

"No."

"I was right!" said Andrea, a cute blonde of twenty-two with a bright future in journalism. She'd be perfect for the cybersex story. "I said if she refuses to dish, then it was more than a fling."

Keely pushed back her chair. She really didn't need this. "It's flu, is what it is, and if you guys aren't careful I'll plant a big kiss full of icky germs on each one of you."

Denise, the outer-office receptionist, poked her head in

the conference-room door. "Excuse me, but I have a guy out here who needs to deliver his singing telegram, and he's late for his next gig. Can you spare Keely for a minute?"

Keely groaned. "You guys didn't have to do this. I promise to cheer up. Just don't make me face a singing telegram."

Carolyn looked around the room, her eyebrows raised. "Well, *I* didn't order the singing telegram. Did one of you?"

Their chorus of denials didn't convince Keely. She leveled a stern look at all of them, but nobody cracked. She sighed. "Okay, I might as well get this over with." She stood and headed for the door. "Note to self—stay perky on the job or you'll be sent a singing telegram and be embarrassed like you wouldn't believe."

Her cohorts trailed out after her, the better to view her humiliation, she assumed. She'd never received a singing telegram before, so she didn't know exactly what to expect, but definitely not a black guy who looked as if he played pro football. He wore a baseball cap backward, a T-shirt and rapper shorts. He held a boom box on one broad shoulder.

"Miz Keely Branscom?" he asked.

Keely grimaced. "I'm afraid so."

The man nodded and punched a button on his boom box. As a steady rap beat filled the office, he gyrated to the rhythm and began to chant.

"Well, you gotta come home, 'cause your sister's gettin' hitched.

Girl, the knot will be tied and the rice will be pitched.

So we just wanna know if you're comin' or you're not,

'Cause to give it to you straight, we been missin' you a lot."

Keely's first reaction was shock, because a singing telegram was so not what she'd expected from her family, but as the significance of the message sank in, tears pushed at the back of her eyes. "Th-thank you," she told the guy as she blinked to clear her vision.

"No problem." With a little bow, the man turned and sauntered out of the office.

"Wow," Carolyn said as she walked over to Keely's desk. "You have a sister who's getting married?"

Keely nodded, not trusting herself to speak. *We been missin' you a lot.* Oh, God, why had she let ten years go by?

Carolyn took a closer look at Keely's face. "I think you have an RSVP call to make."

"Yep." Keely sniffed.

Carolyn tilted her head toward the door of her private office. "Why don't you use my phone?"

Keely gave her a shaky smile of gratitude. "I'd appreciate that," she said, her voice thick with emotion. Swiping at her eyes, she walked quickly into Carolyn's office and closed the door. Then she pressed both hands against her stomach. Ten years. She'd missed ten years of her father's voice and B.J.'s laughter. Ten years of birthdays, Christmas mornings, hugs and memories.

She couldn't imagine how they could ever forgive her. And yet they'd sent a singing telegram with a corny, touching, homemade rap verse just for her.

With trembling hands she picked up the receiver of Carolyn's telephone and dialed an outside line. Then she punched in the number that came to her as easily as a favorite nursery rhyme, even though she hadn't used it in ten years.

B.J. answered, sounding older. Of course she was older. She'd been only seventeen the last time Keely had seen her.

"B.J., it's Keely." Tears poured down her cheeks.

"Keely? Is it really you?"

"Oh, God, yes. I'm so sorry, B.J." Her words tumbled out

between choked little sobs. "I've missed you so much. So much. Can I really come to your wedding?"

B.J. started crying, too. "You'd better! You'd better come or I'll send another singing-telegram guy, and this one will be armed!" Laughter mixed in with her jerky sobs. "You hear me, Keely Marie?"

"I hear you," Keely said, smiling despite the tears that didn't seem to want to stop. She fumbled for the box of tissues on Carolyn's desk. "I'll be there. So, was the singing telegram your idea?"

"Nope."

"Dad's?" Keely had a hard time picturing that.

"No, but he was all for it."

"Okay, I know. Jonas was behind it. He's just the type."

B.J. laughed. "You're right, he is, but Noah's actually the one who thought it up. He said we couldn't just send a letter because it would be too boring."

"Noah?" Keely's heart squeezed. Lord, how she loved that man. "Well, tell him I wasn't bored." *Tell him I'm crazy about him.* "Who made up the rap thing?"

"Oh, we all worked on that. Pretty cool, huh?"

"Very cool." Her throat tightened with a fresh surge of emotion. "I loved it."

"Dad wanted to make it country instead, but we thought rap fit L.A. better, and maybe it wouldn't be *quite* so embarrassing for you at the office."

"Oh, it was plenty embarrassing, but I don't care a bit."

"Good. I was hoping that would be the way you'd react. Listen, Dad's out in the west pasture, but if you want to call back tonight—"

"You know what? When I talk to Dad, I'd like to be standing right in front of him. I think I'll wait until I get there."

B.J.'s voice was gentle. "His bark is worse than his bite, Keely. He's missed you something awful. We all have. Noah told us about your job. I can't believe I've never seen your name in that magazine, but you know me, I mostly read State Line Tack catalogs for fun." She paused and chuckled. "Or I did. Lately my tastes run more toward *Playgirl*."

"B.J.!" Keely wasn't sure what she thought about her little sister ogling naked men.

B.J. laughed. "I'm not the same uptight woman I was when you left, Keely."

"Well, I guess not!"

"In fact, I think we're overdue for a long, sisterly talk."

Keely gulped back a fresh onslaught of tears. "We sure are," she said.

"When can you get here?"

Keely had been eyeing her schedule ever since she'd returned from her trip. It was packed with work. "Coming in the day before is the best I can do. I know that sucks, but this was unexpected. I'll have to juggle a few things to even take that Friday off, but I'm determined to do it."

"Then Friday it is. Want me to pick you up at the airport?"

"Absolutely not. You're the bride and you have things to do."

"I'll bet Noah could."

Not on your life, babe. "You know what? Let me rent a car." A convertible, she was thinking. The prodigal daughter needed to make a splash when she arrived back in Saguaro Junction after a ten-year absence.

"Renting a car seems silly," B.J. said. "I'm sure that Noah—"

"I want to rent the car," Keely said. "Think red Mustang convertible. Think top down, radio blaring, going down Main Street past the feed store, past the café, past the bench in front of the post office…"

"Okay." There was a grin in B.J.'s voice. "I get it. God, it's

gonna be great to see you again. Set those tongues to waggin',
Keely. It's been duller than dust around here without you."

Keely had a sudden moment of uncertainty. "Maybe I
shouldn't do the convertible thing. I don't want to upstage
the bride."

That really made B.J. laugh. "There was a time I would
have been worried about that. But I have Jonas right where I
want him, and that's all I care about. Come back in full sail,
Keely. This girl can take it."

"I can hardly wait."

"Me neither. See you soon."

Keely couldn't stop grinning as she hung up the phone. She
was dying to see what sort of transformation had taken place
with B.J., who'd been the quintessential tomboy the whole
time they'd been growing up. Keely had always thought that
B.J. took that role in self-defense because Keely had grabbed
the sex-symbol image so early on and B.J. hadn't wanted to
compete.

But maybe Keely's long absence had been a good thing for
B.J. Without Keely around, she might have felt more free to
try her sexual wings. It was majorly weird to think about that,
but it was comforting to imagine that the separation might
have produced something positive. And Keely was thrilled
to be forewarned, so she wouldn't head to the ranch expecting her sister to be an Annie Oakley look-alike.

Then Keely's mind circled back to the topic it couldn't
seem to leave alone. Noah. She still couldn't believe he'd in-
stigated the rapper stunt. The guy was full of surprises, and
she was a sucker for surprises. Leaving him strictly alone
next weekend was not going to be easy.

NOAH GOT HOME AFTER dark to find Jonas and B.J. cozied up
on the front-porch swing. "Okay, keep it clean," he said as

he walked up the steps. "I want all your hands out where I can see them."

Jonas flashed him a dry smile. "You're just jealous because you don't have a babe like B.J. to make out with."

"Keely called," B.J. said. "She loved the rapper telegram and she's definitely coming to the wedding. You must have stayed well out of sight, because obviously she didn't have a clue you were there."

"That's good." Noah leaned against the porch railing. In a way, he'd been disappointed that she hadn't seen him just outside the door of the office. He wasn't sure what he'd have done if she'd caught him standing there, but he'd had a tough time being so close and not making contact. Damn, but she'd looked incredible in her silk blouse and tight little skirt.

"Was the office nice?" B.J. asked.

"I guess." He'd barely noticed the office once Keely had walked out of that conference room looking so efficient, with her hair scooped up on top of her head and a pencil stuck through her red curls. The spiral notebook in her hand had reminded him of teenage fantasies in which a full-breasted secretary invited him to have sex on the top of a wide executive desk. Come to think of it, he had a desk like that in his office at the ranch....

"How was L.A.?" Jonas asked.

"Smoggy." He wondered if Keely noticed the smog, or if she was so caught up in all that a big city had to offer that she didn't care what the air was like or how bad the traffic was. After seeing her in the bright, bustling office he was beginning to doubt himself again. But he'd needed to see her in that environment so that he had a better idea of what he was up against. She probably liked that hectic pace. She must like it if she'd stayed there for ten years.

"Dad's excited that she's coming home," B.J. said. "You know him, he doesn't want to let on that he's excited, but he's

over at our place cleaning like I've never seen him clean. I offered to help, but he wouldn't let me. He still thinks he does
it better than anybody, and he wants the house to be perfect."

Noah nodded. He understood the urge. He'd left the inside
of the ranch house to their housekeeper, Lupita, but he'd spent
his spare time trimming the mesquite trees that surrounded
the house and raking up the beans. Jonas had talked him out
of slapping a new coat of paint on the front door, but he still
might get around to that.

Jonas chuckled. "I wish I could've been there to see her
face when the guy started his routine. Now that it's over, I'm
glad you decided to fly over and supervise, so we could be
sure it was done right."

"If I'd been able to locate somebody I had confidence
would do the job the way we wanted it done, I wouldn't have,"
he said.

"Uh-huh," Jonas said. "I think you wanted to go over and
check things out, is what I think. I know you better than you
realize, big brother."

Noah thought of all the things Jonas didn't know about
him. But Keely knew. She was the only person who had
tapped into his deepest fantasies, the only person he trusted
with them. She'd shown him a whole new world, and he'd
fallen in love with her vision and with her. He needed her by
his side so they could continue to explore that world together.
If only he could be sure that she needed him just as much.

KEELY'S ONE-WOMAN PARADE through Saguaro Junction the
following Friday turned heads exactly as she'd hoped. What
she hadn't expected were the shouts of greeting and the enthusiastic waves of welcome. She'd had to stop the car four
different times to talk with folks, or risk running them over
as they hurried toward her car.

Not a single person had insulted her. Quite the contrary.

They'd made her feel like a celebrity. Apparently the good people of Saguaro Junction had mellowed toward her. More likely her little sister, and maybe even her father, had spread the word that she was published nationwide in *Attitude!* magazine. From every indication, her earlier transgression of posing nude had been forgiven.

Of course, they didn't know that she was still a sexual risk-taker, a fact she'd proven to herself and Noah in Vegas. She didn't really fit in here any better than she had before.

And yet she couldn't stop the rush of nostalgia when she drove past the small park and swimming pool where she'd hung out with her friends back in high school. High-school kids clustered there now, their shouts and laughter carrying to the road on the clear desert air.

She remembered what a hot August day was like for a teenager in Saguaro Junction, and she felt a stab of envy for their uncomplicated existence. At the time she'd thought her world was terminally boring, but now she sort of missed the simplicity of a life where the Roadrunner Theater had only one screen and the Cactus Café was your only choice if you wanted to eat out.

Yes, she'd stirred things up nicely, she thought as she drove on out of town past the gas station and the Elks Lodge. She'd forgotten what it was like to cause a commotion on a major thoroughfare, and she rather enjoyed it. In L.A. you could find auburn-haired, well-endowed women in convertibles at every intersection. She fit in there, all right. Yessir, fit right in. She might be wild by Saguaro Junction standards, but in L.A. she was like everybody else.

If she lived here she'd be unique again. Not that she would really consider such a thing, but there was a certain appeal. Of course, her father had never wanted her to be unique.

As she continued down the two-lane highway and glimpsed the arched iron gate over the entrance to the Twin Boulders

Ranch, the bravado that had taken her through town with a flourish began to disappear. In a few minutes she'd have to face Arch Branscom, and she was scared to death.

Even the prospect of dealing with Noah again didn't worry her as much as this meeting with her father after all these years. Their parting words had been bitter. He'd flung a copy of *Macho* in the fire and said that she had way too much of her mother in her for her own good. Then he'd as much as told her to leave his house.

She'd planned to use the money she'd earned from the photo session to get out of town, anyway. But she'd counted on it being her idea, not his. Packing a bag, she'd bought a bus ticket for L.A. She'd said goodbye to B.J., Jonas and Jonas's father. Noah had been out of town at the time, which had been just as well.

But she'd left without telling her own father goodbye. These would be the first words she'd spoken to him since he'd declared her a disgrace to the family ten long, lonely years ago.

And she had been lonely, she finally admitted to herself as she drove toward the ranch. Her car kicked up a rooster tail of dust on the dirt road as she passed the two large boulders on the left that gave the ranch its name. She'd made friends and had lovers in L.A., but nobody had filled the empty place where her family used to be. She wanted her family back, but not at the expense of her self-esteem. If her father showed any signs of disapproval, she'd leave right after the wedding Saturday night and never come back.

Passing the ranch house, she wondered if Noah was inside and if he might be watching for her. As she drove around the main house toward the smaller cabin where her father lived, she noticed a man on horseback cantering over a cactus-studded hill on his way toward the ranch. Even from this distance she recognized Noah.

Her already stressed heart kicked into an even faster rhythm. But she could only deal with one of these men at a time, and her father was first on her list. She parked beside a battered pickup that she assumed belonged to him. He'd bought different trucks through the years, but Arch Branscom's transportation always looked about the same—a light-colored paint job so it wouldn't show the dust and an assortment of dings and scratches where he'd taken it through the brush in pursuit of cattle, horses and even a few lost dogs.

She left her suitcase in the back seat of the Mustang and took only her purse with her. If her reception was too chilly, she could always stay in Saguaro Junction's only motel. As she walked up to the small covered porch, she noticed that the bushes were trimmed and the porch had been swept recently. The woven straw mat in front of the door looked new.

Maybe her dad had spruced up the place for the wedding. She could hardly believe he'd done it for her. Heart pounding, she stood in front of the door and couldn't decide whether to go in or knock. Although she'd sailed in and out of this door with complete ease for the first nineteen years of her life, she didn't live here anymore.

But knocking at the door of her father's house seemed ridiculous. She reached for the knob then pulled her hand back. Then she raised her fist to knock and couldn't make herself do that, either.

Finally the door opened and her father stood there staring at her.

She stared back. Although logic should have told her he'd look older, she hadn't expected him to. His hair and mustache used to be dark red sprinkled with gray. Now they were nearly white. His face was more weathered and he seemed... shorter. She'd always imagined him towering over her, but in her three-inch heels she could look him straight in the eye.

Those piercing blue eyes of his hadn't changed at all. They

still seemed to look clear into her heart. She wondered if he could tell how scared she was. Probably.

"Hello, Keely," he said in his deep, gruff voice.

"Hello, Dad."

"Figured I'd better open the door for you. You seemed to have forgotten how to do it."

"I...couldn't decide if I should knock."

And just like that, the fierceness left his expression. "No," he said softly. "You should never knock." His voice shook. "You're always welcome here."

A dam broke inside her as she flung herself into his arms. "I'm sorry," she sobbed, pressing her face against his shirt. He smelled so achingly familiar, a mixture of sunshine, soap and pipe tobacco.

He held her close and patted her back. "I'm the one who's sorry," he said, his voice even gruffer than before. "I didn't really mean for you to go away, Keely-girl. I was...hasty."

"You were just being a dad," she said, her voice muffled against his shirt. "I couldn't expect you to be overjoyed with what I did."

"I'll admit you did test my patience."

She smiled against his shirt. "You tested mine, too." She lifted her head and gazed at his beloved face with watery eyes. "But maybe we can start over."

He shook his head. "That would mean throwing out all the good things along with the bad. You gave me plenty of joy, too. So we aren't starting over. We're just going on from here."

"Okay." She took a deep breath and felt her body fill with a kind of peace she hadn't known in years. "Where's B.J.?"

"Right here."

Keely disengaged herself from her father and turned to see her sister standing there with tears in her eyes. Keely barely recognized B.J. She was actually wearing *makeup,* and she'd cut her hair. No more single braid down the back. Instead, her hair curled softly around her face. She hadn't given up her jeans, but she'd replaced her usual faded denim shirt with a sexy halter top.

With a squeal of delight, Keely ran over to grab her. "My God, look at you!" She hugged her sister, held her away to admire her some more, then hugged her again. "Jonas is *so* lucky."

"I think so," B.J. said.

"I definitely think so," Jonas said from the doorway. "How're you doing, Keely?"

"Fabulous." Her heart full, she walked over and gave Jonas a hug, too. He'd always been a little too handsome for his own good, with his thick brown hair and laughing hazel eyes. In the ten years since she'd last seen him he'd become even more attractive. He and B.J. were a stunning couple.

"Now that Jonas has shown up, I'm gonna go find us some beers," her father announced as he started toward the kitchen.

"Need help?" B.J. asked.

Keely wished she had the nerve to offer, but the truce was too new and fragile to risk being alone again with her father.

"I'll take care of it," her father said. "You kids go on out to the porch and catch up on your news."

"He sounds so happy," Keely said as they trooped outside the way they used to when her dad had promised them a Popsicle.

"He is happy," B.J. said. "All he's been talking about for the past week is you coming home."

"Oh, he's added a few comments on the wedding," Jonas said with a chuckle as he pulled B.J. down next to him on the swing. "Especially about how much we're spending on it." He glanced up at Keely and patted the swing. "Come on. There's plenty of room, and I've never been opposed to having a babe on each side of me."

"Thanks, anyway." Keely leaned up against the porch railing. "I just want to stand here and get used to the sight of you two together."

"Amazing, isn't it?" Jonas said with a grin. "Who'd have thought I'd end up with such a goddess?"

"Not me, that's for sure," said a deep male voice behind Keely.

She turned to see Noah coming up the walk. Immediately her heart began to pound. "Hi, there," she said, trying to sound all breezy and big-city.

"Hi, yourself." He gave her an easy smile. "I might have known you'd roll up in a red Mustang convertible. I'll bet you had the top down and the RPMs up all the way through town."

It sounded like a perfectly innocent comment, but when she glanced into his eyes, she knew there was sexual innuendo written all over it. And her body heated, right on schedule. So that was how he intended to play it.

Well, she knew how to play that game, too. She might even be better at it than he was. "Of course," she said, smiling back at him. "And if you're a good boy maybe I'll give you a ride before I leave."

Noah gulped and Keely mentally chalked up one for her side.

"Woo-hoo!" Jonas yelled. "Keely's back!"

19

AT FOUR THE NEXT AFTERNOON Noah stood next to his brother at the altar of the Saguaro Junction Community Church. All eyes were supposed to be on the bride coming down the aisle on her father's arm, but Noah's attention kept straying to the woman sitting in the left front pew.

He wondered if she stood out in this crowd as much as he imagined, or if his agitated state of mind only made it seem that way. No, it wasn't his imagination. She really did look like an orchid plopped in the middle of a field of daisies and sunflowers. Her color-of-sin hair was one reason. That deep, foxy red wasn't common in these parts. Add in her traffic-stopping figure wrapped in a leaf-green halter dress and gold hoop earrings that nearly touched the golden skin of her shoulders, and you had a spectacular sight.

If he'd expected her to melt into the landscape so he could kid himself that she belonged here, he could forget that fantasy right now. The minute he'd seen that cherry-red car, he'd realized his mistake. That red car had flashed like a stoplight, warning him to back off.

Of course, he hadn't been able to do that, obsessed as he was with her. So instead he'd needled her every chance he could get, and she'd fired right back at him with that smart mouth of hers. He was pretty well disgusted with himself.

His tactics for getting her attention weren't much more sophisticated than they had been at sixteen when he'd put a frog
down her blouse.

Still, he couldn't seem to stop his sophomoric attempts to
get her riled, and none of them seemed to be working worth
a damn. So here they were at his brother's wedding, Keely
sitting in that wooden pew looking totally together and rav-
ishing, and him turning into a heat-seeking missile counting
down to launch. His need to make love to her was making
him irrational about their relationship, or lack of one, and
he vaguely realized that just enough to know that a hot babe
like Keely was not interested in settling down on the ranch
to play erotic games with him for the rest of her life. So now
with that dream in the toilet, all he could think was that she'd
leave tomorrow and return to her big-city job, and he would
never, ever touch her naked body again.

Oh, sure, she'd come back once in a while for a visit, but by
then the gulf between them would be like the Grand Canyon.
His last opportunity was tonight, when they only had to cross
a little irrigation ditch.

He thought he could talk her into an encore performance if
he could get her alone. She'd been avoiding being alone with
him, but avoidance had been easy with all the wedding stuff
going on. The wedding would be over soon. Maybe sometime
during the reception he'd get his chance. They had already set
a precedent for wedding-reception hanky-panky. She might
still be tuned to that channel.

If he got lucky—and for the first time in his life that phrase
really meant something to him—then he only had to remember
one thing: He must not, under any circumstances, no matter
how fantastic the experience, let it slip that he loved her.

KEELY HAD FORGOTTEN how hot an Arizona summer could
be, even at nine o'clock at night. Noah, Jonas and Arch had

installed a misting system under the canopy they'd erected for the reception, but it didn't affect the temperature much. Still, having the reception at the ranch in an outdoor setting had allowed more people to come, and the whole town had turned out. Apparently everyone was perfectly willing to sweat in order to be here.

To be fair, part of her discomfort was her own fault. She would have stayed *mucho* cooler if she hadn't insisted on dancing every blessed number the band played. But that wouldn't have been her style.

Besides, she needed to stay busy in order to forget that look she'd seen today on Noah's face. He'd spent a fair amount of time glancing her way during the ceremony, and his speculative, worried frown told her more clearly than any words could have that he'd figured out she really didn't belong here.

The rebel in her had decided to underline that opinion and put about five exclamation points after it. The woman in her was trying to hold her heart together. Just about the time Noah had formed his opinion that she had no business staying in Saguaro Junction, she'd begun to think maybe she wanted to, after all. Murphy's Law.

She'd enjoyed being home more than she ever would have imagined and had begun to think of what it would be like to live here again. Yes, she would stand out, but while that had seemed terrible at nineteen, it sounded like fun at twenty-nine. She seemed to have outgrown the need to blend in.

Nor would she have to give up her career. She could use the move to reposition herself at a different type of magazine, maybe one that ran exotic-travel features. Two publications she was thinking of were based in New York, but now that she had a decent résumé, she wouldn't necessarily have to spend much time at the office. In fact, she could live anywhere there was internet access. Twin Boulders had internet access.

But she'd figured out from Noah's expression during

the wedding that he didn't share any part of her reworked vision for the future. And so at the reception she'd flirted and laughed and completely ignored the only man she cared to build a future with. Outrageous behavior had always been her protection and it would serve her well again.

Inevitably the band took a break. Thanking her latest conquest, she slipped away from him and headed over toward her sister. In her effort to forget Noah, she didn't want to miss spending time with B.J. On the way over, she grabbed a glass of champagne and a paper napkin from a table. She wiped the napkin over the cool moisture on the flute and dabbed it against her throat.

B.J. motioned her to a couple of folding chairs. "Whew," she said, sinking down to the chair and arranging the full skirt of her wedding dress. "Maybe we should have waited until November for this shindig."

"Jonas wouldn't have stood for it," Keely said with a grin. "That man wants you bad."

"Yeah, he does." B.J.'s gaze wandered over to where Jonas stood talking with Noah. "But I had to get around his preconceptions before he realized he was crazy about me."

"Now that you've brought it up, I'm dying to know how you managed that."

B.J. turned to her, looking virginal and pure in her white dress and lacy veil. "Anonymous sex."

Keely nearly dropped her champagne flute. "Excuse me?"

"In a bad rainstorm I dodged into one of those caves we used to play in when we were kids. My horse had run away, so when Jonas ducked into the same dark cave, he didn't know anyone was in there."

Keely laughed. "You must have scared the living daylights out of him."

"I did, but when I realized he didn't know it was me, I pretended to be someone else and seduced him."

"No way!"

"Yep. I did."

Keely stared at her sister in admiration. "Way to go, sis!"

B.J. grinned. "It gets better. Before he left the cave, we agreed to meet secretly, and each time I made him wear a blindfold so he wouldn't know who I was."

"Get outta town!" Keely shook her head in amazement. "You had total control of the situation. Now, that sounds like something I'd do."

"I know." B.J. looked smug. "In fact, many times along the way I asked myself what you would do, and I did that. I had a blast."

"Cool." She smiled at her sister. "I'm so glad you made it happen. You're perfect for each other."

"So it seems." B.J. gazed at Keely. "Listen, you can tell me to mind my own business if you want, but...what's up with you and Noah? I keep picking up on all kinds of tension between you two."

Keely swallowed, thinking how much she longed for a confidante. And after all, her sister had confessed her secret. "We, um, sort of got involved in Vegas."

"You *did?*" B.J.'s blue eyes glowed with eagerness. "That sure explains a lot about his weird mood lately, and the singing telegram."

"Yeah, you told me he was the one who thought of that."

"He not only thought of it, he was there."

Keely was sure she must have misunderstood. "What do you mean?"

"I mean that he flew to L.A. and supervised the whole stunt, to make sure it went the way we'd planned. He stood just outside the door of your office where he could see you, but I guess you never noticed him."

Keely was stunned. "No. No, I sure didn't."

"He pretended his being there was necessary, and we went

along with it because we could tell from the beginning that he wanted to go over there and see you. I wondered at the time if something had happened in Vegas."

"Yeah, something happened in Vegas." Keely sighed. "But we don't belong together. He doesn't want a wild child like me."

"Oh, you're dead wrong there."

"Trust me, I'm not. His expression when he looks at me tells it all."

"Mmm." B.J. glanced over to where Jonas and Noah stood. "By the way, can I have a sip of your champagne?"

"Sure, but I can get you a whole glass. I—"

"Don't want a whole glass. I plan to treat Jonas to some fun and games tonight, and I don't want to be fuzzy headed for that." She winked as she handed the flute back to Keely. "Which brings me back to your comment. I don't know what you're reading into Noah's expression, but it's my opinion every man wants a wild child. Jonas sure does, and I'm having a great time turning into one."

"But that's just it—on the outside you don't seem wild at all. You know that old saying about being a naughty girl in the bedroom and a lady in the parlor. That's what a man wants in a wife."

"Did Noah tell you that?"

"No, but—"

"Excuse me for saying so, Keely, but for a big sister and a city girl, you have some ideas that are seriously out of date. From what I've seen, Noah would take you any way he could get you."

"Then you're not looking close enough," Keely said. "Haven't you noticed how standoffish and stuffy he's been tonight?"

"Well, duh!" B.J. said. "That's *exactly* how he acted after that incident in the barn when you were sixteen and, according to Jonas, Noah wanted you so bad that summer he finally went rodeoing to try and get you out of his system. That's how he gets when he wants something he thinks he can't have—stuffy."

Keely stared at her sister. "He wanted me? But he was so awful to me!"

"You were sixteen," B.J. said gently. "A guy with principles as strong as Noah's couldn't have taken you up on your offer. But turning you down nearly killed him, which he disguised by being standoffish."

"Wow." Keely thought of how she'd tortured herself with that rejection. Then she'd tortured Noah for revenge. "I guess I was so wrapped up in my own pain I didn't even think he might be suffering, too."

"Feel better now?" B.J. asked.

"You have no idea." Her self-esteem felt healthier by the minute.

"Oh, I think I do. I needed to know Jonas had suffered a little, too, after all he'd put me through."

"I understand." Keely cast a sideways glance at Noah. Was it really possible that he not only wanted her, but that he loved her?

"Listen, I have to warn you that Noah's superglued to this place," B.J. said. "So the question is, could you come back?"

"Maybe." Keely desperately wanted to believe B.J. was right about Noah's feelings, but if she acted on the information and her sister was wrong, life wouldn't be worth living. "I mean, I might come back, if it wouldn't freak everybody out."

"I would dearly love it and so would Dad. And this town could use some freaking out, if you know what I mean."

Keely took a sip of champagne. "Are you sure? From what I've heard, Mom was kinda flamboyant, and I don't think she was all that well received."

"The town's grown up a lot," B.J. said. "Besides, you've already done the ultimate with that centerfold," she added with a grin. "Whatever else you come up with will be anticlimactic."

"Well, shoot, that's no fun."

B.J. chuckled. "Or maybe not anticlimactic. What do I know? Anyway, here's the deal—you have to take a chance and come on to Noah, instead of ignoring him like you've been doing. That won't work."

Keely opened her mouth to object on the grounds that she might not survive the crash if Noah rejected her again.

B.J. held up her hand to stave off her comment. "You don't have to say it. Believe me, I know what it could cost you if the plan turns sour. I had to gamble, too, with no guarantee of winning." She reached for Keely's hand and gave it a squeeze. "Can a little sister offer a big sister some advice?"

Keely managed a smile, although her chest was tight with anxiety. "Sure."

"That stuff we were told when we were teenagers is wrong. The way to a man's heart is not through his stomach. You have to aim a little lower."

Keely looked at B.J. and they both began to giggle. It felt like old times.

Noah had been looking for an opportunity to get Keely alone all night, but she seemed determined to dance with every man at the reception except him, and when she wasn't doing that she was hanging out with B.J. or talking with Arch. Apparently she was still trying to avoid him.

As he was wondering how to work around that, lo and behold, she walked in his direction. He knew he'd better act fast before she veered off to ask some other cowboy to dance, or one of them trotted over to ask her. Striding forward, he caught her arm.

Sensation zinged straight to his crotch. It was the first time he'd touched her since Vegas, and his body certainly remembered what to do with the information transmitted by her warm skin.

He looked into her eyes and was encouraged by the glow he saw there. "Could we go somewhere to talk?"

"We could." Her voice was low and seductive. "But let's not start any gossip like we did at the last reception."

That had to mean her mind was on the same track as his. His blood heated.

"Let me leave first," she murmured. "Give me five minutes or so before you leave. I'll tell people I'm going back over to Dad's to freshen up. I'll meet you there."

"In your dad's house?" He wasn't so sure about that. He'd feel damn uncomfortable doing what he had in mind in her father's little cabin.

"Of course not, silly. I'll meet you by my car."

Her car. Now, that had possibilities. "Okay."

"See you in a few." Then she walked away from him with that little swing to her hips that always drove him around the bend.

Noah had never spent a longer five minutes in his life. He had no idea what he said to the people he talked to during those five minutes, and he hoped nobody noticed how often he glanced at his watch. He checked his pocket at least twenty times to make sure the condom he'd stashed there earlier hadn't somehow disappeared. Once again he was wearing rented clothes, and rented pockets could have holes.

Finally he figured he could start after her. His excuse for leaving was to go find a bottle of aspirin. Consequently he walked in the front door of the ranch house and then slipped out the back. On the short trek over to her dad's, he recited instructions to himself. *Enjoy the moment. Remember the condom. Don't tell her you love her.*

He didn't see her beside the car, but he sure as heck saw a pair of black lace panties dangling from the radio antenna. His heart beat like crazy. Softly he called her name.

"Back here," she said in a low voice.

He could barely breathe as he peered into the back seat of

the Mustang. The light wasn't very good, but good enough that he could see that she lay there naked, her dress rolled neatly and tucked under her head for a pillow, her knees bent delicately so that she'd fit on the seat.

Smiling at him, she cupped her breasts in both hands. "It's so hot. I could hardly wait to get out of those clothes."

His tongue didn't seem to want to work.

"Is this what you had in mind when you said we needed to talk?" she asked.

Still unable to speak, he nodded.

"I thought so." Then she slid one hand between her thighs and caressed herself. "This weather just makes you want to be bad, doesn't it?"

With a soft moan, he reached for the car's door handle.

"Wait."

"Wait?" Now, there was a terrible word if he'd ever heard one.

"Not yet," she whispered.

Not yet. Two more words that should be wiped right out of the language. He gripped the handle and his voice was a harsh croak. "What do you mean, not yet?"

"What's the password?"

He felt like someone was trying to strangle him. "Password?"

"Tell me the password and you can come in. I'll give you a hint. It has four letters." Her hand fluttered between her thighs. "Mmm, that feels good."

"Keely."

"Four letters, Noah."

He gripped the door handle so hard his fingers hurt. And all the while he was drawn to the indistinct but riveting sight of her fingers gliding into the place that he'd had wet dreams about. "I'm thinking of a four-letter word, all right," he ground out, struggling for breath. "What is this game, Keely?"

"It's a shakedown, Noah. Here's a big hint. The word rhymes with the name of a bird."

His jaw clenched. "A duck."

Her soft, musical laughter rode the night breeze. "Now, there's a man for you. Not a duck. A different bird."

"Damn it, I don't know anything about birds. And I—"

"A dove."

"A *dove?*" His brain stalled. Only one four-letter word rhymed with dove. And last he knew, she hadn't been interested in hearing that word. Hope surged in his chest. "Okay, a dove it is." He opened the door.

"What are you doing?" she said. "You didn't say the password."

"I will," he said fervently. "Trust me, I will." He nudged off his shoes, grateful that he wasn't wearing boots. Then he took off the rest of his clothes, heaving them piece by piece into the front seat of the car. At the last minute he remembered to take the condom out of his pants pocket.

"But that's the rule," she said. "No password, no nooky."

"That's what you think." He put on the condom and climbed into the car, hoping she wasn't serious enough about this rule business to kick him in the balls. "I'm the kind of guy who breaks rules." Kneeling on the edge of the seat, he braced one hand against the convertible's boot as he leaned over her. "And I happen to think that's the kind of guy who turns you on."

"Is that right?" She gazed up at him, seeming disinclined to kick him. In fact, she seemed quite glad to have him there.

"Yeah, that's right." If only he could see her face better. He tried to plan his next move, but he couldn't see much of her at all. His body was casting a shadow over the very spot he was aiming for. He drew back. "Put your foot down."

"I was trying to put my foot down by making you say the password, but you're not playing by the rules, so—"

"I mean your actual foot. Put it on the floor."

"Oh." She followed his directions.

Okay. He had clearance. It was cramped quarters, yet worth every charley horse he might get in the process. But as he leaned toward her, his shadow fell on her willing body once again and he fumbled a bit.

And then, wonder of wonders, she took his sheathed penis in her hand and guided him toward paradise. But right before he reached heaven, she stopped.

"What's the password?" she whispered. "You promised to say it."

"Love," he murmured, rolling the word on his tongue, tasting its sweetness. "I love you, Keely."

"That's the password," she said, guiding him forward. "Now you can come in."

He slid home with a sigh. Nothing was equal to the feeling of being right here. Nothing. But a million questions buzzed in his brain. "Now what?"

She stroked his back. "I thought we had that part down. In, out, in, out. It works very well with us."

In spite of the enormous significance of the moment, he couldn't keep from grinning. "I mean, now what do we do about us? You don't want to live here."

"Yes, I do."

He leaned down, trying to see her face better. "You do? Just like that? Why?"

"Because I love *you,* you big dope."

"You love me?" Incredible. She'd said it. He decided to ignore the *big dope* part and focus on the *I love you* part. Besides, she was right. He was a big dope for not tracking her down years ago.

"Yes, I really, really love you," she said. "And I know I stick out like a sore thumb in this town, but if you can deal with that, I sure can."

"You love me." He couldn't believe that a man could be this happy. What a perfect night. He began gently to rock. "If you love me, I can deal with anything. Besides, you're not a sore thumb. You're a Ferrari in a world of Fords. This town needs you in it. And I need to be in you. It all works out."

"That sounds nice."

"I'll think up more nice things to say when I'm not so busy. Oh, God, but you feel good. Let's have a small wedding."

She picked up his rhythm and tightened around him in that special way of hers. "Let's have a big one. A blowout."

"Fine." He was through being chatty. He just wanted to revel in the sensation of pushing into the warmest place on earth while a cool breeze tickled his butt. "A big wedding it is."

"That was easy."

"You keep letting me do this and you can have anything you want."

"Then stop right this minute."

He froze in mid-thrust. "Stop?"

"Pull out a minute. Then I promise you can come back, and you'll have oh so much more fun. Please, Noah. If you love me."

He did love her, so he pulled out.

Before he realized what she meant to do, she'd reached between them and slid the condom right off, slick as a whistle. Then she tossed it out of the car.

"Hey!" he said. "That was my only one! I thought you liked the ribbed kind."

"Well, I did, but you said I could have whatever I wanted, right?"

"Yeah, but—"

"I want babies, Noah. Now come to momma, big boy."

With a groan of pure bliss, he did exactly that.

Epilogue

"YES!" KEELY GRINNED in triumph as she read an e-mail from her editor, Jim Stevens, at *Prime Destinations* magazine.

"That sounds like my cue." Noah appeared in the doorway of the ranch-house bedroom he'd converted into an office for Keely. "Have you been downloading from that Kama Sutra site again?"

"Nope. This is better." She glanced up as he leaned casually against the door frame and wondered how she'd ever imagined life on this ranch could be boring. She'd enjoyed more innovative sex and pure bliss in the past six months with Noah than in all her years of being single.

What she hadn't thought of he had. They'd made love in every room inside and most of the secluded areas outside. A major bathroom remodel had resulted in a large whirlpool bath plus a huge shower with nozzles at interesting levels and bench seats at an appropriate height for fun and games. Mirrored closet doors in the bedroom reflected a four-poster bed dressed in satin sheets.

They'd also enjoyed some spectacular, sensual episodes when he'd gone along on some of her travel assignments. But he'd never encountered an assignment like the one she'd landed this time. She smiled and hit the print command on her computer.

"Better, huh?" His gaze warmed as it slid over her. "Am I going to need props for this one?"

"Only a suitcase."

His eyebrows lifted. "If I'm going to make love to you on top of a suitcase, we'd better look around and see if I have any hard-sided ones left. Those soft-sided jobs will cave in for sure."

With a laugh she reached for the hard copy of the e-mail. "I don't know what benefit we could get from making love on a suitcase, but I'm willing to give it some thought. In the meantime, take a look at this." She handed him the piece of paper.

He scanned it before meeting her gaze. "A nude beach resort?"

"I've always been curious about those places, so I proposed the idea to Jim. I just got clearance." She challenged him with a bold glance.

"And I suppose as the writer covering this you will have to be…"

"Naked. Yes. But that's okay. Then I won't have to buy any maternity beachwear." She paused. "Wanna come along, cowboy?"

She watched him struggle with the concept of a nude vacation destination. No doubt he would always approach unusual sexual ideas with some hesitation. That made him Noah, after all, and made his eventual capitulation even more exciting. She'd also learned that once he embraced a new idea, he gave it all he had.

"I double dare you," she said softly.

His eyes sparkled in response to her taunt, yet still he hesitated. "I don't know, Keely. I mean, walking around without any—"

"Don't think of it as walking around. Think of it as lying on a towel on soft, warm sand, rubbing oil all over my body, me rubbing oil all over yours." She stood and moved toward him.

"I'd have to spend the whole vacation on my stomach. I'd have to dig a little hole in the sand for my—"

"A private stretch of warm sand." She began unbuttoning her blouse. When they weren't expecting visitors, like this afternoon, she skipped wearing a bra. "I checked out the site online, and they have all sorts of intimate spots where couples can be alone."

"They do?" His attention drifted to her unbuttoned blouse. "You're not playing fair, Keely. You know I can't think when you do that."

"Don't think. Use your imagination. Picture a secluded little cove, soft sand, thick towels, each of us warm and slick with oil…everywhere…." She pulled her blouse from the waistband of her jeans. Lately she'd had to leave the top button of her jeans unfastened to accommodate the baby growing inside her. Noah liked that, because then she was even more accessible to him. He loved to pull the zipper of her jeans down and stroke her round belly whenever he had a chance.

With a gusty sigh he reached for her, slipping his hands inside the lapels of her blouse and caressing her breasts. "Okay, you win. I'm going."

"Good." She tingled with anticipation of pleasures to come, both long range and more immediate ones. He would make love to her now, because he was surely thinking about that nude beach and getting hot. She closed her eyes the better to enjoy his touch. "I promise you won't be sorry."

"Easy for you to say." He pulled her close and leaned down to nuzzle her neck. "I'll probably sunburn my ass and won't be able to ride for a week."

His mouth could make her crazy, no matter where on her body he chose to place it. "And that would be bad because…?"

"Because then I wouldn't be able to work. I'd have to let

Jonas do everything while I hung around here, and—" He paused and began to laugh. "I see your point."

"I thought you might." She drew him toward her desk. "Now let me emphasize it."

"On the desk?" His voice vibrated with excitement.

"On your big, old executive desk." With a sweep of her hand she sent pages flying. "After all, it's on the list."

He unzipped his jeans. "I love that list," he said in a voice roughened with desire. "Think we'll ever get through it?"

She shoved her jeans and panties down and stepped out of them. "Not if we keep adding to it like we've been doing."

He lifted her to the polished surface of the desk. "Think the baby will slow us down?"

"Nope."

"Me neither. Now open your legs for me, woman. Time to cross this one off the list." As she complied, he cupped her bottom in both hands and held her gaze as he slid deep. "Ahhh…that is so sweet, Keely. Every time. Every blessed time."

"I know."

He settled in tighter. "Think we'll be this crazy when we're eighty?"

"Crazier," she murmured. "Now love me, you wild man. Love me good."

And he did.

* * * * *

COMING NEXT MONTH

Available August 30, 2011

#633 TOO WILD TO HOLD
Legendary Lovers
Julie Leto

#634 NIGHT MANEUVERS
Uniformly Hot!
Jillian Burns

#635 JUST GIVE IN...
Harts of Texas
Kathleen O'Reilly

#636 MAKING A SPLASH
The Wrong Bed: Again and Again
Joanne Rock

#637 WITNESS SEDUCTION
Elle Kennedy

#638 ROYALLY ROMANCED
A Real Prince
Marie Donovan

You can find more information on upcoming
Harlequin® titles, free excerpts and more at
www.HarlequinInsideRomance.com.

REQUEST YOUR FREE BOOKS!
2 FREE NOVELS PLUS 2 FREE GIFTS!

red-hot reads!

New York Times *and* USA TODAY *bestselling author*
Maya Banks presents a brand-new miniseries

PREGNANCY & PASSION

When four irresistible tycoons face
the consequences of temptation.

Book 1—ENTICED BY HIS FORGOTTEN LOVER

Available September 2011 from Harlequin® Desire®!

Rafael de Luca had been in bad situations before. A crowded ballroom could never make him sweat.

These people would never know that he had no memory of any of them.

He surveyed the party with grim tolerance, searching for the source of his unease.

At first his gaze flickered past her, but he yanked his attention back to a woman across the room. Her stare bored holes through him. Unflinching and steady, even when his eyes locked with hers.

Petite, even in heels, she had a creamy olive complexion. A wealth of inky-black curls cascaded over her shoulders and her eyes were equally dark.

She looked at him as if she'd already judged him and found him lacking. He'd never seen her before in his life. Or had he?

He cursed the gaping hole in his memory. He'd been diagnosed with selective amnesia after his accident four months ago. Which seemed like complete and utter bull. No one got amnesia except hysterical women in bad soap operas.

With a smile, he disengaged himself from the group

around him and made his way to the mystery woman.

She wasn't coy. She stared straight at him as he approached, her chin thrust upward in defiance.

"Excuse me, but have we met?" he asked in his smoothest voice.

His gaze moved over the generous swell of her breasts pushed up by the empire waist of her black cocktail dress.

When he glanced back up at her face, he saw fury in her eyes.

"Have we *met?*" Her voice was barely a whisper, but he felt each word like the crack of a whip.

Before he could process her response, she nailed him with a right hook. He stumbled back, holding his nose.

One of his guards stepped between Rafe and the woman, accidentally sending her to one knee. Her hand flew to the folds of her dress.

It was then, as she cupped her belly, that the realization hit him. She was pregnant.

Her eyes flashing, she turned and ran down the marble hallway.

Rafael ran after her. He burst from the hotel lobby, and saw two shoes sparkling in the moonlight, twinkling at him.

He blew out his breath in frustration and then shoved the pair of sparkly, ultrafeminine heels at his head of security.

"Find the woman who wore these shoes."

Will Rafael find his mystery woman?
Find out in Maya Banks's passionate new novel
ENTICED BY HIS FORGOTTEN LOVER
Available September 2011 from Harlequin® Desire®!

HDEXP0911

Harlequin *Desire*

ALWAYS POWERFUL, PASSIONATE AND PROVOCATIVE.

NEW YORK TIMES AND *USA TODAY*
BESTSELLING AUTHOR

MAYA BANKS

BRINGS YOU THE FIRST STORY
IN A BRAND-NEW MINISERIES

PASSION & PREGNANCY
*When irresistible tycoons
face the consequences of temptation.*

ENTICED BY HIS FORGOTTEN LOVER

A bout of amnesia…a mysterious woman
he can't resist…a pregnancy shocker.

When Rafael de Luca's memory comes
crashing back, it will change everything.

*Available September
wherever books are sold.*

SD73120R